D0406853

MIDNIGHT GRAFFITI

MIDNIGHT GRAFFITI

WITH STORIES BY

STEPHEN KING

HARLAN ELLISON

DAN SIMMONS

DAVID J. SCHOW

NANCY COLLINS

EDITED BY JESSICA HORSTING AND JAMES VAN HISE

A Time Warner Company

WARNER BOOKS EDITION

Cover design by Don Puckey
Cover illustration by Martin Cannon

Warner Books, Inc.
1271 Avenue of the Americas
New York, NY 10020
 A Time Warner Company

Printed in the United States of America

0-446-36307-3

Introduction

Many of the stories collected in this book first appeared in Midnight Graffiti *magazine, a publication dedicated to the idea that there* is *a Twilight Zone and we live in it.*

BUT FIRST, A WORD FROM OUR SPONSORS . . .

This is a book about fear, and if you want to take the measure of fear in America, watch television. I don't mean the news, or those PBS documentaries, or Charles Kuralt, or afternoon talk shows, although I'll admit *Geraldo* is pretty darn scary—I mean the amalgam. Television has shaped and influenced the majority of people now leading and providing for the country, and understanding what scares us means understanding what our other parent, the box, has been teaching us to fear.

Television has evolved over the last forty years, though basically it still lies, diverts, informs, and entertains as it always has. *Texaco Star Theater* has merely mutated into *Late Night With David Letterman*, *I Love Lucy* into *Roseanne*, and tragically, Edward R. Murrow has been replaced by Dan Rather. But what it teaches us continues to rest between the programs, in those thirty- and sixty-second cultural time capsules called commercials. They're the body language of America, unerringly reflecting our fears and concerns regardless of what the ad agencies are peddling.

In the fifties, clearly the group mind was as swollen and monstrous as the fins on a '58 Caddy, while outwardly, the suits were sharply creased and the ties rigidly narrow, indicating a nation suffering from both penis envy and penis anxiety. Commercials addressed the hidden agony of a nation in the throes of prosperity and peace. Homemakers across America took stock: We own our own home, we have the new Oldsmobile, I have modernized my kitchen, we have 2.5 children—what is making me so damn unhappy? Detergents! Detergents that leave my whites dingy gray!

Advertising executives were on firm territory here. They sensed society's vague malaise, and persuaded us the problem certainly was *not* the hydrogen bomb. America was suffering from the humiliation of not having frost-free refrigerators and matching washers and dryers. Is nuclear fission causing you to lose valuable sleep? Buy something! The answer to being consumed is consume! Consume Hi-Test gas, get Hi-fidelity, stop rot with Fluoride Toothpaste, more suck with Electrolux, Lucky Strike Means Fine Tobacco. Of course, America was afraid of the bomb, and commercials clearly reflected the sublimation of our fear as an unquantifiable uneasiness that something was wrong, and perhaps it *was* the Ivory soap flakes.

Being terrified of sex didn't help either.

Only in fiction and film, particularly horror, were the issues squarely addressed. Horror then was not the industry it is today, but it was the genre where the scientist would finally utter the unspeakable.

> I'm not against progress, but these stubborn fools are searching for atomic power in the wrong place. If they continue . . . do you realize what the people of the future will be? What they'll look like? Monsters! Grotesque, misshapen frightening fiends. Isotopes and fallout . . . in our lungs, in our glands, distorting natural growth and proportions. Nobody can calculate the hazards of radiation monsters. What reckless fools! They search in the wrong place when I can demonstrate that a power strong enough to destroy the world is buried in each of us. I can release a destructive power in a human being that would make a split atom look like a blessing.
>
> *Blood of Dracula*, 1957

Whew. There it was, our true fears, all wet and squirmy. Another quintessential expression was found in the John Campbell story *Who Goes There?* eventually translated to film as Howard Hawks's *The Thing*, a near-perfect exploitation of our fears of otherness and technology germinating since Hiroshima. Though *The Thing* had the trappings of science fiction, its soul was horror, and it crystallized our dread: what have we wrought, and is it going to kill us in our sleep?

In the sixties, we seemed to gain enough cultural sophistication to admit that sex and drugs were an unavoidable part of American life, although we weren't so sure about rock and roll. Commercials reflected the phenomenon by advertising a lot of booze and personal hygiene products. It was okay to be drunk, but not drunk and smelly. The fins on cars disappeared and manufacturers introduced smaller cars with bigger engines, embracing the notion that size really didn't matter, it was all in the technique, er, horsepower.

Though advertising now seemed to suggest that sex actually occurred between men and women, they were just pretending it was okay. Our real concern, blossoming fully at the end of the decade, was not our relationships but ourselves: our clothes, our hair, our body odor, our shaves, our cellulite, our bad breath, our headaches and cold symptoms. All that stress from worrying about the bomb made our personal appearance deteriorate and our noses run. Young people were slovenly, impudent, their hair was unmanageable, and they had never been in the same time zone with Halston. The generation gap was only superficially over politics and lifestyle—the real issue was grooming. Are we natural creatures or not? Shave the body hair, or let it grow? The underlying fear was of ourselves. We have seen the enemy, and he is us. He is hairy, smelly, and something kind of bothers me about him. It bothers me a lot.

Horror was again the constant chronicler—the granddaddy of the medium as it exists today was published on the brink of the sixties, Robert Bloch's *Psycho*. The ensuing film adaptation by Alfred Hitchcock ushered in an era of horror that has not yet been exhausted, the era of anthrophobia: "My God, that's not a monster, that's my neighbor Bill . . ." *Psycho* begat *Rosemary's Baby*, which begat *The Exorcist*, which begat Stephen King, whose singular voice continues dominating popular horror because he understands so well what scares us.

The introspection that began in the sixties continues maturing in the nineties. We are certainly fascinated by ourselves and our capacity for bad deeds. We know things are wrong, though gauging just how off-kilter things have become is sometimes impossible. But there are commercials to guide us. They reveal that things have become very strange indeed.

We fear litigation—and we also fear we have missed an opportunity for a lawsuit. We fear health care costs. We fear all manner of drug dependencies, unless they are over-the-counter drugs, in which case we're afraid we may be taking the wrong one. However, we show no fear of beer. AT&T obviously fears we're not calling our loved ones enough, although they're really afraid that we're using some other carrier when we do. We seem to be worried about driving the wrong car to the wrong supermarket. (Food and grocery commercials outnumber car commercials by about two to one, and car commercials outnumber everything else by about ten to one.) Sex is still pretty scary, but at least now we can call and talk about it. We still think we stink, and apparently we are a nation that needs to lose a few pounds to get into our bathing suit.

But what we're really scared of will be found on the following pages, in these stories. These are the writers who cut through the shit, real and imagined; writers who understand that although we may be concerned about personal hygiene, we're horrified by the prospect of a generation of crack-addicted offspring. Those children, in the tens of thousands, who are emotional equivalents of thalidomide babies. Because of their inability to bond with other human beings, each of them is a potential Ted Bundy. (Now, there's a concept to sink your molars into.)

We pay a great deal of attention to the plague of sexually transmitted disease, but we are terrified of random violence. What good is a condom, if someone may pull up next to your new Infiniti Lexus on the freeway and fire a .44 slug right through your factory-tinted glass?

We're worried about the collapse of the S&Ls and the FDIC, but we're petrified that we may be one fumbled test tube away from a plague or a cancer so virulent, AIDS will seem like a summer cold. And who is the source of all this free-floating anxiety? We is. We is doing it to us. As we lurch into the nineties, America is waking up, sleepy-eyed, to the truth that we are our own worst nightmare. Boil off all the crap, the rhetoric, the bureaucracy, and the mechanics of every conceivable societal ill, and beneath it you find a person or persons who, through indifference, ignorance, or greed have caused some misery for those who follow.

In the past year, with the controversy surrounding Bret Easton Ellis's *American Psycho*, and Thomas Harris's novel and the subsequent film adaptation of *Silence of the Lambs*, the media has suddenly discovered the public's intense attraction/repulsion for violence and horror. Critics and commentators have rushed to quantify the trend, mistaking their increased awareness of the phenomenon for the revelation of something new and sinister about our culture, congealing after decades of television violence and mayhem into some sort of new zeitgeist of the nineties. Please, someone alert the media that there is nothing new here, it is simply our ancient companions, fear and loathing, dressed in some gnarly jams for the new decade. *Silence of the Lambs* dips from the same well as *Psycho*, whose esteemed heritage can be traced to *Beowulf* and further to our hindbrain fears of pain, dark, and loss. Our capacity for fear has not diminished in the age of information, it has simply diffused into a million capillaries of anxiety correlating directly to the complexity of our lives.

Fear is a sort of emotional chaos that can often be overwhelming, so we try controlling it in a variety of ways: organized religion, astrology, est, scientology, computer classes, aerobics, housecleaning—basically, I see everything as a sublimation of fear, except horror, which is a fairly uncorrupted expression of it. Horror is the only medium that regularly succeeds in relating the monumental strangeness of the world in an accessible, cathartic manner. It's good for you—trust me.

Silence of the Lambs is pro-survival, and better for your soul in the long run than, say, *Home Alone* or *Ghost*, the other major films of the past year. Just as Thomas Harris is more honest reading than Danielle Steel, *Home Alone* and

Ghost were, of course, diverting and likable films—but they sustain the illusion that bad guys are simpleminded and predictable, money *is* everything, or that love is the Prozac for that nasty depression you get from waking up in the morning. *Silence of the Lambs* is a much more plausible and likely film—based on real occurrences and characters we unfortunately have a good chance of encountering in one form or another. (The only unreal expectation set up by the film is it implies people like Hannibal Lector are behind bars. The truth is, most serial killers operate randomly and freely for a long, long time.)

Of course we need the deceptions offered by happy endings and soothing prose. I defend creations like Speedy Alka-Seltzer, Spuds MacKenzie, and that dopey-looking Pillsbury Doughboy. Similarly, Flannery O'Connor and Charles Dickens and Gabriel Garcia Marquez are a necessary part of one's minimal mental diet. Life would be pretty dismal without Terry Gilliam and Walt Disney and Chuck Jones, and a thousand more like them.

But fear is inescapable and vital. History demonstrates how little is accomplished without it. The polio vaccine wasn't sought out of boredom and fat research grants, it was sought out of fear. Ditto the smallpox vaccine, quinine, anesthesia, nuclear fission, and fire—which is why we need the writers and artists and filmmakers who deal directly with the things that scare us, if only to allow us to inspect them at a safe distance. Better to contemplate madness than to experience it. Better to know the gut-tightening, sweaty-palmed adrenaline rush of a good scare in a movie theater, or in the pages of this book, than discovering firsthand what it feels like to be on the business end of a large-caliber handgun, or a lethal virus, or the heat flash of a hydrogen bomb, or, God forbid, you could be a featured segment on *60 Minutes*.

The writers in these pages will guide you on a tour of their imaginations—they take reality and stretch it here and there for you, giving you a perspective on what things might be like on the other side of your skin, in another time or place. Maybe they will give some perspective on the fears you face. The book has been sectioned into what I perceive to be major areas of concern as we come to the close of the century. These categories aren't necessarily the top five—but I suspect they are in the top ten.

And listen, stop worrying so much about dietary fiber. As Julia Child recently pointed out: "It's our fear-of-food period. There is definitely life after oat bran. All our nation has to show after years of concern is diarrhea."

There's things out there that are worse. Much worse.

Have fun, and may all your worries be over oat bran.

—Jessica Horsting
Los Angeles, 1991

Contents

Acknowledgements

"Introduction" by Jessica Horsting. Copyright © 1992 by Jessica Horsting
"Rainy Season" by Stephen King. Copyright © 1989 by Stephen King
"Say Hello, Mr. Quigley" by J. Michael Straczynski. Copyright © 1992 by J. Michael Straczynski
"Sinus Fiction" by Gil Lamont. Copyright © 1992 by Gil Lamont
"Emerald City Blues" by Steven R. Boyett. Copyright © 1989 by Steven R. Boyett
"Cattletruck" by Cliff Burns. Copyright © 1989 by Cliff Burns
"Bad Guy Hats" by David J. Schow. Copyright © 1989 by David J. Schow
"I Want to Get Married!' Says the World's Smallest Man" by John Shirley. Copyright © 1992 by John Shirley
"Spike Jones and the Reverend Claudine" by Rex Miller. Copyright © 1992 by Rex Miller

It Came From Beyond

If you are like most people, you're more worried about things you don't know than things you do know. This fear surfaces often, usually resulting in strange, ritualistic behavior—like religion, or betting the same Lotto numbers week after week, even though the statistics indicate that your numbers will only come up once in 12,273,458 drawings. But you know, if you don't bet those numbers, they will positively be drawn and some other slob is going to win all your money. Now the fear has taken on a rather perverse quality. You don't expect to win, but you have the talisman to prevent others from winning. You have gained some measure of control in a chaotic universe.

We also possess an intense curiosity about the unknown. I treated this character flaw in part by studying philosophy, which is a great way to snoop around in other people's thoughts and see what hangs from the rafters. Philosophers and scholars were worried about the same things I was: what is it we don't know about the universe, mankind, subatomic particles, paranormal experience, gestalt, dating, those kinds of things. Halfway through graduate school, it seemed apparent they didn't have the answers. I can condense five years of study pretty succinctly: there's a heck of a lot we don't know about the universe and we're usually guessing about the rest.

As a result, I'm willing to accept the possibilities of the supernatural. There may be a God—and we may be in deep trouble. I think there probably are giant squid. I believe in Carl Sagan. I'm willing to bet there is other sentient life in the universe, though it doesn't mean I'm going to be first in line when they arrive. I'll probably stand a little to one side and count their teeth first.

Possibility is the seduction of the "what if" story, though most stories are "what if" stories at their core. The difference is in the rest of the question. Jackie Collins usually asks "what if two incredibly attractive and successful people happened to merge in a glamorous, sophisticated city wearing fabulous clothes at all the right places?" Though this is a question that interests many people, I am not one of them. But I will always be sucked in by questions such as the one Mary Shelley posed: what if a scientist could create a living man? It's safe to say Mary Shelley's answer will continue to interest readers long after Jackie Collins has become a footnote in a historical overview.

Following are some very imaginative questions and answers.

—J.H.

STEPHEN KING

Stephen King is as unlikely a celebrity as one could encounter. He is an unpretentious, good-hearted guy who seems as if he would be happier at the local garage than at an author's reception. His writing has the same character. It is writing that is honest, heartfelt, intelligent, and unerring in its ability to evoke the deepest levels of fear, yet at the same time is filled with hope and a sense of just conclusions. That such a fine writer can also be one of the world's most popular writers gives me great optimism about the public's taste. Good guys can finish first.

Stephen is also a funny guy. He offers here a fast, wry, and relentless story about a small New England town and its best-kept secret.

Rainy Season
by Stephen King

It was half past five in the afternoon by the time John and Elise Graham finally found their way into the little town of Willow, Maine. It was less than five miles from the Hempstead Place, but they took two wrong turns on the way. When they finally arrived on Main Street, both of them were hot and out of sorts. The Ford's air conditioner had packed it in on the trip from St. Louis, and it felt about a hundred and ten outside. Of course, it wasn't anything at all like that, John Graham thought. As the old-timers said, it wasn't the heat, it was the humidity. It felt as if you could twist your hands in the air and wring water out of it. The sky overhead was a cloudless, faded blue, but that high humidity made it feel as if it was going to rain any minute. Fuck that—it felt as if it were raining already.

"There's the market Milly Cousins told us about," Elise said, and pointed.

John grunted. "Doesn't exactly look like the supermarket of the future."

"No," Elise said carefully. They were both being careful. They had been married almost two years and they still loved each other, but it had been a long trip across country from St. Louis, especially in a car with no air conditioner and no FM radio. John had every hope they would enjoy the summer here in Willow (they ought to, with the University of Missouri picking up the tab), but he thought it might take as long as a week for them to settle in and settle down . . . and when the weather was yellow-dog hot like this, an argument could spin itself out of thin air. Neither of them wanted that kind of start to their summer.

John drove slowly down Main Street toward the Willow General Mercantile and Hardware. There was a rusty sign with a blue eagle on it hanging from one corner of the porch, and he understood this was also the postal substation. The Willow Mercantile looked sleepy in the afternoon light, with one single car, a Volvo, parked beside the sign advertising ITALIAN SANDWICHES PIZZA GROCERIES FISHING LICENSES, but compared to the rest of the town, it seemed to be fairly bursting with life. There was a neon beer sign fizzing away in the window, although it would not be dark for almost three hours yet. Pretty radical, John thought. *Sure hope the owner cleared that sign with the Board of Selectmen before he put it in.*

"I thought Maine turned into Vacationland in the summer," Elise murmured.

"I think that's mostly along the seacoast," John said, turning in. "The tourists sure missed Willow, anyway."

They got out of the car and walked up the porch steps. An elderly man in a straw hat sat in a rocking chair, looking at them from shrewd little blue eyes. He was fiddling a home-made cigarette together and dribbling little bits of tobacco on the dog which lay crashed out at his feet. It was a big yellow dog of no particular make or model. Its paws lay directly beneath one of the rocker's curved runners. The old man took no notice of the dog, seemed not even to realize it was there, but the runner stopped a quarter of an inch from the vulnerable paws each time the old man rocked forward. Elise found this unaccountably fascinating.

"Howdy, folks," the old man said.

"Hello," Elise answered.

"Hi," John said. "I'm—"

"Mr. Graham," the old man finished placidly. "Mr. and Missus Graham. Ones that took the Hempstead Place for the summer. Heard you was writin' some kind of book."

"On the in-migration of the French during the seventeenth century," John agreed. "Word sure gets around, doesn't it?"

"It does travel," the old party agreed. "Small town, you know." He stuck the cigarette in his mouth, where it promptly fell apart, sprinkling tobacco all over his legs and the dog's limp hide. The dog didn't stir. "Aw, doodly," the old man said, and peeled the uncoiling paper from his lower lip. "Wife doesn't want me to smoke nummore anyway. She says she read it's given her cancer as well as m'ownself."

"We came into town to get a few supplies," Elise said. "It's a wonderful place, but the cupboard is bare."

"Ayuh," the old man said. "Name's Henry Eden." He held out one bunched hand. John shook with him, and Elise followed suit. They both did so with care, and the old man nodded as if to say he appreciated it. "I expected you half an hour ago. Must have taken a wrong turn or two, I guess. Got a lot of roads for such a small town, you know." He laughed. It was a hollow, bronchial sound that turned into a phlegmy smoker's cough. "Got a power of roads in Willow, oh, ayuh!" And laughed some more.

John was frowning a little. "You were . . . expecting us?"

''Lucy Ducet called, and said she saw the new folks go by,'' Eden told them. He took out his pouch of Top tobacco and opened it. He reached inside and fished out a packet of rolling papers. ''You don't know Lucy, but she says you know her grandniece, Missus.''

''Milly's great-aunt?'' Elise asked. ''Milly *Cousins's* great-aunt?''

''Ayuh,'' Eden agreed. He began to sprinkle tobacco. Some of it landed on the cigarette paper, but most went onto the dog below. As John Graham began to wonder if perhaps the dog was dead, it lifted its tail and farted. So much for *that* idea, John thought. ''In Willow, just about everybody's related to everybody else. Lucy lives down at the foot of the hill. I was gonna call you m'self, but since she said you was comin' in anyway . . .''

''How did you know we'd be coming here?'' John asked.

Henry Eden shrugged, as if to say *Where else is there to go?*

''Did you want to talk to us?'' Elise asked.

''Well, I kinda have to,'' Eden said. He sealed his cigarette and stuck it in his mouth. John waited to see if it would fall apart. He felt mildly disoriented by all this, as if he had walked unknowingly into some rustic spy network.

The cigarette somehow held together. Eden produced a wooden match from one of his shirt pockets. There was a charred scrap of sandpaper tacked to one of the arms of the rocker. Eden struck the match on it and applied the flame to his cigarette, half of which incinerated on contact with the flame.

''I think you and your Missus might want to spend the night out of town,'' Eden finally said.

John blinked at him, bewildered. ''Out of town? But . . . we just got here.''

''Good idea, though, mister,'' a voice said from behind Eden.

The Grahams looked up and saw a tall woman with slumped shoulders standing inside the Mercantile's rusty screen door. Her face looked out at them from just above an old tin sign advertising Chesterfield cigarettes—Twenty-One Great Tobaccos Make Twenty Wonderful Smokes. She opened the door and came out on the porch. Her face looked sallow and tired but not stupid. She had a loaf of bread in one hand and a six-pack of Dawson's Ale in the other.

"I'm Laura Stanton," she said. "It's very nice to meet you. We don't like to seem unsociable in Willow, but it's the rainy season here tonight."

John and Elise exchanged bewildered glances. Elise looked at the sky. Except for a few small fair-weather clouds, it was a lucid, unblemished blue.

"I know how it looks," the Stanton woman said, "but that doesn't mean anything, does it, Henry?"

"Nope," Eden said. He took one giant drag on his eroded cigarette and then pitched it over the porch rail.

"You can feel the humidity in the air," the Stanton woman said. "That's the key, isn't it, Henry?"

"Well," Eden allowed, "ayuh. But it *is* seven years. To the day."

"To the day," Laura Stanton agreed.

They both looked expectantly at the Grahams.

"Pardon me," Elise said at last. "I don't understand any of this. Is it a joke?"

This time Henry Eden and Laura Stanton exchanged a glance. They sighed at exactly the same moment, as if on cue.

"I *hate* this," Laura Stanton said, although whether to the old man or to herself John Graham had no idea.

"Got to be done," Eden replied.

She nodded, then sighed. It was the sign of a woman who has set down a heavy burden and knows she must now pick it up again.

"This doesn't come up very often," she said, "because the rainy season only comes in Willow every seven years—"

"June 17th," Eden put in. "Rainy season every seven years on June 17th. It's only one night, but rainy season's what it's always been called. Damned if I know why. Do you know why, Laura?"

"No," she said, "and I wish you'd stop interrupting, Henry. I think you're getting senile."

"Well, pardon me all the way to hell and back," the old man said, clearly nettled.

Elise threw John a glance that was a little frightened. Are these people having us on? it asked. *Or are they both crazy?*

John didn't know. But he wished heartily they had just found a clam-stand beside the road and gone into Augusta for supplies in the morning.

"Now, listen," the Stanton woman said kindly. "We reserved a room for you at the Castle Motel out on Route 130, if you want it. The place was full, but the manager's my cousin, and he was able to clear one room out for me. You could come back tomorrow and spend the rest of the summer with us. We'd be glad to have you."

"If this is a joke, I'm not getting the point," John said.

"No, it's not a joke," she said. "Every seven years, it rains toads here in Willow."

"Toads," Elise said in a distant, musing, I-am-dreaming-all-this voice.

"Toads!" Henry Eden affirmed cheerfully.

John was looking cautiously around for help, if help should be needed. But Main Street was utterly deserted. Not only that, he saw, but shuttered. Not a car moved on the road. Not a single pedestrian was visible on either sidewalk.

We could be in trouble here, he thought, and for the first time he was afraid as well as bewildered.

"Now, I'm just doing my duty," Laura Stanton said. "Henry, too. You see, it doesn't just *sprinkle* toads. It *pours*

. . . It can be frightening if you're not prepared for it. In fact, it can be dangerous.''

''Come on,'' John said to Elise, taking her arm above the elbow. ''It was nice to meet both of you people,'' he added. He guided his wife down the porch steps, wondering if his nose was growing yet. He kept looking back at the old man and the slump-shouldered, pallid woman standing beside him. It didn't seem like a good idea to turn his back on them completely. Not at all like a good idea.

The woman took a step toward them, and John almost stumbled and fell off the last step.

''It *is* a little hard to believe,'' she agreed. ''You probably think I am just as nutty as a fruitcake.''

''Not at all,'' John said. A large, insincere smile surfaced on his face and froze there. Dear Jesus, why had he ever left St. Louis? He had driven nearly fifteen hundred miles with a busted air conditioner to meet Dr. Jekyll and Mrs. Hyde.

''That's fine,'' she said with a weird serenity that made him stop by the ITALIAN SANDWICHES sign, still six feet from the Ford. ''Even people who have heard of rains of frogs and toads and birds and such don't have a very clear idea of what happens in Willow every seven years on the 17th of June. If you are going to stay, I'd stay in the house. You'll most likely be all right in the house.''

''Might want to close y'shutters, though,'' Eden said, and the dog lifted his tail and articulated another long and groaning dog fart.

''We'll . . . we'll do that,'' Elise said faintly, and then John had the Ford's passenger door open and was nearly shoveling her inside.

''You bet,'' he said through his large frozen grin.

''And come back and see us tomorrow,'' Eden called as John hurried around the front of the Ford to his side. ''You'll feel a mite safer around us tomorrow, I think.''

John waved, got behind the wheel, and pulled out.

There was silence on the porch for a moment as the old man and the woman with the pallid, unhealthy skin watched the Ford head back up Main Street, at a considerably higher speed than that at which it had come.

"Well, we done it," the old man said contentedly.

"Yes," she agreed, "and I feel like a horse's ass. I *always* feel like a horse's ass."

"Well," he said, "it's only once every seven years. And it's the ritual."

As if agreeing it was so, the dog flipped up his tail and farted.

"I *know* it's the ritual," she said crossly, and booted the dog. "That is the *stinkiest* mutt in four towns, Henry Eden!"

The dog arose with a grunt and staggered down the porch stairs, pausing only long enough to favor Laura Stanton with a reproachful gaze.

"He can't help it," Eden said.

She sighed, looking up the road after the Ford. "It's too bad," she said. "They seem like such *nice* people."

"Nor can *we* help that," Henry Eden said, and began to roll another smoke.

That was why the Grahams ended up eating dinner at a clam-stand after all. They found one in the neighboring town of Woolwich and sat at a picnic table in a little clearing beside it to eat. The clam-stand was in sharp, almost jarring contrast to Willow's Main Street. The parking lot was nearly full (most of the cars, like theirs, had out-of-state license plates), and yelling kids with ice cream on their faces chased after one another while their parents strolled about, slapped black-flies, and waited for their orders to come up. The stand had a fairly wide menu. In fact, John thought, you could have just about anything you wanted, as long as it wasn't too big to fit in a deep-fat fryer.

"I don't know if I can spend two days in that town, let alone two months," Elise said. "The bloom is off the rose for this mother's daughter, Johnny."

"It was a joke," John said. "Just the kind of thing the natives like to play on the tourists. They just went too far with it. They're probably kicking themselves for that right now."

"They looked serious," she said. "How am I supposed to go back there and face that old man after that?"

"He probably won't even remember we were there," John said. "He looked like he might need a roadmap to find his way to the bathroom, to tell you the truth."

"Well, where was everybody?"

"Bean supper at the Grange or the Eastern Star, probably," John said, stretching. He peeked into her clam basket. "You didn't eat much, love."

"Love wasn't very hungry."

"I tell you it was just a joke," he said, taking her hand and speaking earnestly. "They carried it further than they meant to, that's all."

"You're sure of that?"

"Yes," he said. "I mean, every seven years it rains toads in Willow, Maine?"

She smiled wanly. "It doesn't rain," she said, "it pours."

"Yeah, that's what she said, isn't it? Well, I don't believe it, and I don't think you do, either. When I was a kid at sleep-away camp, it used to be snipe hunts. This really isn't much different. And when you stop to think about it, it really isn't that surprising."

"What isn't?"

"That people who make most of their yearly income dealing with summer people should develop a summer camp mentality."

"That woman . . . sort of scared me."

John Graham's normally pleasant face grew stern and hard. The expression did not look at home on his face, but neither did it look faked or insincere.

''I know,'' he said, picking up their wrappings and napkins and plastic baskets. ''And there's going to be an apology made for that. I find foolishness for the sake of foolishness agreeable enough, but when someone scares my wife—hell, they scared *me* a little, too—I draw the line. Ready to go back?''

''Can you find it again?''

He grinned, and immediately looked more like himself. ''I left a trail of breadcrumbs.''

''How wise you are,'' she said, and got up. She was smiling again, and John was glad to see it. She drew a deep breath and let it out. ''The humidity seems to have dropped.''

''Yeah.'' John deposited their waste into a trash basket with a left-handed hook shot. He winked at her. ''So much for rainy season.''

But by the time they turned onto the Hempstead Road, the humidity had returned, and with a vengeance. John felt as if his tee-shirt had turned into a clammy mass of cobweb clinging to his chest and back. The sky, now turning a delicate shade of evening violet, was still perfectly clear, but he felt that if he'd had a straw, he could have drunk directly from the air.

There was only one other house on the road, at the foot of the long hill with the Hempstead Place at the top. As they drove past it, John saw the silhouette of a woman standing motionless at one of the windows and looking out at them.

''Well, there's your friend Milly's great-aunt,'' John said. ''She sure was a great sport to call the local crazies down at the general store and tell them we were coming. I wonder if they would have dragged out the whoopee cushions and the joy-buzzers if we'd stayed a little longer.''

''That dog had his own built-in joy-buzzer.''

John laughed and nodded.

Five minutes later they were turning into their own driveway. It was badly overgrown with weeds and dwarf bushes, and John intended to take care of *that* little situation before the summer got much older. The Hempstead Place itself was a rambling country farmhouse, added to by succeeding generations whenever the urge—or the need—to do some building happened to strike. A barn stood behind it, connected to the house by three rambling, zigzag sheds. In this flush of early summer, two of the three sheds were almost buried by fragrant drifts of honeysuckle.

It commanded a gorgeous view of the town, especially on a clear night like this one. John wondered briefly just how it could *be* so clear when the humidity was so high, and dismissed the thought.

Elise joined him in front of the car and they stood there for a moment, arms around each other's waists, looking at the hills which rolled gently off in the direction of Augusta, losing themselves in the shadows of evening.

''It's beautiful,'' she murmured.

''And listen,'' he said.

There was a marshy area of reeds and high grass fifty yards or so behind the barn, and in it a chorus of frogs sang and thumped and snapped the elastics God had for some reason stretched in their throats.

''Well,'' she said, ''the frogs are all present and accounted for, anyway.''

''No toads, though.'' He looked up at the clear sky, in which Venus had opened her coldly burning eye. ''There they are, Elise! Up there! Clouds of toads!''

She giggled.

" 'Tonight in the small town of Willow,' " he intoned, " 'a cold front of toads met a warm front of newts, and the result was—' "

She elbowed him. "You," she said. "Let's go in."

They went in. And they did not pass Go. And they did not collect two hundred dollars.

They went directly to bed.

Elise was startled out of a satisfying drowse about an hour later by a thump on the roof. She got up on her elbows. "What was that, Johnny?"

"Huzz," John said, and turned over on his side.

Toads, she thought, and giggled . . . but it was a nervous giggle. She got up and went to the window, and before she looked for anything which might have fallen on the ground, she found herself looking up at the sky.

It was still cloudless, and now shot with a trillion spangled stars. She looked at them, for a moment hypnotized by their simple silent beauty.

Thud.

She jerked back from the window and looked up at the ceiling. Whatever it was, it had hit the roof just overhead.

"John! Johnny! Wake up!"

"Huh? What." He sat up, his hair all tangled tufts and clocksprings.

"It's started," she said, and giggled shrilly. "The rain of frogs."

"Toads," he corrected. "Ellie, what are you talking ab—"

Thud-thud.

He looked around, then swung his feet out of bed.

"This is ridiculous," he said softly and angrily.

"What do you m—"

Thud-CRASH! There was a tinkle of glass downstairs.

"Oh, goddam," he said, getting up and yanking on his blue jeans. "Enough. This is just . . . fucking . . . enough."

Several soft thuds hit the side of the house and the roof. She cringed against him, frightened now. ''What do you mean?''

''I mean that crazy woman and probably the old man and some of their friends are out there throwing things at the house,'' he said, ''and I am going to put a stop to it right now. Maybe they've held on to the custom of shivareeing the new folks in this little town, but—''

THUD! SMASH! From the kitchen.

''God-DAM!'' John yelled, and ran out into the hall.

''Don't leave me!'' Elise cried, and ran after him.

He flicked up the hallway light switch before plunging downstairs. Soft thumps and thuds struck the house in an increasing rhythm, and Elise had time to think, *How many people from town are out there? How many does it take to do that? And what are they throwing? Rocks wrapped in pillowcases?*

John reached the foot of the stairs and went into the living room. There was a large window in there which gave on the same view of the long, descending hills which they had admired earlier. The window was broken. Shards and splinters of glass lay all over the rug. He started toward the window, meaning to yell something at them about how he was going to get his shotgun. Then he looked at the broken glass again, remembered that his feet were bare, and stopped. For a moment he didn't know what to do. Then he saw a dark shape lying in the broken glass—the rock one of the imbecilic, interbred bastards had used to break the window, he assumed—and saw red. He might have charged to the window anyway, bare feet or no bare feet, but just then the rock twitched and moved.

Why, it's not a rock at all, he thought. *It's a . . .*

''John?'' Elise asked. The house rang with those soft thuds now. It was as if they were being bombarded with large, rotten-soft hailstones. ''John, what is it?''

"It's a toad," he said stupidly. He was still looking at the dark, twitching shape in the litter of broken glass, and spoke more to himself than to his wife.

He raised his eyes and looked out the window. What he saw out there struck him mute with horror and incredulity. He could no longer see the hills or the horizon—hell, he could barely see the barn, and that was less than forty feet away.

The air was stuffed with falling shapes.

Three more of them came in through the broken window. One landed on the floor, not far from its twitching mate. It landed on a sharp sliver of glass and black fluid burst from its body in thick ropes.

Elise screamed.

The other two caught in the curtains, which began to twist and jerk as if in a fitful breeze. One of them managed to disentangle itself. It struck the floor and then hopped toward John.

He groped at the wall with a hand which felt as if it were no part of him at all. His fingers stumbled across the light switch and flipped it up.

The thing hopping across the glass-littered floor toward him was a toad, but it was also not a toad. Its green-black body was too large, too lumpy. Its black and gold eyes bulged and lolled like freakish eggs. And bursting from its mouth, unhinging the jaw, was a bouquet of large, needle-sharp teeth.

It made a thick croaking noise and bounded at John as if on springs. Behind it, more toads were falling in through the window. The ones which struck the floor were either crippled or died outright, but many others—too many others—caught in the curtains and tumbled to the floor unharmed.

"*Get* out of here!" John yelled to his wife, and kicked at the toad which—it was insane, but it was true—was attacking him. It did not flinch back from his foot, but sank that mouthful of crooked needles first over and then into his toes. The pain was immediate, fiery, and immense. Without thinking, he made a half turn and kicked the wall as hard as he could. He felt his toes break, but the toad broke, as well, splattering its black blood onto the wainscotting in a half circle, like a fan. His toes had become a crazy road sign, pointing in all directions at once.

Elise was standing frozen in the hall doorway. She could hear window glass shattering all over the house. She had put on one of John's tee-shirts after they had finished making love, and now she was clutching the neck of it with both hands. The air was full of ugly croaking sounds.

"Get out!" John screamed. He turned, shaking his bloody foot. The toad which had sunk the grappling hook of its mouth into it was dead, but its huge and improbable teeth were still buried deep in him. This time he kicked at the air, like a man punting a football, and the toad finally flew free.

The faded living-room carpet was now covered with bloated, hopping bodies. And they were all hopping at them.

John ran to the doorway. His foot came down on one of the toads and burst it open. His heel skidded in the cold jelly which popped out of its body and he almost fell. Elise relinquished her death grip on the neck of her tee-shirt and grabbed him. They stumbled into the hall, and John slammed the door, catching one of the toads in the act of hopping through. The door hacked it in half. The top half twitched and juddered on the floor, its toothy, black-lipped mouth opening and closing, its black and golden pop-eyes goggling at them.

Elise clapped her hands to the sides of her face and began to wail hysterically. John reached out to her. She shook her head and cringed away from him, her hair falling over her face.

The sound of the toads hitting the roof was bad, but the croakings and chirrupings were worse, because these latter sounds were coming from inside the house . . . and *all over* the house. He thought of the old man sitting on the porch of the Willow Mercantile in his rocker, calling after them: *Might want to close y' shutters.*

Christ, why didn't I believe him?

And, on the heels of that: *How was I supposed to believe him? Nothing in my whole life prepared me to believe him!*

And, below the sound of toads thudding onto the ground outside and toads squashing themselves to guts and goo on the roof, he heard a more ominous sound: the chewing, splintering sound of toads in the living room starting to bite their way through the door. He could actually see it settling more firmly against its hinges as more and more toads crowded their weight against it.

He turned around and saw toads hopping down the main staircase by the dozens.

"Elise!" He grabbed at her. She kept shrieking and pulling away from him. A sleeve of the tee-shirt tore free. He looked at the ragged chunk of cloth in his hand with perfect stupidity for a moment and then let it drop.

"Elise!"

She shrieked and drew back again.

Now the first toads had reached the hall floor and were hopping eagerly toward them. There was a brittle tinkle of glass as the fanlight over the door shattered. A toad whizzed through it, struck the carpet, and lay on its back, mottled pink belly exposed, webbed feet twitching in the air.

He grabbed his wife, shook her. "We have to go down to the cellar! We'll be safer in the cellar!"

"No!" Elise screamed at him. Her eyes were giant floating zeros, and he understood she was not refusing his idea of retreating to the cellar but refusing everything.

There was no time for gentle measures or soothing words. He bunched the front of the shirt she was wearing in his fist and yanked her down the hall like a cop dragging a recalcitrant prisoner to a squad-car. One of the toads which had been in the vanguard of those hopping and tumbling down the stairs leaped gigantically and snicked its mouth of darning needles shut around a chunk of space occupied by Elise's bare heel a second before.

Halfway down the hall, she got the idea and began to come with him of her own accord. They reached the door. John turned the knob and yanked it, but the door wouldn't move.

"Goddam!" he cried, and yanked it again. No good. Nothing.

"John, hurry!"

She looked back over her shoulder and saw toads flooding down the hall toward them, leaping crazily as if on springs, landing on each other, striking the walls with their faded rambler-rose wallpaper, landing on their backs and being overrun by their mates. They were all teeth and gold-black eyes and heaving, leathery bodies.

"JOHN, PLEASE! PL—"

Then one of them leaped and battened on her left thigh just above the knee. Elise screamed and seized it, her fingers punching through its skin and into its dark liquid workings. She tore it free and for a moment, as she raised her arms, the thing was right in front of her eyes, its teeth gnashing like a piece of some small but homicidal factory machine. She threw it as hard as she could. It cartwheeled in the air and then splattered against the wall just opposite the kitchen door. It did not fall but stuck fast in the glue of its own guts.

"JOHN! OH JESUS, JOHN!"

John Graham suddenly realized what he was doing wrong. He reversed the direction of his effort, pushing on the door instead of pulling it. It flew open, almost spilling him forward and down the stairs, and he wondered briefly if his mother had had any kids that lived. He flailed at the railing, caught hold of it, and then Elise almost knocked him down again, bolting past him and down the stairs, screaming like a fireball in the night.

Oh she's going to fall, she's going to break her neck—

But, somehow, she did not. She reached the cellar's earth floor and collapsed in a sobbing heap, clutching at her torn thigh.

Toads were leaping and hopping in through the open cellar doorway.

John caught his balance, turned, and slapped the door shut. Several of the toads caught on their side of the door leaped right off the landing, struck the stairs, and fell through the spaces between the risers. Another took an almost vertical leap straight up, and John was suddenly shaken by wild laughter—a sudden bright image of a toad on a pogo stick had come to him. Still laughing, he balled his right hand into a fist and punched the toad dead center in its pulsing, flabby chest at the top of its leap, while it hung in perfect equilibrium between gravity and its own expended energy. It zoomed off into the shadows, and John heard a soft *bonk*! as it struck the furnace.

He scrabbled at the wall in the dark, and his fingers found the raised cylinder which was the old-fashioned toggle light switch. He flipped it, and that was when Elise began to scream again. A toad had gotten tangled in her hair. It croaked and twisted and turned and bit at her neck, rolling itself into something which resembled a large, misshapen curler.

Elise lurched to her feet and ran in a large circle, miraculously avoiding a tumble over the boxes which had been stacked and stored down here. She struck one of the cellar's support posts, rebounded, then turned and banged the back of her head twice, briskly, against it. There was a thick squishing sound and the toad's curl unrolled. It hung there for a moment and then fell out of her hair, tumbling down the back of her tee-shirt, leaving dribbles of ichor.

She screamed, nearly mad with fear and pain and revulsion. John half ran, half stumbled down the cellar stairs and enfolded her in his arms. She fought against him at first and then surrendered. Her screams gradually dissolved into steady weeping.

Then, over the soft thunder of the toads striking the house and the grounds, they heard the croaking of the toads which had fallen down here.

She drew away from him, her eyes shifting wildly from side to side.

"Where are they," she panted. Her voice was hoarse, almost a bark, from all the screaming she had done. "Where are they, John?"

But they didn't have to look; the toads had already seen them, and came hopping eagerly toward them.

The Grahams retreated, and John saw a rusty shovel leaning against the wall. He grabbed it and beat the toads to death with it as they came. Only one got past him. It leaped from the floor to a box and from the box it jumped at Elise, catching the cloth of her shirt in its teeth and dangling there between her breasts, legs kicking.

"Stand still!" John barked at her. He dropped the shovel, took two steps forward, grabbed the toad, and hauled it off her shirt. It took a chunk of cloth with it. The cotton strip hung from one of its fangs as it twisted and pulsed and wriggled in John's hands. Its hide was warty, dry but horribly warm and somehow busy. He snapped his hands into fists, popping the toad. Blood and slime squirted out from between his fingers.

Less than a dozen of the little monsters had actually made it through the cellar door, and soon they were all dead. John and Elise stood together, arms around each other's waists, listening to the steady rain of toads outside.

John looked over at the low cellar windows. They were packed and dark, and he suddenly saw the house as it must look from the outside, buried in a drift of squirming, lunging, leaping toads.

"We've got to block the windows," he said hoarsely.

"Their weight is going to break them, and if that happens, they'll *pour* in."

"With what?" Elise asked in her hoarse bark of a voice. "With what?"

He looked around and saw several sheets of plywood, elderly and dark, leaning against one wall. Not much, perhaps, but something.

"That," he said. "Help me to break it up into smaller pieces."

They worked quickly and frantically. There were only four windows in the cellar, and their very narrowness probably caused the panes to hold longer than the larger windows upstairs would have done. They were just finishing the last when they heard the glass of the first shatter behind the plywood . . . but the plywood held.

They staggered into the middle of the cellar again, John limping on his broken foot.

From the top of the stairway came the sound of the toads eating their way through the cellar door.

"What do we do if they eat all the way through it?" Elise whispered.

"I don't know," he said . . . and that was when the door of the coal-chute, which had not been used for years but which was still intact, suddenly swung open under the weight of all the toads which had fallen or hopped into it, and thousands of them poured out in a high-pressure jet.

Elise could not scream; she had damaged her vocal cords too badly for that.

It did not last long for the Grahams in the cellar after the coal-chute gave way, but until it was over, John Graham screamed quite adequately for both of them.

By midnight, the downpour of toads in Willow had slacked off to a mild, croaking drizzle.

At one-thirty in the morning, the last toad fell out of the

dark, starry sky, landed in a pine tree near the lake, hopped to the ground, and disappeared into the night. It was over for another seven years.

Around quarter past five, the first light began to creep into the sky and over the land. Willow was buried beneath a writhing, hopping, complaining carpet of toads. The buildings on Main Street had lost their angles and corners, everything was rounded and hunched and twitching. The sign on Route 9 which read WELCOME TO WILLOW, MAINE, THE *FRIENDLY* PLACE! looked as if someone had put about thirty shotgun shells through it. The holes, of course, had been made by flying toads. The sign in front of the General Mercantile which advertised ITALIAN SANDWICHES PIZZA GROCERIES FISHING LICENSES had been knocked over. Toads played leapfrog on and around it. There was a small toad convention going on atop each of the gas pumps at Sonny's Sunoco. Two toads sat upon the slowly swinging iron arm of the weather-vane atop the Willow Hardware Store like small misshapen children on a merry-go-round.

At the lake, the few floats which had been put out this early (only the hardiest swimmers dared the waters of Lake Willow before July 4th, toads or no toads) were piled high with toads, and the fish were going crazy with so much food almost within reach. Every now and then there was a *plip! plip*! sound as one or two of the toads jostling for place on the floats were knocked off and some hungry trout or salmon's breakfast was served. The roads in and out of town—there were a lot of them for such a small town, as Henry Eden had said—were paved with toads. The power was out for the nonce; fast-falling toads had broken the power lines in any number of places. Most of the gardens were ruined, but Willow wasn't much of a farming community, anyway. Several people kept fairly large dairy herds, but they had all been safely tucked away for the night. Dairy farmers in Willow knew all about rainy season and had no wish to lose their milkers to the hordes of leaping, carnivorous toads. What in the hell would you tell the insurance company?

As the light brightened over the Hempstead Place, it revealed drifts of dead toads on the roof, rain gutters which had been splintered loose by dive-bombing toads, a dooryard that was alive with toads. They hopped in and out of the barn, they stuffed the chimneys, they hopped nonchalantly about John Graham's Ford and sat in croaking rows on the front seat like a church congregation waiting for the services to start. Heaps of toads, mostly dead, lay in drifts against the building. Some of these drifts were six feet deep.

At 6:05, the sun cleared the horizon, and as its rays struck them, the toads began to melt.

Their skins bleached, turned white, then appeared to become transparent. Soon a smoky vapor which gave off a vaguely swampy smell began to trail up from the bodies and little bubbly rivulets of moisture began to course down them. Their eyes fell in or fell out, depending on their positions when the sun hit them. Their skins popped with an audible sound, and for perhaps ten minutes it sounded as if champagne corks were popping all over Willow.

They decomposed rapidly after that, melting into puddles of cloudy white *shmeg* that looked like human semen. This liquid ran down the pitches of the Hempstead Place's roof in little creeks and dripped from the eaves like pus.

The living toads died; the dead ones simply rotted to white liquid which bubbled and then sank slowly into the ground. The earth sent up tiny ribands of steam, and for a little while every field in Willow looked like the site of a dying volcano.

By quarter of seven it was over, except for the repairs, and the residents were used to them.

It seemed a small price to pay for another seven years of quiet prosperity in this mostly forgotten Maine backwater.

* * *

At five minutes past eight, Laura Stanton's old Volvo turned into the dooryard of the General Mercantile. When Laura got out, she looked paler and sicker than ever. She *was* sick, in fact; she still had the six-pack of Dawson's Ale in one hand, but now all the bottles were empty. She had a vicious hangover.

Henry Eden came out on the porch. His dog walked behind him.

''Get that mutt inside, or I'm gonna turn right around and go home,'' Laura said from the foot of the stairs.

''He can't help passing gas, Laura.''

''That doesn't mean I have to be around when he lets rip,'' Laura said. ''I mean it, now, Henry. My head hurts like a bastard, and the last thing I need this morning is listening to that dog play *Hail Columbia* out of its asshole.''

''Go inside, Toby,'' Henry said, holding the door open.

Toby looked up at him with wet eyes, as if to say *Do I have to? Things were just getting interesting out here*.

''Go on, now,'' Henry said.

Tony walked back inside, and Henry shut the door. Laura waited until she heard the latch snick firmly shut, and then she mounted the steps.

''Your sign fell over,'' she said, handing him the carton of empties.

''I got eyes, woman,'' Henry said. He was not in the best temper this morning, himself. Few people in Willow would be. Sleeping through a rain of toads was a goddam hard piece of work. Thank God it only came once every seven years, or a man would be apt to go shit out of his mind.

''You should have taken it in,'' she said.

Henry muttered something she didn't quite catch.

''What was that?''

''I said we should have tried harder,'' Henry said defiantly.

"They was a nice young couple. We should have tried harder."

She felt a touch of compassion for the old man in spite of her thudding head, and laid a hand on his arm. "It's the ritual," she said.

"Well, sometimes I just feel like saying frig the ritual!"

"Henry!" She drew her hand back, shocked in spite of herself. But he wasn't getting any younger, she reminded herself. The wheels were getting a little rusty upstairs, no doubt.

"I don't care," he said stubbornly. "They seemed like a real nice young couple. You said so, too, and don't try to say you didn't."

"I *did* think they were nice," she said. "But we can't help that, Henry. Why, you said so yourself just last night."

"I know," he sighed.

"We don't make them stay," she said. "Just the opposite. We warn them out of town. They decide to stay themselves. They *always* decide to stay. They make their own decisions. That's part of the ritual, too."

"I know," he repeated. He drew a deep breath and grimaced. "I hate the smell . . . afterward. Smells a little like clabbered milk."

"It'll be gone by noon. You know that."

"Ayuh. But I just about hope I'm underground when it comes around again, Laura. And if I ain't, I hope somebody else gets the job of meetin' whoever comes just before the rainy season. I like bein' able to pay m'bills when they come due just as well as anybody else, but I tell you, a man gets tired of toads. Even if it is only once every seven years, a man can get damned tired of toads."

"A woman, too," she said softly.

"Well," he said with a sigh, "I guess it's time to start cleanin' up for the summer, ain't it?"

"I guess it is," she said. "And, you know, Henry, we

don't make ritual, we only follow it. And things could change. There's no telling when or why, but they could. This might be the last time we have rainy season. Or next time no one from out of town might come—"

"Don't say that," he said fearfully. "If no one comes, the toads might not go away like they do when the sun hits 'em."

"There, you see?" she asked. "You have come around to my side of it, after all."

"Well," he said, "it's a long time. Ain't it. Seven years is a long time."

"Yes."

"They *was* a nice young couple, weren't they?"

"Yes," she said again.

"Nasty way to go," Henry Eden said with a slight hitch in his voice, and this time she said nothing. After a moment, Henry asked her if she would help him set his sign up again. In spite of her nasty headache, Laura said she would—she didn't like to see Henry so low, especially when he was feeling low over something he could control no more than he could control the tides, or the phases of the moon.

By the time they finished, he seemed to feel a little better.

"Ayuh," he said. "Seven years is a *hell* of a long time."

It is, she thought, but it always passes, and rainy season always comes around again, and the outsiders always come with it, always two of them, and we always tell them exactly what is going to happen, and they don't believe it, and what happens . . . happens.

"Come on, you old crock," she said, "offer me a cup of coffee before my head splits wide open."

He offered her a cup, and before they had finished, the sounds of hammers and saws had begun in town. Outside the window they could look down Main Street and see people folding back their shutters, talking and laughing.

The air was warm and dry, the sky overhead was a pale and flawless blue, and in Willow, rainy season was over.

J. MICHAEL STRACZYNSKI

J. Michael Straczynski is doing the things many writers only dream of: he is a successful novelist, screenwriter, television series story editor (first for CBS's revamped *Twilight Zone* and currently for *Murder She Wrote*), and fledgling series creator. His two novels, *Othersyde* and *Demon Night*, were well received, and he is currently editing the ongoing anthology series *Tales From the Twilight Zone*. (In his spare time, he also does brain surgery, ballet, is a professional mime, and acts as a consultant for the Pentagon.)

Joe's great strength as a writer is storytelling. He has the ability to take the conventional and make it surprising, with a skilled sense of structure and characterization, as the following story will chillingly illustrate.

Say Hello, Mister Quigley

by J. Michael Straczynski

It was almost noon by the time they got to the house. For the last two miles, Liz hadn't bothered to check the map. The town had changed in fifteen years, but the shape of it, the *feel* of it, remained the same.

"There," she said, and pointed across the street. Already past it when she called out, Jim turned into a driveway farther down, did a U-turn, and parked in front of the house.

He shut off the engine. "Nice place."

Liz nodded absently. From here, it still looked reasonably well kept, but the lack of attention characterized by six months of unoccupancy left it a little ragged around the edges. It had taken Liz that long to decide whether or not to keep the house, or if she was going to personally go and take possession, or if it would be better just to sign the papers long distance.

Fifteen years. Don't be such a baby.

The interior would also need work. After her father had died, her mother had tried to keep up appearances, but more often than not things that needed doing just got postponed in anticipation of a vaguely foreseen day when she'd "get around to it all." But that appointment had been missed permanently, and in her mother's absence the list of demands remained: paint and caulking and a dozen small repairs, wiring desperately in need of an overhaul, she guessed that there was probably asbestos that would have to be removed—

It was a lot of work. But the house could be made clean again.

She would *make* it clean again. And in the process—

She glanced across at Jim, vaguely aware that he was speaking to her. "—do you think? She's all yours now."

"It's so much smaller than I remembered."

"Liz, that was ages ago. Of course it seemed bigger. And granted, it needs a little TLC—well, make that a lot of TLC—but it'll be fine. Then you can move in, if you still want to."

She nodded. "My mother wanted me to have the house. And I intend to."

"Then let's get started." He climbed out of the pickup and went to the back of the cab. She popped the door and followed him out onto the street, standing back as he unloaded boxes of tools and wires.

She stuffed her hands in the pockets of her sweater. She felt cold despite the sun on her face. Standing outside the house, she wondered if this was really a good idea. Maybe it would have been better if she'd just signed it over. . . .

Jim turned toward her, hefting the boxes of tools. "Ready to get to work, Madame Assistant Carpenter, First Class?"

"Yeah," she said, and smiled, though it felt false across her lips. "I'm ready."

He crossed the lawn and started up the porch steps to the door. Liz hesitated, then followed.

It was a long time ago, she thought. *Long time gone. Long time dead.*

Time to get to work.

Everywhere was the smell of dust and old furniture and carefully hidden bags of cedar chips to keep away the moths. And here and there, almost a year after her mother had closed up the house to go and stay with her aunt, there was still the fragile scent of her perfume. Jasmine.

Liz moved through the house room by room, opening windows and snapping the sheets off furniture, each step revealing some new artifact of her parents' lives. In the living room she found his favorite chair. She remembered how her mother had been unable to get rid of it even after he passed away. There were too many memories in that chair for her to throw it out, and too many memories filling the house to let her stay.

I'll take care of that soon enough, Liz thought.

She moved to the fireplace, and the mantel covered with a flurry of framed photos, the glass stained by a fine patina of dust. Her graduation pictures from high school and college. Her grandparents. Photographs of the neighborhood, the house—

She stopped. Carefully picking through the frames, she pulled a photo with her face on it out from the back row. She remembered when it was taken. She was twelve. Her father sat next to her in the photo. He was grinning broadly for the camera, holding her in his lap, an arm around her waist. Her own smile was wrong, staring past the camera, looking back at her across the years, trying to sit still, there beside him, and he was holding her—

She threw it across the room. The frame smashed into a wall and rained down in a shower of glass and shredded paper.

Why didn't they see? It was so obvious. It was right there on her face. Why didn't they SEE?

"You okay?"

She turned, and saw Jim standing in the doorway. "Thought I heard something break," he said, and then noticed the glass.

"Just a picture. It fell. Nothing important." She found a broom and stepped toward the debris. "This place is a real hazard. But it'll be okay, once we get rid of—once we clear it out."

She glanced up to meet his gaze. If he doubted her story, he gave no sign of it. "So what's your prognosis?"

"Like I said, it needs a lot of work. You've got some pipes that have to be replaced, with copper if you're smart. The foundation looks pretty solid, but the roof needs some reshingling, and the wiring is pretty much shot. I wouldn't suggest you run any heavy equipment on the wires until you get someone in to check it out thoroughly. Other than that, there's just a lot of stuff that needs to be sorted, kept, or thrown out. Where do you want to start?"

"The attic, I guess. We'll work our way down."

He nodded, and headed back out of the room. She scooped up the broken frame and carried it to the trash box. A fragment of her face stared up at her. *Can't tell, can't tell, no, never tell, there'll be trouble, there'll be—*

She let it fall into the box, shook out the dustpan, and moved on.

The attic was musty and dark, an explosion of boxes and crates and trunks and piles of old clothes. Jim volunteered to start at one end, she'd start at the other, and they'd meet in the middle.

She plowed her way through the first three boxes, making good time. There were stacks of old *Life* magazines, broken toys, glassware and crockery, books and clothes, some in need of repair, or too worn to wear and too familiar to throw away, finally just stashed out of sight in lieu of a decision. Most of it could be trashed, but some was in good enough shape to donate.

"Hey, slugger," Jim called. She looked up to see him waving a baseball bat he'd found in one of the boxes.

She smiled at the sight of it. "Thirteenth birthday present," she said, "from my uncle."

"Save it or throw it?"

"Save it," she said, and turned her attention back to the task at hand.

She closed up the third cardboard box and reached for the next, like the rest sealed with tape long gone yellow. She tugged at the top. For a moment it refused to yield. She pulled harder. With a sudden tearing of rotten cardboard it ripped open and down one side, spilling its contents, musty piles of clothes, and something large and soft that jingled as it fell into her lap.

It landed with its face turned up to her own, a grey and white cloth face with oversize stitching, too large eyes, and a grin that ran from ear to ear,

(mister quigley)

its limbs long and gangly and dressed in a green-and-black checked motley, stained by food and age, a three-foot-tall jester with bells on his arms and bells on his feet and bells sewn into the cap that was sewn onto his head,

(Mister Quigley)

and she automatically tried to shove it away, but it shifted in her grip, soft and resilient, folding back at her, and now she was batting at it, only distantly aware of the noise that came from the back of her throat, guttural and hungry for air,

(say hello, Mister Quigley)

as she finally kicked it away, and it jingled as it fell,

bells clattering against the hardwood floor of the attic. She scrabbled away from it as she would from a spider.

Jim looked up from his pile of boxes, started toward her. "Liz? Are you—"

She stood hurriedly, brushing off the dust. "I'm fine."

"You sure?" He came up alongside her and looked down at the cloth-and-stuffing jester dumped upside down on the floor. "Who's that?"

Liz glanced down only for a second. "Mister Quigley," she said, barely loud enough for him to hear. "Mister—"

She fled from the attic, careening against the doorway but not feeling it, frantic to get to any place that was not this room.

Liz found the coffeepot where it had always been, and pulled out the fresh-ground coffee they'd brought in from town. She would give the pot a thorough cleaning later. Right now, a quick wash would have to do. She needed something to drink, and something to do with her hands that would make them stop shaking, make them feel warm again.

A few minutes later, sensing perhaps that she needed some time to herself, Jim came down from the attic, brushing dust off his work shirt as he entered the kitchen. She sat at the Formica table, facing the wall as he appeared in the doorway. She could feel him looking at her. "You want to talk about it?"

She shook her head. "No."

He waited.

She set down the cup and pressed her hands down flat on the table, letting the coolness seep into her palms. "His name was Mister Quigley," she said. "He belonged to my father when he was a boy. It was one of the few things he still had from that time. He used to keep it propped up in a chair in a corner of the living room. It always made the other kids nervous. I mean, it was nearly as tall as they were, and to see it sitting there, sometimes at night—no, they didn't like Mister Quigley. Not one bit.''

''And you?''

''I felt the same way, at first. My father used to tease me about it. In the mornings, I'd come out, and he'd say, 'Well, Liz, say ''Good morning, Mister Quigley.'' ' And I'd do it. And then he'd look at it and say, 'Now say hello to Liz, Mister Quigley.' It gave me the creeps. But eventually, I guess I got used to him. He was just another part of the family. After a while, we ran out of space in the living room, and my father decided to put Mister Quigley in my room. Since he was good at scaring the other kids, I figured he'd be my guardian. I used to pretend he was there to protect me against monsters. Right before I went to sleep, I'd whisper, 'Watch out for the monsters, Mister Quigley. Keep them far away from my bed.' ''

''And did he?''

She opened her mouth to answer, but nothing came out. She stood and carried her cup to the sink. The china rattled in her hands.

''Liz?''

She dropped her cup into the water. ''I don't want to talk about it anymore, all right?''

She began washing out the cup, letting the water run until it was so hot it scalded her, even through the gloves. She had to make it clean, wipe it all away. She felt moisture on her cheeks, distantly aware that she was crying. *Can't tell, can't tell, no, never. . . .*

Jim came behind her, put his hands gently on her shoulders. ''Liz?''

''I'm sorry.'' She wiped furiously at the tears. ''I always feel so stupid when this happens. I told myself I wasn't going to cry over this anymore. But when I saw him upstairs, I—''

She closed her eyes, squeezing them tight until they hurt,

shutting out the tears. She turned away from him and walked back toward the table. She couldn't bear to look at him and tell him.

Make it clean, wash it over and over and over and over.

"You remember I told you how I ran away from home when I was fifteen?"

He nodded. "Some problem with you and your dad. You never said much about it."

She nodded. "Well, see, my mom got sick when I was about twelve, thirteen. She was sick for a long time. And then my dad—my dad would come into my room at night, when she was asleep, and—and he would *touch* me, and he would—he would *do* things to me, and there was nothing I could do except lie there . . . and all the time, there was Mister Quigley in the corner, looking at me, and he saw everything, over and over, and he didn't do anything. He didn't protect me. He just sat there, and watched, and I swear he was laughing, *he was looking at me and he was laughing because he didn't belong to me he belonged to my dad and he was supposed to protect me, he was supposed to—*"

She slammed a fist into the table, hit it again and again, then Jim was there beside her. He reached for her, but she moved away. "No. Please. Don't."

He stopped. "I'm sorry."

She shrugged, looked away.

"Did you ever tell your mother?"

"No. It would've killed her. But after a while I just couldn't take it anymore. There were times I thought about killing myself, just so I could make it stop. But I couldn't bring myself to do it. So I ran away, and tried as best I could to pretend he didn't exist. It was the only way I could stay sane. My mom and I didn't talk for almost a year after I left. She didn't understand why I did this to them, and I couldn't tell her. Later, when I got my own place, and things calmed down a little, I'd call and talk to her, sometimes, but never to him. Not once. If he answered the phone, I just hung up. Never talked to him. Never came back to visit."

She met his gaze briefly, then looked away. "When he was dying a few years ago, my mom called. She said he wanted to talk to me. I wouldn't do it. She said . . . she said he couldn't die without just seeing me once more. I told her, 'Yes, he can.' And he did."

The silence hung between them for a moment. "Maybe your father wanted to—"

"I don't *care* what he wanted to do," she said, "or what he wanted to say. My God, hadn't he done enough to me already? I'd killed him in my head a thousand times already, what was one more? Now he's dead, and he's gone, and I'm glad. He can't hurt me anymore, and now this is MY house, my *mother's* house, and I'll do what I want with it. I'm going to clean it, and erase every trace of him. The best thing I can do to him is make him vanish, to go over this house and get rid of every trace of his existence, to take from him just like he took from me. As far as I'm concerned, he's got nothing to do with me or this house anymore."

She turned away, then felt his hand on her shoulder. This time she permitted the touch. Then she turned and held him, tight, trying for the warmth that would make her whole again. Clean again.

Somehow, it was never quite enough.

It was getting dark outside when Jim deposited the last of the boxes from the attic on the living-room floor. Mister Quigley was in one of them. She tried not to notice.

"Okay, that's the last of it," he said. "These go to the dump tomorrow, those over here you can either sell or keep, and this bunch we can give to charity." He glanced at the box containing Mister Quigley. "I was thinking about it, and well, he's still in pretty good shape. Maybe there's some kid out there who might enjoy him, give him a clean slate. Unless you'd rather—''

''No,'' she said, too quickly, ''that's all right. I agree.''

He stood silently in the hall for a moment. ''I can stay a little longer if you like.''

''No. It's a three-hour drive back to town, and you've got work tomorrow.''

''I could always call in sick. Spend the night here.''

She sighed. ''Jim, we've discussed this before. I'm just—I'm not ready for that yet. Give me a little more time, okay?''

He nodded, forced a smile. ''Okay. You're sure you wouldn't prefer staying in a hotel for a while?''

''No. There's a perfectly good bedroom here. My bedroom.''

''I was just thinking, with all the bad memories . . .''

''I'm going to wash them away,'' she said. ''This is *my* house now, the only thing I've ever really owned, and I'm not going to be put out of it.''

''All right,'' he said, and headed for the door. ''I'll be back tomorrow. Then we'll finish the inside, and start on the wiring and the plumbing. I'll make an engineer out of you yet.''

He paused to kiss her, then stepped out onto the porch.

''Wait,'' she said. ''I'll walk you to the car.''

She followed after him, pausing by the box containing Mister Quigley. She took a sheet she'd pulled off the sofa and draped it over the mute jester's form. Satisfied that it could not be seen, she hurried after Jim.

Dinner was quick and simple. Salad, a slice of tenderloin and some vegetables tossed into the wok she'd brought from her apartment. She scraped the plate clean into the sink, and headed back to the living room. She figured she could spend the next half hour taping up boxes, and the rest of the evening sorting through shelves and closets.

She switched on the living-room light. It flickered, then held. She stepped inside, and stopped in the middle of the room.

The sheet she'd thrown over the box containing Mister Quigley had shifted, and now lay gathered about him in folds. Its garish painted face was turned up and toward the door, reflecting the overhead light. It seemed almost to be looking at her.

Tentatively, as though touching something unpleasant, she snatched at the sheet and threw it over Mister Quigley. She gave the box a little kick with her toe. This time the sheet stayed put.

And stay there, she thought, and began assembling boxes.

She was standing on a high cliff, overlooking the sea. It churned and boiled far below, the sound roaring up at her. She looked out at the horizon, and over the surge of the surf she could hear something behind her, moving slowly toward her, swaying from side to side as it advanced, and she was too frightened to turn, but there was nowhere to run, just the cliff before her and the jagged rocks below, and it was so much closer now, just behind her, and now she could hear the sound of bells, small and tinny, and a shadow—

Liz sat up in bed, wet with perspiration, a cry on her lips. She ran a hand across her face, forced herself to breathe easier, slow the triphammer beating of her heart. *A nightmare, that's all, just a nightmare*.

As the blood roaring in her temples died away, she became aware of a sound. At first she'd thought it only a carryover from the dream, but as she glanced up and stared into the night, straining to hear, she could just make it out.

Bells.

Small and tinny.

And a sense of movement outside in the hall, a rustling like something soft being dragged past her door.

She slid out of bed, and the sound stopped. She sat still for several minutes, trying to decide if it was really gone, and if it had even been there at all. Finally, she nudged on her slippers and stood. She slowly opened the bedroom door, heard nothing, then stepped into the hallway.

She flicked on the light. It revealed nothing. The hall was deserted, as it had been earlier. She considered going back to bed, then decided to make a fast check of the house, just to be sure. She came to the end of the hallway, and the darkened living room. Switched on another light. It flickered, then held.

She instantly saw the writing scrawled in chalk on the far wall.

GET OUT OF HERE, LIZZY

She stepped back as though slapped and almost fell, her foot tangled in a sheet that hadn't been there earlier, she was sure it hadn't been. She turned, and despite herself cried out at the sight of Mister Quigley in his box, staring vacantly upward.

She looked down at her feet. The sheet was the one she'd draped over his box.

The box was at least two feet from where the sheet

(*had been thrown*)

had fallen.

Say hello, she thought, her gaze drawn against her will back to the garishly painted jester's face. *Say hello, Mister Quigley*.

She was scrubbing the wall for a third time when Jim came back inside. No matter how hard she scraped, enough traces of the chalk remained to make the words visible. *Then I'll wash it a fourth time, and a fifth*, she thought, *and if that doesn't work I'll paint it over or rip out the whole damned wall*.

"I checked all around the house and out back," Jim said. "I found a window unlocked, but it's too small for anybody but a kid to have climbed through. If you like, I can talk to the neighbors, see if any of their kids were out late."

She didn't look up from her work. "It said Lizzy, Jim. No one's called me Lizzy in fifteen years."

"That's because it's a kid's name."

"It's *my* name."

"Yes, and it's also a name that a kid might use to try and annoy an adult," he said. "It must've been one of the neighbors' kids. Look. . . ."

He walked up beside her, and used his palms to measure the distance from the writing to the ground. "About three feet," he said. "If it was an adult, he'd have to lean way down like this to write it. So we're talking a kid, close to the same height."

Mister Quigley is three feet tall, she thought, but cut it off before she said it aloud. *Stop it. You're being foolish*.

"I'm sure you must be right," she said.

"My offer still stands. I can stay over," he said, then added quickly, "on the couch. Just to keep an eye on things. Or we can get you a room somewhere else. If you don't think it's safe—"

She considered it for a moment, then shook her head. "No. If anybody'd meant me harm, they had every chance to do it last night. It's just kids, that's all. I'll make sure everything's locked up this time." She looked up into his eyes. "This is my house now, Jim. I was driven out of it once before, I'm not going to give it up again."

He nodded absently for a moment, then looked away. "You know, I was thinking. Maybe it wasn't such a good idea after all, you coming back here. I think there's still a lot you haven't dealt with, things you *need* to deal with if you intend to live here.''

''I'm doing just fine,'' she said, firmly.

''Are you?'' He pointed at the scrawled writing on the wall. ''Then why did this upset you so much? I've seen you deal with kids and petty vandalism before, you've never gotten this angry, this obsessed.''

She turned away, didn't answer.

''Is Lizzy what your father called you? Is that it?''

''I don't want to talk about it.''

''Well, maybe it's time you did start talking about it. Damn it, Liz, it's been fifteen years. I'm no psychologist, but I do know you can't go around angry for the rest of your life. Maybe . . . well, maybe it's time you forgave your father.''

She wheeled on him, and the rage was there before she could stop herself. ''Time I forgave—FORGAVE him? My God. Don't you understand what he *did* to me?''

''Yes, I do, I—''

''No, you don't,'' she said. ''You know it in your head, but you don't know what it *feels* like. Christ, Jim, it was years before I could let another man even *touch* me. He did more than use me, he took away everything I had, made me powerless. I couldn't say anything, I couldn't do anything, all I could do was take it, and take it, and take it—''

''I know, Liz, but he's dead now. He's dead, and he's buried, and he can't touch you anymore. It's not *him* that's messing you up now, it's you. You have to get past all this. You can't hate your father forever. It's not healthy.''

''Watch me.''

He reached for her. ''Liz, please, just listen to me, you've got to—''

She pulled away. ''Look, Jim, maybe—maybe you should just go away for a while. I know you've got things to do, and

I think I'd just like to deal with this on my own for a while. All right?''

He looked ready to debate the question, then finally shrugged. Looked away. ''All right. I guess the wiring can wait another day.''

He started across the room, grabbing his jacket off the sofa. ''The truck'll be by tomorrow morning to pick up the rest of this stuff. I'll be home if you need me.''

''Thanks,'' she said, and went back to scrubbing the wall again. The screen door clattered shut behind her, followed a moment later by the sound of Jim's car starting and then driving away. She looked at the barely visible letters. *Almost gone. Just a little more and it'll be clean again.*

First, though, she would need more detergent.

She started across the room, and passed the box that contained Mister Quigley. The sheet covering it was exactly where she'd left it last night. She hesitated, then ripped off the sheet and, in one move, grabbed the stuffed jester by the shoulder and lifted him to eye level. She studied him for a moment with the detached curiosity she might exhibit at some curious insect splattered on her windshield.

''He's right,'' she said, very softly, very quietly. ''You're dead. You're dead, and you're buried, and you can't touch me anymore. I hope you rot in hell for all eternity for what you did to me, 'Daddy.' ''

With that, she threw him back into the box, bells jingling with the impact. Then she replaced the sheet, and went in search of the detergent.

This time, there was no dream. Only a black, mindless sleep suddenly broken with a sound in the darkened bedroom. It vibrated on the edge of her hearing, gone now, but it had definitely been there.

Liz reached for the flashlight beside her bed, and flicked it on. There were chalk letters scrawled on the bedroom wall.

Get out of here, Lizzy

And then, from somewhere down the hall . . . the sound of tiny bells.

This time, she did not cry out.

She climbed out of bed and pulled on her robe, never letting go of the flashlight. She eased past the writing on the wall, careful not to brush her robe against it, and moved toward the door. She grasped the knob, turned it without pulling, then yanked it suddenly open.

The jingling stopped.

She switched on the hallway light. As before, it flickered, but she could clearly make out the words written in chalk, jagged letters scrawled on both sides of the hall.

GET OUT OF HERE, LIZZY
GET OUT OF HERE, LIZZY
GET OUT OF HERE, LIZZY

Again, the sound of bells, this time coming from the living room.

She started down the hall, switching on lights as she went. Every few feet revealed more of the writing. It covered the walls and doors and sloped down at strange angles. She followed the sound of bells. Came to the living-room door, and flung it open. The jingling stopped abruptly. She stepped inside.

Mister Quigley was on the floor, slumped against a wall, directly beneath more of the scrawled writing. His eyes gazed sightlessly into the light above her.

She crossed the room and picked him up. He was limp in her grip. She looked at him carefully.

There was chalk dust on Mister Quigley's hands.

In an instant, her face twisted into a mask of rage. Gripping him harder, she stalked through the kitchen and out the side door. She cut around back, heading for the rusted metal trash can. She lifted the lid, crammed Mister Quigley in among the garbage, and slammed the lid down again. She banged it flush on all sides, so it would stay on.

"Go to hell," she whispered, and turned back to the house.

She was halfway there when there was a sudden *clang* and a rattle behind her. She spun around to see the lid of the trash can on the ground, still moving. She rushed back, peered into the trash can.

Mister Quigley was gone.

Then another sound, a scrape of wood against wood, and she turned to see a window open now that wasn't open a minute ago.

Inside. Damn it, he's inside!

She ran back toward the side of the house, just in time to see the door starting to close. She rushed the door, sticking her hand through the narrow opening to stop it from closing. She pushed against it, feeling the resistance from the other side as something pushed back.

She dug in her heels, put her shoulder to the door, and *pushed*. The door gave way with a sudden motion, as if there were no longer anything on the other side. She grabbed hold of the door frame to keep from stumbling.

Where? she thought. *Where?*

The lights were flickering again, making it hard to focus. There was the pop of a lamp being knocked over somewhere nearby, making it darker, harder to see.

"Come on out," she said, moving into the living room. No sign of him. "Come on!"

She paused long enough to dig through one of the boxes, pulling out the baseball bat they'd found the first day. She hefted it, and moved slowly toward the hallway.

She stepped past several doors that opened only onto darkness. Continued down the hall as suddenly there was a jingling of bells behind her. She spun around in time to see a door slam shut. She raced to it, then waited. Listened.

The doorknob moved, ever so slightly.

She grabbed it and threw the door open.

Nothing. The room was silent, dark. She ventured a step inside. The window at the far end of the room was open, the cool night wind blowing the curtains.

She stepped back into the hall. Two more closed doors were ahead of her.

Think, her mind shrieked at her, *think*!

She lowered herself to the floor, until she could see underneath the doors. She peered beneath the first one, saw nothing but darkness, and moved on to the next.

There was something moving on the other side. She could get just the sense of it, a greyness against the deeper black of the room.

And, ever so faintly, a rustling of motley, and the faint whisper of bells.

Slowly, slowly, she put her hand on the doorknob. Grasped it firmly. Took a deep breath, and threw open the door.

And it was *there*.

Standing.

Turned toward her.

Just a momentary flash before it hurled itself into the shadows.

She ran after it, swinging the bat, not connecting, flailing madly as suddenly she heard it again, across the room. She spun around, brought the bat down, heard a lamp smash, and didn't care, she had to find it, had to—

Another flash of movement.

She swung, and this time connected with a dull thud of wood striking cloth, and a seizure of bells. She slammed it against the wall, heard it bounce, brought the bat down and again found the target.

"Damn you!" she cried, slamming it over and over. "Damn you! *Fifteen years!*"

Pounding.

"I loved you, you bastard. You hurt me! I trusted you! Damn you! Damn you!"

The bat arced down in her hands again and again, as if of its own volition, until her arms ached and she fell to her knees, and she could not raise it any longer. She sobbed, and let the bat fall one last time, and in the darkness she could just make out its form, lying slumped against the wall, battered and broken, stuffing ripped out and scattered on the floor, one leg nearly torn off.

". . . damn you," she cried, exhausted, and let the bat fall to the floor. She sat heavily, sobbing into her hands.

Then: a jingling of bells.

Startled, she glanced up.

Mister Quigley was gone again.

She stood, and stepped back into the hall again. The lights were flickering even more now, but she ignored them, drawn to the sound of bells, only this time the sound was different—slower, duller.

She'd hurt it. There was still a chance—

She no sooner stepped into the living room than suddenly the lights went out altogether. An instant later something whirred past her head and smashed into the wall behind her. The plate shattered and crashed to the floor in shards. She cried out, moved just as another plate sliced through the air, crashing into the wall. More followed, cups and saucers and plates and silverware, a flurry that pushed her back, back toward the front door, each plate thrown with the jingling of small bells behind it.

Each volley came closer, driving her farther and farther until she was up against the door. She fumbled for the knob, found it, and lurched outside, slamming the door behind her.

She could hear another plate smashing against it on the other side.

Then another sound, as the door was locked from the inside.

She rattled the door. It refused to move.

I'm not giving up, she thought, pounding on the door. *He took everything I had, everything I cared about, he took it all away but he's not taking this too! It's mine and he can't have it!*

She stepped away from the door, staggered backward onto the lawn. "I'll be back!" she cried. "Do you understand me!? I'll be back!"

Silence was her only answer.

She turned and stalked away from the house and down the street.

A phone. She had to find a phone. She'd go back there with Jim, and they'd find that thing and that would be *that*.

She was already down the street and out of sight when the first blue-white flash smeared across the front window.

It was almost dawn when she drove back with Jim. They could smell the smoke even before he turned the corner. The crew of the last fire truck remaining were packing their gear, dragging hoses across the waterlogged and soot-blackened street.

"Oh, Christ," she whispered as he stopped the car. She dove out and raced across the street to what was left of the house. There was almost nothing left, only parts of walls surrounding a black pile of debris where the roof had crashed in. The fireplace chimney still stood, precariously balanced on the edge of what had been the basement. The smell of smoke still clung to the place, and the acrid scent burned at her throat.

She felt her knees go weak as she stepped onto the lawn. "Oh, my God, what happened? What—"

One of the firemen dragging a hose stopped. "Are you the owner, miss?"

She nodded numbly.

"I'm sorry. It looks like a total loss. Do you have any insurance? Anyone you can call?"

"I—I think so," she said. "But how—how did it—"

"As far as we can tell, looks like the wiring." He pointed to the melted wiring, which hung out of the walls and ceiling like thin, blackened tendrils. "The place looked pretty solid from the outside, but it was a real firetrap. We think the blaze started in the bedroom, probably an open circuit. It erupted in the walls and next thing all the wires were burning." He turned to face her. "I know this is a hard time for you right now, but for whatever comfort it might be, you're real lucky."

She focused on him. "What?"

"This was the worst kind of flash fire. A thing like this can consume a house in minutes. Just goes up like a match. If you'd been inside when it went up, you wouldn't have had a chance. You were lucky, real lucky, to get out of there."

With that, he stepped away, joining the others at the fire truck as Jim came up alongside her.

"I was in bed," she said.

"What?"

"The fire started in the bedroom. I would've been asleep." *And I would have died*, she thought.

He kept trying to get me out of there.

He knew. He must have known.

She walked away.

"Liz?"

She didn't answer, heading for the back of the house to examine the damage.

It was even worse back here. The back of the house was made almost entirely of wood paneling.

Nothing left but ashes.

He knew. He must have known.

"Why did you do it?" she asked, looking around. *"What do you want from me?"*

Then, from somewhere close: a tiny jingling of bells.

She followed the sound to the low stone wall that separated her property from the house next door. There, at the foot of the wall, was Mister Quigley . . . or what was left of him. Battered, broken, and seared by flame, his legs were almost totally burned away. Little remained of his face. He no longer looked frightening, only sad and lost and small.

In his hand was a piece of chalk.

She gently nudged him aside, to reveal what was written on the wall behind him.

FORGIVE ME
PLEASE FORGIVE ME
DADDY

She sat back on her heels, and the tears came. Fifteen years' worth of tears. She struggled to speak, but nothing came out but great, gasping sobs.

Finally, when the worst of it had passed, she reached out and touched the cold stone on which the words had been written.

". . . I . . . God, I'll try," she said, then added, "Daddy."

Gathering up what was left of Mister Quigley, she walked back to the front lawn, and Jim.

She held him for a very long time.

GIL LAMONT

Gil Lamont's life has always been books—now he is finally taking the time to create them. An editor for many years, Gil was also a highly regarded commentator and collector. Though a love of prose rarely translates into writing ability, Gil has ably made the transition. He has had several stories published and is at work on a novel titled *No Joke Too Small*.

He offers here a blackly comic look at the conventions of science fiction, with uncommon insight and a deft solution.

Sinus Fiction
by Gil Lamont

I.

The itch began as a tiny pinprick on his right cheek where the bone is most prominent, just below the outside corner of the eye. He brushed idly at the itch and reached for his beer, chugging the rest of the bottle while his stare never left the TV screen. Fourth down and twelve. Then the commercial break came and what the hell had just happened on the field? The bottle, now empty, was still at his lips. The pinprick had enlarged to the size of a needle. He moved the bottle away from his mouth and, frowning, turned his head.

Dust motes stirred in the late afternoon sunlight from the picture window, dancing their fruity way across the neat sheaf of *Playboys* on the coffee table and around the Port-o-Gym he'd blown half a yard on and someday might get around to using. But it gave his apartment such a strong, masculine look, and that impressed the babes he brought home interchangeably every Friday and Saturday night. Sunday afternoons, without exception, were reserved for the ball game and not to be spoiled by anything, least of all an itch.

Thank God it wasn't one of those damned sinus headaches that lately plagued him, when everything inside his face felt like it was rearranging itself. Just an itch.

Idly he scratched at it and was assaulted by incredible pain; pain that tossed the empty bottle to the carpet, lifted him out of his chair, threw his fingers up against his cheek, and lockstepped with him all the way into the bathroom. Lungs panting, heart pounding, he clamped his left hand onto the edge of the sink and peered at his reflected face. His eyes were suddenly bloodshot, his skin pale and waxy beneath its veneer of sunlamp tan. When he pulled his fingers away from his cheek he half expected to see the imprint of loops and whorls; instead, his cheekbone at the epicenter of the itch wore a tiny full moon of puckered skin, like an old scar. But no scar had ever been there. Inside the moon a dark spot lay, surrounded by a uniform iris of white skin. He touched it gingerly with his thumb and felt something hard and unyielding. It did not feel like his cheekbone.

Something weird was going on here.

Didn't he live as clean a life as he could? His only vices were the straightforward: beer, sports, and chicks. His life made no demands on anyone. He was comfortably and thoroughly masculine without being a misogynist, and he never even beat up queers. And now this.

Bracing himself for the pain, he plunged the tip of his right index finger into the dark spot and scratched madly. There was no pain. The skin flecked away like a dead sunburn, revealing a lump hard and unyielding . . . and black. He tugged at the skin and it lifted and came away.

Astonishing. The skin came away.

2.

Until she saw his two thugs just before boarding, she believed her getaway would work. Taking the bus was simple, direct, and unexpected. One connection to make in Kansas City, and the next day she would reach her ship, disinter it, and lift herself off-planet.

She hid in the Ladies' until departure time, secure behind the latched door of the stall, her portfolio case flat over the toilet seat, her feet braced against the door frame. Only once did she have to move so she could throw up.

The nausea convulsed her primary stomach, high under the breastbone, close to her main heart. She bit her lower lip until she tasted blood hot and salty, and her gorge would not be denied; instantly she was off the seat, tossing aside the portfolio case. Her furtive breakfast sandwich threw itself out into the bowl.

A thousand times over she had to remind herself that what mattered was the new life quickening inside her. The new life and the other thing.

The cool of the porcelain rim against her forehead calmed her and slowed her pulse. Drawing herself up, she recalled why she was here and felt the gravity of responsibility press upon her with sobriety and stuffy purpose. She also felt a last good-bye wave of nausea and clamped her teeth together.

She yanked on the flush handle. When the water became still, she dipped a corner of her handkerchief in it and dabbed at her cheeks and upper lip and the insides of her wrists.

Standing at last, she checked her watch. Time to go. She draped her cheap coat over her shoulders, the sleeves dangling empty, and left the stall. No one in the place. Good. At the sink, a last chance to bathe her face in refreshing cold water. A quick look up into the mirror. Ebony features, flattened nose, full lips, hair in tight kinks, a body she'd counted on being anonymous. Too bad she was obviously pregnant. Her eyes were tired and bloodshot, but they stared back at her with adamant resolution. She lifted an ironic *right on!* fist at her reflection.

Then it was out the door, just her and the portfolio case and a cheap handbag. Her free hand held the ticket with its promise of freedom. And she surrendered her ticket at the gate and was almost at the bus before she saw.

Them.

Two of them. One man stood against the bus, a foot bracing him. The other man elaborately studied his manicure as he leaned against the NO LOITERING signpost where the buses pulled in. Both men appeared nondescript and unmemorable. She recognized both of them as killers.

She had never seen them before, but she knew them for the nonhumans they were. The one at the bus kept forgetting to breathe, the other to move his eyes in tandem.

She reached the bus door and without breaking stride brought the portfolio case up and across her chest, into the first man's face. The steel edge of the portfolio slashed across his eyes and shattered the bridge of his nose. Carelessly, as though she had given it as much thought as unwrapping a stick of gum, she swung the portfolio along its arc and let it fly straight at the other man. Her coat fell off and she didn't care.

Already the first man was on his knees, hands cupped to his face. Whimpers came from him in soft rhythmic waves.

The second man was her immediate concern. Before the portfolio reached him he lifted his arm without looking up and casually brushed the case aside. But she had caught his attention. He shifted his weight onto the balls of his feet, hips loose and ready to move in any direction. He pulled his gaze at last from his fingernails and turned it toward her.

His eyes were dead and colorless. He had managed to make everything else look human, everything but the eyes. And still they would not move together.

Her heavy armament had been foolishly concentrated inside the portfolio, which now lay fifteen feet from the second man's side. It might as well have been fifteen miles. All she had left was her handbag. Inside it were lip gloss, wallet, comb, perfume, pens, mascara, a nail file.

While she watched him attempt to keep his eyes parallel she thrust a hand into the bag and closed her fingers on the nail file. She grazed its point with her thumb. It was sharp enough.

As if somnolent the second man yawned, lifting one hand to the inside of his raincoat. In seconds that hand would emerge with a pistol or a phaser or a colloidal gun or worse. She had no time to lose.

Nail file raised high she lunged at the second man, set on taking him with her if she had to go down at all. As she leaped the incongruity struck her: millennia of wisdom and philosophy could not outreason the fist. What, she wondered in flight, do we learn from this?

Before he could draw his weapon she slammed into him, the nail file flashing in her hand. Kill the inhuman in him first, she thought, and aimed for his wandering eyes.

He batted her away as though she were nothing. The nail file slid from her fingers and skittered feet distant.

She tried to swallow past a gigantic lump in her throat. Amazing, how fear stayed with you always. The fear said she was as good as dead. This she would not accept.

She made herself go limp, letting him toss her to one side.

In seconds he would throw himself on top of her, splayed fingers ready to choke the life out of her. She had only seconds to live. She still had a chance.

Fumbling in her purse, her fingers discovered the perfume atomizer. New hope filled her. Her coat was ruined and her back felt as though she'd tried wrestling the bus, but by the Great Mother the game was not over yet. As soon as the second man was close enough she sprayed perfume into his eyes.

He screamed.

She scrambled clear and retrieved her portfolio, took stock of the thugs. The first still lay by the bus, holding his face. The second lay on the sidewalk, pawing at his eyes and moaning. She allowed herself one quick gloat of victory and then she was gone, scurrying from the bus terminal as fast as she dared, disdainful of the waiting passengers and what they thought.

Outside, in the early afternoon, perfectly ordinary people somehow conducted themselves as though it was a perfectly ordinary day.

In her haste to blend with them she did not notice the cadaverous gentleman in the dingy white suit leave his battered 1974 Pinto and sidle after her in an awkward gait. He hid his eyes behind cheap plastic mirror shades. He was loose-limbed and gangly-legged, and easily kept up with her unhurried but desperate flight.

Her mistake was looking over her shoulder *after* she ducked into the alley.

Well, of course, he was the boss of the two at the bus station. Power flowed from him in almost visible waves. She laughed to herself in the sudden understanding that escaping him without her full armament was impossible. Atomizer or nail file would be useless here.

Anyway, the alley had a dead end.

Dead end. Ha. She grimaced at the gallows humor.

Nothing left to her could compete with the cadaverous man in the dingy white suit. Indifference cloaked his spirit like the callus on a heel. He lacked compassion, and therefore his powers far outranked hers.

(Except.)

She let the portfolio case fall to the ground, for there was no saving the portfolio case now. She eased her pregnant self down to sit on the portfolio, resting her wrists on her knees, palms up, for there was no saving herself. Death was her only option, and she would embrace it with her head raised.

(Quitter, accused the undying part of her.)

Mr. Cadaver returned her stare, unblinking. He pointed his beam weapon at her and fired it and she died.

Neither of them knew that somehow she survived.

3.

This was utterly fantastic. The skin was peeling off in long strips, each about half an inch wide. Sunburned skin is tissue thin when it peels, but this stuff was thick as the wedge the rocks on the beach had taken out of his big toe the summer he turned thirteen. As thick as that, and yet the skin came off easily, no pain, no blood. Was this how a snake felt?

No pain, no blood. With every piece of his skin torn away the itch dwindled. By the time it had vanished he was too captivated to notice.

What the peeling skin revealed was hard and black, like onyx yet flexible. A carapace. (Chitin? he wondered.) It followed the contours of his old pink face like an impressionistic painting, a suggestion, a remembrance. First the skin came off the cheekbone, stopping at his right ear with a soft tearing noise. He leaned into the mirror to examine the demarcation line, but was distracted by the skin on the left side of the original puckered scar curling up in invitation. He slid his attention to this new tab of skin with the languor of someone drugged. His thumb and forefinger grabbed the curl and pulled slowly, and the skin lifted up in its strip, traveling smoothly across the territory under the eye and across the fleshy part of the nose, moving down at an angle over the other cheek until it came to a stop at the base left of his jaw.

He still held the first piece in one hand, the new piece in the other. He dropped both pieces into the sink, looked up. The next piece of skin seemed to lead up into the eye itself.

Scared? Hell, this was fascinating.

He braced his forehead in his left hand and tugged slowly at the tab of skin with his right. It eased off his skull with the static resistance of a sock that clings to a shirt in the laundry. Once it reached the eye, the skin formed itself into a spiral around the socket. Circumnavigating the eye, right across the eyebrow ridge, avoiding the eyelid altogether, down and around, it intersected uncovered onyx and tore free.

He opened his eyes wide in delight. Where next? Where next? And his right eyelid fell off. Fluttered into the sink. And he was laughing now, hugely entertained, because the skin of his forehead was bulging and beginning to flap as if air blew behind it. And he tore it straight across as though it were a paper towel perforated at the hairline, and then he threw that handful into the sink, and then it was down the other cheek and under the mouth, swinging back up around to the tip of the nose—and there was no nose *nothing*! beneath it—and his hands had traveled loose skin up to his left eye and bared that and then stripped away his chin and were scrabbling at his neck.

When he stopped for a second and saw what he was becoming.

He stared without moving, except for a tic in his left eye that jettisoned the eyelid and then went away. He studied his face for a long moment.

And he liked what he saw.

And he thought he was beginning to recognize himself.

And the panic he had not known was there began to recede, quashed under growing acceptance. Hell, this was like exploring. No Columbus or Cortés had confronted territory as unfamiliar as this. He slid his fingers under his scalp and the whole damn thing lifted, not a hair out of place. He felt it unsticking at the back of his neck. Into the sink with it! And look at those dreadful ears! Sail with the wind much? He reached up and plucked one off his head. It lay in his hand, a disgusting wrinkled thing, and with a shudder he dropped it. His left hand batted away his other ear and he admired his sleek black shining faceted earless noseless head, turning it with his hand this way to admire the reflection of the bathroom light fixtures bouncing off the mound of cheekbone, turning it with his hand that way to revel in how he could almost see the other eye without the bother of a nose to block his view, turning it with his hand, his hand—

The pinkness of it, the wrinkles, the softness. Bile scurried up his throat. For a few heartbeats he had to look away.

Then it was thank God hard fingernails scraping the inside of one wrist, finding purchase, peeling away skin like peeling away a glove, revealing beautiful armored segments of black, the tips a deeper black. Fascinated, he drew his new fingers negligently across the back of his old hand.

And saw blood well out in sudden redness. In haste he stripped away the other glove of skin, saw the bleeding stop, carried away with the skin.

Skin. He shuddered at the concept.

The only skin left on him was covered by his clothes.

And the sink was getting full.

4.

Being dead held certain advantages denied her former condition. For one, her nausea had vanished completely. For two, pain was a memory. For three—as she was soon to find out—mobility was no problem.

But first she willed her eyes to open. They would not. She willed her eyes to open. They would not.

Ah. No longer was she in control of her body.

She pushed out a sensor from her mind, a tendril of thought that bloomed beyond the confines of her body with a sudden flare of paraconsciousness. So the mind still reigned. She quickly added vision, felt herself above her body and looking down upon it. Damn. She was in a Dumpster. And naked. Angry beam scars covered her chest and abdomen.

The bastards. Mr. Cadaver and his thugs had done an instant autopsy on her after all. She wondered if they'd killed the new life inside her. Or even interfered with the other thing.

Great Mother, she looked terrible. She looked dead. She was dead. And probably her inner secret had been lost, along with what was in the portfolio.

So where was Mr. Cadaver and his dingy white suit? Where was anybody? Was this world of the dead empty and deserted?

She expanded her consciousness in accordion folds, shifting her perceptions outward.

Beyond the Dumpster lay a parking lot on one side, an apartment complex on the other. She moved to the apartment complex, sensing herself passing through walls, simultaneously at room level and above it, as if one eye stayed at eye level and the other looked down through the ceiling. And learned that Mr. Cadaver was not very bright: his own apartment abutted her Dumpster grave. Here was the living room: couch, chairs, table, lamps, no TV, no stereo, one picture on the wall opposite the couch: a landscape of some place that was not Terra. She knew the place well. She recognized it with an inner heartache that transcended the mortal senses.

It was Home.

Time became meaningless. Perhaps in her present condition Time was no longer a constant. So she could not judge how long she stared at that picture. She only knew that had she still worn her human body she would have felt the tears running down her cheeks.

She spread her perceptions further, beyond the walls of Mr. Cadaver's apartment. She found herself in a long corridor, then above it. The night was young and full of new stars, stars she saw as swollen globes of energy, and she a puny thing lost in the vast dark. They sucked at her, the stars did, seducing her spirit off-planet (where she had wanted to be—before), and she rose up and up, halfway to the thin clouds before she shook herself free and looked down and down, and gaped in awe at the grid of the city spread below her. Not just streetlights; anyone in an airplane could see those. She saw more. She saw the power lines that lit the streetlights and electrified the homes. The telephone wires that laced across the city and held the buildings down. As she dropped to treetop level she could see the delicate tracing of a car's electrical system, the faint glimmer of a pedestrian's Walkman radio.

She reached out with a casual tendril of thought and nudged the radio's frequency higher, saw the pedestrian frown, smiled to herself, shifted the tendril, and gave a waiting car's turn signals palpitations. The traffic light turned green and the car moved off and the pedestrian stepped off the curb, and she could see not only the flicker of the relays that told the traffic light when to change but the gas mains beneath the street holding their breath and the water lines muttering to themselves and somewhere off to her right the crimson huffiness of a factory late shift and above her the airplanes along their well-worn highways and beneath it all the unceasing background hum of the planet itself and she knew she was starting to shred and she concentrated all of her will and shut down her perceptions until she could deal with it.

Then she scanned across the city's muted lights, her mind

translating the auras or energy fields or whatever into primary colors that she could understand. Over there, in the east. Something tugged at a childhood memory.

She followed it and found herself above a giant apartment complex in the suburbs. She looked down upon it as if the roof had lifted on a vast, many-roomed dollhouse. Inside were the dolls. She sampled their lives, her perception dipping down and rising up and moving on and dipping down again.

She saw a young woman sitting mesmerized by a book.

She saw a married couple arguing and the wife carried murder in her heart, the aura of death a black cape about her.

She saw a young man stretched out on a bed, corpse for half a day already.

She saw a corpulent man feed himself and his small corpulent dog rich delicacies.

She saw rooms submerged in cigarette smoke, their occupants slowly drowning.

She saw an old woman polishing her furniture over and over in an endless pavane.

She saw a sad-faced man in a leather armchair divide his attention between a clock on the wall and a bottle of pills at his elbow. While she watched, the clock hands did not move. So, Time really was no longer a constant. She could, it seemed, slow it down to an infinite moment. (But the sad-faced man moved to the clock, frowned, consulted the watch on his wrist, frowned, rapped the side of the clock. The hands began to move.)

She saw one person crying, she saw many people laughing.

She saw an odd faceted black creature shedding human clothes in a bathroom. The childhood memory was almost invoked. She settled back on mental haunches to watch this one for a while.

5.

His laughter echoed against walls of tile.

Because his skin was coming off easier than his clothes had. No buttons to fumble with, no zippers to catch the folds of hated epidermis. Just a smooth ecdysiasm that gave him instant rewards: broad shoulders pared themselves away to faceted plates of armor; overpadded chest and hard pecs and useless nipples sloughed off at sternum depth; pucker of navel gave it up with a moist sucking sound; soft washboard of toned bellyfat peeled down to a rock-hard plane flat from throat to belly.

Kicked off his pants, past his shins and ankles and feet. Ripped the skin down from the knees, feeling it cling like socks on a sweaty day. Gone the leg hair, the scars of a thousand summer ball games, the ingrown toenails, the odor.

He lifted up his shoulders in a gigantic shrug and felt all of his back loosen. His inner self writhed and the solid sheet of skin shifted, caught, hung by a shoulder blade, responded to the twisted swipe of his arm up behind him and fell away. It hit the bathtub porcelain with a soft sigh, slid down to join the rest of his skin and clothes.

Thighs quickly diminished to half their girth. The tendons that ran up the insides of his thighs were like piano wire.

His buttocks dropped off like a shed bustle. Now it was a straight line from his nape to the backs of his thighs. His waist and hips were gone.

His crotch refused to come away.

This enraged him. In his life he had desired many things: tight prom queen, sleek sports car, fifty-yard-line tickets, boss's big-breasted secretary. But none of these with the fervor for this final metamorphosis. A keen frustration filled him. Give it up! Tear it off! Have done with it!

He snatched up the scruff of his scrotum and yanked it hard. It barely budged.

He used his best golfing grip on his penis (one hand clutching mostly air) and jerked it just as powerfully as he could, and he felt it resist and he realized then why it resisted and he stopped himself suddenly. Was he crazy? His dick was smarter than he was! His dick was crying *No! Let me stay a man!* Because giving this up was giving up the last of himself, the essence of masculinity.

What kind of man would he be without it? (What kind of man was he now? whispered the errant thought.) Would losing this make him androgynous, or the sort to patronize fern bars?

The thought made him sick to his stomach. For the first time the enormity of what was happening reached him, made him stagger.

And then he found the answer. No. A real man would see this through. Columbus. Cortés. He too was an explorer. One of *them*. A real man down to the marrow. Hey.

And so he slid his hand down his abdomen, slid it under the hypotenuse of pubic hair, felt the whole thing slip away. His genitals shriveled all the way down to the bathtub, became insignificant wrinkles of skin, what the hell had all the fuss been about, it was all about being a man inside, dammit, inside.

He looked down at himself and there was nothing there. No extrusion of cartilage or flesh or skin. No orifice of any kind. Just the smooth juncture of thigh meeting groin, groin meeting thigh.

So what happened when you had to piss? Or maybe you never had to piss. He rather liked that concept.

He lifted his feet out of the mess of useless skin and useless clothes in the bathtub, steadied himself on the shower curtain rod, found he was light enough to chin himself one-handed, found he was strong enough to tear the rod down. He thrust both hands into the sink and picked up the remnants of his face and threw it at the window over the tub, dislodging the shampoo and conditioner on the sill, and he laughed again, caught a sidelong view of himself in the mirror over the sink, laughed even more.

Watched his teeth fall in a linear sequence from his mouth, leaving behind hard-edged black gums and an elongated tongue.

Winked at his image and saw the facade of his eye—pupil, iris, white—unstick and flutter down, this sleight of hand revealing a yellow eye with the vertical pupil of a cat. And the same with the other eye.

This had to be one of the great cosmic jokes.

So. Was he done changing, then? (Funny, he still *thought* human.) Was he complete? In the full-length mirror on the back of the bedroom door he saw his final transformation:

An odd tingling suffused his toes. He stared down without amazement at his feet. (He had abandoned amazement long ago.) The second and third toes on his right foot merged to become one toe. The fourth and fifth toes merged to become one toe. He was left with three little piggies.

His left foot did the same.

No, he had some amazement left after all. He held his hands up in front of his face and watched the index and middle fingers of his right hand merge and become one finger, watched the ring and little fingers merge and become one finger, watched it happen again with his left hand. Three fingers on each hand.

Looked about his bedroom and saw threes everywhere. Three points define a plane. Three rooms defined his apartment. Bedroom (& attached bathroom), living room, kitchen. Kitchen. He wondered if he was hungry.

The Formica of his kitchen counter did not quite meet the wall behind it. A cockroach emerged from this misaligned juncture and without a thought his tongue slithered out and licked up the insect and his jaws ground it to paste.

It tasted like the tiniest morsel of chocolate chalk.
He loved it.

6.

What she watched was fascinating. One part of her mind witnessed this metamorphosis, another part cast and recast her chances of making something of her situation, another part threw guilt up at her for wasting her time watching and doing nothing. Perhaps she was becoming fragmented. Perhaps it was just as well. She felt so hopeless. Soon she would dissolve into the Cosmic All like coffee crystals in water, becoming a thin ersatz spirit before her flavor faded completely.

The other thing: a microdot in the lining of the portfolio case had held theory and schematics for the ultimate weapon: total manipulation of time and matter. Inside her body, lodged uncomfortably between her hearts, had been the plan for the weapon's only defense. Or maybe, she thought wildly, the microdot in the portfolio had contained the greatest epic poem ever written, the finest moment in a billion years of cultural and philosophical evolution, all truths and wisdom encompassed in it, and inside her body had been the thematic key that would unlock the poem's mysteries for everyone. Given her situation, what was the difference now?

Likely the weapon and its defense (the poem and its interpretation) were gone from her forever. She had seen her mutilated carcass, that beautiful brown skin torn open and ineptly sealed shut. All her plans had been undone.

And she wept for the daughter she had conceived more than a century ago and waited until now to grow, the daughter she had meant to succeed her in the great tradition of her line, the daughter she had planned to teach for decades, just as her own mother had done some thousands of years before, the daughter now lost forever.

Damn Cadaver! Damn him for eternity!

If only she could squash him like the bug he was . . .

She saw below her the human finish his metamorphosis and she gave mental utterance to an oath. Her childhood memory restored at last.

In the ancient days, when her race had equated power with violence, they had bred their own warrior caste. This was before even her great-great-grandmother had been young. These warriors were bold and fearless, quite strong and quite invincible (albeit extremely short-lived, even by human standards), thoroughly obedient and devoted, and once they had roamed the galaxy in the millions. The last one had died in a zoo on Home thousands of years ago, before she was even born. As a little girl she had been taken by her mother to see his stuffed remains; all she could remember was what the exhibit card had told her.

Yet before her now was a modern-day example. A warrior!

She was not beaten yet. She could no longer complete her mission but she could show Mr. Cadaver justice.

If. If Mr. Cadaver had not yet left Terra with his booty. If she could communicate with her newfound Champion.

Better to find Mr. Cadaver first, she thought. Her Champion would keep; lost in self-admiration he wasn't going anywhere.

She lifted up her spirit and felt herself pulled back to the other side of town, to the Dumpster where her body lay still. As she sped over the city she expected to perceive the souls of humanity as an assortment of colored auras. Golden shafts would extend up from church spires to pierce the low-hanging clouds. A crowd in the streets would be mostly soft blue, except for the occasional red gleam like a coal before it sinks to ash. Once in a while a brighter color would show itself:

yellow or orange or even copper. Rarely there would be a pure white. That is how it would be.

Instead there were just a thousand thousand dim red firings of synapses packaged neatly in skulls. No colors. No auras.

Instead there were just humans. Humans.

Perhaps humans had no souls.

A pitiful concept, but she had to appreciate its practical advantages: without the human static it should be that much easier to find Mr. Cadaver.

Blanking the nonsentient energies of electricity and gas and water and gravity, she released thought beams to wander over the city. Over there. A cold, cold blue, muffled as if through gauze.

She sped toward it, plummeting her consciousness through clouds, frightening sensitive winging geese, skimming over the tops of trees. As she neared, she discovered that Mr. Cadaver's cold blue aura concealed another aura deep down inside, like a core of rot at the heart of an onion.

She stopped and watched. In this other part of the city, Mr. Cadaver, her portfolio case beside him, sat enjoying the finest in fast-food cuisine and berating in turn each of the men from the bus station. The second man hid his regenerating eyes behind opaque sunglasses. The first man wore across his nose a bandage already stained black crimson and mild pink.

The second man's aura did not vibrate in any frequency. He did not respond to Mr. Cadaver's harangue in any way because he had turned himself off. She sensed that when the need arose he would turn himself on again.

The first man was not listening because all his attention was on his boss devouring french fries. Inside him was a spirit like a small and faithful dog. When kicked he would whine but would always return, eager to please and enormously satisfied with a few words of praise; or just as ready to be kicked again, for that was attention too.

And Mr. Cadaver loved to kick his dog around. No, not true. He just gave his people what they really wanted. His thoughts were indifferent. Unreadable.

Just for fun she moved herself inside his body.

And emerged, shaken, as quickly as was possible.

In the dim and happy days of her childhood, she once wandered into a palace corridor so thick with dust the settling clouds obscured her footprints. Quickly lost, she thought she would never see her mother again. Her immature hearts thudded in anguish; she was ready to drop and die. Then a shadow fell across her. Looking up, and up, she beheld a crone, hooded, caped, one withered claw lowering a mirror to her. The mirror was clouded by dirt. She scrubbed it with the hem of her skirt and peered deep into it:

Her face. Her face grew up, grew older, grew lines. She was going to be very beautiful, even in old age, for the progression did not stop. Her cheeks sank in on themselves. Her hair turned gray, then white, then brittle, then disappeared in uneven patches. Her skin flensed itself away as if invisibly scoured. Her skull grinned back at her.

In terror she shifted her gaze back up to the old crone, who threw back her hood and revealed the face of a very beautiful young woman. Herself. But with a twisted aspect.

She fled. Lacking footprints to guide her, she fled in any direction, and somehow emerged into known territory. The old woman who wore her face seemed so unimaginably evil that not until centuries later did she understand the reason for her fright: that face was of one who would respond to the least of stimuli: that face was of one who was corrupt.

So too the inside of Mr. Cadaver. He was a house that had been shuttered for years. The drapes were musty and rotten and stank of mildew. Crawling things ran over the books and paintings. Furniture fell apart at the caress of a hand. The visible part of Mr. Cadaver was all artifice, and all hollow.

There was nothing there. No morals, no ethics, no sense

of humanity. Not even a lust for power that could redeem this her murderer.

(Not even the love of a little dog.)

But in her brief visit to that crumbling manor, she had found the place where Mr. Cadaver was most vulnerable and most dangerous. She had looked into the pantry and found the heart of the onion, the rotten core: the parasite.

(She did not stay in Mr. Cadaver to meet the parasite because of the wholly irrational fear it would have her face, with a twisted aspect. Unlike Mr. Cadaver, who could sense power yet had no need of it, the parasite lived for power, accepted nothing else. And now, thank the Great Mother for her warrior, the parasite would not be impossible to kill.)

Mr. Cadaver was merely the willing puppet of an organism so palpably evil that she suddenly understood that all the conflict through the ages between Good and Evil came down to people like herself against this one terrible, foul thing.

And she—*she*!—controlled the one instrument that could destroy that parasite, destroy it so utterly it could never seat itself in another corrupt host. She controlled her warrior.

Well, soon enough, anyway. It was her heritage. And his.

Now that she had firmly fixed Mr. Cadaver's aura, knowing she could easily track him, she sped back to her Champion.

7.

He had eaten half the refrigerator—shelves, eggkeeper, icemaker, door handles—when he thought he heard a voice calling him to the bathroom. He put back the mayonnaise jar he'd been about to munch and cocked his head in an attitude of listening. Nothing.

In the bathroom he saw nothing but the person *he* used to be, collapsed in the bathtub. His disarrayed face, what was left of it, was there. But if his face was trying to speak it was hopeless, since it lacked lips, tongue, or palate, or even any arrangement that could resemble them.

But he knew someone wanted to communicate with him. He *knew*. He could not articulate how he knew (perhaps something tugged at a racial memory), but he knew.

He tore off the towel bar and nibbled it idly while pondering the next step. Soon enough a sliver of soap heaved itself up from the dish and began to drift across the mirror. "Help me" appeared in shaky, delicate letters.

He nodded eagerly at the soap, started to say *yes, yes, I understand, what is it you want?* when he realized he had lost the power of speech. Damn. Then inspiration seized him and he plucked the soap out of the air and rubbed the letters away and watched his three-fingered hand write in hasty block letters, "Who are you? What do you want?"

After a beat he rubbed the mirror again and opened his hand. The soap floated up. Time passed. Letters slowly wrote themselves: W A I T, and the soap dropped back into the sink.

Nothing happened for a while. He grew bored. He ate some more towel bar. An idea occurred to him, almost as if he had thought of it himself. He went into the living room. The sky outside the picture window was dark with brooding clouds covering the moon. He snapped on the TV set and turned it to an empty channel. He put a sofa cushion between two 10-kilo weights and munched this sandwich thoughtfully while he sat and stared at colored TV snow. After a while his head drooped, and simultaneously a blurry picture formed on the screen. Haltingly and without speech the blurry picture told him to turn on his radio. This he did.

The needle raced by itself across the dial, back and forth, station to station, pulling in phonemes from a hundred sources, building sentences from fragments in a thousand voices and timbres, some with a snatch of tune, some yanked from the middle of the news or out of a commercial, most from the meaningless chatter of the gospel stations: "HELL tooth *ee* O *my* ch UMMM peon!"

At last the spirit had a voice, and it told him everything.

8.

Who'd have thought it would be so difficult? If she hadn't remembered the pedestrian and his Walkman she'd be playing with that silly soap sliver even now, helpless as Time made her Champion's skin scaly and brittle with old age, sapped him of his special strength, and robbed her of her revenge. Then she would have had no reason to cling to her consciousness this little while longer.

But no. She had remembered, the radio had supplied her with all the sound combinations she'd needed, all was right with the world, she'd told him exactly what he needed to know:

That she was several thousand years old in the way he measured Time. That she had been nearly immortal. Nearly.

That she was the enchanted princess of a far-off land (a fair rendering of the truth), brought to Earth in chains as a slave (an utter falsehood; as courier she had come to Terra to obtain the ultimate weapon/poetry from one of its authors, who had retired here millennia ago).

That her killer, Mr. Cadaver, was of an alien, inimical race whose sole reason for existence was to wrest power from her own people, the Good Guys. (If somewhat true, this was misleading: his race was not so alien nor so inimical, and if his people wanted to wrest power, so did hers.)

That he was her Champion, as had been destined from the first. That he had been bred for this moment; that his transformation was the inevitable result of her appearance in the city; that she owned him body and soul, because she had brought him this wonderful metamorphosis, because he was her Champion.

That at the completion of the mission the finest and sweetest of rewards awaited him. The most sensual of concubines to fulfill every fantasy. The most precious metals and crystals on which to dine. The frothiest acid baths in which to lounge. Glory everlasting.

His eyes had practically glowed with the hunger of his belief, it was almost pitiable. She felt no remorse regarding the manner of his reward, which she had made up entire because her knowledge of the warrior caste was too scanty to go beyond its prime purpose.

Now she directed him to his closet, where he donned raincoat and slouch hat, pulling the latter low over his face. She told him to keep his hands in his pocket, no one would even notice them or his strange feet.

And she led him into the night, to be her Champion truly, to destroy in his special way the thing that pushed and pulled Mr. Cadaver, the thing that lived inside Mr. Cadaver's testicles.

And then she could finish dying.

9.

Concubines, crystals, and baths. Oh, my!

Almost too wonderful to be believed, but believe it he did. After his metamorphosis he was ready to accept almost anything. The trick with the radio had clinched it. What human agency could have that kind of finesse?

Out in the street, clad in only raincoat and hat, he moved through the night wherever she guided him, following a series of beckoning traffic signals and streetlights, store window neon and the running lights of an occasional passing car.

Leading him onward, west, farther into the city. Thunder rattled and it began to rain.

The water on his three-toed feet as he splashed through gutters was warm, amniotic, gelatinous, erotic. Strings of rain hung from street signs and telephone wires. Sound flattened. He tipped his head back and let the rain sluice his tongue and throat, feeling the rain inside and the rain outside, feeling light-headed, wanting to tear off the raincoat and hat and dance through the jelly of the sodden air, wanting to spin down into the sewers and race beneath the city, what was happening, what was happening, he felt giddy, he had to stop, he lowered his head and shut his mouth. Equilibrium returned. Across the street a traffic light blinked yellow at him angrily and he waved back at it, hunched his shoulders, and moved on.

He was beginning to realize that this change was more profound than he'd thought. Sure, rainwater seemed to make him drunk, but that didn't explain why he felt more carnal now than ever before in his life. Everything around him turned him on. The sheen of water on the pavement, silkier than the softest thigh. The squeals and thuds of thunder. People hurrying through the rain, quivering blobs of animation. The spermatic flow of car lights on the elevated highway to his left. The musty tang of a NO PARKING sign as he munched it. The rough caress of the sidewalk under his feet.

And her. Had she been beautiful? he wondered. When she was still alive? He imagined her in harem garb, all diaphanous and frail and he her great protector. (But not a eunuch, never that. No.) She would have responded to him eagerly, bending her lush body beneath him willingly, because he was all male, all powerful, she would have yielded to that, it was what all women wanted, how could she have resisted him . . . ?

So swirled his thoughts as he moved through the streets. Pacing steadily along the wet sidewalk to the fast-food restaurant, his feet titillated by the concrete slabs, he kept looking about him in quick glances, recording everything, missing nothing, tripping briefly over a discarded plastic hamburger box only because it would not stop fellating his toes. And then he stopped outside the golden arches, staring at the back where a tiny red light above something cooking in hot oil winked and blinked and semaphored to him: your target is here.

But he already knew that.

Just as, once inside, he knew immediately who Mr. Cadaver was. Not only because his quarry was the thinnest of the only three customers in the place. There was something else, almost tangible.

The stench of corruption. Of embracing a steadily cheapening sense of values, until what became important was the flashy, the tawdry, the shoddy, the seedy.

(Not that The Warrior could articulate all this, not when a hundred primary smells seduced him and the heavy odor of french fries was all musk and mating. He sat, and the seat cupped him.)

He took off his hat and dropped it on the table, and felt the victim of a thousand cheap theatrics. This was the enemy? This pathetic eater of vultures' leavings?

The man with the bandaged nose glanced his way and said something to Mr. Cadaver. Mr. Cadaver blinked slowly in the direction of the uncovered earless noseless black faceted head, and betraying nothing in his face pulled a projectile weapon from his dingy coat and fired it.

The Warrior's new yellow cat's eyes watched the bullet tumble out of the barrel and lazily fall forward. When at last it reached him he plucked it from the air and ate it. It didn't taste bad at all.

"What's going on?!" cried the man in the opaque sunglasses. "Will somebody please tell me what is going on!"

Mr. Cadaver blinked once, twice, and revealed another

weapon. A beam fanned out from the muzzle of this weapon, and caught the warrior full in its triangle.

Tingling! Ecstasy! Sexual delights surpassing anything his former human state had fantasized. Mindless orgasm rooted him to the spot.

Holding a large flat case, Mr. Cadaver stood up. His retinue stood up. Mr. Cadaver & Crew made to leave the restaurant.

Back over at the grill a radio blared into life. "Stop him, you fool! Break free and stop him!"

And he wanted to reply to her, to the radio, to her spirit, *Hey, babe, it's okay, we got some time here. Feels so good, just five minutes more!* But the radio would not stop its demands, now it called him names, shamed him, denigrated him past and present, and only his overpowering devotion to her kept him from getting really mad. Still he did not move, not until the frightened gum-chewing teenager from behind the counter ran in slow motion into his line of sight and his eyes tracked the bounce of her breasts and the sway of her hips and *oh baby oh baby* his innate maleness asserted itself and he shook himself free of his trance—

—and he was up and out the door, Mr. Cadaver & Crew just a few steps ahead, and had he a voice he would have shouted. Instead he settled for lunging forward at the skeletal figure, hoping by his forward rush to break some legs.

Mr. Cadaver sidestepped him neatly.

"OH, MY CHAMPION!" blared the radio behind him. "DO NOT FALTER NOW! DO NOT DISAPPOINT ME! THE ENEMY HAS A SECRET! A SECRET WEAKNESS! HE PRETENDS TO BE FEARLESS BUT HE IS TERRIBLY AFRAID OF ONE THING, AND ONE THING ONLY! ALL HIS POWER IS BETWEEN HIS LEGS! CASTRATE HIM! BITE HIS BALLS OFF! THEN YOU'LL STOP HIM FOREVER! BITE HIS BALLS OFF! AND THEN GRAB THAT PORTFOLIO CASE, MY CHAMPION!"

He dug in his heels and suddenly stopped. Now hold it right there! He liked to think of himself as an anything-goes kind of guy, but even "anything goes" had its limits. And biting off Mr. Cadaver's genitalia went way beyond those limits, no matter how important she thought it, no matter how erotic his current exalted unhuman condition. He was still all man, dammit. (Wasn't it enough that he never even beat up queers? Did he have to become one?) And real men didn't—

He tried to visualize what she asked, but the thought made him sick to his stomach. He grabbed at a lamppost and swung around it, vomiting up bits of a NO PARKING sign and Port-o-Gym weights and sofa cushion and towel bar.

"NO! NO! NO!" screamed the radio from the restaurant. "YOU'RE LETTING HIM GET AWAY! IF YOU DON'T STOP HIM NOW, THE WAY I SAID, THAT THING INSIDE HIM—"

He stopped listening. His mouth tasted vile, his head buzzed, he felt betrayed.

But she owned him, body and soul. He had been bred for this moment. He was her Champion.

He pulled his fingers free of the lamppost and saw the triple track they had left behind. He cranked his head around and saw the three points that defined Mr. Cadaver and Company hardly more than a block away, slithering and sliding along the wet street. He ran after them casually and was not surprised to catch up to them in no more than three heartbeats.

The one in the sunglasses, still blind, ran into a parking meter and bounced off with a scream, fell face forward, and the man's spine snapped beneath The Warrior's three-toed feet.

The one with the bandaged nose looked back, screamed, was still screaming as The Warrior's three-fingered hand closed around the man's neck and broke something inside.

Two down, one to go, and Mr. Cadaver had not looked

back, not even for an instant, but he was just a few strides away . . .

And *he* was her Champion. She *owned* him. She was his reason for being. So as her Champion he reached out and tapped Mr. Cadaver gently across the back of the head, and The Adversary tumbled down onto the glistening sidewalk and lay still.

But he had to be sure, because he was her Champion and *she owned him*. So, stooping, he placed his black faceted hands one on either side of Mr. Cadaver's head and then brought his hands together. And Mr. Cadaver would never again enslave enchanted princesses from far-off lands.

He grabbed the portfolio case and hurried back to hear her radioed congratulations.

10.

Everything had gone wrong.

Her radio link steadily weakening, she watched helplessly as her Champion failed her. Watched in disbelief as he reverted, *at the last minute*, to that same alien, inimical thinking that characterized Mr. Cadaver's race: maleness.

She had forgotten the unyielding rigidity of male thinking and male behavior, and it had cost her dearly. No wonder her own people had eliminated the male element millennia before.

She had badly misjudged, and although Mr. Cadaver and his toadies were dead, that thing inside him would find another host and this ultimate war between Good (she or her sisters) and Evil (thing thing thing) would go on until another Champion was found. She only hoped the next one found would be female.

And now she would never know if her daughter could have been saved. She would never fire the ultimate poem or delight in all the verses of the ultimate weapon. She couldn't even direct that miserable male warrior to take care of the portfolio case in the unlikely event of a new courier, for already she was fading, and could manage through the radio no more than a weak "I'm sorry. Good-bye . . ."

And then she was moving up and away from the surface of the planet, all the bodies beneath her dwindling and shrinking, and this time, yes, she could sense an infinitude of other souls in all the colors both known and unknown, vibrating across all spectra to become one vibration. And as she blurred to join them she left behind her a last thought that faded like a smile:

All adversity derives from the cell that first divided.

II.

How could he have been such a fool?

He let himself in the door and stared around his apartment in dismay. The refrigerator was half-eaten, the couch was a mess, he'd never use the Port-o-Gym again, thank God he hadn't touched the TV, and his landlord would fix him good for the damage to the bathroom.

The bathroom. There was nothing in the sink or bathtub but a lot of fine ash. No clothes, no skin. Just holes in the wall where the towel bar had been fastened.

Just holes in his heart where she'd fooled him. He had been bred as her Champion, what a laugh that was, as if she knew what motivated him. No woman knew. Fools. All of them fools.

And he the biggest fool of them all. *Believing* her. *Believing* she owned him, body and soul. *Believing* all her lies and promises. Concubines and acid baths indeed! Enchanted princess from a far-off land! She'd enchanted him all right. He'd waited and waited, portfolio case in hand, waited while the counter help returned and, ignoring him, called the police, waited for her to shower rewards upon him—or at least direct him to where they could be found—and all she'd said, finally, was "I'm sorry. Good-bye . . ." Fool!

He'd thrown away the portfolio case and in dejection come home before the police arrived.

Now he looked into the bathroom mirror, past the pathetic soapy letters that read W A I T, and he had to admit that whatever else had happened, he had to admire his black faceted head, had to approve of the changes to his body. Only . . . where did he go from here?

Damn, he looked good. That powerful head, that virile body. Maybe he should go into politics. Become dictator. He could outrun the wind, he could eat anything (well, whatever he *chose* to eat), and bullets couldn't touch him. He nodded his head at himself. Yes. Rule the world.

Rule the world! (Just stay out of the rain.)

An itch began just below the outside corner of his right eye, where the facet of his cheek was most prominent.

Apocalypso

For connoisseurs of doom, the end of the world can lurk around any corner. The possibility of a limited nuclear exchange is pretty small potatoes next to the thought of some virus already in existence that could go critical, gene-wise, at any time and become the pandemic of our nightmares. There is a belt of volcanoes girdling the globe just waiting for the geological burp that will cause them to simultaneously spew out enough ash and smoke to turn the earth into a gigantic ice cube. Just imagine what's percolating in the atmosphere right now, along with acid rain and fluorocarbons. Maybe we're one ingredient away from a chemical reaction that will turn our breathable gases into something I don't even want to think about. And you want to talk about earthquakes? Comet strikes? War? Meltdowns?

You come to realize civilization is a house of cards. For writers, the contemplation of just how fast it could collapse has been fertile territory for centuries and as the options grow, so do the number of stories. We've selected a few for you here, though these are far from your typical survivalist fare. No evolution in action, no post-nuclear Rambos blasting their way through herds of mutant cockroaches nesting in the husk of the Statue of Liberty, no neo-primitives worshiping an ancient, brittle copy of *I'm O.K., You're O.K.* Just stories about the end of life as we knew it, or hoped it could have been.

—J.H.

STEVEN R. BOYETT

Steve is a writer whose stories are savored like a connoisseur savors the elusive truffle. Though he is not a prolific writer, each story he produces is a superb, iconoclastic gem. As the following story illustrates, Steve's work defies classification: you'll find elements of horror, science fiction, fantasy and reality in equal measure.

"Emerald City Blues" was one of the most controversial stories in *Midnight Graffiti*'s history. It was considered "untouchable" by several editors in the field, yet considered by writers such as Stephen King to be "one of the great stories of the last few years." Here's a second chance for readers to discover the talent of Steven Boyett.

Emerald City Blues
by Steven R. Boyett

Lieutenant Rhino loves his F-18.

After thousands of hours nestled in its warm and pressurized cockpit, the Hornet is as responsive to the commands of Lieutenant Rhino's brain as his hands. He enjoys the power at his fingertips and beneath his hard-soled boots. He can make the horizon pinwheel with the slightest turn of gloved wrist. A push will fill the wedge of windshield with the monotony of sea or confusion of land. A pull, and the horizon drains in an even line.

A finger on this button, and the load would lighten beneath his wings, to explode somewhere and someone ahead of him.

Lieutenant Rhino smiles, sliding his rubber cup of oxygen mask a half-inch up his nose. On his nose is the wart that gives Rhino his nickname; the wart that all the kids made fun of in school; the only wart on his body, and in the most conspicuous place possible; the wart he absolutely refuses to have removed.

His oxygen mask irritates the wart.

Rhino thinks about the payload specialists on bombers. They have time to *plan*, to add some style to their button-pushing. A bombardier—payload specialist—can arc out his hand, add a flourish, extend an index finger, and *push*. Or he can jab like a concert pianist attacking ivory, then wait for the welling of megaton timpani. Or simple and direct, the Air Force way. Or better still, simple, direct, and with little finger.

Rhino envies them this time to plan. Fighter-pilot decisions don't allow much planning—in fact, they're hardly conscious decisions at all. Rhino feels he is the perfect man for his job.

He glances right, looking out the Windex-clean window at Kneecap, the 747 with the presidential seal.

There are campfires all over Oz tonight. Gillikins from the north, Quadlings from the south, Munchkins from the east, and Winkies from the west, all flock toward the Emerald City, taking care that their torches, lighted ceremoniously in their home cities, remain burning. They wish to add to the bonfire already blazing in celebration of the imminent return of Dorothy.

The first delegation of Munchkins arrives at the end of the Yellow Brick Road. They are greeted with glee by the revellers, who are becoming a little drunk from the flow of Winkie Country wine.

Wine leaves no hangover in Oz.

The Munchkins bow their short little bows and with great pomp add their torches to the bonfire. The Scarecrow thanks them solemnly from his gilded platform, which is located a respectful distance from the flames.

* * *

Lieutenant Rhino snakes a gloved finger beneath the damnable oxygen mask to scratch at the wart. He wonders—not for the first time, certainly—if he can get one of the masks custom-built, with a rubber dot of a hump for his nose.

Kneecap plods along in its clumsy-graceful way, like a pregnant guppy swimming upside down. "Kneecap" is for NEACP, which is for National Emergency Airborne Command Post.

Rhino frowns, and his oxygen mask lowers snugly where it belongs. Looking at the bulbous-headed airplane, he has just been struck by the notion that the craft looks remarkably like a winged penis. He squashes the thought and glances ahead of the 747. There flies Tee Dee One, the point plane in the Tasmanian Devil Group, spewing a gray contrail. Tasmanian Devil Group is the hastily assembled escort of F-18s flying in a diamond configuration so perfect Euclid would have had an orgasm. In the center of the diamond flies Kneecap, and inside Kneecap sits the President of the ephemerally United States.

In the mid-1970s it had been decreed that, when the Balloon finally went up, so would the President—hence Kneecap. Several hours ago the United States spy satellites peeking in at the escalating situation in the Persian Gulf had politely informed those who get informed that the Balloon was as up as a Pittsburgh Steeler before the Super Bowl and so, up went Kneecap.

A voice crackles in Lieutenant Rhino's ear, the Voice of Kneecap. "Kneecap to Tasmanian Devils. Deploying antenna. The air drag'll slow us up a bit, so stay with us. Tee Dee Three will want to climb a hundred feet. Acknowledge."

Tee Dees One and Two acknowledge. Tee Dee Three adds that he is climbing, since he is flying behind Kneecap and wants no part of the long antenna that is deployed to collect vital information.

Rhino thumbs his radio transmitter. "Tee Dee Four acknowledges. Do we have an ETA, Goldilocks?"

Goldilocks was SAC—Strategic Air Command—headquarters in Omaha, Nebraska; ETA was Estimated Time of Arrival. It was fun to think up names to go with important things.

"We can't give that on the air, Tee Dee Four," answers Kneecap smugly. "It shouldn't be too hard to work out yourself. Keep this channel clear. Kneecap out."

Well! Rhino toys with the idea of peeling off and shoving a bang or six under Kneecap's nose, but dismisses it. If he does and is somehow caught after this mess is over, he will be court-martialed.

The Tin Woodman swims the length of his Olympic-sized pool, breast-stroking his hollow body through the Quaker State forty-weight. He emerges, dripping viscously, and bends his legs and flexes his arms to work the oil into his knees and elbows. A bespectacled assistant hands him the evening edition of the *Green Street Journal*: he turns immediately to Commodities.

Hearing himself scrape as he sits on a stone bench, he thinks, *I ought to do something about that. A little foam padding, perhaps.*

He opens his chest and pulls out his heart. Nine twenty-five already. The revelry will go on for another two and a half hours—until Glinda made everybody go to bed.

Being one of the Good Guys sure has its drawbacks, he reflects. But it's probably for the best, since Dorothy arrives tomorrow.

Dorothy . . .

He looks down and, for the ten thousandth time, curses his incompleteness. "If I only had a hard," he sighs.

* * *

"Tee Dee One." The voice of Kneecap crackles to life, calling the F-18 Hornet leading the diamond formation.

"One here."

"We show activity on long-range. DSB confirms. Speed and signature suggest Soviet cruise missile, type unknown, target Goldilocks probable." Kneecap gives coordinates and velocities, then adds a command that Lieutenant Rhino yearns to hear directed to him: "Go for it, Tee Dee One."

The trail farting from Tee Dee One's tail darkens as the F-18 shoots ahead and veers southwest on an intercept course. *How come I never have any fun?* Lieutenant Rhino whines to himself.

The once-cowardly Lion, king of beasts, ignores the big-breasted woman plaiting his calves as he searches through the matted fur of his emaciated arm. He finds a healthy vein and grins carnivorously. He wraps his tail tightly around his elbow and clenches his fist several times, then slips the needle of a hypodermic syringe into the vein and pushes the plunger.

Euphoria courses up his arm and throughout his undernourished body. *Courage*, he thinks.

The woman gives up plaiting his legs and sits on the polished floor giggling to herself.

The Lion folds his paws behind his head and feels himself beginning to float above the couch. He stares contentedly at the emerald ceiling and thinks of the revelers outside the city wall. *Whatta they got that I ain't got?*

Brightness blossoms in the southwest, where Tee Dee One veered off for his rendezvous with destiny.

The three Tasmanian Devils still escorting Kneecap remain in tight formation until Tee Dee One is sighted, first on radar, then visually. The phrase "visual sighting" is not redundant to a fighter pilot.

The returning fighter-jet banks, and Rhino sees that it has expended only two air-to-air missiles. Tee Dee One resumes formation, and the Tasmanian Devils are a diamond once again. He is back in lead position and reporting before the shock wave reaches them.

Smug-ass bastard, thinks Rhino. Still, he thumbs the "transmit" button and joins the others in congratulating Tee Dee One.

Ninety minutes later Kneecap touches down at SAC headquarters. The four escort jets shoot ahead, fifty feet from the tarmac, then peel off in four directions.

Flight crews glide out to Kneecap on maintenance trucks, sticking long hoses into its delicate underparts.

The President and his staff, including an officer carrying a Little Black Bag known as the Football that contains the codes for launching U.S. nuclear forces, hurry down the roll-up stairway and are quickly bundled away in a van that hurries them to another airplane: Looking Glass, commanded by an Air Force general in charge of directing U.S. ICBMs and bombers.

Fifteen minutes later Kneecap is airborne again, heading north. Looking Glass noses into the air soon afterward, gains a respectful height, and turns south, toward Kansas.

-

The Wicked Witch of the North cackles gleefully. "Melt my sister, will she?" Her voice is a silken *sssliiiding* across a sheen of oil. "Start a housing development on my *other* sister, will she?"

Perched beside her, the King of the Flying Monkeys cocks his capped head. He removes the soggy stump of a Cuba Libre cigar from his mouth and gestures with it. "Dat housing development," he says in a distinct Bronx accent, "is the best thing ever happened to us."

Many items were salvaged from the unintentionally mobile home of Dorothy's Aunt Em and Uncle Henry. In a wire magazine rack next to the flush toilet were Aunt Em's back issues of *Collier's* and *Vanity Fair*, and a Sears & Roebuck catalog (minus the first thirty pages) advertising such novel items as hunting supplies, washing machines, door locks, and shoe lifts for the short-statured. A supplement detailed Sears & Roebuck's generous Credit Plan. On a narrow vanity shelf beneath the medicine-chest mirror were Coty cosmetics, including a cake of rouge in a cameo box with a cracked, ivory-handled, horsetail brush, a thick glass jar of vanishing cream, and lipsticks in various reds. On the scarred maple dresser were books—among them the 1898 edition of the *Home Medical Encyclopaedia* (with a comprehensive listing of drugs, their effects, and methods of administration), Hobbs's *Guide to the Stock Exchange*, Smythe's *Guide to Investments and Agrarian Commodities*, and *The Shooter's Bible* (with a chapter on home loads). Beneath the books, in the top dresser drawer, were a box of Lucifer matches, a package of Diamond rolling papers, and Union Leader tobacco in the Crimson Couch package. Scattered about were fifty-five cents in change and a rumpled dollar bill (which solved the mystery of the hitherto unknown word "dollar" that occurred with such frequency in the Sears & Roebuck catalog, in the back of Aunt Em's magazines, and in the Hobbs and Smythe books). There was also a box of Cuba Libre cigars hand-wrapped in Havana, and beneath this were twelve worn-cornered, black-and-white French postcards, most of them thumb-worn at the lower left edge. In the drawer below this were bras, panties, and elastic girdles.

In the utility room was a gasoline-powered generator. In the living room was a cathedral-arched Philco radio. Discovered beneath a loose board in the larger bedroom were two unlabeled glass jugs of illegally distilled grain alcohol, colloquially known as "hooch."

The house had been picked clean in days.

* * *

The King of the Flying Monkeys waves his fragrant cigar. "Best thing that *ever* happened," he repeats.

The Wicked Witch of the North slits her green eyes at the King of the Flying Monkeys. "The best is yet to come," she grates. She smiles, and the King of the Flying Monkeys finds he must look away.

The Wicked Witch of the North gazes back into her crystal ball.

In it are a river and a rocket.

Held aloft by its short, stubby wings, the Soviet cruise missile amorously hugs the terrain. It is a submarine-launched missile that has come all the way across the western United States, zooming along a scant hundred feet from the ground. Being launched from a submarine means that it has escaped detection by the Ballistic Missile Early Warning System radars in Alaska, and if the Defense Support Program satellites haven't detected it by now, there is little that can be done about it if they do.

Traveling across the continent, its Terrain Contour Matching capability (guided by a preprogrammed minicomputer that uses a radar altimeter to match the contour of the ground with on-board maps obtained from spy-satellite photographs) pilots the cruise missile swiftly toward its programmed destination.

With simpleminded determination it follows the twisting path of the Missouri River, avoiding radar detection, until its pea-brain tells it that it is time to turn now.

The missile veers southwest, whistling to itself as it carries its 300-kiloton nuclear warhead toward Omaha, Nebraska.

What would pass for the sound of a DC-10 crash elsewhere is laughter in the castle of the Wicked Witch of the North. Her Tartar-like guards are used to the sound and do not flinch, but the Flying Monkeys are not, and they cover their enormous ears.

The Wicked Witch of the North turns away from her crystal ball and fixes her evil-eyed gaze on the King of the Flying Monkeys. "Bring me my broom!" she screeches. Her voice is a thousand jagged fingernails dragged across two hundred spotless blackboards.

The awful sound raises the fur of his neck, and the King of the Flying Monkeys turns to obey.

"And make sure it's full this time!" she calls after him. "I don't want to run out of smoke the way I did before!"

She rubs her long-fingered, black-nailed green hands and turns back to the lovely prime-time viewing on the crystal ball.

In it are blackness and stars.

Orbiting high above the earth, a Soviet satellite receives a coded radio signal.

The satellite—with a microchip brain even smaller than that of the Soviet cruise missile—sets in motion the short program that has waited years for this moment.

Four small explosive bolts blow away its small metal shell to expose the warhead beneath. A thick, ceramic heat shield covers its nose; it will be sheared away by friction, and the remainder discarded, during the warhead's descent.

Gyroscopes whir soundlessly in the vacuum of space. The bulbous-headed body pivots until its single cone of rocket exhaust points away from the delicate blue marble of the earth. The engine flares for seventeen seconds, and the pea-brained missile begins its seventy-two-second descent toward Omaha, Nebraska.

God takes a flash picture right behind Lieutenant Rhino's F-18.

"What the *fuck* was that?"

"Cut it, Tee Dee Four," orders the Voice of Looking Glass.

Up yours, Rhino commands silently.

"That," says a radio voice, "was Omaha." Rhino notes the use of the past tense.

"Cut it, Tee Dee Three," orders Looking Glass.

Tee Dee Three, muses Rhino. *Golly gee, Tee Dee Three, see the bee*?

The overpressure wave hits them from behind. The five jets nose up and ride it out nicely. Rhino hangs ten all the way.

Why can't they break piñatas, or hold a parade, or anything else in the goddamned world? the Scarecrow wonders. *But no, they've got to light the biggest damned fire they can make, and I have to preside over it.*

If the wind changes I'm going to go up like a firework. The King of Ahhs.

The Scarecrow bows to a party of Good Witches in Training from the south-southeast. They blush behind thick layers of rouge, duck their heads, and smile shyly with reddened lips. With charming sophomorism they recite spells to light the brands they contribute to the bonfire's blaze. Straightening, the Scarecrow fixes his painted eyes on the white-taffeta-gowned butt of one of the Good Witches.

One of the prudish Munchkins catches him staring at the Good Witch's butt. The Scarecrow stares him down until he turns away, red-faced and muttering apologies.

Short little fuck.

He looks back at the white-clad derriere.

Maybe I shouldn't have asked for brains.

By Lieutenant Rhino's reckoning—as dead a reckoning as ever there was—they have just crossed over into Kansas airspace.

What are they doing down there? he wonders, looking out at vast stretches of farmland. Hiding?

Shooting each other to get into air-raid shelters, probably. There's a missile silo for every cow, 'round here.

What would they think if they knew we were up here?

Be pissed off, he decides. Hell, they *paid* for this. Their money went to build Kneecap and Looking Glass. Somebody picked beans for weeks to pay for the radiation-shielded fuselage. Someone else, some skinny redneck riding a tractor from sunup to sundown, got hemorrhoids plowing from January to the middle of March to contribute to the long-range radar, the teletype printers, the mile-long reel-out antenna.

Hey, down there! he sends telepathically, waving. *Thanks! You guys paid for my F-18!*

He tips his wings in salute.

The Wicked Witch of the North takes to the air on her broom, which leaves a much blacker trail than even the most flatulent of the F-18s. She doesn't need to understand overpressure waves and aftershocks, dynamic pressure and "dirty" bursts and gamma radiation, to know that she will be safer in the air. She doubts even her castle will survive the coming onslaught, and her castle is about as tough a castle as a contractor can build.

Besides, she'll need to be in the air to open the Rainbow Bridge.

She orders all her flying monkeys to take off with her, and they flap around her, shrieking delightedly. It's been a while since the old hag let them cut some air.

She checks her skywriting smoke level. The dipstick shows full. Not that she doesn't trust the King of the Flying Monkeys, but you never know. Good help is pretty hard to find in Oz these days.

"AWACS shows a bogey," announces the electronically dehumanized Voice of Looking Glass.

"Numbers?" Tee Dee One demands quickly, knowing that Looking Glass is talking about an unidentified flying aircraft and not about a film star dead of cancer.

Looking Glass gives Tee Dee some numbers. The numbers tell him the bogey is way up high and dropping fast.

Glory hog, thinks Lieutenant Rhino.

"Tee Dee Four," says Tee Dee One.

Rhino jumps. "Four here."

"Go for it, Tee Dee Four. Short and sweet."

Rhino grins. He guns his engines, rises smartly, and shoots ahead of the Tasmanian Devil formation, pulling back hard on the stick. His contrail darkens behind him.

"Beep-beep," says the F-18's radar.

Rhino glances at it. A tight-packed group of phosphorescent green-white tactical numbers creeps toward a bull's-eye on the screen. Rhino relies on his computers; the bogey is too fast to visually sight—by the time he saw it, it would be long gone.

It looks like there's one whopper of a storm about forty miles to the south. Tornado, maybe. Clouds cover the land like puffy gray fungus.

"Beep-beep," repeats the radar.

"I *know* it's there!" Rhino snaps.

Fifteen seconds later his targeting computer has a radar lock and tells him he can fire. Rhino's F-18 carries a special missile, an ASAT—Anti-Satellite—with the barest smidgen of a nuclear tip to wipe out enemy satellites. But this bogey has managed to sneak right by everybody until almost too late to do anything about it, and Rhino is not sure that his ASAT could maneuver, target-lock, and detonate in time to take care of the satellite-launched missile. If it is an air-burst warhead, it will go off at approximately two thousand feet. But since the bomb that shifted Omaha into the past tense was an air burst, this one will probably be a ground-pounder intended to further pulverize Strategic Air Command Headquarters and get whoever may have cheated by hiding in underground shelters.

The pea-brain of the descending missile, however, is just smart enough to know that it should try to get out of the way if it detects someone trying to stop it. Since it is moving so fast, it can't maneuver so well, but since it *is* moving so fast, even the slightest move will make it harder to intercept.

Rhino frowns at the shifting number group on his tactical display. The missile must have seen him coming, because it is running away.

Rhino runs after it.

In what seems like no time they are over the fungus of the storm. The storm is capped by a huge rainbow, and Rhino thinks of McDonald's.

The rainbow draws closer as the Soviet missile speeds down and the F-18 speeds up and across the sky. Lieutenant Rhino's tactical radar is beeping bloody murder now.

Oh, what the hey, thinks Rhino. ''Bang,'' he says out loud. ''Bang-bang.''

The F-18's Voice Activated Weapons Launcher System hears the words. It asks itself if they are the right words. It asks itself if Rhino is allowed to say them.

Yes, it answers itself. And yes.

Satisfied, it throws out a heat-seeking missile. This missile has a ''conventional'' warhead, meaning that it is not nuclear, but uses the kind of explosive traditional bombers recommend most.

The voice-activated, heat-seeking missile misses, however, and for the strangest of reasons: the satellite-launched Soviet missile dives over the rainbow and disappears.

Targetless, the heat-seeking missile speeds under the rainbow. Lieutenant Rhino and his F-18 sail over it.

* * *

"There she is!" Somebody points upward. The Scarecrow looks at the indicated patch of night sky and sees nothing unusual. But he keeps his gaze fixed unblinkingly and, sure enough, one of the stars is moving. It seems to be coming closer, growing brighter as it does.

"Dorothy!" shouts one of the Good Witches in Training from the south-southeast. The one with the nice butt.

"Dorothy isn't due till tomorrow," says the Scarecrow. But the cry has been taken up: "Dorothy!" shout the Munchkins. "Dorothy!" shout the Good Witches. "Dorothy!" shout the Gillikins, Quadlings, and Winkies.

"Might be the Wicked Witch of the North," mutters the Scarecrow, wishing he weren't so damned smart.

Something's very wrong.

It hits Rhino as his F-18 sails over the rainbow without a ripple: You *can't* get close to a rainbow. They're a phenomenon of refracted sunlight, and must keep pace ahead of you because the angle of refraction must remain constant to the observer in order for the rainbow to be visible at all!

And besides, he remembers, rainbows are *circular* when viewed from the air.

Ahead of Rhino, the Soviet missile is even more confused. Nothing matches the contour signatures contained in its peabrain. The altimeter shows a drastic reduction in height.

Desperate, it switches to infrared tracking and discovers a heat source only a few miles below. It makes a minor course correction and sighs an electronic sigh of relief and fulfillment.

Rhino sees stars through his wedge of windshield. But it can't be night yet! Something is really fucked here.

He follows the missile down through puffy, moonlit clouds

that he knows should be puffy gray fungus. He breaks through them just in time to glimpse a brilliant flash ahead of the plummeting nose of his F-18.

Rhino jinks left, kicks in the afterburners, and pulls up, feeling blood drain from his head. His vision dims even though his flight suit tries to fight the G-forces by squeezing his body like a concerned mother.

Just before the flash he glimpsed something he is not about to believe. There is no way he can believe it, no way it can exist, even though his mother read him to sleep describing it when he was a little boy with a big wart on his nosc; even though it is exactly what he pictured but never bothered to credit with any importance, any weight, any relevance, to his life, his dreams, his heart's desire.

But inside he knows that he really did see it before he'd begun to pull up from the dive, and he knows that, somehow, he's not in Kansas anymore.

Aftershocks buffet his F-18.

And the Emerald City, the slender spires and fragile domes and jeweled gates; the capital of Oz and host to her miracles; the green flint that sparked the imagination of generations; the Emerald City, where the impossible is as ordinary as a Sunday paper beside a china plate of steaming scrambled eggs; the brilliant, delicate, and eternal Emerald City of Oz, shatters under an explosion beyond the mind's containing—fifty times more powerful than that which destroyed Hiroshima, an explosion equal to the simultaneous detonation of one million tons of TNT. But before those pieces of emerald, shaped by small hands and large thoughts, can fall a measurable distance, they are melted to slag by a flash of consuming, voracious heat—ten million degrees Fahrenheit, heat that fuses sand into glass, heat like the surface of the sun.

Seeing the flash, the Tin Woodman extends a metal arm to grab his famous axe and defend his beloved city, but his arm shimmers, glows, and melts in a fraction of a second. Within his melting chest his heart bursts into flame, as if unable to contain its rage.

The Once-Cowardly Lion, hearing a jungle bellow from somewhere outside his chambers deep within the Emerald City, draws a proud breastful of air to respond to the challenge, but no amount of courage could withstand the onslaught that devours him as unthinkingly as a whale devours a plankton cell.

And the Scarecrow, Ruler of the Emerald City and wisest creature in all of Oz, whose greatest fear and enemy is fire, sees all the flames of Creation born before his painted eyes, and has only enough time to rail against the brain that could conceive a device that obliterates minds on a wholesale level, before he ignites and bursts and becomes ash and less than ash, not even a flicker in the terrible conflagration that is his city, not even a tenth of a second's worth of fuel to feed the clenched fist of consumed matter that towers above the heart of the Land of Oz.

Yellow bricks burn. Poppy fields vaporize. Round houses explode. The bodies of Munchkins catch fire by themselves. Good Witches run screaming, white taffeta blazing; are smashed by a compressed wall of air moving faster than the speed of sound—the overpressure wave; are picked up and hurled like so many clots of dirt; are flensed by debris; are slammed into walls and trees or tumbled like broken dolls upon the ground, twisted and bleeding, powerless to help themselves or their burned and blackened and blinded and bleeding countrymen. Everyone is a child again, pleading for help, calling to make it stop, make it go away, but their cries are subsumed by the howl of the wind.

Firestorms feed on the kindling of smashed houses. Those Munchkins, Gillikins, Winkies, and Quadlings who have managed to hide in cellars are asphyxiated by the voracious greed of fire sucking away the air.

The roiling fist swells above the heart of Oz. It unclenches, and leaves not one life untouched by its fingers.

Flying far away—gloating, unaware that the malevolent life within her body ebbs as those billions of body cells destroyed by an onslaught of neutrons and gamma rays encourage the death of surrounding cells—the Wicked Witch of the North straddles her broom and writes triumphantly in the sky.

She has not even completed the first word before she is shot down by a jet fighter.

The next morning a house landed in the middle of a smoking, thousand-feet-wide crater, and Dorothy Gale stepped right from her snaggle-toothed front porch and onto a vast plain of fused emerald and glass. She cradled Toto in one arm and her ungainly lunch pail in the other. Her ruby-slippered feet clacked across a solid sea of green until she stopped before a wall—a lone wall of emerald brick, the only wall standing for a dozen miles.

A hot wind blew among the ruins. Black flakes settled like filthy snow upon Dorothy's gingham-clad shoulders. A lengthening white contrail stretched across the murky sky.

But this can't be Oz, thought Dorothy. *This just can't be*.

And so she walked away from the plain of emerald, letting Toto pick his own way through piles of rubble the height of buildings—the rubble of townships and yellow brick roads and talking trees and tall cornfields and horses of a different color—a little girl with braided pigtails wandering the perpetually twilit corpse of a city she dreamed about every night at her aunt and uncle's farm in Kansas. For mile after mile she saw not one living creature, not one standing building. In a few hours she stumbled upon life: a wasteland of leveled houses writhing with groping, burned figures in charred uniforms of red, yellow, blue, or green. Knowing nothing of fallout, blinded by nuclear flash, deafened by detonation, the People of Oz staggered in private blackness and agony through the soft and deadly rain, calling out to ears that could not hear.

Dorothy cupped her hand to the river that fed Lake Quad and drank radioactive water. Fish floated belly-up. Dorothy looked up from her small, wet palm and saw shadows on a stone wall in the remains of a Munchkin village, but there were no figures to cast them. She recognized the Mayor of Munchkinland from his curled-brim hat and spike goatee. The shadow held a scroll in one hand and gestured to the crowd with the other, burned forever onto the stone.

She chased away rats that fed on the festering corpses of Munchkins, two sources of the plague to come, and walked on.

In one day Dorothy saw more burn victims than there are burn-unit beds in the United States, Canada, and Europe. The burned and unburned alike were afflicted with radiation sickness: vomiting, diarrhea, anemia, hair loss, skin cancers, and infections. There was not one hospital in all of Oz.

The land was growing cold because the airborne debris blocked the sunlight. In a few months the fifteen thousand survivors of Oz—which once boasted a population of one hundred thousand strong—will face the first true winter of their lives. Farmers will watch withering crops that signify the doom of their families. In the land of the Winkies, opposite the easterly wind, surviving cows and goats will give forth radioactive milk; the last normal infants born in Oz will suck at the breasts of mothers eating radioactive food and breathing radioactive air. Only half of the fifteen thousand will see the next summer.

Dorothy will not live to see this grim winter. Within days of her arrival she is dead. Massive radiation poisoning sleeting through her body disrupted its cells beyond repair, forcing her metabolism to work itself to exhaustion, until it simply gives up. She lies against a pile of rubble besides a puddle of her own vomit, lunch pail in hand, a widow's shawl of radioactive ash around her shoulders, small bodies huddled beside her, still forever.

Toto, too.

I've got to get back, Lieutenant Rhino thinks frantically. *I've got to tell them they can't do this, not this.*

Rhino has logged more than a thousand hours in fighter jets. His F-18 fits his body like a tailored suit, and he knows its every tic and tremor. He does not need to look at the gauge to know that he is nearly out of fuel.

But I've got at least an hour left, he thinks. I've got to find it, got to check my course tracker and tactical radar and inertial navigator and trust my dead reckoning to get me back to that rainbow, to get me over that rainbow and back *home*. To tell them, to make them stop. If he could tell them what they'd done, if they could only see what he had seen, surely they'd understand.

He shuts his eyes and remembers what he saw just before pulling his F-18 up and out.

It was tall. God, it was so tall and slender . . ..

Got to get back and get on the radio. If I do one thing, God, one useful thing in my entire life, let me find that rainbow, let me make it back before I run out of fuel. You gave me the speed and the skill and the talent to let me fly like a bluebird, God. Now let me use that skill to find my way back and tell them what I've seen, what we've done.

—slender like the fingers of a lady. And it sparkled like the ocean in the moonlight . . .

Thirty minutes. I can find it in thirty minutes, God.

—and the color, so bright, even in the darkness before the flash, and so green.

CLIFF BURNS

Cliff Burns is a young Canadian writer who made his first professional sale to *Midnight Graffiti* with a story striking in its subtle themes and sensitivity. Cliff has had a busy career since then, and recently moved from Toronto's metropolis to a remote town in British Columbia. ''They don't have a bookstore,'' he reports, ''but they do have a moose.''

Cliff's story ''Cattletruck'' is a suggestive look at the victim of some future holocaust, and the power of innocence.

Cattletruck
by Cliff Burns

''They flutter behind you, your possible pasts
Some bright-eyed and crazy, some frightened and lost
A warning to anyone still in command
Of their possible futures to take care
In derelict sidings the poppies entwine
With cattletrucks lying in wait for the next time . . .''
—Roger Waters (Pink Floyd's ''The Final Cut'')

I watch as the child approaches, swaying and bumping down the aisle as she combats the car's tricky contortions.

She and I have been sneaking looks at each other since I was helped aboard by sickened porters three hours ago.

''Man, you sure in bad shape,'' one of my dark, uniformed aides had mumbled.

I saved myself some pain by just nodding. The skin on my face is so tight that the slightest movement causes it to split open. Despite my efforts the blistered skin voids a good amount of purulent matter into the gauze wound above my head. The dried pus acts as a mortar, encasing my face in a painful papier-mâché mask.

There will be no relief forthcoming. The shortage of medical personnel means that I must travel alone, untended, forgoing luxuries like periodic changes of dressing. It will be a long, excruciating trip to . . . wherever. There is a large displaced persons camp out on the prairies but I hear food is short even in the breadbasket of the world.

"Listen," the doctor insisted, "you can't stay here. We can't do anything more for you and we need the bed. It's as simple as that."

I stared up at him accusatively. He kept his eyes on his clipboard as if he was reading from a prepared statement.

"You must have someone somewhere. Sisters? Brothers? They can take care of you. We're just overwhelmed, *you understand?"*

I turned my face toward the wall.

"It says here you're from out west originally. Well, there you are. They didn't get it too bad out there." He waited for me to say something but I would not oblige him. "We . . . we'll keep you here tonight but tomorrow you'll have to leave. I'm sorry. And I want you to know that I wish you the best."

I heard his shoes squeak on the gymnasium floor as he moved on, his arrival at the next clutter of patients greeted by cries of relief, pitiful pleas for morphine.

Don't ask for too much, I warned silently, because people who need too much—

The train is slowing.

Immediately I recall the reports I've heard of the recent resurrection of a lost art: train robbery. Bands of people crazy with hunger are tearing up tracks, deliberately derailing trains, burrowing in the hissing wreckage for a morsel, a mouthful, anything to line their acidic stomachs with.

They might like me, I come precooked, ready to serve.

The train picks up speed again and the part of me (it grows more persuasive every day) that wants all of this to be over is disappointed.

During my reverie the child has advanced a few more steps, her gaze frank and penetrating.

She is a regular little dervish, this one, whirling in and out of the grasp of everyone in the car, earning indulgent smiles, chin chucks, and the odd hug if the adult is quick enough to catch her. I have enjoyed watching her but have dreaded the moment when her inquisitiveness drew her in this direction.

Somehow she has summoned the courage to shamble toward me—one digit tucked reflectively in her mouth—and for that she is to be congratulated. But I curse her too because I can picture the scene that will transpire: the little girl screaming and crying, her mother rushing to her side to protect her from the mangled boogeyman, the reproachful glares of fellow passengers . . . *AS IF IT'S MY FAULT*.

I shake my head at her.

She pauses.

I thrust out a wrapped hand, waggle it in a shooing gesture. The concealing mitten only widens her eyes and mouth. She takes another step.

I sigh.

She's close now, close enough to smell me. Her little nose wrinkles daintily. But she doesn't run away and she doesn't scream and she doesn't cry.

"You look . . . funny," she says.

And giggles.

The statement is so unexpected, so cogent, so anticlimactic that I laugh along with her, a sibilant wheeze escaping between clenched teeth and out of my nostrils. Good laughter, not bitter. I welcome the pain that flushes my features.

"That's because I am funny," I grate, "the biggest joke of all."

"What do you look like, underneath all that gunk?"

"Funny," I shoot back.

She cackles. "I know, but what do you *LOOK* like."

I think about that.

How do I look?

I recall the poor souls pressed into service as assistants, orderlies, nurses, and sometimes even surgeons in makeshift hospitals throughout the city. Men and women who'd had to acquire torpid hearts, rigid backbones, eyes that saw but refused to comprehend, voices that were filled with cheerful optimism as they cut away dressings and uncovered a person whose humanity had been caricatured by fire or flying glass. A few bodies revolted against the demands being imposed on them by the carnage. A big fellow, over six feet and swollen with muscle, broke down as he removed the last layer of my bandages. He vomited all over the bedclothes, fell to the floor where he proceeded to kick and flail at anyone who tried to restrain him.

"He's a meatloaf!" he screamed. "A fucking meatloaf!"

How do I look?

"I look like . . . like there are big blobs of melted plasticine all over my face."

That earns me an "Ooooo."

I see the little girl's mother preparing to rise from her position opposite a young couple.

"You'd be great at trick 'r treatin', y'know," she advises me.

"Oh yeah, I do it all the time."

"Really?" Her expression is doubtful.

"Yeah. Got two Tootsie Rolls the other day." Actually they've been in my pocket for ages. "Would you like to have them?"

"Sure!"

"Rachel?" Her mother is calling, craning her neck, trying to see the current object of her daughter's attention.

"In my pocket," I whisper.

She is torn between obeying her mother and the promise of a treat. Finally, she moves closer, reaches into my coat pocket, rummages around, and comes up with the candy.

I expect her to retreat from me quickly but she lingers. She reaches down, strokes a wrist, my fingers, cradles my palm, her touch gentle and intuitive.

"Does it hurt much?" she asks.

"Oh . . . sometimes."

She draws the hand up, plants a placating kiss on the yellowed wrapping.

Hot and salty, the tears slip down my cheeks, emblazon a crooked pattern of pain to my chin.

Stinging.

Burning.

"RACHEL!"

Her mother forces the wind out of the girl in her efforts to get her away from me. Rachel begins to cry.

"I'm really sorry—"

"It's okay, she was just—"

"—won't happen again, I'll—"

"—really we were just talking—"

"—for any inconvenience—"

"—please—"

The woman speaks to a conductor who helps her stuff Rachel's toys into a bulging shopping bag, escorts the two of them from the car.

My hands contract into tight, angry fists.

I wasn't going to hurt the kid—

I bring my hands up to my face, stare at them.

A week ago, an hour ago, a minute ago charred skin tissue and soldered cartilage prevented all but the slightest movement of either hand. My fingers had been fused together, ensnared in a web of tough, violet flesh. I required assistance for the simplest tasks like zipping up my coat or using the washroom.

But now . . .

I open-close-open-close my hands, marveling at the complexity of His designs.

DAVID J. SCHOW

Dave Schow's writing has been described as controversial, aggressive, and unflinching. The same could be said of his career—Dave always seems to be living in the eye of a hurricane. His award-winning collections and novels, such as *The Kill Riff, Seeing Red*, and *Lost Angels*, all seemed to birth in the midst of conflict.

Dave coined the word ''Splatterpunk'' to encompass his style of horror, a style that pushed the envelope in terms of its graphic depictions of violence and the examination of taboo themes. Seeding the ground broken by Clive Barker in the eighties, Schow and several other like-minded and talented young writers (John Skipp and Craig Spector, Ray Garton, Robert McCammon, and others) ignored the conventions of genre horror and began writing stories that reflected the realities of their time. Settings were moved from the suburbs to urban streets, heroes were as likely to be addicts as account executives, the music was rock and roll, the influence of pop culture was woven into the backdrop, and the update was done. It seemed a wholly natural process, but the grumblings have yet to cease.

Graphic horror is not everyone's cup of tea, but it is undeniably a style that acknowledges the human animal as being truly capable of the most grotesque and brutal behavior imaginable. But we knew that, didn't we? Schow's story that follows embodies that understanding.

Bad Guy Hats

by David J. Schow

The four young men in bad guy hats sauntered into the Jump Mart on a summer day of record heat and Amazon humidity.

They came packing, hammers down on chambered slugs, mad whoopee dancing in their eyes.

Their bad guy hats made them heartbreakers, life-takers. Hard partyers and dirty fighters.

Dicky's savage grin organized itself around a wooden match, the kind you could strike anywhere. This one was burnt out. Sweat ran into his eyebrows from his black brush cut. He mopped, then drew his piece from the waistband of his jeans. Stonewashed and supertight, those jeans; snug in all the right places, yet soft and broken-in as a mother's nipple. Dicky was proud of the gun. It was an S&M L-frame Combat Magnum, a 586 cut for speedloaders. It took Dicky a moment to haul all eight-plus inches of barrel out of his pants. He dipped the weight of the revolver forward to help his thumb cock it. Smooth.

He told the geezer working the counter to shut up three times. By the third time, he was screaming, and the rest of the store had fallen silent.

Zippo and K-Bar and Toots had drawn and leveled. By the time Dicky demanded money, the tableau was just like that *Twilight Zone* episode about the stopwatch that froze everything timelessly still.

Twilight Zone spoke to Dicky's condition.

Down through desert, they had ridden hard. Past scrub and saguaro, first Phoenix, then Tucson, look out, Cochise County, here we come. Mexico was one potential tidbit for the future. If not, then they would ride east, to Lordsburg, New Mexico. There were convenience stores everywhere. That's why they were called convenience stores.

They faced off against six. Besides the old counterman there was a cowboy, a mommy with a toddler, and a teenage muscle-car metalhead with his chick in tow. The baby was seated in a small shopping cart. The cowboy was farthest from the counter. The couple both wore Metallica T-shirts, and were facing the coolers, trying to guess whether they'd get carded for beer.

Zippo got a vantage and froze them with his mini-Uzi; hypnotized them like a snake charmer. He had used a home conversion kit to bump the weapon to full auto—fifty rounds in five seconds. Zippo was the biggest of them. He wore a yoked western shirt, bright yellow, with no sleeves. His sunburn made his eyes seem to bulge—too white, mildly insane. His temper was as filed down as the pin on his Uzi.

Dicky snapped his fingers and pointed. Toots snatched a basket and began to round up chips, brew, you know—supplies.

The counterman fumbled. He was so shaky he could barely coax the register to pop.

K-Bar drew down on the cowboy while Zippo covered the rest. The cowboy was packing; K-Bar had spotted tooled leather and ivory grips. He ordered the cowboy to unholster, butt-first, using his fingertips. K-Bar kept his own Automag IV steady in a two-handed grip and edged closer; he thought all revolvers to be ancient history and occasionally itched Dicky about sticking with a six-shooter. Good-natured teasing to mask genuine irrational contempt.

The cowboy did as he was ordered. Nice and easy. Toots grabbed cold six-packs as the Metallica twins shrank out of his way.

Then K-Bar saw something he had never seen before, and would never see again in his life. The cowboy *snapped* his wrist, simple as flicking a booger. His pistol spun in a clockwise blur and landed in his grasp with the hammer back. K-Bar's ears registered the *click* about the time the first shot smashed through his right collarbone. He actually heard the gunshot . . . afterward.

Time sped up again.

The Automag became inexplicably heavy; K-Bar tried to drag it up as he fell. Zippo opened up with the Uzi. Chattergun racket drowned the store and a shelf of condiments noisily ceased to exist, ketchup and relish and mustard flying to mix like blood and bile. K-Bar fired, wild, unaimed; he bounced from one knee back to standing and shied the Automag sideways, snapping off. His arm was no longer equal to the recoil. The cowboy sprang up half an aisle from where K-Bar fired and plugged another round through his bicep, disintegrating the bone. K-Bar dropped the Automag.

Zippo hit the cowboy in the ear right before his magazine ran dry. Whatever the cowboy was thinking flew all over the beer cooler in a spray. He folded and piled up on the floor. Zippo hustled over to nab his hogleg and kick the corpse once, for macho's sake.

''Aww, *dammit*.'' His lip curled. They had never really killed anybody before.

Metallica was making huffing noises, like he was about to try something stupid. His girlfriend punched him in the arm and hissed at him to shut up.

K-Bar was wadded up on the floor, his hands making weak, grabbing motions at air. Toots parked his basket and held threatening with his pet 12-gauge, the chopped-off bore glinting a wicked silver.

''God *damn* that hurts!'' K-Bar managed.

Zippo tried to compress K-Bar's wounds with sanitary napkins. He could not be moved; his breath was already coarsening into a whine. K-Bar was leaking his life away, and making a hell of a mess doing it.

The counterman was still fucking around. Dicky told him to step back. Crammed behind a canvas cash-drop sack, Dicky discovered a mickeymouse .32.

''Thought so. That's why you kept fading; dipping down. Wasting our time. Dumb.''

Dicky shot the counterman in the forehead. Bang.

The old fellow flopped backward and cleaned off a bulletin board, going down in a hail of pushpins and for-sale cards.

The mother yelped; her baby had been screaming since the cowboy's first shot. Zippo changed clips and gave up on trying to prevent K-Bar's blood from mixing with the mustard and ketchup.

"Okay." Dicky turned from the mess of the counterman, gun up. "Bound to happen eventually. So that's it for me and Zippo; what about you, Toots."

Toots was watching K-Bar's eyes glaze. "Somebody's gotta watchdog, outside."

"I'll do that," said Dicky. "You do what you have to. Is K-Bar dead?"

"No," said Zippo.

"Fuck." This sort of thing pissed Dicky off.

"I guess you're up, man," Zippo said to Toots. He picked up the basket of goodies. Dicky stuffed the register cash in his back pocket and scored a couple hundred more from the open safe.

The mother had no way to stop her baby from crying; she was crying herself, by now. Toots bowslung his shotgun and broke a Pit Bull from his shoulder rig, but did not point it.

"What's your name?" he asked the woman.

The woman, who had had the misfortune to see *Dog Day Afternoon*, got full up with bogus hope. "Miriam," she said between sobs.

"Okay, Miriam, I think it's time for everybody to get inside the freezer." He let the Pit Bull show the way for Metallica and his girlfriend. "No need for alphabetical order or anything like that."

The possibility for practical resistance was zero. They trooped in, but Miriam hesitated at the door, still pushing her baby ahead of her in the shopping cart.

"Please. Promise me. Promise me you boys won't hurt my baby. He's not even two . . ."

"Shh," said Toots. "Don't worry so much."

When she turned, Toots shot her dead-bang in the occipital ditch. The copper-jacketed slug blew her all over the cart in a shower.

"Classic!" cried Dicky from the counter, where he had selected a baseball hat that read HONK IF YOUR HORNY.

Toots shrugged and spent his remaining seven on the Metallica guy. He only missed once.

After the baby stopped wailing, Dicky shoved the still-smoking muzzle of his auto beneath Lady Metallica's trembling chin. Here in the freezer it was cooler, more reasonable.

"Skip the part where you say you'll do *anything*," he said. "We already know that."

Zippo kneecapped her so she couldn't kick them. They stripped her atop a stack of beer cases, and each one of them picked an orifice. By the time Dicky had his orgasm, the girl was dead.

It always took Dicky the longest.

Between all the ambulances and sheriff's cruisers, the highway patrollers and a van grimly stenciled CORONER, there was just no way for the VW microbus to nose in, so it stopped on the dirt strip bordering the highway. It was the hottest part of the day, and the stench in the parking lot of the Jump Mart was pretty ripe.

"Somebody crapped themself." Conor worked a toothpick from one side of his mouth to the other, over the white scar bisecting his lower lip. He plucked a blue engineer's kerchief from the visor to blot his forehead. The VW's cooling unit was on the blink again.

Grace made a face. It wasn't as though Conor had never smelled death spoor. "I sure hope they have apple juice," she said.

She dropped down her visor mirror to check how she

looked, which was pretty good. She had shorn a lot of her extremely blond hair into a rag cut that could be backswept and forgotten—tousled, casual, not sloppy. She wore a spun black bandanna above Air Force pilot shades as dark as the heart of a silver mine. Grace favored gray work jumpers with a lot of zippered pockets. She was still wearing her BEAM sling; from outside the van it looked like nothing more than a pair of tangled suspenders.

Conor dismounted first. The lowers of his roughout boots matched the dust in the parking lot. It had taken more than a year to break the damned boots in; right now his feet thought that was just fine. The uppers were tooled topgrain and the next best thing to indestructible. Conor wore very tight jeans because Grace liked very tight jeans on him. Across the breast pocket of his denim shirt he wore a row of miniature skull pins, some with crossbones, some engulfed in biker flames. He had scored them all at convenience marts.

His shoulder holster was empty as he got out. He could pick a weapon later.

A deputy was already hustling toward him, one hand riding the butt of a still-snapped automatic. He squinted in the blazing sun; his scowl suggested that the last thing in the universe he'd countenance was an interruption like Conor.

"Looks like a hit," said Conor, friendly.

"Sorry, but you folks gonna have to back on outta here; we got us—"

"A situation," Conor overrode. "Yeah, I can see that. But I truly need some gum, and my lady needs a cold drink, and it looks to me like the bad stuff here is already past tense." Conor smiled big. His nose was hawkish. His beard and mustache, though precisely trimmed, were full and burnt red. Conor could smile like a satyr.

Conor watched the deputy's eyes consider his empty shoulder holster. Practically everyone in the desert carried weapons. The deputy stuck out a hand that would have halted Conor at chest level. Conor stopped short.

Sterner, now: ''I'm sorry, sir, but I'm going to have to ask you to turn around and back on out of here and leave this area. Right now.''

Conor appreciated the improved diction.

''But I still need some gum.'' Conor scoped the ambulance with its doors still open. ''You collected one, didn't you? One of them.''

The deputy summoned his partner. ''Billy? Get on over here.'' He unsnapped his gun strap.

Billy approached. Conor thought he looked put out. From the microbus, Grace had counted four peace officers, total.

''You don't want any trouble, am I right?'' Conor drew a deep breath.

''That's right, sir, so what you want to do is—''

Viper quick, Conor captured the pistol on the updraw, plucking it right out of the deputy's hand, with his right, while clamping the deputy's throat, with his left. Conor had waited until the second deputy, Billy, was within range. Billy stopped two shots to the head before he could get his next footstep down.

While Billy's glasses and hair made a cloud of red, the deputy thrashed against Conor's death grip.

Grace had selected a loaded Steyr Aug assault rifle and clipped it to her BEAM sling. Deftly, she stepped out to cover the whole parking lot and caught the remaining two cops slow and stupid.

''No trouble, deputy.'' Conor hoisted him, one-handed, to tiptoe. ''No trouble at all.''

He let go of the pistol and punched the deputy right in the chest. The deputy's body armor split lengthwise, his ribs caved in, and his heart exploded. The impact made a sound like a tire blowing in the parking lot.

Grace opened up. The highway patroller's vests were no match for her armor-piercing tracers. She greased them and they dropped, still slow, still stupid, weapons sheathed, their viscera flash-fried by incendiaries.

Through it all, ten seconds, max, the medics played statue. By the time Grace's discharge echoes were gone, Conor was through the doors of the Jump Mart.

"You did say apple juice, right?"

Grace nodded, and kept everybody covered.

Conor quickly filled a basket. When he emerged, he headed for the ambulance.

"They took down five that I can see," he told Grace. "Five and a half, if you count the baby."

"Real bad asses," she said.

Conor picked the dead deputy's gun out of the dirt and slid it into his back pocket. He climbed into the ambulance bay, where he found K-Bar strapped to a gurney, immobilized in a traction sling, and packed with freon compresses.

"You look sorta guilty to me." Conor smiled again. "Can you understand me?"

K-Bar said nothing. His eyes paid attention.

"I need the direction your friends went. All you have to do is point. If there's more than three, besides you, I want you to tell me. Okay?"

K-Bar kept his teeth clenched. He was obviously in a lot of pain. He told Conor to go fuck himself.

"Ooh, the f-word. I was afraid of that."

Conor dug around in his basket, displacing a box of fresh toothpicks and at least twenty packs of Black Jack gum. He used paramedic scissors to cut a hole in K-Bar's exposed stomach. Into the hole he poured blue drain cleaner. It fizzed.

K-Bar heaved against the straps, screaming, reopening his wounds.

"You know, I find that effervescent action is a real attention-getter," said Conor. "Now, sweetheart, before you kick,

I still need to know a direction. Scream once for yes and twice for no.''

K-Bar screamed a lot in the next two minutes. Conor only had to use half the can.

He stepped down from the rear of the ambulance and rubbed Grace's shoulders. ''You need this one a little more than I do. I'll be okay.'' What he meant was that the two deputies he'd just waxed would hold him. For a bit.

Grace unclipped the Steyr Aug and Conor gave the medics a gunpoint grin. ''You boys just keep on doing what you're doing. You're doing it real good.'' He broke out a fresh toothpick.

Grace stepped up.

K-Bar was writhing and twitching. Pallid foam lipped the holes Conor had clipped in his chest. His cognizance of Grace was elemental, reptilian.

''Poor baby,'' she said. ''That Conor; he's such a whiz with household ingredients. But you did good. You only have to do one more thing. Don't worry—this one's easy.''

She stripped her shades, unveiling laser-blue eyes. Very arresting, very Aryan. She crouched to hold K-Bar's face in both hands and spoke softly, like a lover.

''Die for me.''

Conor heard K-Bar scream one last time. It was not a sound of injury or torture, despair, loss, or even simple pain. It was the violent unmooring of life itself. Conor knew the difference.

When Grace emerged, she did, in fact, look better.

Conor felt his deputy's final heartbeats replay in his mind. Not food, but vitamins, at least. A fast-burning jolt, to see them through. He handed Grace her apple juice as they waved good-bye to the medics—at gunpoint—and reboarded the microbus.

''I picked me up some more skulls.'' He showed her. ''You better?''

"Better." She donned her glasses. "Which way?"

"South. Just like I thought."

"Here's to first blood."

Dicky raised his Budweiser. Toots clinked cans immediately. Zippo held back.

"*Blood*, yeah!" Toots was a little wasted.

"What the fuck's wrong with you?" Dicky said to Zippo.

"K-Bar." Zippo had been looking toward the floor and his own feet a lot lately. "It cost us K-Bar."

Dicky cleaned out his can and imploded it one-handed. Easier to do, these days—crushing aluminum was like wadding paper. Dicky was not fond of recycling. He popped a fresh Bud.

"So drink to K-Bar, you fuck."

They were holding forth from a transmission shack, inside the fenced and posted confines of a desert power station somewhere south of Tucson. They drank around a brass-faced worktable bolted to the concrete floor. The brass was wincingly old; they'd had to wipe off all the dust.

Tied facedown to the table with bungi cords was a woman they'd collected from the highway. Her mouth was crammed full of cinnamon hots, from the Jump Mart, and sealed with two around-the-head winds of duct tape, also from the Jump Mart. She was trussed so that all she could do was listen to the tea chat of her abductors and stare, straight down, at their case of beer.

The game was that when the last can was drunk, she would be dead chicken.

Her name was Arianne, and there was blood in her mouth. She remembered hearing music coming her way before she or either of her friends could actually see the car that the lunatics with the firearms had called Death Caddy.

That chance encounter had happened about an hour ago.

It's not Nadia's boyfriend, Willy, but Nadia herself, Miz Cautious, who insists on flagging the first car to pass. "This is an emergency, *right?"*

"Goddamn alternator," Willy grumbles. He slams the hood of the old Impala. "I can smell oil burning. We might have fried a gasket, too." Willy hates the idea of soliciting aid from passing motorists in the middle of the desert. His mohawk, his garb, were not popular in this neighborhood . . . as they'd all discovered when they'd gassed up at that convenience mart, two hours back.

The beer cans blurred out of focus as Dicky lifted her head by the hair. "Comfy?"

She had ceased making protest sounds. For what?

"I'll be gentle," Dicky cooed. He licked the free sweat from her forehead. "Is your name really Arianne? Sounds like one of those piss-ant yuppie names ex-hippies give to their litters. It sucks. From now on, your name is Bitch. Like it? Can you say *Bitch*? I knew you could."

Toots drew another beer. One more can down.

"Snatch is dead. She didn't last very long. No legs. City chick; you could tell."

Tears filled Arianne's eyes. Tears for Nadia.

"Keep it warm." Dicky slapped her naked rump. "Eight cans to go."

Her sinuses were packed, and she could barely breathe through her nose. Maybe if she held her breath, she could ace herself. Cheat them.

By noon it's too hot for Willy to wear his jacket, the fabulous patchwork fatigue that he climbs into like a new identity. He is down to jeans, safety pins, canvas combats, and tong shades. His BAD RELIGION shirt now has smears of grime, from the engine.

All he says is, "Just try to get a look at them before you flag 'em down." Then: "I'll do it."

So saying, he sealed their fates.

The music was right. The attitude was right. Their ages were right. None of them could see the bad guy hats.

Arianne can recall saying, "Hey—that guy looks like he has blood on him."

Toots and Zippo took up the back seat of Death Caddy. No one had hurried to claim K-Bar's spot, up front. It was K-Bar's blood, on Zippo, that Arianne had glimpsed.

The pilot of the Cadillac ragtop scabs the road with rubber as he stands on the brakes, slams into reverse, and backs up to rendezvous. Willy steps forward; their rep. Their de facto protector.

The guy in the Wild West shirt—the one with the blood on him—stands with some kind of machine gun and puts nine into Willy, pirouetting him. Arianne freezes, mouth on the hang, eyes large like a shined deer.

Nadia runs.

The handsome one with the long black hair runs after her. He is wearing gray night-fighting pants with an enormous knife sheathed to one thigh. He tackles Nadia, knocks her into a cactus, and breaks her arm taking her down.

Arianne begins to back-pace in welling panic. The driver, wearing a HONK IF YOUR HORNY cap, vaults from behind the wheel, and before she can beg, or promise she'll do anything, he smashes her in the face with a long-barreled revolver.

She wakes up in the trunk of the Caddy. Among her friends, one of whom has shit oneself in the process of roundup. She smells the lube of auto tools and spare tire rubber. Moisture speckles her face; she is afraid it's blood.

The heat and the smell knock her down until she wakes up on the table.

The power station stood a good five miles back from the road, accessed by a dirt track of single-vehicle width. Hotwire towers squared steel shoulders, a row of gigantic Japanese superheroes, and their rows diminished over the mountains in both directions. On chainlink and razor-wire, signs bespoke DANGER and HIGH VOLTAGE and OFF-LIMITS.

The shack was about ten-by-ten, and Arianne was the most interesting thing inside.

"If one kills, we all kill." Dicky felt the need to remind Zippo and Toots of their blood oath. It was the same thrill as forming a monster club, when you were a kid. "The cowboy shot first, so we're all in the clear. We did what we had to do."

For Dicky, so the story ended.

Toots indicated their current harvest. "Three of them. Three of us, now."

"Bitch is mine," said Dicky. "Zippo took the punk ninety percent of the way; he owns him. You nailed Snatch, so she's yours." He nailed Zippo with his Dicky-glare. "We do this for K-Bar, our bro, whom we love. Right?"

"Ain't got nothing else, you don't have your bros." Toots swigged and tried to nod solemnly; he had already drunk too much to nod without bobbing his head.

The bullet-riddled Willy was tied upright to a saguaro outside the station fence. His pupils still reacted to light; some of him was still living. Sprawled in the dirt at his feet, Nadia was naked and dead. As Dicky had predicted, she had not lasted very long.

Willy had witnessed just how long.

"Lemme tell you something about blood, and natural selection." Dicky was pacing, drinking, working up fire. "We are the survivors. We are the hunters. Can't you guys *feel* it? It's almost like . . . when I terminated that geezer back at the store, I could, like, *feel* the charge. Like a battery, powering up." He indicated the power station. "Like *this*, crackling the ozone, all around this place."

"Death rush," said Toots, bobbing.

"No, listen—it's more. It's like angel dust. Like nitrous

oxide for a car engine. Almost like you can *feel* their life, adding to yours as you take it. Man, I don't need to *eat*, I don't need to *sleep*—"

"Count fucking Dracula," said Zippo.

"I feel it," said Toots, with numb lips. Then he averted his head to liberate a quart of acrid beer vomit. Zippo had to laugh.

"You fucks don't understand," said Dicky. "But you will. You'll see." His gaze flickered outside, toward Willy—sunburnt, shot, impaled on cactus spines from his heels to the nape of his neck. "Zippo—we'll do the punk last, as we leave. Right now it's time to do Bitch."

"Do her to death," said Zippo.

"We haven't finished the case yet," protested Toots.

Dicky thought of Arianne, staring down at the beer cans, counting them, keeping track as they dwindled.

"I know," he said.

Conor sniffed the blood on his fingertips. "Couple of hours. They moved inland. No bodies."

They had found the Impala parked on the shoulder, windows up, doors locked. Grace finessed the driver's side door in seconds. "They cleaned out all the documentation."

"They're learning." This was getting good.

Conor spat out his used Black Jack and peeled a new stick. By his reckoning, the sun hung at about four o'clock. As Grace backed out of the car, he circled, less mindful of all the footprints, now that she'd had a shot at reading them. Nine-millimeter shell casings on the road. Blood smear on the flank of the Chevy. The cowboy at the Jump Mart had been killed by the same slugs.

Grace popped the hood. "Vapor lock," she said after a peek. "Needs oil. Alternator's about to go."

Conor leaned in for a peek at the V8 powerhouse.

Grace wiped her hands. "Now, *there's* a position I wish I could catch you in more often."

"Never," he joked. She was eating him with her eyes.

"It's never too hot." She caught him and turned him, hands snugging his butt close and tight, the merciless desert heat that had pounded into her clothing now penetrating his own. They kissed like they really meant it. Their lips knew where to go, and did their devilish best.

"You taste like gum."

"You taste like salt."

"Come sundown, your ass is *mine*."

His hand caressed her neck—perfect—then tracked the zipper of her jumper all the way down, for a gentle squeeze. "You know where I'll be," he said.

Grace gazed past his shoulder. She was getting a mild recharge from holding him so close. She was only an inch or so shorter than Conor, who topped six feet without his boots.

"What are you *grinning* at?" he said.

"Those power towers."

He craned around and saw them, too, marching from the highway into the heart of the scrub and cacti, leading the way like a column of Spartans.

Grace got another kiss for that one.

"Check it out," said Toots.

"Hippie mobile." Zippo buttoned his fly as he walked. Together he and Toots observed the slow, bumpy approach of the VW bus along the dirt path. "God, I hope none of 'em are wearing patchouli oil; I *hate* that shit!"

Toots had been coring Willy with a Randall survival knife that had, until this morning, belonged to the original owner of Death Caddy.

The four of them had just ditched yesterday's truck and purloined virgin plates when Dicky spied the Cadillac in the lot of a highway roadhouse. At that time it had Confederate plates and one hellacious burglar alarm, not to mention the modest arsenal Dicky discovered upon punching the trunk lock. Dicky fell in love. They bushwhacked the owner as he barreled out, gun-first, to answer the call of the alarm—headlong into the muzzles of his own hardware. He skidded to a cartoon character halt, looking rather sheepish and electing not to discharge the nickel-plated whore's pistol that had come out of his waistband.

The four of them had fun. When the owner's buddies looked out, they stayed inside. Dicky bashed the guy's teeth out with his own Automag; that was what you called irony.

He'd been alive when they drove off. He died. But that had been eons ago, back before they had actually murdered anyone.

"How's your clip?"

"Got it." Zippo jacked the primer round on the Uzi.

The VW microbus puttered to a stop, bringing a thunderhead of dust with it. Glare blanked the windshield. Dead bugs, grit, and mileage. The doors opened simultaneously like the pathetically flapping wings of some obese insect.

"Tell Dicky."

Zippo doubletimed away while Toots sheathed the Randall on his thigh. There was no way to conceal poor old Willy, staked to his cactus, leaking the rest of his life out.

The shotgun was leaning against Willy's cactus, out of sight. The Pit Bull was snugged down in the small of Toots's back, ditto. He let his hand ride the hilt of the Randall. He saw a rangy man, a tall blonde in a jumper. They didn't look armed.

"Sure hope you fellas ain't planning on using any of that firepower on us," said the man. He smiled. Friendly.

Toots felt Zippo return. He knew he was covered.

"You lost?"

The man spat out a black wad of gum and replaced it with

a toothpick. Toots watched it travel from one side of the man's mouth to the other.

"No."

Zippo was close enough to play Grim Reaper.

"Where's Dicky?" Toots kept his eyes on the pair.

"He told me to tell you that you and me should take care of it."

Shit, thought Toots. Dicky thinks we'll cluck without him. He's probably watching us. To see if we buy all his mung about nitrous and angel dust and death.

The blonde had her hands on her hips. Toots saw her lick her lower lip. Hot out today. He could see himself and Zippo reflected in her pilot shades.

"Mini-Uzi," she said. "That's a nice little piece."

Zippo actually looked at his own gun. He had just gotten to the stage where he was fantasizing about what he'd do to this babe once he sliced off her jumper.

Toots moved forward, drawing the Randall.

When Zippo looked back, the woman had already whip-drawn a Colt Trooper from behind her. She fired once from a distance of about ten feet. Her lead semi-wad hollow point hit Toots in the cheek below his right eye, expanding to .69 caliber on impact and kicking a five-inch entryway.

There was no need for a second shot.

Little moist hunks of Toots's face and red strands of his hair spattered Zippo, who squeezed convulsively and fired into the sky over Conor's head. Conor was in his face before Toots could fall all the way to the ground. He flat-handed the Uzi back into Zippo's face, shattering teeth. Then he jerked him forward on the gun strap, right into his fist. Zippo's lips halved. His nose pancaked in a splurt of blood. His left eye was welded shut; the sclera crimsoned as it filled.

Conor let Zippo drop as Dicky's face appeared in the transmission shack doorway. It ducked instantly as Conor brought up the Uzi and emptied the magazine, peppering the doorway.

Grace was on her knees, cradling Toots, getting the last out of him.

"You want that 12-gauge?" Grace nodded toward the cactus.

"What for?" Conor dropped the exhausted Uzi and pointed at the doorway. "Just keep him in there for me, baby."

Conor hared over while Grace spaced out her remaining rounds from the Trooper. By five, Conor was past the gate and hugging cover against the shack.

His back to the corrugated steel, he called toward the doorway. "Hey! Why don't you and I chat a bit, first?"

Inside, Dicky still had his pants off, and had thumbed back the hammer on his Combat Magnum. He held it near his face, as if it could give him wisdom.

"Yeah, so?"

"Take a look," said Conor. "Isn't she great?"

Anything past the gate was too dicey to hit with accuracy from the shack, no, not with a bad guy crouching mere feet from the door. Dicky saw Toots, crumpled unmoving in his own mud puddle of red. He saw the woman, who did not appear to have any trouble dragging Zippo by the scruff even though he was the biggest of them. He saw Zippo paw at her grip, once or twice. She dumped him upright behind the wheel of Death Caddy.

"Zippo!"

No response. Dicky saw her pop the trunk. Faster than he had, this morning. She took out the jerry can and funnel.

"Zippo! Goddammit!"

"Kinda elegant, ain't it?" said Conor, from somewhere down and to the right, outside, out of view.

"Zippo!" Dicky hazarded shots, one-two-three, but it was pretty hopeless.

Grace liberally doused Zippo and the front seat of the Caddy with five gallons of Super Unleaded.

"Zippo? That's real cute. You're the forgotten Marx Brother, hon."

His good eye followed her. He got a hand on the door, weakly. She broke his thumb with the butt of the Trooper.

Zippo curled and convulsed. The pain had deadened his senses to animal, reactive instinct. He could not make his body comply with the urge to escape. He could not even smell the gas drenching him.

"Please . . ." he croaked.

"What's that?" She seemed genuinely sympathetic.

From the shack, Dicky hollered and fired two or three more times. Zippo heard his name. The closest shot struck sparks off the chrome near the wipers.

"I'll do anything . . . you want . . ."

Grace frowned. "Somehow, I knew you were going to say that." Now she looked disappointed, almost sad. "I thought you had the stuff, baby. I guess not. Happy cooking."

Zippo tried. He could not prevent her from reaching into Death Caddy and pressing the cigarette lighter inward, *clink*.

Zippo tried. He heard her steps as she walked away, calm, measured paces.

He heard the lighter pop out, *clink*. His eye widened. He tried.

He heard his own hair frying and felt his ears fuse to his scalp one heartbeat before Death Caddy blew up, scattering jumbo car-part shrapnel and impromptu napalm. Grace hugged the saguaro for cover; the Willy side. The ammo in the car discharged uselessly and the air filled up with the stink of smoking oil and barbecued Zippo.

Conor called toward the door. "You want to know something really funny? You've been blockaded in there, and you just let your pal up and *die*, because you're afraid that if you poke your nose out, I might shoot you . . . and you know what? I don't even have a gun!"

The veins in Dicky's temples banged feverishly as he watched Zippo burn. Toots had not moved. This was all bullshit. This was wrong. *They* wore the bad guy hats around here.

He thumbed a speedloader into the open cylinder of the Magnum. Think fast, move fast.

"I have a hostage in here."

"So what? I don't give a shit. Hey, Grace!"

Grace had reloaded her Trooper just as fast as Dicky. She waved A-OK.

"Is Mister Mohawk still kicking on the cactus, there?"

She gave the high sign. Willy was, believe it or don't, still among the living. Flies were lunching on him, afloat on updrafts of excrement and clotting blood and the last dregs of dehydrated sweat.

"Grace, show our buddy here how much we care about *hostages*."

Grace shot Willy in the temple. He stiffed. She enjoyed a tiny internal twinge as he was finally released. Willy was no predator, however—he had been into punk fashion, not punk thought.

"Okeydoke, chief." Conor was savoring this. It was what he had come for. "No hostages. You don't win a helicopter. No barter. *Now* what are you gonna do?"

Dicky could hear his own breathing too much. Too defensive. His extra loaders had gone up with Death Caddy. Six shots left; he should have stolen a Beretta.

"Hey, you listening? You asleep? Have you got a name? What do we call you?"

The stranger's civil tone made Dicky want to kill everybody. He itched to murder the world and feel the empowerment. Zippo and Toots had been so *close* to seeing, to feeling as he felt.

"Fuck you!"

Conor chewed on that one. ''Okay, fuck you. From the hole I saw in the old man's head back at the Jump Mart, I figure you're clutching a .45 revolver like your dick and wondering where to get more ammo, am I right?''

Six shots. Dicky edged nearer the door, pacing his heart, his racing pulse a metronome.

''Getting adrenalated? I can smell you getting ready to blow, man.''

Hammer back. Dicky thought about blasting through the corrugated wall . . . but the interloper's invisible position was not guaranteed, and there were no bonus shots to squander. His lady partner stayed behind the cactus, behind Willy's cloud of insect vermin.

Behind him, Bitch groaned against the tape sealing her mouth. Nobody home there, not anymore.

''I can wait all day,'' said Conor. ''I've got gum.'' From his shirt pocket, below the line of skulls, he pulled a coil of rasp wire, a bit nastier than the kind campers use to saw firewood. He toyed with it, passing one ring through the other, making a little noose in which he trapped his finger. ''You're the big deal around here. Mister Fuck You.''

Dicky gauged the open door. Getting ready. He could fall against the jamb in a crouch and fire in half a second. He wiped his hands on his black T-shirt, to keep a better grip on the Magnum. His teeth were locked, his lips back in a snarl, and he could now feel the power accumulated within him come rushing forth, to shake him like a climax.

Eyes ablaze, he sprang, twisted, impacted back and down, trigger finger cutting loose, screeching.

Fuck THIS you fucking DIE scumbag asshole—!

His first two shots ate dirt. And hit nothing.

The razor noose looped in from behind Dicky's left shoulder and snugged tight with a hiss, trapping both of his hands around the gun butt. Conor, who had deftly circumvented the shack while Dicky was pumping up, wrenched the wire hard, lifting Dicky straight up into his waiting fist.

"Howdy!"

Said the man.

When Dicky woke up, he had a hard-on.

When Dicky woke up, he had a hard-on because he could see a blond woman.

When Dicky woke up, he had a hard-on because he could see a blond woman masturbating him. She held up her hand to show him: slick, coated, maroon. She smiled at Dicky and pumped away.

"Don't come yet, honey," she said.

"Howdy again," said the man.

Conor gave the free loop of razor wire a savage yank.

The incoming pain was astonishing. It arched Dicky right off the table. Now he could see his erect cock, going from crimson to violet, bulging. Painfully.

Dicky found himself right next to Bitch, still unmoving on the brass-topped surface.

"Here's the game," said Conor. "Me and Grace, we don't approve of rape. You understand hydrostatic pressure? You'll stay hard as long as this wire around your balls stays cinched. Your victim here won't stay wet forever."

Conor rolled Dicky over into doggy position and guided him in. It was akin to making two hand puppets copulate.

"The moment you stop—or come—I whipcrack this wire and you're gonna need the world's most absorbent Kotex."

Dicky tried to say *fuck you* but was not sure whether the words ever left his mouth. He saw Grace kneel at the head of the table and point the Colt Trooper right at his nose, range less than two feet. She steadied her aim between the girl's shoulder blades as Dicky began thrusting. Grace's hands were saturated in blood; Dicky had no idea whose.

"Shouldn't we take off that tape?" said Conor. "Maybe she can't breathe."

"She's alive so far," said Grace, dead eye-to-eye with Dicky. "I don't want to listen to her carrying on." She held down on Dicky while she lifted Arianne's head by the hair. "You *are* still alive, right? Don't you know any better than to stop for strangers in the middle of the desert?" She emitted a cluck of disgust. "Sweet Jesus—don't you find all this just a tad *humiliating*?"

Dicky and Arianne both began voiding fresher blood.

"You oughtta be flattered," Conor told Dicky. "You caught *our* eye. I knew that mess at the Jump Mart wasn't the end product of a buncha ratpackers on the wild. Nope. Just one mind at work, there. Yours, am I right?"

"The son we never had." Grace said it mock-operatic.

"It's sorta like that joke about the minnow getting eaten by the fish. Then a shark eats the fish. A whale eats the shark. Your love partner here is one of the minnows of the world. And, as I'm sure you're beginning to find out, minnows *can* provide sustenance . . . but not much in the way of real nourishment." Conor chewed his gum.

"And the people out there . . ." Grace shrugged. "Nine times out of ten they confuse carnivores with avengers."

Dicky could no longer pump, period. He sagged. His penis was rigid and well sunk . . . but he just couldn't, anymore.

Grace backed off, holstered her Colt, and held up a slim, long-barreled rifle so Dicky could see it.

"Now, your sadists and sickos," Conor continued, "would use a scattergun for this sorta thing. Y'know—one kaboom, serious gauge, and you kind of rain down all over the place. What Grace has there is just a plain ole .22."

She reached down to where Dicky and Arianne were joined, and used a handful of blood to lubricate the barrel.

"We've been waiting to find someone like you for a long time," she said, almost lovingly.

Dicky got out a scream where the sight on the barrel tore his rectal tissue. When Conor worked the bolt, Dicky could feel the *click* in his throat.

The first shot ripped sideways, tumbled, skinned a lung, cracked a rib, then lodged dead to bulge Dicky's right nipple from beneath the skin. The second shot made it almost all the way to his shoulder socket.

Conor was nearly gasping by now. "Waiting. A long time."

The third shot imploded Dicky's left lung. He could feel the barrel inside of him, choosing targets, and his penis inside of Bitch, formerly Arianne, as empty as his useless weapons.

Grace collected Dicky's face into her hands. She looked right on the teetering brink of orgasm, herself. "Come on, baby—you *hate* us. Fight it. Fight it. You're one of the *bad* guys, you hate us, fight it, fight it, you're a *fighter*—"

Dicky, the fighter, lasted nine rounds.

"You don't want to look at this," said the highway patrolman. He spoke to a middle-aged man who had entered the Jump Mart parking lot on foot.

"It looks like some officers died." Concern colored his tone.

The patrolman was a kid, twenty-three, tops, with no wartime or street experience to compare with the shock sight of so many corpses in uniform. Two fellow hypos, Nick Bonaventure and Dallas Reese, blown down by an assault rifle. A deputy sheriff, Billy Simons, facedown in his own brains, most of his head gone.

And what had happened to Carter Strawn . . . Jesus fucking Christ. He had been hit in the chest so hard his Kevlar had ruptured and his internals mashed into pulp.

And that wasn't even counting five dead civilians *inside* the store. Including a baby.

The stranger had a kind face. Mild prescription glasses.

Graying hair. Fatherly. He read the patrolman's nameplate. "Officer Fremont," he said, "would you like a smoke?"

"Yeah. Thanks." Fremont was having trouble working up spit. Talk was okay. "You are . . . ?"

"Pike. Are you okay?"

Fremont sniffed. "Yeah." Then, a vast exhalation. "First, we hear it's four raiders. Blitzkriegers clipping a convenience mart. Then we hear six. Then we hear nothing, because all the responding officers have been capped. Then we hear *three* perps and two vigilantes . . . shit, I sure can't tell you what happened here, Mr. Pike."

"It's going to start raining," said Pike. "Summer monsoons are rolling in." He pondered a moment, scratched his upper lip. "You know what we need, officer, is like in those old westerns. A way to tell. White and black. Good guys wore white. Bad guys wore bad guy hats."

"It's not that simple anymore."

Pike arched an eyebrow at the carnage all around. "You're telling me."

"Sir, they killed cops wearing bulletproof vests. They killed a fucking *baby*. Whoever they were, they were maximal bad asses."

"It could have been worse," said Pike.

"I don't see how. How much worse could this get?"

Pike patted Fremont on the shoulder; he rather liked this naive and idealistic child. "You'll make out okay, I think. I'll just be getting out of your hair."

"Thanks for the smoke."

Pike acknowledged by making a little pistol of his thumb and forefinger. Then he strolled out of the parking lot, his running shoes crunching gravel softly. He turned his nose south, toward the rising storm front. He smiled. He always smiled when he felt good, and he always felt good when he knew it was close to feeding time.

Graffiti

There is no real niche for the stories in this section. They are bright flashes of color and substance, drawn with flair and imagination, the kind of stories that will always find a home in *Midnight Graffiti*. They feature a quirky, unusual examination of the contemporary landscape, a landscape known as the . . .

CUE NARRATOR

NARRATOR
(V.O.)
(sounding uncannily like Rod Serling)

At first, the faces seem strange and unfamiliar, but then, a glimmer of recognition. You've seen them someplace before. There, in the mirror. You will find the world's smallest man in pursuit of happiness; a transvestite nun whose congregation consists of junkies, the homeless, and the dead of a decaying ghetto; a dinosaur with a dream. All denizens of the shadowy world that lies between dusk and the . . .

FADE. CUE MUSIC. AVOID COPYRIGHT INFRINGEMENT.

—J.H.

JOHN SHIRLEY

John Shirley long had the reputation of being an angry, confrontational, intense, and gifted young writer. If horror and science fiction can be said to have an underground, John Shirley was one of the chief terrorists. Collections such as *Heatseeker* and projects such as *Journal Wired* gave John's vision free rein.

But with maturity, like it or not, comes some respectability. So many now plow the field John staked, he has come to be looked upon with regard and, yes, some reverence: an iconoclast turned icon. Included here is a look at human relationships from the angry, confrontational, intense, gifted, and revered John Shirley.

"I Want to Get Married," Says the World's Smallest Man!*

by John Shirley

"You a fucking whore," Delbert said. "You even got the sores on you skin."

"It's no way from that," Brandy said. "It's from tweakin', I thought there was bugs, okay? Like you never did it? And fuck you, Delbert, who turned me out? You had me out there on Capp Street when it was fucking thirty degrees—I ain't a fucking whore like yo' nigger bitch cousins, I'm a white girl, motherfucker, I don't come out of that—"

"Don't be talkin' that shit. You was already a fucking whore, you fucked that greaser motherfucker CheeChee—"

*The character herein referred to as "World's Smallest Man" is purely imaginary and is in no way related to anyone who may hold that title anywhere.

"Sure so he didn't beat my fucking head in. Where were you? Hittin' the fuckin' pipe, Delbert. Shit you knew what was going on— Where you going now goddammit?"

Delbert was mumbling over the loose knob of the piss-in-the-sink hotel room's door, trying to get out into the hall. The knob was about ready to come off. Brandy was glad Delbert was going because that meant he wasn't going to work himself up to knocking her around, but at the same time she didn't want to be left alone, just her and the fucked-up black and white TV that was more or less a radio now because the picture was so slanty you couldn't make it out, a two-weeks-old *Weekly World Inquirer*, and one can of Colt Malt stashed on the window ledge. And something else, he was going to get some money, maybe get an advance from his posse, and do some rock. She shouted after him, "You going to hit that pipe without me again? You suckin' it all up, microwavin' that pipe, fuckin' it up the way you do it, and Terrence going to kick yo' ass if you smoke what he give you to sell—"

But he'd got the door open, yelling, "SHUT UP WOMAN I BITCH-SLAP YOU!" as he slammed it behind him with that soap-opera timing.

"*Fuck* you, you better bring me some fuckin' "—she let her voice trail off as his steps receded down the hall—"dope."

She felt that plunge feeling again, like nothing was any use so why try and what she wanted was to go back to bed. She thought, maybe I get my baby out of Foster Care Hold, that place's just like prison. Shit, Candy's not a baby anymore, she's twelve, and she's half-white, looks more white than anything else, she'll be okay.

Brandy got up off the edge of the bed, walked across the chilly room, hugging her gut, feeling her sharp hips under her fingers, as she went to the window. She looked out through the little cigarette burn-hole, just in time to see Delbert walk his skinny black ass out the front door, across the street to the Projects, right up to Terrence. "The man's going to go off on you one of these days, Delbert, you be a dead nigger before you hit the emergency room, you fucking asshole," she said, aloud, taking satisfaction in it.

There was no reason, she thought, to be looking out the burn-hole instead of just lifting the shade; she didn't have anything to be paranoid about, there wasn't even any fucking crumbles of dope in the house, she hadn't had any hubba in two days, and now she was lying awake at night thinking about it, not wanting to go out and turn a trick for it because she had that really bad lady trouble, the infection—

There it was, soon as she started thinking about it, the itching starts up bad again, itching and burning in her cunt. Ow. Ow. Ow. Shit, go to the clinic, go to the clinic. She didn't have the energy. They made you wait so long. Treated you like a fucking whore.

She turned to the burn-hole again, saw Terrence walking along with Delbert, Terrence shaking his head. No more credit. Delbert'd be back up here, beat her till she'd hit the streets again. She turned away from the cigarette hole. Looking out through the tiny burn-hole was a tweakin' habit. Once she'd spent a whole day, eight hours straight staring out through that hole, turning away only to hit the pipe. That was when Delbert was dealing and they were flush with dope.

Fucking cocaine made you tweaky, it was funny stuff.

Maybe Delbert's cousin Darius would give her some. For some head.

Her stomach lurched.

She went back to the bed, looked again at the *Inquirer* article she'd been reading:

"I WANT TO GET MARRIED,"
SAYS WORLD'S SMALLEST MAN!

Ross Taraval, the world's smallest man, wants to get married—and he's one eligible bachelor! He weighs only seventeen pounds and is only twenty-eight inches high but he has a budding career as an entertainer and he's got plenty of love to give, he tells us. "I want a woman to share my success," said Ross, twenty-four, who has starred in two films shot in Mexico, making him a star in his native Trinidad. Recently he was given a "small" role in a Hollywood film. "There's more to me than meets the eye," Ross said. "The doctors say I could have children—and I'd support my new wife in real style! And listen, I want a full-sized wife, not a little lady small like me. That's what a real man wants—and I can handle her! I've got so much love to give and there's a real man inside this little body wanting to give it to the right woman!"

Ross, who was abandoned at three years old, was raised by Catholic missionaries in Trinidad. After attracting attention in the *Trafalgar Book of World Records*, Ross was contacted by his manager, six-foot five-inch Benny Chafin, who could carry Ross in his overcoat pocket if he wanted to. Chafin trained Ross in singing and dancing and soon found him work in nightclubs and TV endorsements.

"I've got my eye on a beautiful house in the Hollywood hills for the right lady," Ross said.

There was a picture of the little guy standing next to his manager—not even coming up to the manager's crotch-height. The manager, now, was cute, he looked kind of like Geraldo Rivera, Brandy thought. There was a little box at the bottom of the article. It said,

If you'd like to get in touch with Ross Taraval, you may write him care of the Weekly World Inquirer *and we'll forward your letter to him. Address your correspondence to . . .*

Huh. Stupid idea.

She heard Delbert's footsteps in the hall . . .

There was a stamp on the letter from her sister that hadn't been canceled. She could peel it off.

"I think I got you a job at Universal Studios!" Benny said, striding breathlessly in.

"Really?" Ross's heart thumped. He climbed laboriously down off the chair he'd been squatting in to watch TV. The Sleepytime Inn had a Playboy Channel.

He hurried over to Benny, who was taking off his coat. It was May in Los Angeles, and sort of cold there. The cold made Ross's joints ache. Benny had said it was always warm in L.A. but it wasn't now. It was cloudy and windy.

It took Benny a long time to get across the floor to Ross, and Ross was impatient to know what was going on, so he started shouting questions through his wheezing before he got there.

"What movie am I in?" he asked. "It has Arnold Schwarzenegger?"

"Ross, slow down, you'll get your asthma started. No, it's not a movie. It's at their theme park. They want you to play King of the Wonksters for the tourists. It's a live show."

Ross stopped in the middle of the floor, panting, confused. "What is Wonksters?"

"They're . . . sort of like Eewoks. Little outer space guys. Universal's got a movie coming out about 'em at Christmas so this'd be next summer—if the movie hits—and—"

"Next summer! I need some work now! Pendajo bastards! You said I could be in a buddy picture with Arnold Schwarzenegger!"

"I spoke to his agent. He already did a buddy picture with a little guy. He doesn't want to do that again."

"You said I could meet him!"

''You're going to be around Hollywood for a long time, you'll meet your hero, Ross, calm down, all right? You don't want to have an attack. Maybe we can get a photo op or something with him—''

Benny had turned away, was frowning over the papers in his briefcase.

''We are not sleeping even in Hollywood!'' Ross burst out. He'd been saving this all morning, having heard it from the maid. ''We're . . .''

''Hey, we're in *L.A.*, okay? It doesn't matter where you live as long as you can drive to the studios. Most of 'em aren't actually in Hollywood anymore, Ross, they're in Burbank or—''

''Mary, Mother of God! I want to going out in Hollywood! You are out there being a pig with all the girls! No? You are! You're pigging and leaving me here!''

Benny turned to him, his cheeks mottling. He cocked a hip, slightly, and Ross backed away. He knew, from when he was a boy, the times he had run away from the Jesuit Mission, how people stood when they were going to kick you.

He'd spent six weeks in the Mission hospital, after one kick stoved in his ribs, and he wasn't quite right from it yet. He most definitely knew when they were going to kick you . . .

But Benny made that long exhalation through his nose that meant he was trying to keep his temper. He'd never kicked Ross, or hurt him at all, he probably never would. He'd done nothing but help him, after all.

''I'm sorry, Benny,'' Ross said. ''Can we have some Jacks in the Box and watch Playboy Channel?''

''Sure. We deserve a break, right?'' He'd turned back to his briefcase, sorting papers. ''I had a letter here for you, from those people at the *World Inquirer*.''

''I am not like those people.''

"They're bloodsuckers. But the publicity is good, so whatever it is, we play along. We'll get a TV commercial or something out of it. What do you want from Jack in the Box?"

"Finger Food. I am hope you are not mad at me, Benny . . ."

"I'm not mad at you. Hey, here it is. Your letter."

There was something off about his face, Brandy thought. His nose seemed crooked or something. His features a little distorted. Must be from being a dwarf, or a midget, or whatever he was.

She tried to picture cuddling with him, think of him as cute, like a kid, but when she pictured him unzipping his pants, she got a skin-crawling feeling . . .

Hit the pipe a few times, anything's all right.

She pushed the pipe to the back of her mind. She had to play this carefully.

They were sitting in the corner booth of a Denny's restaurant. Ross, actually, was standing on the leatherette seat, leaning on the table like it was a bar, but the people who passed probably thought he was sitting. They also probably thought he was her kid. Shit, he was twenty-eight inches high. His head, though, was almost normal-sized. Too big for his body. He was wearing a stiffly pressed suit and tie, with a hankie tucked in the pocket; he looked like a little kid going to Sunday school. "Did a lot of women write to you?" she asked.

"Not too many. They are all having too big and fat or old, except you. Or they were having black. I don't want a black wife. I liked you, because your hair is blond, and you are not fat, and your letter was very nice, the handwriting very nice, the stationery very nice. Smelled nice too."

But he was talking sort of distractedly. She could tell that even through his Mexy accent and his goofy grammar. She could see he was staring at the scabs on her cheeks. There were only a few, really.

"I guess you're looking at my skin—" she began.

"No no no! It's fine. Fine." His voice sounded like it was coming through a little tube from the next room. He smiled at her. He had nice teeth.

"It's okay to notice it," Brandy said. "My . . . my sister has this crazy Siamese cat. You know how the little fuh—" Watch your language, she told herself. "You know how they are. I bent over to pet him and he jumped up and scratched me . . ."

Ross nodded. He seemed to buy it. Maybe they didn't have a lot of Hubba-heads in Trinidad picking at their skin all the time.

"There was a cat," he said absently, "who scared me very much, at the Mission. Big and fat and mean." He scowled and added something in Spanish.

"It's nice of you to buy me dinner," Brandy said. A fucking Denny's, she thought. Well maybe it was like he said, it was just the nearest one and he was hungry. But she'd pictured some really fancy place . . .

The waitress brought their order, steak for Brandy—who knew if this was going to work out? Get what you can now—and a milk shake and fries for the little guy, which was kind of a funny dinner, Brandy thought. The waitress had done a double take when she'd first come to take their order; now she didn't look at Ross directly. But she stared at Brandy when she thought Brandy wouldn't notice.

Fuck you, bitch, you think I'm sick for chilling with the little dude.

"You really do look nice," Ross said as the waitress walked away. Like he was trying to convince himself.

She'd done her best. Her hair was almost naturally blond, that was good, but it was a little thin and dry from all the hubba, and when she'd washed it, with that shitty hand soap that was all Delbert had, it'd frizzed out, so she'd had to cornrow it. She'd handwashed her dress and borrowed Carmen's pumps and ripped off a pair of new panty hose and some makeup from the Payless drugstore. Getting the bus down here was harder, but she'd conned a guy at the San Francisco station into helping her out, and then she'd ditched him at the L.A. station when he'd gone to the men's room, and she'd got twelve dollars for the guy's luggage, so it was beginning to click.

Ross started to cough. "Are you choking on something?" she asked, dreading it, because she didn't want to attract even more attention.

"No—my asthma." He was fishing in his pocket with one of his little doll hands. He found an inhaler, and sucked at it.

"Just rest a bit, you don't have to talk or nothin," she said, smiling at him.

So his health was not that great. It wouldn't seem too weird or anything, then, if he died or something.

"You just swept me off my feet, I guess," Brandy said. "I thought you were hella cute at the wedding. I was surprised you didn't have your manager over to be, like, best man or something."

"We had to be married first, because I have knowing what he would say, he doesn't want me to getting married till he check everything you know. But him, he has many girls. Come on in, come on in, this is our room, our own room . . ."

"Wow, it even has a kitchen! Anyway, look, it's got a bar and a microwave and a little refrigerator . . ." She noticed that the microwave oven wasn't bolted to the wall. It was pretty old, though, she probably couldn't get shit for it.

"I do like this refrigerator, this is good for Ross, little refrigerator by the floor. When we get a big house we will be having real kitchen!"

"Yeah? Uhhh . . . When do you think—"

He interrupted her with a nervous dance of excitement, spreading his arms to gesture at the whole place. "You have like it, this place? Las Vegas, it is so beautiful, everything like a palace, so much money, everything beautiful."

"Uh-huh." She started to sit on the edge of the bed, then noticed his eyes got all round and buggy when he saw her there. She moved over to the vinyl sofa, and sat down, kicked off her shoes. "It would've been nice if we coulda stayed in the Golden Nugget or one of them places—this Lucky Jack's is okay, but they don't got their own casino, they don't got room service . . ."

"Oh—we stay in the best, very fine, when Benny is find some work for me in Hollywood."

He toddled toward her, unbuttoning his coat. What did he think he was going to do?

She wondered where you copped rocks in Vegas. She knew there'd be a place. Crack cocaine is everywhere there's money. Maybe the edge of town out by the airport. She could find it. She needed the cash . . .

And then it hit her, and she stood up, sharply. He took several sudden steps back, almost stumbling. She looked down at him, feeling unreal. Had she been hustled by this little creature? "When Benny finds you some work? What do you mean?"

She felt the tightening in her gut, the tease of imagined taste in her mouth: the taste of vaporized cocaine and the God-knows-what-else they put in it. She could almost feel the glass pipe in her hand; see the white smoke flowering in the glass tube, coming to her. Her heart started pounding, hands twitching, fuck, going on a tweak with no dope to hit, one hand plucking at a scab on the back of her left forearm.

The little guy was chattering something. "Oh, I'm working in Hollywood!" He actually puffed out his chest. "I'm going to star in Arnold Schwarzenegger movie!"

"You mean you're going to costar with him. Okay. How much did you get paid—"

"I am not have the check yet—"

"Jesus fucking Christ."

He looked at her with his mouth open, so round and red and wet it looked like it had been punched in his head with a tool. "That is a blaspheme!"

"Look—we're married now. We share everything right? *How much we got to share?* I need some cash, lover—for one thing, we didn't get a ring yet, you said we'd get a diamond ring—"

Ross was pacing back and forth, looking like a small child waiting for the men's room, trying not to wet his pants. "I am not have very much money now—thirty dollars—"

"Thirty dollars! Jesus fuh . . . that's a kick in the butt. What about credit cards?"

He wrung his little hands. Made her think of a squirrel messing with a peanut. "I already am paying too much with American Express for the airplane and hotel—Benny will stop the card!"

"American Express? Can you draw cash on the card?"

He stopped scuttling around and blinked up at her. "I don't know."

"Come on, we're gonna find out. We're going out."

"But we are just married!"

"It's not even dark out yet, Ross. Hold your horses, okay? First things first. We can't do anything without a ring, can we? We're gonna do something, don't worry. I'm hella horny. But we can't do it without a ring. That'd be weird, don't you think?"

When she came in, the little guy was sitting in the middle of the bed, with his legs crossed Indian style, in a pair of red silk pajamas. There was a St. Christopher's medal around his neck. Probably couldn't get shit for that either.

It was after midnight, sometime. He had the overhead lights dialed down low, and the tall floor lamp in the corner was unplugged. In the dimness he looked like a doll somebody had left on the bed, some stuffed toy, till he leaned back on the pillow in a pose he'd maybe seen on the Playboy Channel.

They'd got the limit for the account, three hundred cash on the American Express Card. They'd endured all the stares in the American Express office, and she'd kept her temper with the giggly fat guy who thought they were performing at Circus Circus, but the hard part had been making Ross swallow the *amazingly* bullshit story about how it was a tradition in California for the girl to go shopping for the ring alone . . .

She'd had to cuddle him and stroke his crotch a few times. His dick was hard as a pocket knife down there and unnaturally big for his body. Then she'd left him here with a bottle of cheap André champagne, watching some shit about big-tit girls shooting each other with Uzis. He'd made kissy faces at her as she left.

Right now, stoned, she thought maybe she could give him a blow job or something, if she closed her eyes. She had gone through two hundred fifty dollars in hubba; her mouth was dry as a baked potato skin from hitting the pipe.

''Let me seeing beautiful ring on beautiful girl,'' he said, his voice slurred. He said something else in Spanish as she crossed the room to him and sat on the bed, just out of reach.

''Hey, you know what? Whoa, slow down, not so fast, *compadre*,'' she said, fending his clammy little hands away. She pointed at the girl on the wall-mounted TV screen, a girl in lavender lingerie. ''How'd you like me to dress up like that, huh? I need something like that. I'd look hella good, just hella sexy in that. I know where I can get some, there's an adult bookstore that's got some lingerie, they're open all night, you can go in and look at movies and I'll—''

''No!'' His voice was unexpectedly low. He said something in Spanish; she could tell he was cursing her. She caught the word *puta*.

"Hey, cool off—what I'm saying, you could call Benny and ask him to wire you some money, we need some things. He could send it to the all-night check-cashing place on Las Vegas Boulevard, they got Western Union—" She picked up her purse and went unsteadily toward the bathroom. The room was warped, because of the darkness and what the crack had done to her eyes. It always did weird shit to her eyes.

"Where you go?"

"Just to the bathroom, do some lady's business." I could tell him I'm in my period, Latin guys will steer clear from that, she thought. Maybe get another girl in here, give her a twenty to keep him occupied. "Why don't you call Benny while I'm in here, ask for some money, we need some stuff, hon!" she called as she closed the bathroom door and fumbled through her purse with trembling fingers. Found the pipe, found the torn piece of copper scrubbing pad she was using for a pipe-screen, found the Bic lighter. Her thumb was already blackened and callused from flicking. Her heart was pounding in her ears as she took the yellowish-white dove of crack from the inner pocket of the purse, broke it in half with a thumbnail, dropped it in the pipe bowl, melted it down with the lighter . . .

There was a pounding on the door, near her knee. She stared at the lower part of the door, holding the smoke in for a moment, then slowly exhaled. Her vision shrank and expanded, shrank and expanded, and then she heard, "You come out here, be with your husband!" Trying to make his voice all gravelly. She had to laugh. She took another hit. It wasn't getting her off much now. And she was feeling on the edge of that plunge into depression that waited around the corner of the high; she felt the tweaky paranoia prod her with its hot ice pick.

Someone was going to hear him yell; they were going to come in and see the pipe and she'd be busted in a Vegas jail. She'd heard about Vegas cops. Lot of times they raped the women they brought in. If they didn't like your looks, or you pissed them off more than once, they'd take you out to the desert and use you for target practice instead of highway signs or bottles, and just leave you out there . . .

"SHUT THE FUCK UP, ROSS!" she bellowed. Then thought: Oh, great, that's even worse. She hissed: "Be quiet! I don't want anybody in here—"

"They were here, to bring towels, and they told me"—something insulting in Spanish—"women don't go alone to buy ring! You come out, Ross is not stupid, no more little jokes!"

"*You're* a fucking little joke!" she yelled as he started kicking the door. She turned the knob and slammed the door outward. Felt him bounce off it on the other side. Heard him slide across the rug, stop against the bed frame. A wail, then a shout of rage.

She thought again about a will. He might have more money stashed someplace, or some coming. But there was no way this thing was going to last out the night and she couldn't get him to a lawyer tonight and he was already suspicious. She'd have to just get his Rolex and his thirty bucks—twenty some now after the champagne—and maybe those little pajamas, sell that shit, no first get—

She paused to hit the pipe again. Part of her, tweakin', listened intensely for the hotel's manager or the cops.

—get that call through to his manager, make him give the manager dude some bullshit story, have him send the most cash possible. Maybe hustle a thousand bucks. Or maybe the little guy could be sold himself somewhere, Circus Circus or someplace, or some kind of pervert. No, too hard to handle. Just make the call and then he should get a heart attack or something. He deserved it, he'd hustled *her*, telling her he had money, was a big star, but all the time he wasn't doing shit, getting her to marry him under false pretenses, fucking little parasite, kick his miniature ass . . .

A pounding low on the bathroom door again. Angrier now. The door was partly open. Little fucker was scared to put a limb through, but he stood to one side and peered in at her. "What is that? What is that in your hands? Drogs! Coca-enn?" Spanish cursing. "You are be going to jail soon! You are make my reputation bad! Puta bitch!"

She kicked the door open. He jumped back, narrowly avoiding its swishing arc. Fell on his little butt. For a moment she felt bad because he looked so much like one of her kids, then, like he was going to cry, and then for some reason that made her even madder, and she stepped out, pipe in one hand and lighter in the other, and kicked at him, clipping him on the side of the head with her heel. He spun, and blood spattered the yellow bedspread. She paused to hit the pipe, melting another rock. Then she came slowly at him as she took a hit. Her mouth was starting to taste like the pipe filter more than coke, she wasn't getting good hits, she needed cash, get some cash and get a cab.

He was up on his feet, scuttling toward the door to the hall. He was just tall enough to operate the knob. There was no way she could let the little fucker go, and no way she was going to let the rollers get her in Vegas, fuck that. She crossed the room in three strides, exhaling as she went, trailing smoke like a locomotive, doing an end run around him, turning to block the door. He backed away, his face in darkness. He was making some kind of ugly hiccuping noise. He didn't look like a human being now, in the dimness and through the dope; he looked like some kind of little gnome, or like one of those little fuckers in that movie *Gremlins*, which was what he was like, some sneaky little gremlin thing going to run around in the dark spots and pull shit on you.

Maybe the microwave. If you didn't turn it up much it just

sort of boiled things inside, it could look like he'd had a stroke. She had persuaded him to check in without her; they didn't know she was here. Unless he'd told the girl with the towels.

"You tell anybody I was here?"

He didn't answer. Probably, Brandy decided, he wouldn't have told much to some cheap hotel maid. So there was nothing stopping it.

He turned and scrambled under the bed. "That ain't gonna do you no good you little fucker," she whispered.

Ross heard her moving around up there. The dust under the bed was furring his throat, his lungs. He wheezed with asthma. She was going to get him into a corner, and kick him. She'd kick him and kick him with those hard, pointy shoes until his ribs stoved in and he spit up blood. He tried to shout for help, but it came out a coarse whisper between wheezes. He sobbed and prayed to the Virgin and St. Jude.

He heard the giantess muttering to herself. He heard her move purposefully, now, to a corner of the room. He heard glass break. Surely someone would hear that and come?

What was she doing? What had she broken?

"Little hustlin' tight-ass motherfucker," she hissed, down on her knees now, somewhere behind him. Something scraped across the rug; he squirmed about to see. It was the tall floor lamp. She'd broken the top of it, broken the bulb, and now she was wielding it like an old widow with a broom handle trying to get at a rat, sliding it under the bed, shoving the long brass pole of it at him.

It was still plugged in. A cluster of blue sparks jumped from the bulb jags broken off in the socket as she shoved it at his face.

He tried to scream and rolled aside. The lopsided king's crown of glass swung to follow him, sparking. He could smell shreds of rug burning.

He thought he could feel his heart bruising against his breastbone. She shoved the thing at him again, forcing him back farther . . . Then it stopped moving. She had moved away. Giggling. Moving around the bed—

Ross felt her fingers close around his ankle. Felt himself dragged backward, his face burning in the dusty rug; the back of his head smacking against the bed slats. He gave out a wail that tightened into a shriek of frustration, as she jerked him out from under the bed.

He clawed and kicked at her. She was just a great blur, a strange medicinal smell, big slapping hands. One of the hands connected hard and his head rang with it. He began to gag, and found himself unable to lift his arms. Like one of those dreams where you are trapped by a great beast, you want to run but your limbs won't work. She was carrying him somewhere, clasped against her, trapped in her arms like a dog to be washed.

He gagged again. Heard her say, from somewhere above, "Don't you fucking puke on me you little freak."

His eyes cleared. He saw she was carrying him toward a big white box, open on this side. The place had an old, used, cheap microwave oven. The early ones had been rather big . . .

"*Bennnnnyyyyyyyy!*" But it never quite made it out of his throat.

In less than a second she had crammed him inside it. He could feel his arms and legs again, feel the glass lining of the microwave oven against the skin of his hands and face; his head crammed into a corner, his cheek smashed up against the cold glass. He found some strength and kicked and she swore at him and grabbed his ankles in both her hands, stuffed his legs in far enough so she could press against his feet with the closing door. He could feel her whole weight against the door.

Crushed into a little box. A little box. Crushed into a little . . .

Absolutely not.

He pressed his palms flat against the glass, tucked his knees in against his chest, deliberately pulling deeper into the oven. Felt her using the opportunity to close the door on him.

But now he had some leverage. He used all his strength and a lifetime of frustration, and *kicked*.

The door smacked outward, banging against her chest. She lost her footing; he heard her fall backward, even as he scrambled back and dropped out of the oven, fell to the floor himself, landing painfully on his small feet. She was confused, cursing incoherently, trying to get up. He laughed, feeling light-headed and happy.

He sprinted for the living room, jumping over her outstretched leg, and ran into the bedroom area. He could see the door, the way out, clearly ahead of him, unobstructed.

Brandy got up. It was like she was climbing a mountain to do it. Something wet on the back of her head. The little fucker. The pipe. When had it got broken? It was broken, beside the sink. She grabbed the stem. It'd make a knife.

Shit—maybe the little fucker had already gotten out the door.

She felt her lip curl into a snarl, and ran toward the door—her ankle hooked on the wire stretched across the rug, about three inches over it, drawn from the bed frame to the dresser. The lamp cord, she thought, as she pitched facefirst onto the rug. She hadn't left the cord that way . . .

The air knocked out of her, she turned onto her back, gasping, choking, trying to orient herself.

The little fucker was standing over her, laughing, with the champagne bottle in his little hands; he clasped the bottle by the neck. A narrow bar of light came in between the curtains, spotlighting his round red mouth.

He was towering over her, from that angle, as he brought the champagne bottle down hard on her forehead.

"A BURGLAR KILLED MY NEW BRIDE!"
SOBS WORLD'S SMALLEST MAN

The newlywed bride of Ross Taraval, the world's smallest man, was murdered by an intruder on the first night of their Las Vegas honeymoon. Ross himself was battered senseless by the mystery man—and woke to find that his wife had been struck unconscious, raped, and murdered. Her throat had been cut by the broken glass of the drug-crazed killer's "crack" pipe. The burglar so far has not been located by police.

"It broke my heart," said the game little rooster of a man, "but I have learned that to survive in this world when you are my size, you must be stronger than other men! So I will go on. And I have not given up my search for the right woman, to share my fame and fortune . . ."

Ross hints that he's on the verge of signing a deal to do a buddy movie with his hero, Arnold Schwarzenegger. A big career looms up ahead for a small guy! "I'd like to share it with some deserving woman!" Ross says.

If you'd like to send a letter to Ross Taraval, the world's smallest man, you can write to him care of the Weekly World Inquirer, *and we'll forward the letter on to him . . .*

REX MILLER

Rex Miller caused quite a stir in the horror field when his controversial first novel, *Slob*, was released. Here was a narration that changed tense and point of view at the drop of a comma, featured a surly, ex-alcoholic detective named Jack Eichord, a gargantuan serial killer known as Chaingang, and a story that simply picked you up and carried you away. Though critics weren't quite sure what Miller was up to, his readers demanded, and got, five more novels featuring Eichord, and another that resurrected the unstoppable Chaingang. There is no doubt, however, about Miller's pyrotechnic prose, or his ability to precisely capture on the page our fear and loathing.

In the following story, Miller evokes a reluctant hero who unwillingly becomes the patron saint of the homeless, the hopeless, and the dead.

Spike Jones and Reverend Sister Claudine

by Rex Miller

It was October in the bottoms, the predominantly black ghetto, the place where Spike Jones crashed.

The stench began in whitey's city across the river, and it wafted over the contaminated waters into which industrial and human waste constantly streamed, mixing with the swirling fumes into a noxious blend of unbreathable pollution that settled over the bottoms like a stinking shroud.

Two persons of color walked by talking about the October weather.

"Listen," the first man said as a distant rumble penetrated

the ever-present vehicle and machine noise, "hear that thunder?"

"I hear it, bro." They walked by an obvious street person, one of the desperately homeless who populated Erie River Avenue. He had the look of a terminal junkie, slouched on the half nod, mumbling incoherently at the traffic, and they avoided looking directly at this creature.

Had these passersby been a little closer they would have heard the junkie, who was called Spike Jones by those who knew him, cursing them in the same vile terms he usually reserved for whitey and dark narcs.

"High yeller snot-faced Tommin' turd-packin' assholes," he said, effortlessly and without serious malice, scratching his nonexistent but transpunkrifying skinpopper itch, adjusting his fruitbasket, watching the October rain clouds darken.

Another crash split the sky, this time it was closer, and the junkie laughed in the direction of a Bronco II four-by-four with dented right fender.

"Street lightning," he said ominously. A shiny, new Bird cruised past. "Gon' *GETCHA*!" He laughed again just as the first hard, wet raindrops smashed down.

He didn't move at first, still on the half nod. He could sometimes stand like this for hours, mesmerized by the lowriders with their outrageous hydraulics, and the boogie boomers, the vehicles with sound systems that rattled the windows of the storefronts as they passed. Rain? No strain, Jane.

A chromehome bounced through the potholes, box blasting Sudden Death Overtime, rattling the grimy windows of the storefronts along Erie River Avenue.

"Oh, mo' fuck *yes*! *POUNDER!*" Spike Jones screamed. "Pound that pud. All right! Streetbeater." His eyes momentarily flickered with enthusiasm.

Black-brown, wasted, gaunt, filthy under the heavy coat,

oblivious to heat or cold, itching and feeling something strike his face, he gave his fruitbasket a final tug, and started ambling down the street.

The garish vehicle, caught again inert at the corner stop sign, got the light and lurched on down the thoroughfare, and Spike Jones yelled after it,

"*BOOMER*." Causing a very obese, short, black sister who was coming out of one of the nearby storefronts to jump nervously as if goosed.

Then Reverend Sister Claudine recognized the owner of the voice, realizing it was not someone out to threaten him or do him bodily violence, but only a harmless junkie known by the street handle of Spike Jones.

This Spike Jones had never heard of the bandleader Spike Jones. Nor was the musician his namesake. They called him that because he, one Prentice Tyrell by name, *had* one.

Long ago he'd become inured to packing his honker with "about a trey of eight-balls" a day. Translated, this was in the vicinity of ten and a half grams; a six- to seven-hundred-dollar-a-day junk habit. When snorting lost its kick he started slamming. He was now slamming a small fortune into his poor, collapsed veins. Spike Jones had himself a deadly serious spike jones.

"Blood," Reverend Sister Claudine signified, in a voice like the deepest sustained note on a fine church Hammond.

"Um-cool," Spike Jones said nervously, going up to the corpulent figure in the nun's habit and slap-dapping.

"Mojo power."

"Mojo," the hype said as they gave the mojo power dap, where one does a dap like a straight Dignity-for-Afro-People fist-to-fist, two on the back, a high five, a blow on the dice, and then the blood shake with the fingertips.

The immense nun looked up as a long black car with privacy glass shot past, tires singing lowdown, dirty blues on the wet street. Lightning struck and for just that split second the nun got an impression of two men in the front seat. He knew the driver, and he could imagine who would be on the passenger side.

"Walker," he said the name in a whisper, shivering as he scurried across the street.

"Say what?" the junkie called out to his fat back, but the massive nun was waddling away. He'd heard the fat one whisper a name. He'd concentrate real hard now and make himself remember it, because down here information was golden. And when you sometimes trade in information, the name can mean the game, lame. "Walker. Dude said Walker." This was valuable intelligence.

Spike Jones was, among other things, a police snitch, with a rat jacket as big as a monkey, and he was currently working to snitch his way out of a jackpot where they'd nailed him splitting down with heat. No biggie. He'd trade something.

Reverend Sister Claudine had a jones, too. Only a righteously clawing need like his would bring such a soul out into the rain. He was on his way across the street to get a takeout dinner from the Switch, and go back and scarf it in the shop, in case he got a cash customer. The last few months had been slow.

His was a vision of that bad sweet corn with melted butter, twice-baked Virginia ham with red-eye, breaded homeboy okra, and sweet taters in sugar syrup. That was *his* jones, and he could taste it in his nose the way a whorehound can taste that nasty stale tuna.

As he went through the door of the Chitlin' Switch, shrugging off October rain, he heard the junkie scream into the traffic: "Rattlers snakefuck yo' mama!"

November and Christmas blew past, and January roared down through the bottoms. Reverend Sister Claudine was open for business, and in fact had already turned a ten spot for a palm reading, and sold a jar of GIT-RITE ROOT for a pound, when Shortnin' Bread and Gypsy the Fighter came in.

"Yar-dough," it sounded like Reverend Sister Claudine said by way of greeting, booming it out to them in his deep and unmistakably masculine register.

"Mornin', Reverend Sister Claudine," the small man said respectfully, satching as he shook from the cold, the two black men stepping into the small, storefront root and herb emporium, and closing the door on the cold wind. Gypsy nodded woodenly, seemingly impervious to the external woes that plague lesser mortals.

"Y'all get in 'fo you freeze."

"That hawk be *talkin'*!"

"Amen." The hugely overweight man behind the counter agreed. "What cha all doin' so early in the mornin', Shortnin'?"

"We puttin' our promotional advertising up." The one called Shortnin' Bread said, reaching for one of the cardboard signs Gypsy the Fighter was carrying, and lying it on the glass showcase in front of the nun. "Will you put this in your window for us?"

"Nothin' to it," the proprietor said amiably, and the diminutive fight hustler thanked him and the two men left. Reverend Sister Claudine held the sign far enough away from him so that he could see it without glasses, reading "The bronze gladiator Gypsy Joe Jackson and Pigfoot Davis FIGHT for the Regional Welterweight Crown Saturday Night—at Toughie's Club in the bottoms."

He was not thinking about the upcoming fight. He was thinking about his monetary situation, which had developed a number ten hitch in its gitalong, which is not a good thing, especially when you have a demanding woman. The thought made him shiver.

Reverend Sister Claudine, whose name was Claude Ammons, did not like the cold. He hated the hawk, that mean mutha coming off the stinking river from the direction of the white folks' office buildings on the other side. It was nothing for that hawk to drive the chill factor down to thirty below.

It was truly cold this January. The frost was on the pumpkin. It was Tishri. Muharram. Your basic eighteen brutal days after the coming of the Winter Solstice.

The hawk was out looking for black skin. He hoped another blizzard wasn't on the way. How frigid was it? It was colder than a turn-down from Vanessa DuPree, who was standing in the bedroom doorway that adjoined the storefront, pouting and purring in a see-through teddy, and sniffing.

''Daddy, gimmee somethin','' she purred.

''I don't got it.'' He knew what she wanted.

''Well gimmee *SOME*THIN', then.'' She pouted.

''I don't have none of that neither.'' He shrugged, apologetically.

His woman enunciated the four-letter word for defecation, giving it five syllables, putting a whole nasty message in there as she turned, letting him see what would be walking out on his big, fat, black butt if he didn't get hisself together and *COP*, DIG?

Under the flimsy blue thing the big, fleshy watermelons teased Reverend Sister Claudine with the promise of hot times or the threat of a cold and empty bed.

He forgot about signs and promotions and money and concentrated on rummaging around in a cigar box he kept below the counter until he found what he wanted, after which he started in the direction of Vanessa DuPree, waddling through the door to the bedroom like some big puppy dog in heat.

She flopped back on the bed carelessly, pulling the spread halfway over her, eyeing the big black man sullenly as he fired up a joint.

''Umm,'' he grunted deeply, handing it to her as he held

the smoke. "Do dis." She took it and inhaled, as he sat beside her, the springs groaning.

Reverend Sister Claudine, a name he'd had as an inspiration after watching Claudine Longet on a television show, gently pulled the covers away from one of Vanessa's beautiful, light tan breasts, touching pudgy fingers to the large purple-black nipple. She slapped his hand away.

"Hey!"

"Don't be touchin' what you can't take care of."

"I be doing that so fine, lover," he tried to sweet-talk her, leaning in.

"You *gets* me somethin' first, though," she said, with a sneer on her thick, cushiony smoocher. "Y'all T.C.O.B. for T.L.C." The little bell on the door rang.

"Damn," he sighed, forcing his mounds of pounds off the bed, and waddling back out the doorway.

What he saw chilled him worse than any hawk ever could.

It was the one they called Driver, and one of *them*—bastard always had one with him for company. Driver was small. Skinny. Mean as "*bob* wie-yuh." Driver standing in the doorway, the dead one outside, waiting, patient and motionless, staring in at the fat figure in the huge nun's getup.

Ammons knew the dead one was staring right at him, even though they always had the damn blue sunglasses on so you couldn't see their eyes, but he could tell.

"Bah-zoh," he rumbled, making the deep organ notes fill his tiny store with false bravado. "Cold out there, ain't it?" Driver said nothing, only moved toward him in quick silent steps, radiating terrible karma and total ruthlessness.

"Gimme some licorice hair," he whispered. It frightened Reverend Sister Claudine, who was still chilled to the bone but could suddenly feel an icy trickle of sweat dripping down from under his Afrique Glamour Wig—Claudine Longet Model. He didn't have any licorice hair and in fact had never heard of the shit.

"I ain't got none, my man. I never heard of it," he said, apologetically.

"You got it," Driver whispered in his deadly soft voice. Claude Ammons could see the killer zombie out of the corner of his eye, watching him, just waiting for a sign from Driver.

The Driver brought them in from God knows where. Some said Haiti, some said the D.R., others believed they came from South America. They were black men who'd been made into dead men. Soul kamikazes who would sacrifice themselves to make a hit. And some hit. They like to *devour* their victims. One guy a zombie did, they couldn't find anything but his bones. Ammons would never forget the way it had been described on the street: the coppers found a pile of bones and they only ID'd the dead guy by some *fatty tissue* that hadn't been sucked off one of the bones. Lord, God! The phrase "fatty tissue" had haunted Claude Ammons ever since he'd heard it.

"I swear, I ain't never heard of no licorice hair," he pleaded.

" '*LEC*-TRIC CHAIR," the one called Driver repeated patiently.

"Oh! ELECTRIC CHAIR! Certainly, my man. I fix you right up." The fat con artist breathed a deep sigh of relief as he threw his bulk into motion and started sacking up the potion. Man don't even bother to open his mouth when he talk how you s'pose to understand him.

Driver was said to use a sap. One of those jobs with a spring-loaded handle, leather sewn around lead and steel, the kind of a sap that could bust a skull right open. Expose the gray matter and all the brain goo, let them walking dead chow right down.

Bastards couldn't jones for no chitterlings, or hamburgers with radishes baked in 'em, or buttermilk cornbread with country butter or fried okra or stewed tomatoes or green onions and candied yams or hot sweet barbecued ribs—no, they liked to eat *BROTHERS*. Nice fat brothers with plenty of dark meat on their bones. And he knew that one eyeing him right now was jonesin' for his *fatty tissue*.

"That'll be twelve-fifty, sir. I won't even charge you no tax."

The man just stared a hole through him, slowly peeling a ten spot and some bullets out of a big roll of green.

"Y'all hurry back, now," Reverend Sister Claudine called cheerfully to Driver's skinny back as he left, thrilled to be rid of him, the one with the dark blue sunglasses never averting his gaze from Claude Ammons until Driver was back outside, then turning and following him like a vicious attack dog trained to heel and follow off the leash.

They weren't exactly dead men, these walking dead. But they'd been fed datura and different stuff, and got themselves a nice big jones for zombie cucumber and whatnot, and Driver kept them strung out on various things.

Reverend Sister Claudine didn't know from datura and the obscure zombie toxins. He knew from GIT-RITE ROOT and ELECTRIC CHAIR.

He shrugged off the incident, realizing as he looked at the money in his hand that Driver had left him a fifty-cent tip. Thirteen dollars.

He allowed himself to think about Vanessa's big, delicious, velvety, purple-black cherries. He could just about get laid for thirteen bullets. Driver done brought him about thirteen bullets' worth of GIT-RITE.

By Saturday he was lower than snake shit. His main event, his bottom bitch, his primary puss, his el primo numero, his bodacious curvaceous velvet glove of love had just told him to go fuck himself. If he couldn't T.C.O.B. any better than *this*, well he could just unzip them pants and give his *OWN* self T.L.C. next time he needed it. Also, he was gettin' too freakin' fat to cut it. She could do better. *LOTS* better, you dig? Kiss it good-bye, baby.

Life could be so cruel. Life could sting. He was on a diet and it had him lowdown. He couldn't think straight without pussy and food. It got him all screwy like bad acid. He had to have her back. She knew things to do to a man nobody else ever thought of. She could make that little thing catch *fire*, squire, and grow a whole lot higher.

He'd lose a lot of weight. Be handsome again. He was smart. He'd scheme on it and come up with something. He'd make the bitch beg to come back. The bell above the door intruded on his orgy of self-pity.

"Come in," he said, more expansively than he meant to. A frightening-looking brother clomped in. Reverend Sister Claudine immediately clocked him for a narc.

"Hey."

"Help you, sir?"

"I need something, and the word is out on the street you the sister can bust the blister."

"Say what?" He felt a trickle of sweat drip down from under the wig, which was sitting slightly askew atop Claude Ammons's fat, black dome.

"I hear you got a lot of rare remedies for whatever ails a man." He looked around at all the bottles and jars of junk on the shelves.

"Thass right." Ammons surreptitiously wiped a bead of perspiration off his noggin.

"I'm a little under the weather." Uh-huh. He knew how that felt all right. He was under that shit too. Right at the moment he just wanted this narc to go away and he'd take his habit across Erie River Avenue and get hisself a couple three hamburgers with them baked radishes in them, he was so starved—maybe get four—and some ribs while he was at it. Something to keep his stomach bile from eating a hole in his gut and givin' him a big bloody ulcer. Fuck that twat if she don't like him a trifle plump. "I got me an unusual problem."

"Bah-zoh?" he asked in his rumbling basso. One of his all-purpose reflexive responses to anything.

"I need something that'll stop a monkey for a junkie." Ammons just stared at the tough-looking narc. "You got anything?" Here it comes, he thought.

"Um." The Reverend Sister Claudine, wig atilt, looked around innocently at the roots and herbs. "I got Jinx 'Em, and Jinx Off, Dragon's Blood, De-Hex, Good Luck, Curse Nullifier—that's good. I got your Anti-Rattlesnake Spell Protector . . ."

"That sounds good, too. Auntie somebody." The narc was just jiving with him.

"You want some Anti-Rattlesnake Spell?"

"Will it make a junkie zombie straighten out?"

"It'll make a rattlesnake spell get off you." He wasn't playing no jive game with no bogus narc.

"You must know a lot about zombies, eh?"

"I know about the black candle sickness." Reverend Sister Claudine, now sweating profusely, shrugged. Stonewalling it out. "Juju. High John the Conqueror. Git-Rite . . ." He trailed off into his chins.

"You know these boys here?" He slid a glossy rectangle across the counter. A Polaroid. He tapped it with a big black finger. "Hmm?"

"Say what?"

"You know these boys?"

"No. I ain't never seen them."

"You ain't even *looked* at the niggers yet! Look at 'em." The cop adjusted his tone, working to keep it nice and friendly. "See if you don't recognize these here, sport."

Claude Ammons squinted at the picture. It was the one

called Driver and one of *them*. Blue glasses. The house of blue lights in the background. Driver getting in a black car.

"I never seen them that I recall."

"You look again, sport. We know this boy here been in this store buying some of that voodoo shit you sell. You best straighten up, Sister, or your nasty habit gon' be slammed down hard, can you be with that?"

"I didn't do *nothing*, man."

"Aiding and abetting, sport. Ever hear of that shit? That's a felony crime, homes."

"I don't know what you *talkin'* about, man—"

"This one here he *KILLS* black folks, Sister. His name is Walker. And we wanna know where he hangs. Now you get right."

Ammons shrugged and wiped. His name wasn't Walker, he thought, vastly vexed. He *was* a walker. They called them dead folks WALKERS, *SPORT*. "Never paid no attention."

"You better change your tune."

"I swear. I'd tell you if I knew. If he come in here I didn't ever see it," he said, telling the truth. Far as it went.

"It'd be worth a hundred bullets if you got yourself a sudden memory attack," the narc told him, peeling off a couple of crisp fifties.

"I could *use* a hundred bullets," Ammons said, smiling, the wig low over his right eye, fake hair stuck in the gluey sweat. "Wish I knew these boys."

"Um-hm."

"Surely do wish I could help you, sir." Selling hard. In fact for a couple of seconds he thought about trying to pick up a hundred bullets. Old Vanessa be gettin' her nose open for that shit real quick. Thing is—ain't no hot snatch in the world worth snitchin' out no *zombies*. "No skin off my nose if some no-account lowlife get hisself in trouble. Sure wish I could help.'' The cop just looked at him real hard for a beat or two, turned and left. Claude didn't touch the man's card, which was sitting on the glass counter.

Bad enough to rat some brother out, but you go dropping a dime on some of *them*—whew! Huh-uh. He knew his place on the food chain and he was an eat-*er*, not no eat-*ee*. Claude's mama didn't raise no dummies.

That evening early Shortnin' Bread and Little Doc dropped around, lookin' around like two dealers at a narc convention.

''Hey, bloods, what it is?'' Reverend Sister Claudine boomed in old-time jive.

''Same old,'' Shortnin' told him.

''Uh-huh,'' Doc agreed. ''We gots to get some root. Gypsy Joe says he got a curse on him and he wants GIT-RITE and GIT-OFF.''

''We fix him up, then.'' The fat man in the habit started reaching for things.

''Say, er, uh, my man, you think you can let us have some on the cuff? You know—just till the fight's over? I done run up all my pocket change on various promotional materials and advertising. That shit's high, ya dig?''

''I can dig it, bros. Thing is''—Claude Ammons scratched under his itchy, witchy wig—''I'm strictly cash and carry.''

''How about two free ringsides to the fight? They scalpin' 'em for a twenty at Toughie's right now.''

''I'll take one free ringside and y'all comp my dinner.'' His diet was already out the window at the thought of free food from Toughie's grille. The club made a steak sandwich a man could sink his pearly whites into.

''You got it, my man,'' Shortnin' said, expansively producing a ringside ticket to the ''Regional World Championship Fight,'' and handing it across the counter with a flourish. Ammons pocketed it and filled the root order. Maybe the fight would take his mind off his troubles.

* * *

The evening wasn't as much fun as he'd hoped. First to his irritation Ammons discovered that Toughie's Club was jam-packed for the fight and he hated crowds. Especially crowds where everybody had a beautiful bitch with them. Everybody but *him*. He had to sit there at his ringside table, everybody looking at his sorry black ass—he imagined—with Vanessa gone off to greener pastures. Even the *Grille* was shut down! Here he was supposed to be eatin' steak sandwiches and enjoying his black self and what was he doin'? Eatin' his *heart* out and drivin' a stake in his *heart* for Vanessa DuPree and them big juicy milk machines.

Shortnin' Bread apologized for the food, but they comped him free drinks and by the time he'd knocked back a couple of straight 151-proof rums he was mellowing out some. The bell rang and Gypsy Joe Jackson came out dancing like Ali, ready to "float like a butterfly and sting like a bee." Pigfoot Davis came shuffling out to meet him, lookin' like he'd done trained too close to the buffet table, big meaty slabs of dark lard swingin' here and there, shufflin' flat-footed and slow, Gypsy the Fighter movin', dancin, lookin' ten years younger and about fifty pounds lighter.

Gypsy was floatin' and stingin' and suddenly he just run right into Pigfoot's right hand, which hit him so hard even his cousins down in Mississippi must have felt it. Next sound before the crowd noise was Gypsy's head—the back of it—smacking that canvas. Damn!

Shortnin' and Little Doc was out there, fannin' him, pourin' water on him, pinchin' him—finally the salts brought him around and they carried him out of the club. The GIT-RITE and the GIT-OFF hadn't done the trick this time. Claude Ammons looked at his watch. The Regional World Championship Fight of the Century had lasted about a minute and a half.

If it wasn't one thing it was another. Vanessa walked out on his ass. He was on a diet. He couldn't eat nothin'. He was miserable. He went to the fights to enjoy hisself and . . . this! What a world. He was caught up in his wallow of self-pity and didn't see Prentice Tyrell née Spike Jones coming out of the alley near Twenty-eighth and Erie.

"Hey!" Spike Jones said, seeing a familiar face.

"AH!" Claude Ammons jumped as if he'd been goosed again. "*JEEZ*US DON'T DO THAT YOU SCARE A MAN TO DEATH THAT WAY HOLY FUCKIN' *SHIT*!" He grabbed his fat chest more or less in the vicinity of his pounding heart. "Oh, man, you scared me." He was blowing like a whale.

"I'm sorry."

"You always comin' outta some alley or somethin', man. Jeezus. A brother could have a heart attack. Make some NOISE or . . ." he trailed off, trying to calm down. Wouldn't that be the way? Some fuckin' junkie come out and go boo and give him a damn coronary and he'd *die* and nobody'd find his ass. Just his luck. "Whew!"

"I wasn't sure it was you without that nun's dress and shit."

"Uh-huh."

"I need help, man. I'm in bad trouble."

"Tap city, bro—" Ammons was already dissembling out of habit, pantomiming the money gesture with finger and thumb, then pretending to show empty pockets, which indeed he had plenty of.

"I gotta have someplace to hide."

"Yeah?" Claude wasn't the least bit interested. He just wanted to go find a rib joint and get some decent chow in him before he collapsed right there on the street. The potent rum was sloshing around his innards and he was getting sick looking at this ugly junkie.

"The one called Walker—you know—got them zombie

killers? He knows I dropped a dime on him, man. He's gonna do me, man. I got to hide.''

''Walker?'' It suddenly came together in his head, floating across the surface of that fine and nasty Jamaican 151-proof. A bunch of images, random flashes of insight, blurred by too fast to analyze: Walker—the cop thought ''Driver's'' name was Walker; Spike Jones must have heard him call his zombie pal a walker and misunderstood. What do you put in a Zombie Kamikaze? 151-proof rum. He had zombies on the brain.

''He probably don't know it was you snitched him off. I wouldn't sweat it none.''

''He knows. Believe me. I know a dealer sells to them Datura junkies over at the house of blue lights. Them cops is in his pocket. They *told* him who ratted him out. I'd gon' be *dead* if he finds me.''

''Walker ain't even his name, man.''

''It don't matter what his name is I'm one dead motherfucking nigger if he finds me. Can I hide at your place. *PLEASE?* He wouldn't look there.''

''Fuck no, man. I ain't got no room,'' he lied. The last thing Claude Ammons needed was some funkie junkie for a roommate. If he was gonna shack up with somebody had a spike jones, it was gonna be a *bitch* not no rusty-butt, shanky, skuzzy raggedy-ass old Prentice fucking TY-rell, no fuckin' way.

''I know where he puts 'em when he kills 'em and I told the cops. They'll tell him. He's gonna *have* to kill me, man.'' The hype's eyes were as wide as Stepin Fetchit's in the old B movies where he acts scared in the haunted house and says 'Feets, do yo' stuff!' '' But Spike Jones was scared to the bone and Ammons could smell it.

''What chew mean you know where he *puts* 'em?'' He didn't really want to know that tidbit of information either. How did *he* get involved with this lunatic dope fiend? DAMN!

''Right there in the slaughter yard.'' Spike Jones pointed

down the alley toward Twenty-seventh and the local abattoir. "Come on—I seen 'em myself—I'll show you right now!"

What ever made him go? It was against everything in his makeup. Later when Ammons got to thinking about it he figured it was because he knew Spike Jones was just a full-of-shit junkie, and he was bluffing, talking his trash to get a free crash pad for his next nod. But something led him down the dark alley to see these imaginary bodies.

"You know how it always stinks so bad over there?"

"It stinks bad everywhere in the bottoms, bro," Ammons said.

"Yeah, but it's superfunky over there, man. You know why?"

"Uh-huh. They throw all the shit in the back. Animal shits itself when it gets killed is why it stinks so bad, 'n' they make soap or somethin'. Slaughterhouses always stink. That's why they're called slaughterhouses."

"That ain't it. Just check it out. You'll see," Spike urged. "He puts the leftovers back there when they done with 'em."

Claude Ammons didn't say anything more because soon they were crossing the darkened street and entering the lot that led to the slaughter yards. The stench was unusually bad that evening, or maybe this hype had got him psyched out about dead bodies an' zombies an' shit.

"Not that way. C'mon." Spike Jones started down a path between stacks of packing crates flanking the paved entrance to the slaughter yard's loading dock. Spike ducked through a flap in the wire fence and over to two huge Dumpsters where the day's trims and castoffs were stored for rendering, in violation of every city code known to man. The rotten meat stink was overpowering. Ammons wanted to gag.

He should have been home with Vanessa DuPree and them humongously beautiful cherries, a-humpin' and a-bumpin'. Saturday night—and he was where? Sneakin' around the slaughterhouse with a damn dope fiend snitch.

"There. In there. Pull that lid back and see for yourself, man."

"I ain't touching shit," Ammons whispered.

"I gotta eat, y'know," Spike said, shrugging apologetically. He threw open the half lid. He reached in, poked around, shifting, moving, searching, then stood back triumphantly. Ammons stepped forward and peered over the side of the Dumpster.

For a few seconds, Claude Ammons's head just couldn't deal with it. He refused to assimilate or accept the thing he was seeing. He told himself he was looking at parts of dead horses and cows. But his eyes, his no-good lyin' eyes, told him he was looking at a foot, not a hoof. Plain as day. There a cow bone, there a leg bone. When they were rendered, they'd be in the same bar of Lifebuoy together.

"Come on," he said. The junkie did not have to be told twice. He didn't know what he was going to do—if anything. But he knew he had to help this poor cat if he could. When they were back in the alleyway across the street he whispered softly, "We'll go over and you can stay inna back until we get this mess figured out."

"Yeah, man. Okay. All right. Yeah. Thank you, man—you're a stand-up bro. Absolutely. Yeah." Spike Jones scurried along beside his protector.

They went back to the storefront and Ammons unlocked his shop and showed Prentice Tyrell where he could bunk down.

"You can stay here tonight. Tomorrow we gonna have to come up with somethin' else—dig?"

"Yeah. Right. You bet."

"You're *outta* here tomorrow, Jim. Dig?"

"Yes, sir. You bet. Thanks!"

Ammons pulled out his keys again.

"Don't touch nothing. Don't turn on no lights. Stay in the back. Just keep out of sight until tomorrow morning. I'll come up with something."

"Yeah. Okay."

Ammons locked up again. Walking down the street. Trying to figure how to play it. What was he going to do? Where was an *angle*? He wasn't used to putting hisself at risk like this. It was a fool move. Still, he hadn't eaten anything and his stomach had stopped the bad rumbling. He hadn't broken his diet. *That* was a good sign.

Suddenly it dawned on him. Tomorrow was Sunday. He had a delivery on Sunday morning. They might come around and knock or ring before he opened up and Spike Jones would think it was him and show hisself. He started back to the store to warn the junkie and got a glimpse of movement behind the glass.

Cautiously, he inched close enough where he could see into the shadows of the storefront without being seen. Prentice Tyrell was dashing around taking things off the shelves. That fucking lowlife scumbag sonofabitching dope fiend was *robbing* his ass!

Normally Claude Ammons was among the more eloquent exponents of the four-letter words and all the longer mutations, imprecations, and soul-searing combinations—but he was stressed out beyond his tolerances. The sight of the human bones and decomposed flesh, this mini-Holocaust to which his central nervous system had been subjected, had driven him into a dangerous state of overload.

Now—inserting his key into the lock—turning and entering, flipping the light as a bottle of rare potions crashed to the floor—the idea that his single charitable act had been rammed up his exhaust pipe pushed him all the way over the edge. Articulation failed him.

"You no-dick, baby-raping, turd-skinned, marger-flecking ship-cravling sotter-merging low-rent suck fuck shit piss god mother dammerdingdongpussy cuntlipped bubbleassed skag-shooting hymen-sisting fommle-grating. . . ." He ran out of air finally, like a pricked balloon.

"I *HAD* TO, MAN. I GOTTA GET SOME 'LECTRIC CHAIR OR THAT MOTHU'FUCKIN' ZOMBIE DRIVER GONNA KILL MY SORRY ASS!"

"He ain't gonna get the chance. I'M GONNA KILL YOUR SORRY ASS!" Claude picked up a bottle of MAKE HIM B-TRU and hurled it with all his might at Spike Jones's head.

"Ahh!" He ducked as the bottle splintered into a thousand tiny shards. "I gotta get some 'LECTRIC CHAIR an' I ain't got no money, man."

"I be giving you the fuckin' Electric Chair all right," Ammons said, looking around for something heavy to clobber the junkie over the head with.

"Go ahead, man. Kill me. I don't care." Spike Jones crumpled in a sobbing heap amid the broken jars and bottles. "I'm a dead man anyway." He was obviously beyond defending himself.

Ammons just stood there, shaking, wanting to kill the no-good sorry fuck, but too bummed out to get upside his head. He knew it wouldn't do no good. He wouldn't feel any better for it. Besides, the pitiful wreck of a junkie was so pathetic-looking it made him thankful HE wasn't strung out on something, or running from no Driver.

"Get up from there," he said.

"Go on ahead and do it. Go on. Kill me. I don't give a shit anymore. What I got to live for? Them zombies gonna do me anywhichaway."

"Get up from there. And wipe your nose for crissakes. Pathetic piece of dogshit. Get up 'fore I change my mind." He went into the back and got a broom and started sweeping up broken glass.

"Kill me if you want to," the man said. Still on the floor.

"Nobody's gonna kill you."

"Walker's gonna. Walker's gonna kill me and nobody's gonna even notice, don't you get it?" Spike said, hitching his breath, snot running freely from his nose. "They're gonna put me in that Dumpster and nobody's gonna miss me and somebody's gonna take all my stuff and that will be that." Spike was bawling now, and Claude Ammons felt the tiniest constriction in his size twenty-one throat, a slight flutter in the thump of his cantaloupe-sized heart.

"Spike, you are the sorriest thing I've ever seen. Wipe your damn nose. Walker ain't gonna shit. Ain't no Walker anyway. His name is Driver and the one he's with is a walker. Never mind that shit. Tell the truth now or I will get upside your mangy black ass: you was ripping me off for dope, right?"

"Dope?" The dope fiend wiped his nose like he never heard the word 'fore. "You got dope here?"

"Fuck no I ain't got no dope here. But you be *lookin'* for it—right?"

"Shit no, man. I be lookin' for what I toll ya. 'Lectric Chair. Them zombies is *datura* junkies, man. That shit is like LSD to them motherfuckers. And dat Walker dude he hooked on it worst of all!"

"No shit," Ammons said sarcastically. Now the hype was telling him his own business. "Don't tell your old granny how to suck eggs, all right?" Spike Jones just looked at him.

"If you gimme some of that 'Lectric Chair shit I can buy my way outta this jackpot. Man, I pay you back for it I *swear* I will."

Claude Ammons kept sweeping up tiny bits of glass. Thinking. Boiling inside. Cooking. It was coming to a head. All the times he had been accused of satchin', all the lies his bitches had told him, all the times he'd been shat upon by the white devil, all the Mercedes he would never buy, all the thirty-five-inch color TVs he would never watch, all the places he would never go, all the nameless and faceless that shuffled in the streets and alleys, so much fatty tissue with a shopping cart. He could remember the fear when Driver came in and scared his nigger ass so bad he almost made the brown job in his pants. Shit was hard enough without a bunch of junkie zombie assholes fucking up the neighborhood.

He looked at Spike, curled up on the floor beside him, still shaking with fear and self-pity.

"You gonna be free, my man," Claude said. "You ain't gotta worry no more. The zombies gonna be free, too." Everybody's gonna be free, he thought. He picked up the phone and searched through his notes written on the wall for a number and a name he had hoped never to use in this lifetime. Without hesitation he dialed.

"I'm a dead man," the hype insisted.

"You ain't jumpin' shit . . . Hello? Driver? Awright, well lemme talk to him. . . . Driver? This is— Reverend Sister Claudine. . . . Yeah. That's right. I got something for you. Um-hum . . . Um-hmm, well I ain't. I got a shipment of that special stuff y'all like—but it's right from the source. Never been stepped on and it will kick a gorilla's ass. Serious stuff . . . Thass right. *ELEC-TRICK-CHAIR*." He said it nice and clear for the mumbly motherfucker. "Uh-huh. All you got to say is the magic number." They haggled for a bit and Claude told the voice at the other end of the line to come around and "bring plenty to get plenty." The phone went dead. He'd told Driver to come alone.

Prentice Tyrell was back in the bathroom. Trying to keep quiet and not get a bad case of the dry heaves while he waited for the crazy one out front to make his play. He was sure they was all dead anyway. It was just a matter of time. Ammons had found a little this and that which he administered to Spike Jones to keep him from getting too sick, but Spike's illness was the kind that you couldn't cure.

Meanwhile, out front, the good sister was calm and cool—well, fairly cool—waiting for the man in her Reverend Sister Claudine getup. A huge container of ELECTRIC CHAIR under the counter in front of her. It was beginning to feel a bit warm in the store and she fanned herself with an old dreambook.

The bell rang and a shadow entered, followed by the slight and fearsome physiognomy of one Driver, looking all badass threatening and ready to deal out the hurt.

"This shit better be for real," he snarled.

"Real as Don Steele," the immense nun replied quietly.

Back in the john Claudine was sure she had heard Spike Jones cough and a chill trickle of sweat escaped from under the wig on his head. He wasn't so cool anymore. Thing about messin' with junkies so many ways you can get hurt: dope burns, poison in the blow, robbers with Uzis—shit you even in the same time zone with junkies you in trouble. He'd violated one of his cardinal survival rules. Never fuck around with junkies. Also—another rule—never do a good turn for nobody. No good turn goes unpunished was a cliché that even the folks in the bottoms had heard of. You ask for it—well shit, fool, you gon' get it. It's that simple.

"Let's see that shit." Driver flung a stack of bills. Reverend Sister Claudine gently sat the huge container of 'LECTRIC CHAIR in front of the man.

"Have a freebie. Go ahead. On the house."

"No. I *know* you ain't that stupid." Driver took the shit and turned. Claudine never reached for the money. He watched the small, deadly man turn and ease on out the door. Saw him move toward the car. Open the door. Get in. Goodbye.

Claudine had everything packed in less than a half hour. Spike spent most of the time puking in the toilet. He was feeling thin as thin gets, every bone in his body aching and every hole leaking. He staggered out of the john, wiping his mouth with the sleeve of his shirt.

"Pick up that bag there, Jim, take it out back, then get

invisible,'' Claude Ammons told Spike. ''You didn't make no friends today.''

''I make it up to you, Claudine, I swear,'' Spike said, scuttling toward the back of the shop, dragging a seabag full of the surviving bottles of GIT-RITE ROOT, SLO-DOWN, JUMPUP, Vallerion, and ginger root, sweetpea, and a dozen other potions and powders that, all together, couldn't do an ounce of good for Claudine at the moment.

In Claudine's head, the clock was ticking—screaming off every second. Driver would be trying that mix right about now, maybe all the walkers would be havin' themselves a little snoot/toot/hypeful of what was mostly 'LECTRIC CHAIR, but also a lot of STOP-'EM-COLD and B-DEAD, a mess of broken glass and rat turds and roach legs and anything else that Claude had swept up off the floor and ground in fine to that big jar of 'LECTRIC CHAIR. To tell the truth, Claude Ammons didn't have a lot of faith that the mix would *stop* anybody *cold*—but he was positive his lease on breathing would be up for review shortly.

He packed up the last of his belongings in the last of his grocery bags. He was sweating so much, his wig kept slipping off his head and right now was dangling precariously over one ear. He pulled it off and shoved it deep in a bag. Paranoia slipped into an empty space in his thoughts, right next to the space occupied by cold-eyed, pointy-toothed junkie killer zombies sniffing around for a Claude Ammons supper. Nowhere to run to baby, nowhere to hide.

''Move 'em out, cut 'em in, move 'em out,'' he hummed nervously, looking around the store to see if anything important had been forgotten. ''Git goin' little doggies. Got to be someplace else right now, right *now*.'' On Claudine's mental clock, the hands were pointing straight up, the whole face bulging like a cartoon clock, bells and springs and works splitting out the seams, with an air-raid siren whooping out the alarm.

Claudine stripped off her huge black cloak and white surplice and shoved them in the bag along with her wig. He pulled on an old pea jacket to cut the wind. His life was worth shit now, but there was a chance he could slip away out of character. He hitched up the last of the bags in his arms and was stepping behind the counter toward the back door when the sound of squealing tires, very close, made him glance back. Filling his view was the huge, shiny grille and quadruple headlights of Driver's Caddy, tire smoke billowing around the hood, the thunder of the 454 filling his ears. Claude was momentarily transfixed by the sight of the car looming impossibly large before exploding through the front wall of the store.

Claude dove to the floor behind the counter. He could hear the back wall being sprayed with glass and chunks of metal. He felt the impact of the Caddy's front bumper against the front glass of the counter. He heard the glass shatter, watched while the counter frame seemed to stretch, holding for a moment before giving way. Claude futilely covered his head with his arms and kissed his ass good-bye.

The next seconds were ticked off by the cooling engine of the Caddy. Claude held his breath, waited a few seconds more until he was sure he was breathing, his arms and legs were working, he was more or less alive. He got to his knees, glass tinkling off the back of his jacket, and cautiously pulled himself up between the counter and the wall so he could peer out over the top of the counter.

Through a plume of steam jetting out from the front of the Caddy, he saw movement in the front seat. Saw the man fighting to get out of the car. Heard him bellow with rage and then saw him—blood pouring out of his nose, his mouth, probably every other hole on the zombie-making, brother-killing sack of scum. That poison and all those tiny shards of ground glass were tearing Driver a new asshole inside his nasty carcass.

"AAARRRRRRRRR!" Driver screamed, almost made it around the front of the car tough as he was—but this was STOP-'EM-COLD and B-DEAD and broken glass out the ass—and Driver was a red gusher by the time he collapsed facedown on the hood of the smashed Caddy. Claude watched as he twitched a couple times, then was still. Claude stood and reached for the telephone.

"Hello?" Claude Ammons said into the phone. "Is this 9-1-1? Er, uh—I'd like to report an automobile accident . . . Yeah, that's right . . . Just one person. Um-hmmm. The driver was killed."

Claude hung up the phone, picked up his bags, and left through the back. He scanned the alley. Spike had indeed become invisible, along with all of Claude's pawnable belongings. "Shit," Claude said, trying to muster some anger, but could only manage a feeble "Whafuck." Driver's money was in his pocket and he had always wanted to go to New Orleans.

He threw his bags in a nearby Dumpster. He turned down the alley, pulling his collar up against the wind, though the sun seemed to be taking some of the chill out of the air. He was whistling by the time he reached the street, and he was gone by the time the first faint sounds of a siren drifted down the alley.

"You d'Man! GETCHA SOME!" the junkie hooted, laughing, as a particularly cherry Chevy rolled by on East Erie. Though Prentice Tyrell would get careless and OD by Labor Day, that summer in the bottoms seemed the most pleasant in memory. The dope was good and plentiful. The street people were amiable, mothers sat on their landings with their babies and the old men walked down to the HEW Senior Center to play dominoes. No one was found eaten. The weather was moderate and for once the wind blew the stink from the river back uptown.

JOE LANSDALE

Texan Joe Lansdale staked his claim in horror a few years ago when his story "Tight Little Stitches in a Dead Man's Back" won just about every award for fiction around. The story established the young writer as a heavyweight in both horror and mystery. Every year since, Joe has been acknowledged by critics and committees alike for his relentless brand of prose, which typically begins with an easygoing, aw-shucks kind of feel, and ends with readers gripping the pages in mortal dread.

But Joe also has a soft, mushy side coupled with a great sense of whimsy. His story that follows is one of our favorites, an odd sort of tale about growing up, and how the pain of adolescence is truly universal.

Bob the Dinosaur Goes to Disneyland

by Joe Lansdale

(For Jeff Banks)

For a birthday present, Fred's wife, Karen, bought him a plastic, inflatable dinosaur—a Tyrannosaurus Rex. It was in a cardboard box, and Fred thanked her and took the dinosaur downstairs to his study and took it out of the box and spent twenty minutes taking deep breaths and blowing air into it.

When the dinosaur was inflated, he set it in front of his bookshelves, and, as a joke, got a mouse ear hat he had bought at Disneyland three years before, and put it on the dinosaur's head and named it Bob.

Immediately, Bob wanted to go to Disneyland. There was no snuffing the ambition. He talked about it night and day, and it got so the study was no place to visit, because Bob would become most unpleasant on the matter. He scrounged around downstairs at night, pacing the floor, singing the Mouseketeer theme loud and long, waking up Fred and Karen, and when Fred would come downstairs to reason with Bob, Bob wouldn't listen. He wouldn't have a minute's worth of it. No, sir, he by golly wanted to go to Disneyland.

Fred said to Karen, "You should have bought me a Brontosaurus, or maybe a Stegosaurus. I have a feeling they'd have been easier to reason with."

Bob kept it up night and day. "Disneyland, Disneyland. I want to go to Disneyland. I want to see Mickey. I want to see Donald." It was like some kind of mantra, Bob said it so much. He even found some old brochures on Disneyland that Fred had stored in his closet, and Bob spread those out on the floor and lay down near them and looked at the pictures and wagged his great tail and looked wistful.

"Disneyland," he would whisper. "I want to go to Disneyland."

And when he wasn't talking about it, he was mooning. He'd come up to breakfast and sit in two chairs at the table and stare blankly into the syrup on his pancakes, possibly visualizing the Matterhorn ride or Sleeping Beauty's castle. It got so it was a painful thing to see. And Bob got mean. He chased the neighbor's dogs and tore open garbage sacks and fought with the kids on the bus and argued with his teachers and took up slovenly habits, like throwing his used Kleenex on the floor of the study. There was no living with that dinosaur.

Finally, Fred had had enough, and one morning at breakfast, while Bob was staring into his pancakes, moving his fork through them lazily, but not really trying to eat them (and Fred had noticed that Bob had lost weight and looked as if he needed air), Fred said, "Bob, we've decided that you may go to Disneyland."

"What?" Bob said, jerking his head up so fast his mouse hat flew off and his fork scraped across his plate with a sound like a fingernail on a blackboard. "Really?"

"Yes, but you must wait until school is out for the summer, and you really have to act better."

"Oh, I will, I will," Bob said.

Well now, Bob was one happy dinosaur. He quit throwing Kleenex down and bothering the dogs and the kids on the bus and his teachers, and in fact, he became a model citizen. His school grades even picked up.

Finally, the big day came, and Fred and Karen bought Bob a suit of clothes and a nice John Deere cap, but Bob would have nothing to do with the new duds. He wore his mouse ear hat and a sweatshirt he had bought at Goodwill with a faded picture of Mickey Mouse on it with the word Disneyland inscribed above it. He even insisted on carrying a battered Disney lunchbox he had picked up at the Salvation Army, but other than that, he was very cooperative.

Fred gave Bob plenty of money and Karen gave him some tips on how to eat a balanced meal daily, and then they drove him to the airport in the back of the pickup. Bob was so excited he could hardly sit still in the airport lounge, and when his seat section was called, he gave Bob and Karen quick kisses and pushed in front of an old lady and darted onto the plane.

As the plane lifted into the sky, heading for California and Disneyland, Karen said, "He's so happy. Do you think he'll be all right by himself?"

"He's very mature," Fred said. "He has his hotel arrangements, plenty of money, a snack in his lunchbox, and lots of common sense. He'll be all right."

At the end of the week, when it was time for Bob to return, Fred and Karen were not available to pick him up at the airport. They made arrangements with their next-door neighbor Sally to do the job for them. When they got home, they could hear Bob playing the stereo in the study, and they went down to see him.

The music was loud and heavy metal and Bob had never listened to that sort of thing before. The room smelled of smoke, and not cigarettes. Bob was lying on the floor reading, and at first, Fred and Karen thought it was the Disney brochures, but then they saw those wadded up in the trash can by the door.

Bob was looking at a girlie magazine and a reefer was hanging out of his mouth. Fred looked at Karen and Karen was clearly shaken.

"Bob?" Fred said.

"Yeah," Bob said without looking up from the foldout, and his tone was surly.

"Did you enjoy Disneyland?"

Bob carefully took the reefer out of his mouth and thumped ash on the carpet. There was the faintest impression of tears in his eyes. He stood up and tossed the reefer down and ground it into the carpet with his foot.

"Did . . . did you see Mickey Mouse?" Karen asked.

"Shit," Bob said, "there isn't any goddam mouse. It's just some guy in a suit. The same with the duck." And with that, Bob stalked into the bathroom and slammed the door and they couldn't get him out of there for the rest of the day.

LAWRENCE PERSON

An editor and small-press publisher, Lawrence Person has a wide range of experience to bring to one of the most difficult formats in writing: the short short. Lawrence not only succeeds but excels in this compact, powerful piece about the dread possibilities of the future.

Salvation
by Lawrence Person

In Dublin, One almost got away.

He was halfway out the door when they caught Him, the spikes cast aside, His wounds already healed. It took five strong men to hold Him to the cross while the others drove the nails back in.

I know how hard it must have been. I had cross-watch duty at our church (St. Luke's) last Friday when Ours awoke and I had to hammer back the spikes. I'll never forget the look of betrayal on His face, the blood from His crown of thorns trickling down into His accusing eyes. He turned back to wood that way, still facing me.

He didn't stop bleeding.

We've grown used to the blood, all of us. When the crisis first started, we had to dump the buckets once a week. Now we have to do it twice a day, and soon we'll be doing it every hour.

But the worst time was when He came alive Sunday morning, while Minister Farley was reading from John. It took Him almost a half hour to turn back, the sound of the hammers and His screams drowning out the sermon. The congregation had left as fast as they could, their eyes wide with terror and shock.

I pray every night, and when I pray I think about the look in His eyes. I pray desperately for guidance, for a sign that I'm doing the right thing, that I'm still worthy of salvation. And yet I still feel the fear, the cold uncertainty that grips my every waking hour.

But we dare not stop now. I saw pictures of the congregation of St. Jude, the one who let Him escape, the blood oozing from the wounds that appeared in their hands and legs. I saw their faces twisted in pain from the stigmata, their eyes blinded with blood from their invisible crown of thorns, and knew what we had to do.

And so I watch when I have to watch, and nail when I have to nail.

And pray.

In fact, I pray now more than ever, four or five hours every night. I pray fervently that Our Lord's bleeding would stop, and that neither I nor anyone else would have to see those accusing eyes, or drive in those nails, ever again. And most of all, I pray that there is still salvation, that mankind has not filled our world with so much blood that even the infinite mercy of Our Savior can no longer contain it all.

And still the words of Luke 23:34 haunt me, for though those Roman soldiers may not have known what they were doing, dear God, *we* most certainly do.

Psychos

For me, the word "psychos" sums up the last half of this century. The spikes on the graph of recent history are largely assassins, weirdos, and mass murderers—Oswald, Ray, Sirhan Sirhan, Richard Speck, Charles Manson, John Wayne Gacy, Mark David Chapman, Hinckley—you catch the drift. The bad guys have all the flash, and for every Edison there are a dozen Ted Bundys. The good that men do seems to change and evolve as technology does, but the lineage of psychotic behavior has survived unaltered throughout history. A heritage of brutality, cruelty, murder, mutilation: man against man, man against many, man against animal. We seem to be the only species who truly goes crazy without benefit of disease or a sharp blow to the head. As the data accumulates, a picture starts to come into focus. These are individuals whose brains are a couple table-spoons off the original recipe. Low blood salt, high blood sugar, a few crippled segments in the old DNA strand.

The scary thing is, there is no telling who these people are and when they're going to erupt. They are indistinguishable from the rest of us (and I'm not so sure about you). They eat, they sleep, they work, they have pets, shop at the corner market, and mow the grass on weekends—until one day when the frayed binding holding it all together finally snaps. You can only hope you're somewhere else when it happens.

—J.H.

NANCY COLLINS

In the last two years, Nancy Collins has become a significant force in the field of horror. Her debut novel, *Sunglasses After Dark*, not only won first novel honors from Horror Writers of America, but seemed to single-handedly catalyze a renaissance in vampire literature. *Sunglasses After Dark* is a bold renovation of vampire mythology, moving the setting from Gothic camp to urban punk, and spawning a host of imitators. What other writers cannot capture is her blowtorch prose and the deadly accuracy of her observations.

Collins offers here a prime example of the wit and imagination that makes hers a singular talent.

Rant
by Nancy Collins

THEY will never understand. THEY will see my actions from the outside; sitting in their breakfast nooks, yawning over their newspapers, wrapped in floral pink housecoats, fake dead animals on their feet and frozen orange juice cans wrapped in their tinted hair. Stupid cows.

THEY dare to judge me—me!—the savior of their petty, useless, pitiful lives!—and revile me as a monster! Just like THEY did Hitler, Manson, Torquemada, and King Herod! THEY will pass judgment on me and dismiss me from their memories by the time THEY reach the funny papers. But I will not strike them down for that. I am a merciful god. I will not reach out and swat them like the flies they are. I shall bear my cross as my elder brother did before me. No one understood his actions, either.

I will bide my time until I decide it is right. Then I will shed my mortal guise as a lizard does its skin and stand revealed, horrible in my wrath. My face will split, the glory of my divine beauty bursting forth, and their eyes will melt in their sockets. No handcuffs will hold me. I will have too many hands. No jail will contain me. I will be bigger than the Sears Tower. THEY will scream and point at me, cowering like extras in a Godzilla film. I will crush a hundred with each step. I will drown whole suburbs in a scalding baptism of piss. When I walk the world will tremble and all living things will bow down before me and sing my praises or I will destroy them with a single glance. But not yet. Not yet.

I will wait and play their games. I will look at their inkblots and talk about my mother. It will do them no good. My motives are beyond their understanding. THEY will find long Latin words to describe what their hobbled minds perceive as the method of my ''madness.'' I will not lie. I will not deceive them, although it would be pathetically easy to do so. I will tell them the Truth. THEY will hear my words but their brains will not comprehend what I say. THEY have been programmed from birth to believe what the International Jewish Conspiracy wants them to. THEY see the Truth every day and their Conspiracy-conditioned logic circuits edit out all reference to ''forbidden knowledge.''

When I finally elect to reveal myself to the masses, the scales will drop from their eyes and the synaptic blockades will collapse and centuries of Truth will flood their grey matter. THEY will realize that THEY were played for dupes, sold into slavery by the filthy, scheming Jews who killed my brother and tried to divert the wrath of the righteous by spreading the Lie that he was born of a Jewess. THEY took all the evidence that he was an Aryan, born of a White mother, and sealed it in the Ark of the Covenant along with the *real* Ten Commandments; the ones that say *None Shall Suffer A Jew To Live* and that fornication between the races is an

Abomination in the eyes of the Lord. The Truth shall set them *free! I* will set them free! And the gutters shall run with the blood of the money-lenders and the sky will once more grow black with their ashes!

I'm getting ahead of myself. How is it that I, the Second Coming, the Messiah Reborn, am in prison, watched by cold-eyed Jews in white coats? I was protecting myself from the Anti-Christ, that's all.

I wasn't born aware of my godhood. Now that I look back on my early years, the signs were everywhere for my childish eyes to see. But I was still too young to grasp their implications. I did not understand how impossible it was for two squat, swarthy trolls to produce a tall, fair-skinned boy. I never felt comfortable with my "parents," and when my "father" took to beating me, I realized I wasn't their natural son. I was adopted. I first became suspicious when THEY destroyed my collection of World War Two comics, claiming THEY were saving me from brainrot. The cow that claimed to be my "mother" said I was morbid. That I had unhealthy interests. When THEY found the cache of clippings about the so-called Nazi "War Crimes" I'd culled from various men's magazines, the man who called himself my "father" beat me until I bled.

While I was unconscious I had a vision. It revealed to me the exact nature of my conception and birth. My mother was a beautiful, Aryan virgin with long blond hair and blue eyes. My father was God. But not the fierce, storm-eyed God of the Old Testament. He was far older and much weaker now. The Jews and their master, Satan, have made great progress since the Second World War, wringing sympathy from bleeding-heart dupes of the Conspiracy by convincing the world that six million Jews were exterminated in the camps. God is now a senile old deity who drools in His beard. He is disgusting to watch and really quite pathetic. The first thing I will do after revealing myself to the multitudes is depose the old fool. I will banish Him to a suitable limbo. I won't kill Him, like Jupiter did Saturn, although that would be the prudent thing to do. But, after all, He *is* my father.

Anyway, my Divine Father had become forgetful and after I was born I was stolen from my real mother by Jews, who placed me amongst their own to raise, hoping I would remain ignorant of my birthright. Ultimately, THEY failed and I came to manhood aware that I was the Second Coming foretold in the Book of Revelations.

My older brother made the mistake of trying for the hearts and minds of the cows by becoming mortal. He told the parables, performed low-key, tasteful miracles, and ended up nailed to a stick for his troubles. I know better than to follow in his stigmatized footsteps. Benevolence, humanitarianism, and tolerance are the tools of the Conspiracy. THEY mollycoddle the cows into believing that the Lord doesn't mind what you do as long as you keep it to yourself. When I ascend to my rightful inheritance, I will be a god washed in blood and tempered by fire. The Righteous shall be spared while the Communist Jew Humanist Slut Whore Niggers erupt into flame, their skins crackling like bacon in the pan!

Soft words do not work. The only way to get a cow's attention is to goose it with a cattle prod. My brother tried it before me and failed. I shall not fail. My success is secured.

The Anti-Christ. I must tell you about the Anti-Christ!

The Jew bastards were upset when I saw through their mind games. THEY were unprepared for the immensity of my intellect. THEY are crafty, I'll give them that. Seeing that I would one day ascend to my father's throne, THEY got to work creating their Anti-Christ.

I have known for years what THEY were planning, but I was uncertain as to where to begin my search. The Holy Land? Hyperborea? Des Moines? The possibilities were endless. I used my X-ray vision, scanning the bellies of all the pregnant women on the street. I knew that their Anti-Virgin would be a Jewess, but THEY might use cosmetic surgery on her nose and bleach her hair to throw me off the track. As much as it disgusted me, I stared into the pelvic cradles of thousands of lumbering, milk-laden cows, seeking my ancient enemy. I knew my future would be in doubt for as long as the Anti-Christ lived. It took me three years, but at last I found the Beast!

I was at a McDonald's, toying with the idea of turning my strawberry shake into wine, when a grossly pregnant woman waddled past with a Filet-O-Fish and a large order of fries. She wore a bright pink sweatshirt and matching running pants. Across her bloated belly was printed BABY. An arrow stabbed her uterus.

Out of habit, I turned on my X-ray vision and followed the arrow, peering into the red darkness of her womb. There, curled in its cage of bone and flesh like a hibernating toad, was my adversary. The Beast. The Anti-Christ. The Son of Satan. The King of the Jews.

Its head was bulbous, the flesh a sickly white. It had no nose, only fleshless slits set under two sunken jaundiced eyes. Its mouth was lipless and full of tiny, needle-sharp teeth. The mouth of a moray eel. And it was grinning at me! I could make out the fabled "666," the Mark of the Beast, traced in fire on the corpse-pale expanse of its bulging forehead. Its body was folded under the malformed head like a Japanese lantern. The arms were long, like those of an ape, and its tiny hands were complete with yellowed talons. Its legs were the crooked, hairy shanks of an infant goat. I was revolted by the glimpse of unnaturally large genitals. I noticed the Abomination sported an erection. I nearly gagged on my strawberry shake.

I knew the unholy fetus was aware that I had recognized it. And it was laughing at me from within the Anti-Virgin's unhallowed womb. I felt hate and fear boil inside me and the voices of the Archangels—broadcast from their secret staging base within the Hollow Earth—raged in my head. By the time Satan's whore finished her meal I had decided on my course of action.

I followed her home.

She lived in one of those bland, pasteurized suburban mushroom colonies the Conspiracy-controlled lies of the television and radio have conditioned the cows to want. Let them numb their minds with useless consumer goods. *Let* the cows sate themselves with split-level ranches, wall-to-wall shag, microwaves, Jacuzzis, food processors, and remote-control VCRs! THEY have pulled the wool over their own eyes, blinding themselves with animal comfort, ignoring the signs traced in fire and ice, semen and blood that I Have Come and their time is at hand!

I wandered the neighborhood, making sure I would be able to locate the Anti-Manger after dark. I had little doubt that the Anti-Christ Child's aura would be a beacon, even without my infrared vision. But it doesn't hurt to make sure. All those clapboard hellholes look alike, especially at night. Just like the soul-less cows who live in them.

I had a couple of bad minutes waiting for the bus to take me back to the city. I was certain the Men In Black, the Conspiracy's elite secret police, were watching me. I have never been able to really *see* them. THEY manifest themselves as the dark flickerings at the corners of my eyes. Just when I turn my head to try to get a better look at them—they're gone. I pretended not to notice them and began reciting the Lord's Prayer under my breath. THEY hate that and usually don't hang around to hear me finish.

I rode home on the bus, contemplating my next move. I hate city buses. Hate the smelly old crones in their faded shifts, hairy warts sprouting from their chins. Hate their flaccid lips, their liver-spotted talons wrapped around the handles of ancient shopping bags overflowing with meaningless Conspiracy-approved junk. Just like their huge, overinflated bosoms.

I hate the niggers, especially the slut drug addict mothers with their gaggle of pickaninny bastards who go out to the malls and let their little Tyrones and LaTonyas run wild, just like fucking animals. Bad enough THEY chased the Whites out of the city, now they're spilling into the suburbs. Dragging everything down to their level.

I hate the giggling, pimply-faced little teenaged girls who ride the bus because their daddys won't let them drive the 280Z. THEY sit in clumps like heifers, giggling at me when THEY think I'm not looking because of my hair, my clothes, my complexion, the tape on my glasses. I try to ignore them, shut out the smell of their Baby Soft body perfume, the sound of their caged-bird twittering, the sight of their pert young breasts straining against their blouses, their rounded buttocks sheathed in skintight designer jeans. I know that soon—oh, so *very* soon—I shall stand Revealed and all the high school princesses and prick teasers in the world will be mine. THEY will flock to me, fighting like cats in heat for the privilege of tasting my sperm. Even though my mighty penis shall disembowel them like pigs in a slaughterhouse, still they will writhe and yowl in delight and beg for more!

I felt safe at home. I knew the Men In Black could not see me once I entered my room. I disappeared from their demonic radar as soon as I set foot inside the door. That was because I papered the walls of my room with pages torn from the Bible. But not *all* the Bible. The Old Testament is useless trash, nothing more than Jew propaganda. The New Testament has been tampered with and is untrustworthy. No, I papered my apartment with pages torn from a hundred Bibles; King James, New King James, Revised Standard, St. Joseph's Edition, The Good News for Modern Man . . . Pages torn from the Book of Revelations.

I prayed for two hours, scourging myself with the cord from a steam iron whenever visions of designer jeans intruded on my devotions. My earlier anxiety had passed, leaving a confidence that glowed like a hot coal. My Father was with me. I had nothing to fear. I felt the mantle of my power crackling about my shoulders and sparking from my fingertips. I was eager to go forth and slay my enemy. Still, it could prove fatal to be overconfident. I was going up against Satan, the Anti-Christ, and the International Jewish Conspiracy, not a gang of lunchroom toughs.

It was dark when I left. I caught the last bus out to the suburbs. It was empty, for once. I was pleased. I did not need any further distractions from my holy mission.

I found the neighborhood easily enough. I needn't have worried. The Anti-Christ's aura spilled from the windows, an infernal lamplight the color of a ripe bruise. I hunkered in the shrubbery, watching the sickly purple-black glow flit from room to room. It would be a long wait, but I couldn't leave even if I wanted to. I was caught up in the machinery of Destiny. I had taken the first step toward godhead and there was no turning back.

The bruise-light finally moved into what my X-ray vision revealed to be the bedroom. I followed the side of the house, keeping in shadow. I found the window I was looking for. I polarized my magnetic field, the energy leaping from my fingertips in a shower of emerald sparks, and the window latch sprang open silently.

I started creepy-crawling back in high school. I enjoyed walking through houses while the owners were away, looking through their private lives. Secrets were laid bare to my all-seeing eyes. The gin bottles hidden in the Greers' planter. The bundle of magazines featuring nude boys squirreled away in Reverend Sanderson's study. The diverse collection of sex toys in Widow Maynard's dresser. It was like being God. I saw it as a form of on-the-job training. Then, during my senior year, I began creepy-crawling while the owners were home, asleep in their beds of sin.

I eased up the window, levering myself over the sill and slithering into the house on my belly and elbows. Creepy-crawl. Wall-to-wall shag brushed my stomach. Creepy-crawl. Energy coursed through me. I felt it building up in the pit of my stomach and radiating throughout my body. When I exhaled a fine mist of golden light escaped from my nostrils. My hair stood on end, sparks snapping from every follicle. As my fingers closed on the doorknob, tiny lightning bolts the color of blood shot from my palm. My skin felt impossibly tight, as if barely able to contain my divinity. The bruise-light oozed from under the door frame and washed my face in its unholy glow as I opened the door.

I saw the king-size bed and the two figures curled within the covers. I had not expected a husband. For a heartbeat I was confronted by my own doubt, tempted by Satan to entertain the possibility I had made a mistake. The sickly, unwarming light pulled me back to Reality. I knew then how my older brother must have felt, standing on the mountaintop while the Father of Jews whispered in his ears. I was sweating and trembling like a man in the grip of malaria. I had to get it over with before my resolve weakened and I fled.

Ghosting along the edge of the mattress, I reached out and touched the bedside lamp. Heavenly choirs sang in my ears, urging me onward to my destiny. One hundred watts lit the bedroom and the dark blots that swam before my eyes had the wings of bats.

The Anti-Joseph started awake as if doused with water. His eyelids flew open, the eyeballs jerking about wildly in their sockets. He saw me standing next to the bed and the fear that radiated from him was the sweetest thing I have ever known. The Anti-Virgin mumbled something from inside her blankets and was still.

The Anti-Joseph gained his footing, his sleep-stupid face

showing fright and anger. I stepped back, uncertain as to whether he was mortal or some form of incubus watchdog in charge of protecting the unborn Anti-Christ. The bald spot and junior executive's paunch hanging over the waistband of his underwear looked human enough, but you can't be too sure about these things.

He made a clumsy lunge for the nightstand, clawing at the drawer. The heavy blade of my machete bit through his wrist and tasted the wood underneath. The Anti-Joseph recoiled so fast it was like running a film backward. His right hand remained on the nightstand.

He stood holding the stump of his wrist before his horrified eyes, his left hand clamped around the severed ganglia. The blood was redder than the heart of the sun. Each beat of his heart covered the eggshell-white walls in ideograms proclaiming my divinity. Shock glazed his eyes and he collapsed onto the wall-to-wall shag. Satan had erred in his choice of a guardian for his heir apparent.

I kicked the body to make sure the Anti-Joseph wasn't feigning unconsciousness. He rolled onto his back, as slack as an oversize bag of suet. His skin was white, bordering on blue, and his eyelids fluttered in shock. The eyeballs, rolled back in their sockets, were bloodless. I tugged at the waistband of his shorts and pulled the soiled underwear down around his knees.

Even though he had not shown the strength and wiliness of an incubus, I couldn't take a chance. I'd seen those movies where the heroes turn their backs on supposedly "dead" vampires and werewolves.

The Anti-Joseph shuddered once when the machete sliced off his penis. Like all servants of the Lord of Hell, he was circumcised. I thrust my fingers between the dying Jew's blue lips and pried open his jaws. There was something close to sentience flickering in his eyes, but it fled when I stuffed the slippery wet redness of his sex into his mouth. He died with his own blood and semen pooling in his lungs, all hopes of resurrection crushed.

The Anti-Virgin was sitting up in bed, flattened against the headboard. Her eyes were huge and mouth a wide, trembling O. Her swollen belly was crisscrossed with pale blue veins. A roadmap to Hell. She stared at her false husband as he died on the floor. Her thin, tight screams were ultrasonic, the frantic shrieks of a bat. I wasn't fooled by her display. I knew who the *real* husband was. I knew who'd fathered the Beast inside her. In my mind's eye I saw her offering her loathsome, hairy sex to the Black Goat of the Wood. I saw his mammoth, foreskin-less member, engorged with venom. Whore. Whore of Babylon.

She scuttled off the bed as I moved for her, her eyes never leaving me. Her mouth moved spasmodically, but no sound came out. One hand was raised in a feeble attempt to blot me out of her world. She was crying, the tears streaming down her face. The tears of a witch. If I licked the tears from her face I would taste no salt. But I had no need for such crude witchfinding, I already knew *who* and *what* she was. She was working a spell, attempting to conjure forth her lover's minions. Had to work fast. Not much time. Had an erection. Her work. Devil's work. Had to stop her. Stop the Anti-Virgin.

My fist slammed into her mouth and I felt teeth shatter and abrade my knuckles. It was wet and red and warm. She fell, and I heard her cry out for the first and last time.

"My baby!"

I stood over her, staring at her pale face and blood-smeared mouth. Painted mouth. Whore of Babylon. Red laughing mouths. Designer jeans. Floral print housecoats. I saw the Anti-Christ struggling within his mother's pelvic cage, shrieking the foulest obscenities. His tongue was forked and covered with fur. The pale loop of the umbilical cord had become a hangman's noose, throttling the unborn demon as he clawed at the pink walls of his uterine prison. I began to laugh.

The machete had undergone a miraculous transformation. It was a burning sword. Not surprising, considering it was forged from a sliver of the original Sword of Righteousness my Father used to chase those ingrates from the Garden. It sent shock waves of ice-cold heat up my arm and into my brain.

She screamed when I slit her open, totally ruining the moment. Her scream jarred against the bones of my inner ear like a dentist's drill bit, rattling my teeth in their moorings. Bitch. Cow. Purple-pink entrails unraveled onto the carpet like party streamers. The odor of bile was strong. The Anti-Virgin stared up at me, still alive and conscious. Even though she was beyond speaking, I knew she was asking "why." As if *I* had to justify my actions to the whore of the Prince of Lies! I was disappointed. It had been too easy. Satan's wife was just another cow, ignorant of the malignancy she carried in her womb.

In answer to her silent plea, I reached into her and pulled out my nemesis.

The thing I removed from the Anti-Virgin's belly was not what I had expected. Gone were the horns, the crooked shanks and pinioned wings. What I held in my hands did not look very human, but neither did it resemble the Abomination I had glimpsed earlier.

Tiny matchstick legs jerked in feeble protest and something inside its brittle rib cage shuddered. It was soft and squishy, like an octopus, with rubber bones and skin as translucent as rice paper. The eyes bulged in the oversize head and opened wide enough for me to glimpse colorless irises and a dark-adapted pupil. I was overwhelmed by a desire to hurl the half-formed thing against the wall. I had been cheated.

The Host spoke unto me then, their crystalline voices melding into one. The Host told me I was being deceived. My faith was being tested to its utmost. To turn back now would extinguish all hope of achieving my divine inheritance. I had to prove that I was stronger than my rival. I had to take his dark power and make it mine.

I looked into the Anti-Virgin's dumb, uncomprehending eyes as she died. I knew that she would take what she saw to Hell. It made me feel better knowing that.

I was reminded of a poster I used to have as a kid, before my so-called "father" found it and tore it to shreds. It was called *Satan Devouring His Children*.

It was a lot like veal.

THEY tell me I was apprehended walking down the street, laughing and crying at the top of my lungs and that it took six policemen to subdue me. I really don't remember.

THEY've kept me in this damn straightjacket ever since I was arrested. THEY don't even take it off during mealtimes. A burly orderly—a flunky working for the Conspiracy—feeds me spaghetti with a plastic spoon.

When THEY aren't asking me questions, I'm left alone in a room without windows or furniture. It doesn't matter, since I can sleep on the heavy padding as easily as I could on a bed.

I have endured these indignities because I must marshal my energies for the Transfiguration. The time is near. Very near. I can feel my musculature restructuring under cover of the canvas. Soon I will burst my restraints like a butterfly its cocoon and the Archangels shall emerge from their secret staging bases deep inside the Hollow Earth and drive their flaming UFO chariots across the night sky.

Rebirth—like birth—is a painful process. I was not aware just how agonizing it would be. My teeth ache constantly, especially the canines. My eyes feel hot and dry and it's a struggle simply to blink. My spine feels like it's turning into a question mark. Sometimes I suffer immense, painful erections that threaten to tear the seams of my pants.

I have been visited by the Host on at least two occasions, its multitude of voices begging me to have patience and wait out the Transfiguration. I shall bear my agony in silence, as befits a god on earth. But even a god incarnate has moments of doubt, and this is one of them. The pain that attends the discarding of my mortal form has weakened me.

I've begun to wonder if I was mistaken, after all. Not about the unborn thing being my nemesis. Of that I'm certain. But maybe . . . just maybe, mind you . . . I got my wires crossed concerning my origins . . . about who, or what, my Father *really* is . . .

I wish I had something to drink. The fur on my tongue tickles something awful.

K. W. JETER

Along with John Shirley, K.W. Jeter is one of horror's best-kept secrets—something we aim to change. Jeter first won an audience with his now-classic novel *Dr. Adder*, and received further acclaim in England with several subsequent novels. Jeter is finally coming into his own here in the U.S. with his smashing novel *In the Land of the Dead*, and debuted in *Midnight Graffiti* with the following story, a terse psychological tale of quiet desperation.

Blue on One End, Yellow on the Other

by K.W. Jeter

Drinking was good. Drinking was good because it allowed him to fine-tune the process, to stretch out the delicious, scary, on-edge moment, to play with it as though it were some infinitely elastic substance, thinning from a rope to a cord to a string to a thread . . . the words danced in a happy nonsense song inside his skull . . . to a line of atoms, one right after another . . .

Until the elastic string, the delicious moment snapped. That was the whole game: to see how far he could stretch it, without it snapping. Without screwing up. Without going over the edge. He most definitely did *not* want to screw up. Not again, not another time. That part was no fun at all.

He sat at the bar, rolling the capsule with the tip of his finger across the scarred and cigarette-burnt wood grain. (*Very* interesting wood grain; he'd looked at it, times before, long and hard enough to read the microscopic words hidden there.) He had to be careful about that, too. If he pushed down on the capsule too hard, it could split and break open, the bitter white powder spilling out. Which was uncool, as everyone would be able to see him and watch him scraping up the powder and sucking it off the end of his finger. They all knew already, all of them, the bartender working the beer taps and eyeing him, the other customers scattered around, with their sneaky gazes tapping at his spine . . . They all knew, but he wasn't supposed to fuck up and be *obvious* about it. That was part of the game, too. So he pressed down on the capsule just hard enough, just light enough, rolling it away from him, avoiding the wet circles where he'd set his own glass down, then drawing it back the same way.

With his other hand, he raised his glass and took a sip. He could, if he wanted to, pick up the cap between his thumb and forefinger and set it gently on his tongue, and wash it down, the little bullet sliding down his throat. He was in a position to do that: glass with beer, warm and flat, in one hand, the outstretched finger of his other hand pinning the capsule down on the bar. He looked at himself in the mirror behind the ranks of bottles. The reflections of his hands were hidden behind the stacked-up glasses, but he knew they were there. It'd be the smart thing to do; all he had to do was swallow the cap, and the world would be a safer place. And duller. That was the problem. If he swallowed it, the game would be over, at least until the morning. He might as well go home and let the grey wash of the TV rise over his head, a mumbling tide through which he would gaze up as though he were at the bottom of some luminous sea.

A glass squeaked as the bartender rubbed it with a towel. The bartender glanced up from the pink hands doing their work and looked at him sitting there; the hands went on smearing the damp cloth inside the glass. Behind him, out among the bar's tables, the other drinkers fell silent, sounding like birds then . . . like the silence of birds sitting on a wire overhead . . . he closed his own eyes and saw the telephone lines splitting a heat-shimmering sky, the small black shapes suspended there and watching him . . . a crushed insect, perfect down to the spines on its stiff paper legs, scrabbling in the clamp of a bird's beak, the silence of the others scanning the dust and road for their small prey . . .

He opened his eyes. He could see them in the mirror, just barely. But they were there, behind him; the shapes of birds, with their dark, glossy wings, claws gripping the glasses on the tables . . . their bead eyes staring at him with incalculable hate and appetite . . .

He had to bend down low over his own glass to hide the smile that was threatening to split his face open. You weren't supposed to—wherever you went—you weren't supposed to sit by yourself and let some big loony, shit-eating grin break out. That'd be like pinning the hospital commitment papers to your chest and walking around with them like a neon sign. But it really *was* funny: thinking about crows sitting around a table, nursing their beers. Heckle and Jeckyll Tie One On. They knew he was laughing about them, inside himself, and he could feel, without looking up at the mirror, their scowls growing more jagged and hateful.

That's what playing was all about. He watched his fingertip rolling the capsule back and forth a couple of inches. Sailing so close to the edge that you saw things like that—*really* saw them—things you'd never see otherwise. Things they didn't want you to see, that they gave you the caps for, so you wouldn't see them. He tilted his head back for another swallow, and let the beer uncoil, a benign liquid snake, inside his stomach.

When he'd been married . . . and weren't there a lot of stories that started out *that* way . . . ancient saga time, the other epic opening line being *When he'd been in the hospital*

. . . He took another swallow, down to the last half inch in the glass, and concentrated, working the little splinter of memory out of his waltzing brain.

When he'd still been married, and she'd come to see him at the hospital . . . *that* story . . . he'd had the idea in his head that he'd gotten it from her, the way you catch the flu from somebody else. As though it were a virus, something he'd tasted in her sweat or in some pink recess. A sexually transmitted disease, as it were. He hadn't told the doctors and therapists about that, because he didn't want them to take it away from him. The secret hope, that took a long time to die—the memory of it soured the beer in his stomach—was that when he got out they'd be together, he and his wife, in this new world all their own.

It hadn't worked out that way. That made him sad. He leaned his numbed face against the knuckles of one hand and watched the capsule being rolled back and forth on the bar. The capsule was two bright colors, blue and yellow, with the name of the pharmaceutical company in tiny white letters along the side. They must love their work, he figured, to paint their name on every little blue-and-yellow capsule that came rolling off the assembly line, painting on the letters with a one-hair brush, delicate as an eyelash . . . He bore them no ill-will; they just didn't know.

And it was too bad about his wife. It would've been fun. She would've thought the black birds at the table behind him were funny, with their ragged, water-dripping feathers and glitter-eyed malevolence. She had thought all sorts of things were funny . . . That had been the problem; he had to admit it.

The sound of a knife and something wet broke into his head, sending all the old memories flying. He looked up and saw the bartender cutting a lime into wedges, filling up the little plastic bin with the bright red cherries and all the other garnishes, skinned-raw little onions and the like. The bartender looked at him over the wet hands pressing down the knife's point, and he felt the hand of sudden panic grip his bowels.

What if—

(his brain had little rat feet that went scurrying around the walls of his skull, looking for any way out)

—it wasn't a bartender at all, but something *inside* a bartender, something that had crawled in there through a long slit in the back, that had pulled down the bartender head like a helmet, with *its* hands inside the fat bartender hands—

The eyes inside the bartender's head looked at him. *Her* eyes looked at him. And he was afraid.

He scooped the capsule off the bar and put it on his tongue. But his tongue was dry and his throat wouldn't work. They were all staring at him, the bartender and the rag-winged birds behind him, and he couldn't swallow. He knew it wasn't a good idea to take a mouthful from the beer glass—he'd just spew it out, and the capsule with it. He had to get away from them, away from the weight of their gaze, and quick before he strangled.

The barstool rocked and nearly toppled over as he stood up. Heart racing, but moving slowly so they wouldn't see that he was afraid (it'd be death, they'd fall on him if they knew), he squeezed past the tables and chairs. With the capsule on his swelling tongue, locking behind his gritting teeth.

Smart to leave the half-full beer glass on the bar! *They'd think he was coming back!* Already he'd fooled them—again!

He made it to the men's room, down a little hallway with a pay phone and a cigarette machine that had buckled and swayed around him. He collapsed against the wall, his palms smearing on the slick white tile. The whole room was white and smelled like disinfectant—it brought back memories.

Not safe yet. He fumbled behind himself and found the lock on the door, a simple little bolt to shove into the hole on the other side. When he'd done that, his spine relaxed and he could breathe. He could have swallowed, too, taking the capsule safely down into his stomach—but he didn't. He was safe here, he could play just a little while longer.

Rolling the cap around on the tip of his tongue, its little round end tapping against his teeth. Fuck those bastards out there, anyway—they knew that this was off-limits, neutral territory. And he had a lead on them; if they tried to follow him, to get in here, he had plenty of time, to swallow the cap and defeat them, reduce them to the dull, normal things they pretended to be.

He'd have to end the game soon, he knew. This was sailing too close to fucking up in a major way. And he didn't want that—it had gotten bad enough already. He didn't want to see Mister Bad Daddy again, or the Guy with the Red Wet Face, or the one he always called Throw Worm. He'd take a pass on *all* that shit. And especially on seeing *her* again—he super didn't want that.

All that beer he'd been drinking, through the long hours of the game—he stepped over to the urinal, pulling down the tag on his fly.

The white porcelain glistened, a baroque pearl, his own reflection glimpsed faintly on the luminous surface. And the chrome bits, the pipe and handle on top, the drain cover like a vented coin—he wanted to lay his forehead against the cold metal, and weep for their beauty.

A knot of anger tightened in his chest when he saw that somebody had run an X of masking tape across the urinal, with an OUT OF ORDER sign at its center. Those bastards.

He stood in front of the toilet bowl, tugging the zipper the rest of the way down, reaching inside. The capsule had started to grow slick on the tip of his tongue, the blue-and-yellow skin dissolving in his spit. He'd have to swallow it soon or taste the bitter powder as it leaked out.

Head tilted back, he opened his mouth, letting the capsule ride out into the air on the tip of his tongue. Then, suddenly, it wasn't there. The cap was gone, the tiny weight vanished, mystifying him until he heard a bell-like sound, the plink of the tiny object hitting the water.

Shit— He looked down in dismay and saw it, underneath the ripples spreading in rings across the bowl's surface. The cap was still drifting, blue end up, then the yellow, falling through the water. Frozen, he watched, until it came to rest on the porcelain's inner curve.

The cap hung on the lip of the dark, smooth-edged hole; the soft currents of the toilet bowl rocked it back and forth, teetering.

A shiver of apprehension crossed his shoulders as he knelt on the floor and reached in. The chill liquid soaked through his sleeve, wetting him to the elbow as he groped—cautiously—for the capsule.

His fingertips grazed the cap; it scooted out of his grasp, falling farther into the bowl's secret recesses.

Heartsick and afraid, he lowered the side of his face onto the bowl's rim. *I'm sorry*, he whispered inside his head—he had played the game too long, had stretched it past the breaking point, and now he didn't want to play anymore. All he wanted now was to get the cap, bring it up out of the depths, rinse it off in the sink, swallow it, and get out of here. To someplace—that other place—where he'd be safe.

The rim came up under his arm as he reached farther in. The porcelain had turned soft, swelling in time to his own breath. But still cold, and white, like long-dead flesh. He could feel the moist gullet at the bottom spread apart, accepting his hand, squeezing back down along his wrist.

Dancing in the blind water, the capsule eluded him, teasing

him to reach even farther. With his other hand, he braced himself against the tank above the bowl. The water came all the way up to his armpit now. He could hear its murmur and sigh close to his ear.

The capsule had to be just an inch away—a faint electric spark from its surface to his outstretched fingertips. Was it dissolving, leaking away the medicine inside? He wept, biting his lip, as his arm strained to its limit.

Miles away, right behind him, he heard scraping and flutterings at the restroom door. Something was trying to get in, to get at him—they knew he was helpless now. His other hand scraped its nails along the sweating tank. He didn't want to be found like this, to die this way.

The bowl's rim changed shape underneath his ribs, collapsing from a nearly round oval to a tapered ellipse. Then further, to a long, smooth-edged slit, the edges touching his arm. The slit narrowed, the porcelain lips squeezing into his biceps. Below, where he could no longer see his forearm, the water had warmed and thickened, sealing itself tight to his skin.

Come on, you bastard— He moaned, sweat oozing over his face, fingers straining forward in the pipe under the floor. A fingernail grazed the melting skin of the capsule.

Behind him, the things outside the door were battering at it now, their claws scraping and clashing, the beaks and wild staring eyes frenzied beyond control.

The pipe softened and closed around his arm, up to his elbow, closing and releasing a fraction of an inch, with a surging rhythmic contraction. He could feel the veined surface, blood trembling behind the membrane walls, the warmth growing to heat as the contractions sped up in time to his own pulse.

The restroom door started to splinter from the impact of the blows.

You fucker, you sonuvabitch— He wept, anger rolling up from his heart. The contractions shivered into his spine, a snake tightening and burning, blinding him.

He caught hold of something, his hand squeezing into a fist, the knuckles sliding against the soft walls. Not the capsule, but something bigger, that yielded as he hardened his grip. Its center pulsed, then exploded, down in the darkness hidden to him.

The same black explosion blossomed in his chest, snapping his ribs apart. Even as the door fell and the terrible faces rushed upon him, he fell into the darkness, knowing that he'd cheated them, and had been cheated himself, of everything.

He came to as they were loading him into the ambulance. The bad things had gone back into their hiding places—he couldn't see them anymore, for which he was grateful. Maybe they had given him a shot of something, one of the major tranquilizers, which worked even faster and better than the capsules did.

A paramedic with a coffee-colored, smiling face leaned over him. "Don't worry—you've just had yourself a little cardiac arrest. That's all. We're gonna take you someplace where they'll take good care of you."

The gurney's straps bound his arms close to his sides, but he didn't mind. It was nice to be an object again, in the care of others. Let *them* make all the decisions. He closed his eyes, enjoying the flying sensation as they lifted the gurney up. Somebody climbed in after him and pulled the doors closed.

He opened his eyes, looking around at the intricate fixtures. Asphalt rolled beneath the wheels; he could hear it. Behind the chrome and black rubber bits, everything was as white as the restroom's porcelain, the last thing he remembered from before.

His heart crawled under his throat. He was all the way inside now, he realized. Not just his arm. All of him.

The nurse turned around and looked at him with his ex-wife's face.

She smiled and already he felt the warm, soft walls closing in on him, wrapping him in their fierce, endless embrace.

PHIL TISO

Somewhere in the wilds of central California, Phil Tiso now resides. This gifted newcomer makes his professional debut with the following story.

The Domino Man

by Phil Tiso

His teeth are white and his boots are black like his skin. The whites of his eyes are very white, like his mood, but unlike his hood. He absconds with the earth and he eats a mouthful. He is the Domino Man and he says, ''Mmmm.''

The law wants him, like many women do. The Domino Man is a lover of women, and his rich smell is the smell of topsoil. Women love him and smell him and say, ''Mmmm.''

The sun forever favors the Domino Man, and her rays glance off his white teeth and his white eyes. His hood absorbs the warmth, and mingles it with his own. He walks down the road, kicking the dust skyward and headward. He breathes deep and he sighs, ''Mmmm.''

Last night, the geologists were digging in the dirt and the Domino Man forbade it. He told them that it was okay to dig in the dirt, but not with their shovels. He told them to use their hands and feel the dirt in the breaks between the fingers and to love it. They listened in the way that all people listen to the Domino Man. They cocked their heads skyward and looked at his shadow. He walked around and collected all of their proferred shovels and with his hands he buried them. He gave the corrupted earth back to the earth and he smiled. Then he absconded with the earth, and clocked down the road measuring his steps to the beat of the falling sirens.

He spends a week in the trees, and another on the bottom of a lake blowing conversation at the fish.

The police are not happy with the Domino Man. They drive on their roads and put up signs and read them to their partners. "Get the Domino Man," they say, "he is an outlaw."

The Domino Man sees one of these signs and laughs and throws dirt on it and goes up and dances on the high road. He decides to play the part of an outlaw.

He pulls a battered black hat over his hood, and puts on a longer black cloak. He tries an occasional grimace. He walks along the shoulder of the road, sticking his tongue out at the cars passing by. The men shriek in terror and pull their hair, but the women admire the Domino Man's figure and whistle to themselves and say, "Mmmm."

The Domino Man stands on the mountainside overlooking the police capital. Metalmen slinky down steps and chip up steps and fritter along paths and chainsaw out doors. Elevators plummet up and crash down into the earth. The occupants step up onto the metal patio, steel sparking steel into the metalbuiltbox office thing. Some come out, and the officebox, propelled by a hydraulic shaft, circles the patio hurriedly. It bounces up and down springing up on the tincan crushed metalmen that leave to go into police cars and look, search and seek and patrol for the Domino Man. The Domino Man laughs and dances on the mountainside. He whistles a little tune and sits down to watch the solid lava flow traffic of the conqueror beast. After a while, he tires and dances a slow, rhythmic step. He occasionally stops and throws dirt to the air. The metal eardrums hear the earth coming, granite boulders showing through the dark wave like teeth in a savoring smile. The Domino Man surveyed the mound of dirt over the fresh tomb and mumbled a little eulogy, "Mmmm."

The high road is full of excitement and determination. Police cars scrape the surface blue. Signs adorn the walkways and flip over and over in the sky. "Down with the Domino Man," they demand. Citizens are in a panic, because they never know when the wind will kick the Domino Man back into town. Even the women act as if they bend to the will of their men, but they don't really. Occasionally one might drift off into a daydream while at work, her workmate thinking her busy concentrating, only other women grasping the significance when her eyes cloud further and she mumbles, "Mmmm."

For a long while, nobody hears anything of the Domino Man, except the weekly reports of the policc, "We shall have him soon, soon now we shall have him." Not everyone believes this, and many still live in fear, cringing slightly whenever an unfamiliar voice laughs aloud.

The Domino Man has split town, but not for good. He decides that he will set up camp out in the plains, with his stolen earth. Drunken backpackers kick him awake during the night, and shower him with empty beer cans. He stands up and they recognize him, and look up at him the way that all men do. He tells them that they are certainly free to do what they want, and he throws dirt in their eyes. He kicks them all powerfully in their groins and then again in their buttocks. Their heads hit the dirt and the Domino Man dances on their backs. He smiles broadly, his white teeth chomping up and down, and sings. He strides off into the night.

One morning, the Domino Man awakens with a powerful thirst. He wanders through the forests and comes upon his favorite lake. He smiles down at the reflection of the sun, and he bends to take the water in his hand. He drinks and leans back. He feels not so nice as he should here in the sun, his thirst slaked. He scowls, unhappy with the bitter taste of the water. Laughter drifts across the lake, and the policemen there hoot and laugh and jump up and point at the Domino Man. They walk around the lake slowly, rolling the empty drum of poison in front of them. The Domino Man closes his eyes, and the approaching police continue to howl with their hysteria. They reach the Domino Man and they slap their cuffs on him. He passes out when the metal bands close on his deep brown wrists. The policemen slap themselves on the back and congratulate each other, saying that this wasn't too hard was it, and this Domino Man isn't so tough, is he?

The police-car radio informs the station that they have the Domino Man, and instantly the news leaks to the press. In a minute, everybody knows and the signs flip out into the sky, "We got him. We got the damned Domino Man!" It turns into a parade, and the men cheer when the Domino Man bumps his head getting out of the car. Small children laugh at his silly black clothing, and his white eyes.

The trial takes three days to set up and one hour to try the Domino Man.

"You are guilty of absconding with the earth." The judge tries his best to thunder, "How dare you abscond with that which rightly belongs to all the people?"

The Domino Man sneaks a handful of dirt, looks at the judge, and says, "Mmmm."

"I shall pass sentence on you now," the judge intones, passionately, he thinks. "Death by firing squad in the town coliseum today at noon. May God have mercy on your soul, and so forth."

The judge stands up and with, he thinks, a mighty swish of his robes he walks into his chambers directly behind the bench.

They put the Domino Man in the customary place, and open the doors to the colliseum. Hundreds of women swarm the doors, pounding the guards into unconsciousness, and rush down the seats and rows and aisles and such to reach the poor Domino Man.

"We'll save you," the closest croon into his black ears. "We know who you are."

Some women stand back and say, "Mmmm."

The police inform the commissioner and the commissioner informs the judge and the judge calls the president and the president turns on his viewer and sees his favorite wife helping untie the Domino Man's hands and he picks up the communication thing and yells into it, "Kill 'em, kill 'em all!"

The order is received immediately and the police open fire using their automatic weapons like long-handled scythes. They reap the harvest, and the floor of the coliseum is bloodier than it has ever been and the janitors grumble about that. The weapons reduce most anybody to blood, and they did that here, so it was impossible to tell who was a woman and who was the Domino Man, and none of the blood was any darker or any lighter than any other blood.

Well, the president decides that he has made a good call, and he orders the deaths of all the rest of the women. Most of the men say, "right on," except the janitors, who grumble, thinking of the mess. The police go and raze the traditional women hangouts.

The first place to go is the maternity ward.

Mmmm.

R. V. BRANHAM

Though R. V. Branham is still early in his career as a writer, he has already defined his own turf. His style is unconventional and demanding, and reflects a mind that knows the rules and structures of storytelling well enough to break them. He is imaginative and outlandish, conjuring images that are both frighteningly accurate and deeply disturbing. Branham seems to tap into a gestalt informing the nineties—raw, violent, whimsical, and demented. We have included two of his stories in this anthology, one light and one dark, both twisted.

The New Order: 3 Moral Fictions
by R. V. *Branham*

WIFE: "The sleep of reason produces monsters." Goya said that.
HUSBAND: Then marry Goya!
—Geraldine Chaplin & Harvey Keitel, "Welcome to L.A."

ONE: THE PROFESSIONAL
New York City

You crouch in the linen closet silently. You feel a certain remorse and a queasiness—like anyone else trapped in a lucrative but hateful job; like anyone who just drank six Coronas and ate three lamb's heart burritos. You imagine what you'd put down if your Field Super ever asked for a job description: "Bad alchemy . . . transmuting shit into gold."

You listen intently, waiting for the maternity nurse to finish her rounds. A jangle of keys signals her arrival. A belch rises in your throat, suddenly, so you take a pillowcase from a shelf to muffle it.

She draws closer. You have a thought, to say, image of her waddling down the linoleum-squared hall as her shoes, orthopedic, incessantly squeal. You time her. Fifteen secs. . . . Thirty. . . . Forty-five; a door opens, then shuts. The sound of breaking glass, then the door opening, then the nurse: "*Santo culo*. . . ."

You stop the timer. Shit, outta luck tonight. By the time the janitor's finished with the mess the graveyard shift nurse will be on. She's a wild card, and that worries you . . . since they never stick to schedule.

You take a deep breath, gag on the smell of musty linen and ammonia, and stifle a cough. It's awfully quiet out there. Should you take a chance and go ahead with the god-awful procedure, and risk having to retire half the night staff? You toss a coin, forgetting it's a two-tail dime you'd palmed from Div. Jesu Joy.

Tails it is. You lose, the luck of the draw, bad timing, inexorable fate, a real hand job. Cut the bathetic horseshit, you tell yourself. It's not you that's gonna lose it, just some poor little fucking bundle of joy.

You crack the door open, slowly. It squeaks anyway, but slowly. You wait a sec or fifteen hundred. Open it wider. No squeaks this time. Damn, almost forgot.

You switch on the portapak cryo, built into a briefcase, and proceed. Creeping through the hall, you manage to side-step the glass, a blood sample, by all appearances. You consider retrieving a piece to grind to fine powdered crystal, an old 'Nam trick, Operation Phoenix.

You pass a window that reveals the maternity ward and, sliding and jiggling a credit card against the catch, manage to open a side door.

You scan the room, seeing the beatific slumbering demiurges, some smiling the infant's idiot bliss. You take a Swiss Army knife from your pocket, set it on your tray.

Eenee. Meenee. Miney. Moe. You count off, settling on the two cribs nearest you. Without looking at them, cool pro that you are, you read their ID cards to determine sex . . . male . . . each one. You think of your mantra, a private mantra you'd never given to anyone, though offers have been made.

Fast finger stretches, then wham! you slam each palm between mouths and noses, smashing everything back up into their skulls. It goes well tonight; they flop briefly, noiselessly, plotz, and expire. You open the briefcase.

Using a scalpel, you peel the skull back, then you quickly slice the cerebellum in half, slashing to the corpus callosum and using the spoon from your Swiss Army knife to scoop out the gorgeous epiphysis, a.k.a. pineal gland. You toss it in the cryo.

Again using your scalpel, you remove scrotum and testes, also tossing them in the cryo. You're about to repeat the procedure on the second subject when the door opens and a big bad mama of a night nurse discovers this scene of horror. "Oh, my God. . . ." She is appalled.

An infant wakes up, crying. Then the pheromones go into action.

She advances on you, licking her lips, stretching her arms for a come-hither embrace. "I love you," she says, then tries a lunge. You dodge her and she crashes into several cribs, sends them skidding and colliding, waking up all the infants, all the darling babies, who, practicing their chops for the baby choir, aiming for C above high C, begin to yowl and scream and wail. She tries to get up, but her prosthetic leg comes off. "Fuck me," she begs you. "Beat me! Whip me!" The nurse advances, crawling, and grabs your leg, tears your pants cuff. You kick her away, then grab a chair and throw it at, through, and out the window. You leap out after it, using the briefcase as a shield. "Eat from my linoleum!" she screams, climaxing several times as you vanish around a corner.

You hate this crap, but heckshitgoshfuck, somebody's got to do the dirty work.

You hardly ever go out in the day; the last time you caused a gargantuan group grope, safe sex thrown to the wind, a daisychain from Sheridan Square to the midtown tunnel. Synergistic effects of homo sapien infant epiphysis and testes, ionized, centrifuged, spliced with reproductive protocols—a.k.a. pheromones—of bacteriophage, psychotropic spore, mammal, marsupial, reptile, insect, of flamingo and hammerhead shark, of Venus's-flytrap, a recombinance of phyla for a new genus, then finally freeze-dried for further utilization, make for lethal situations; and it has gotten worse . . . in spite of what Pauline said. She was with you, eleven months, four weeks, a day, ten hours, eleven minutes, and two seconds ago, the first time it happened; she had to use the licorice whip in her valise like a cunt to beat back the pet shop boys and manic macaws and febrile gerbils, huskies with hard-ons and crazed korats. . . . Pheromone-shit, she called it—apeshit cubed; contamination was rare, but for good. Powdered with garlic or oregano you can get about quickly with no worry of being gangbanged in every orifice, but if you stop for more than a moment you're in serious trouble. Your employers never see you. After a pheromone run you get the last LaGuardia-Logan shuttle, and then a cab across the dirty Charles to Cambridge, and then do your drop in a chute by a P-4 Lab. Pauline's Op—once; but now, Isao's. You wonder about him, after what Pauline'd said. Does he have letters, Polaroids? Just what is the furtive shit working on, if not pheromones? Is he still splicing *E. coli* to Simian Virus 40? And what is he doing at those bars? And what did Pauline see in him? It's hardly been a week and already you miss her.

What would she have said about that L.A. Zoo run, the way the coyotes tracked you to the flamingos, and, when you'd escaped, fucked them to death? You hear your mail carrier: Payroll sends that postcard with salt mines of Kansas on the front, and Lithuanian invective on the back. It tells you, in acrostics of course, what classified from what periodical to read for further instructions. A day later you get a disability check for $234,567.89, made out to a Mr. Vortex. That Sas, 's some sort of whimsical guy; wifey Pauline was some sort of whimsical gal. You'd metaphorically like to do him the way you literally did her, but somehow can't.

This time the periodical is *The Village Voice*; the advert within reads "THE NEW ORDER." The Avuncular Old Fart Of The Newsstand, wearing a "Duke Lives" T-shirt with a mug of John Wayne on it, is instantly smitten by you. Being less than one standard deviation from the norm, the Avuncular Old Fart is a rather macho sort with a taste for tampon strings. This changes when he goes pheromone-shit.

"How much?" you ask, holding up the *Voice*.

"It's free." The A.O.F. conspires to brush against you and rub your rhythm stick.

"How much," you say again.

". . . Doin' anything later," the A.O.F. says.

"Here's five." You hand him the five, wanting so desperately to leave.

"Please." The A.O.F. kneels. You find him trying to open your fly, fumble with your padlock. He tugs at it. You start to leave. The A.O.F. won't let go.

You try kicking the A.O.F. The old leather enema.

And the A.O.F. begs for more: "Fistfuck?"

You read the advert, then the *Washington* cartoon strip, and are about to shuck it away, when an advert, quarter page in size, attracts you. A cute Canadian seal pup appeals with wide eyes. You make a check out to the Greenpeace Foundation.

You rush to pick up your dry-cleaning. The Chinawoman makes goo goo eyes at you. You retrieve your jacket as quickly as possible, pay and leave.

An infant seal was clubbed to death to make the collar of your jacket.

In dreams you dream: you're a typical baby boy in a typical baby crib atop a typical Mayan temple. You wear 3-D glasses.

So does your daddy.

Your daddy reminds you of how you will find your mommy with her head in the oven on your eighth birthday. You cry, and your daddy, he says to shut up. You do so. Then your daddy lays a Swiss Army knife on a tray. You are taken from a crib, and tied spread-eagled to a wagon wheel. Your right arm points north to water, house of life; your left west to air, house of vocation; your right leg east to earth, house of death; your left leg south to fire, house of records. Your daddy unsheathes his sword. Your daddy raises his sword, and to the strobing of the northern lights, you are sliced in half, instantly, and it pours a deluge, words made images, images words, a deluge of signs, symbols, passwords, culled from route sheets, order of the retina, order of the day, modem passwords to the Top Secret Codices of Langley, VA:

And your mommy's crisped & burnt hair is whisked from inside the oven by your Mayan daddy. *(& your maelstrom of a fever dream reaches critical mass, tumbles past & future into your present, names dates facts lies incidents rumors archetypes totems & tabus all tossed into the 14-screen cineplex mulch-mix: wheat, golden icons, port, swastikas, wafers, worry beads, chalices, rings, coins, lava, placentas, stars of david . . . matinee prices for all showings before six. & the VU meter slams into red. . . .)*

And you wonder what's the what of a Buddhist vegetarian you'd made the two-backed beast with? Why'd your field super Sas want her iced? & who did he hire? And why'd your Sicilian connections clam up behind this?

Is she in the blue Fiat with the ex-ambassador when it explodes? Is her watch ground into & through her wrist? *(& the mayan dream projectionists mix up the reels: & Pauline leads a cast of flying monkey monks from a certain childhood night-light nightmare, silhouetted by eruptions from backlot calderas, monk orangutans in velvet robes, hot in pursuit of polaroids spirited by insincere rice christians now across the dream ice floes, and, lit by aurora mandalas, the dreaming christians clutch bowls of larva, gestating corruptions of spirit; & the dream frame freezes on one of the virgins. . . . & the image frame sets off a Defcon Alert: take no bombings! we begin prisoners in five minutes!)*

Why does all her exposed body hair, though intact, crumble to dust at the Mayan coroner's touch?

(The dream mayan projectionists rub vaseline onto their projector lenses: too late, the dream smoke goes up in film.)

And why do the faces of the Buddhist vegetarian & Pauline's fade into each other's?

And then. You were in a bar in Mombasa. You'd escaped the sub-sub-Saharan heat. You were with your World Anti-Communist League contact.

You'd returned infected monkeys from the U.C. Davis Primate Center, after the polio melitis disaster. *(The dream mayan 14-screen cineplex goes up: iguanas escape, followed by incense, feathers, gypsy moths . . . the projectionist's stash of peyote is consumed, liana shrivel in the wall of dream fire, barbed wire melts, menstrual fluids boil toward a dream mayan meltdown. . . .)*

You sat in a bar in Mombasa. You drank holy waters & watched Bobby Kennedy die, the kindled flag & the folded flame . . . and an eternal silence of moment, please; some sort of prayer. *(& the dream mayan reactor beneath the ditto 14-screen cineplex reaches a po-po-structuralist Meltdown:*

orangutanslongboxesbulletclipspiltdownmanflowersfallen leaderslandslides. . . .)

And then piltdown man rushed into that Mombasa bar & accused your contact of having infected his young daughter; a crowd gathers, & before it will metastasize into an angry mob of ghost dancers from ghost forests felled for print media you've wasted the fascist shit—you never liked paisley bow ties anyway.

(Only the dream mayan alchemical stashes of librium and speiss escape. . . .)

And the Mayan coroner sips yage tea & checks the time on his pocket watch, clips a feather & then writes his report, using the victim's menstrual fluid while absently stroking his iguana. *(& the radioactive dream wind blows: ganja, hammers & sickle cells, wild eyes & a love beyond comprehension.)*

There is a particular dream, more familiar, comforting:

You dream of a machine, suspended in the air, above the Mekong. A delta spewing life.

The machine, suspended, makes a sound, constantly. The machine says chop. And chop. It goes chop-chop.

The pilot says chop. Pilot Pauline slams her crop, says chop. And chop. The pilot goes chop-chop.

You're in the back, opening an envelope, with instructions from the highest bidder. To the highest bidder goes the contract. *The Contract*. It reads drop. And drop. Drop drop.

You turn to the hogtied General with five stars. The five stars are of no use, when hogtied, hogtied in a machine suspended above the Mekong, a machine going chop, and chop, saying chop chop . . . and with instructions, instructing the General's captors, reading drop, and drop, drop drop.

"—Let's make a deal," the General pleads. And for one brief moment the mask slips and you are not facing the General, but are instead facing Sas . . . but Sas never did 'Nam. Sas did the Law School Deferment Shuffle. And the mask slips again, and it is the General again. "Name that tune!"

You reply: "No, siree, General Morelandwest, I have properties to buy back home; barrels to pork, bribes to pay—"

"The Price Is Right, and I'll even throw in my collection of ears!"

You reply that seed money is needed, not ears; that he's turned Vietnam into a nation of Van Goghs, which does the Vietnamese no good without the French to run art courses.

The General protests that Van Gogh was Dutch.

Too late: The pilot goes chop-chop; he goes drop, and drop; and the General goes fall. And fall. Like your asshole buddy who fell on the grenade intended for the General, jumped on it like some fucking Gunga Din. Fell. Fell becomes fall.

Fall fall.

You run.

On down grunged East Village alleyways, absorbed in your motions. You enter into a shop. Pauline loved this shop; she found a pair of handcuffs here. A beam of light has captured your motions. (Crows sing.)

El Viejo Ciego, shoulders weighed with the knowledge of what you seek, shuffles to the back of the musty shop and returns with a long box. "Each time you come back, you seem more and more like your papa," he says. "*Bruto, pero sincero*." God, not Tales of the Guatemalan Coup again. You say nothing. "He was the quiet kind, too."

You give *El Viejo Ciego* five twenties. Opening the box,

you take out a rifle, find a talisman that you put around your neck.

A Nicaraguan child was castrated by a coked-out Moral Equivalent of our Founding Fathers to make this talisman.

From the roof of the General Assembly you spy on an apartment in the U.N. tower, and adjust the telescopic sight. The Subject reads a magazine; you like to think it is "The Talk of the Town" section of *The New Yorker*. All your subjects read *The New Yorker*.

Just as you're psyching yourself up to pull the trigger, an act of infinite tenderness and finesse, the Subject gets up and closes the blinds.

Shit-shat-shoot-shut, you say to yourself. It's time to Play Dirty.

Powdered with oregano and garlic, you consumate your interview with the Maid who services the Subject's floor. There is an exchange of gifts.

You give the Maid twenty fives.

The Maid gives you the key to the Subject's apartment. You slap the key into a mold, and, quickly pressing, take the key out and give it back to the Maid, saying you can't use it.

The Maid reluctantly gives you the twenty twenties back.

You slip the copy into the doorknob; and it acquiesces, turns over, tumblers unlocking. You turn the knob, gently, and enter, quick, quiet; shutting the door behind you.

You do a quick survey of the Subject's apartment. Chic yet simple, with white urinallike tiles everywhere, modern Danish furniture, back issues of *GEO* with articles on the latest growth industry (desertification), a CD player and a CD library of baroque music (the usual suspects—da Gagliano, Salieri, Handel, Nyman), Navajo throw rugs, a Rembrandt litho—nineteenth century, and a dominatrix Madonna in a bondage triptych with the Three Wise Men. You throttle a sob . . . why is it that everywhere you go, everywhere you look, you see Pauline? You open cabinets in the kitchenette—empty but for a row of long-stemmed wineglasses. There are two refrigerators, one of them a three-temperature wine cellar.

You check the bedroom, find a Louis XIV desk repro, and doing something you've never done on the job before, you open drawers. You find a State Dept. passport, a NATO security pass, a blood- and semen-soaked copy of *Puritan: The Adult American Dream Book*, some new seventy-five-cent stamps, and white-out thinner.

You slam the drawer shut. Time to go to work. You enter the bathroom and decide to examine the medicine cabinet. A bottle of Maalox. Stress tabs. Ginseng pills. A tiny bottle of nitroglycerin. Denture cleaner. Preparation-H. A vial of pharmaceutical cocaine with the Subject's name and a label from a pharmacy in Lausanne. Q-Tips.

You shut the mirror. Slap the shower curtain aside. Turn on the shower. Count to five. And turn it off. Wait for the run-off. Then take out a vial containing a few ounces of powdered glass.

You put on gloves and sprinkle the glass all over the floor of the bathtub. That should do the job (working its way up through the Subject's soles, into his capillaries, and onward via the aorta to shred the auricules and ventricles of his heart), if the Subject doesn't run the water too long before hopping in.

To be on the safe side, you go back to the kitchen and fill the salt shaker with arsenic . . . just in case.

You turn on your full-spectrum kiva lights to chase off any errant bugs and make your monthly call to the Field Supervisor, using a rather coy code name assigned you, Deep

Throat. But you know him; having ages ago been assigned by CREEP to do a standard surveillance, you know things that men in high places would pay small fortunes for.

You'd tailed Woodstein from the *Post*, and your Field Super, took pictures of meetings in public garages, intercepted parcels hidden on front steps, and kept this info for your own files: "S.A.S." Right next to another insurance file: "Missing Letters: Pauline/Deeper Throat." A couple's files belong together.

That was a dumb code name Sas gave you. Pauline agreed. You want a raise, a big one. You think you'll get it.

You turn on the TV, then hopscotch your way across the band. There's a lesbian vampire film you've seen too many times, and a Marxist real estate western you're glad to have missed; so you watch Cable News Network in hope of hearing some item on your assignment. You finish the daily crossword puzzle in minutes, you kick back and massage your temples. You remember Pauline's favorite top position, "Husking the Corn," and you're hardening when you remember that that particular Polariod is missing, along with "Drowned Corpse," "Turkish Prison," and "Sharon Tate." You wonder what Sas'd pay. . . .

You're so involved in your migraine attack and hard-on, you almost miss the item. "—ish Ambassador to the U.N. was killed today—" You rush to the volume knob, and turn it up. The smiling anchorbitch continues, teeth gleaming: "—when his car exploded in an ether fire. The F.B.I. has declined comment, though the P.L.O. is suspected." Still smiling, she moves on. You know who wanted his ambassadorial head on a platter: Sas's Op, or the Sicilian Connection. "Next we have Chris with Consumer Tips on . . ." A pregnant pause. "Oven Cleaners! Which are safe, which aren't, which are—"

You turn the TV set off, fuming. A thought comes to you. You grab your wallet, powder yourself with garlic and oregano, and, to be on the safe side, you take a bag of rotting fish from the refrigerator. And a Teflon thermos.

Thus prepared, you leave your apartment and go into the night.

You stand before your Automated 24-Hour Bankteller, your worst fears confirmed. You have just punched *Balance*, and are informed that the disability check to Mr. Vortex for the amount of $234,567.89 has been canceled, *Stop Payment*, and that you're overdrawn. The machine keeps your card.

In a pique, you carefully take the cap off the thermos and pour hydrofluoric acid on the console, which billows white clouds of smoke as the HF begins to feast on it, leaving the plastic shell untouched.

Of all the nerve! you think. A social contract's a social contract's a social contract. What would this society be like if every Tom, Dick, and Hari Krishna simply reneged on their contractual obligations, verbal or written? Civilization would simply collapse; it would be back to the jungle again.

You decide you'd best not go home; but, rather, go crosstown. You take a shortcut, passing near Central Park. The path, woven with crossed shadows of shadows from the avenue and the park, is penumbral. People never do lunch in places of this sort, though they can do murder or mugging or rape transactions. A short latino, with a motor strapped on his shoulders, waves a hose before him: leaves, dust, and candy wrappers are blown into your face. And this, you realize, is how it has always been: we can only move the dirt, hide the mess. Well hell then, bring on the meek cucarachas. You cut across the lawn: this is a big mistake, one you recognize when it is much too late. From the treetops a swarm of monarch butterflies approaches: their flutterings subsonically rend the air.

You run to the nearest subway entrance, the monarchs in pursuit. You zip through the turnstile, after fumbling with a token. As luck has it, the D train arrives. You board it. Time, you think, to visit Sas. You think so.

Butterflies begin attacking the train. Smashing themselves against windows and doors. A few slip past and land on you.

You wonder if it's the herring.

TWO: MISSING LETTERS
Cambridge, MA

Isao Chieko stood under the marquee of the rep cinema in Harvard Square, shielded from a demiacid drizzle, waiting for a Contact. *His* Contact. Well, quasi-Contact. Isao again read the marquee, THE AM-RICA- --EAM . . . again wondered which frat house had stolen the letters, with which they surely must have arranged on some mantelpiece "R-E-N-D." Or "N-E-R-D." Some time ago he'd watched a lesbian vampire film and a Marxist real estate western while being fellated in the back row, and could not remember their titles.

He sneezed, feeling his rib cage constricting around his lungs and his heart. Isao looked to the subway entrance. The cows caught his attention. Sacred cows, painted by the anonymous Back Bay artisans, onto the concrete islands that divided the traffic of Harvard Square. Cubist cows. Abstract expressionist cows. Kitsch cows with bathetic Keane eyes. Ground zero cows. Nagasaki cows.

He thought of his grandmother, and her potion for burns. She said one had to place a toad in an imported Deutschlander gingerbread dollhouse lined with prisms and mirrors. The toad, hopping about, would be confounded at confronting its ten-legged reflections, and would excrete an oil that—after many years of fermenting—would be the most effective of ointments.

He thought of how she'd been deported back to Japan during the war, to Nagasaki—her brother, after all, was doing research for the Japanese government, according to O.S.S. files.

He thought of how his mother and father sometimes said that they'd rather be in Nagasaki than in the desert, than in Manzanar, in some fucking forsaken desert concentration camp.

He remembered everything as Before Manzanar and After Manzanar. He'd been ten, in Methodist Sunday school, when *those Nips* attacked Pearl Harbor. A week before they were sent into exile, placed under arrest, a Mexican boy had nearly poked his right eye out, blinding him in that eye. Manzanar and After was a movie. With one eye *every*thing became a movie. Except for *The* Movies, which became all too real.

A hand grabbed his shoulder and Isao nearly fainted.

"Sorry I'm late." It was Sas, Pauline's husband. He looked a good ten pounds lighter than his photos—Pauline had always called Sas a tennis slut, a health-and-fitness whore, like some of the men Isao had been forced to meet in back rooms of bars, ten years ago now. Business. Research. On viral vectors. He had through the years come to find himself *liking* this research, and had indeed continued after the terms of the new order had expired, a secret sharer lost in a tactile assemblage, and he hated liking it and liked hating it.

"Jesus, Sas, you half scared me to death."

"Sorry about that—I, ah, had to shake *him*—"

"You mean your goon, your *contract*or—I heard on the news, about that ambassador."

"Someone *else* did that."

"Who? You Sicilian associates?"

Sas shook his head. "At this point, I just don't care that much." Then: "How's the P-4 Lab going?"

Isao admired Sas's casualness, his nonchalance. Isao had

schtupped Pauline, possibly even exposed her to that Haitian swine bug—Isao even had letters, and bondage Polaroids from Pauline—some love letters, some regarding M.I.T. research; Isao would not for one moment talk shop, given the circumstances.

One letter, which he'd intercepted, was to a researcher at the Pasteur Institute in Paris, who was also dying of a cancer, about those crackpot pheromone experiments going to shit in a rickshaw. The letter was missing, as were others. But Isao was not about to bother Sas with this.

"You don't look well, Isao."

"You wouldn't look well, either, if you only had one lung, bed sores, lesions, and a flu bug that wouldn't quit."

"You should see a doctor."

Isao laughed, which hurt his chest. "I have. The same doctor who treated Pauline."

"The doctor tell you to cruise gay bars?"

Isao turned, astonished; frozen.

"You know, Isao, I thought, for a while, that you'd been having an affair with Pauline. I hired a cop, private, to keep tabs on you. He observed you going to *gay* bars."

Isao did not know whether to laugh or cry, shit or go blind, fart or wink. But, still. His visits to those bars. The New Order. Sas was not in on this. Shouldn't be in on this. Half the administrative route sheets had passed through his office and he did not even know. This decision. Whose decision, Isao didn't know. All he knew was that the homosexual population would be the vector, in America. *Some new order*. A researcher who'd done postgrad with Isao had spoken of returning from a World Health Organization assignment in Africa, where he found that half the hospital admissions were due to AIDS. And how an editor at the *New England Journal of Medicine* had killed three letters he'd written on the topic, and had left several phone calls unreturned.

Isao took Pauline's letters, scented with "Opium," from his pocket, and handed them to Sas. "I'm tired. I shall, I think, go home." He turned and walked.

"HOW DO I KNOW THAT THESE ARE ALL HER LETTERS—?!"

Isao wanted to turn around and to scream: You don't, you ambulatory life-support system for an asshole, you don't!

He was too tired.

He would have to skip that last bar.

At the bottom of the steps, Isao felt dizzy; he nearly fell. His hands clung to the railing; he could not pull himself up.

A young boy, no older than fourteen, came to his rescue.

The boy's shoes were worn to tatters, as were all his other garments. His T-shirt read, "He Who Dies With The Most Toys *Sins*." He looked vaguely Mexican-American, reminded him of the boy who'd tried to poke his eye out, so long ago.

Isao decided. "Would you like to earn fifty dollars?"

The boy agreed; they went to the rest room.

While the boy earned his fifty dollars, Isao thought of his uncle the scientist. About how he'd been appalled to read that, during the war, he'd been involved in Unit 731, a death camp, near Harbin, in Manchuria, where thousands and thousands of Chinese, Russians, and even a few Americans had died for Science.

His uncle had escaped prosecution, as had *all* the scientists. Isao, as a present for earning his doctorate, had received a coded diary: Iceman had had his arms stuck in dry ice; Plagueman had been exposed to typhus—and, after barely surviving that, anthrax bacteria; Horseman had received a blood transfusion from a horse.

To drown out the screams, the scientists usually played Mozart.

That, decided Isao, was what he needed. Eine Kleine Nachtmusik.

THREE: THE FATHER-IN-LAW SPEAKS
Brooklyn, New York

Here's shit in your eye, Sas! C'mon, don't be a stupid wop. Have another drinky. We could both use a few belts. Don't worry about it, they'll scrape that maniac off the ceiling. I hope this makes ya see the sense in moving; this place has too *many* bad memories.

Sweet Jesus, not again. . . . *Come in!*

Hello, Occifer. Doc just gave him medication, said try to keep him quiet. No, Occifer, his name's not "Segretti," it's *San*gretti. Samuel Anthony Sangretti . . . yeah, the Watergate Sangretti. What? Listen, Occifer; I'd appreciate it if ya'd lay off; he's paid his debt to socie—

Shut up, Sas! I'll handle it. Sit down!

Gotta 'xcuse him, Occifer his wife, my little girl, died a few days ago, and then . . . this. What, Occifer? I'm his—his father-in-law; I just told ya. Me? Grayle; what's it to ya? I *know* there's a stiff in the other room, made me want to paint the toilet with my tongue, especially the way that Spic medical examiner tried to rape the stiff, it really did, I'd heard about those coroners—but my son-in-law, he's already given a report . . . to the F.B.I. Ask the medical examiner. Or the F.B.I. Please close the door. *Thank ya!*

Stupid mick flatfoot; makes me embarrassed to be Irish. Oh, please, Sas, c'mon, don't cry; I can't handle this. I can't cope if people start crying; it—just—tears me up to see ya like this, what good is a roomful of cryin' men gonna do? First the Little Lady cracks up, and then this. Be strong; Pauline'd want it like that. That's what she saw in ya . . . your ability to grab a couple of stilts and just wade through the horsylala.

The way ya zipped through that Senate committee circus on Allende and I.T.T.—ya slipped through that like shit through a goose. And that Church Committee Hearing, where they tried to blame you for the ambassador and his girlfriend getting blown up. And that closed-door Contra-Gate committee. My da, he had a saying: "The best men are made of faults." Of course he never lived to see Nixon.

And speaking of pricks, I wish ya'd zipped your fly or worn underwear at the wake—

What's it with this, "They sent him!"—Who sent who? What missing letters? That's Loony Tunes talk. Why would they do something like that, after pulling ya that consultancy with Dupont when ya'd been disbarred, and then the hefty honorarium from that crackpot Liberty Lobby. They are dangerous—I was at Auschwitz, with Ike and Casey—I saw what those Nazis and their New Order did—nobody's gonna tell me it didn't happen.

I feel a draft . . . did one of those fat-headed flatfeet leave a window open? Let me check—!

Christ on a crutch, I found four windows open!

Your da, I wish he could be here; a man needs all the family he can cling to. But God, Country, and State Department call. I guess.

Well, at least you've quieted down.

If only the Little Lady wasn't taking it so hard. When ya told us about coming home the day Pauline went—the day she died—and about Pauline's Chihuahua—God she loved that dog, I never knew what she saw in that yapper with a perpetual hard-on—how it jumped on her suitcase when ya'd laid it on the couch and would not leave it or shut up, even when ya went into the kitchen and opened some dog food. The little boogers love the noise a can opener makes. And the Little Lady began to cry, like some Diva at the Met, saying "the dog knows!" and "poor poor poochy!" and starts tearing at her hair, until the doc sedated her. And now she's gonna need a good wig. Nervous exhaustion. I really think it was at the wake where she snapped; it was bad enough that they'd gotten Pauline's coffin mixed up with that old black guy's and didn't do anything about it until the Little Lady screamed there was a porter in her daughter's coffin, which really was like our Pauline getting her appointments mixed to the absolutely frigging last, but oh boy when your zipper went down and your gas pump, as the Little Lady calls it, bobbed in and out as ya sat. Or rose. . . . I'm glad I got your attention. Ya sure as fuck got the Father's attention, and the altar boys'—probably scarred 'em for life, turned 'em into fruit loops. I'm *sure* the Little Lady noticed, too.

Ah, fuck funerals, I hate 'em. A wake, with good catering, that's another matter. No more funerals for me.

Funerals are too barbaric, anyway. Pauline Sangretti, née Grayle, decked out like some college drama Juliet. Ya wouldn't have known by seeing her like that that she'd run a research lab. Paid her own way through college, too; insisted. Pauline could pinch a penny until old Abe would scream for Booth to pull the trigger. Got her degree and became a researcher, and then got another degree and became an administrator, with her own research lab. P-4. Pheromones, she said when I asked about her work. Pheromones. I bet that's what killed her.

And that damn lab—they sent the biggest frigging wreath I have ever seen in my life, and I have been to a few too many funerals in my day—but the only one to show up is that Isao you'd thought was having an affair with Pauline until your dick found out he was a fag. He didn't look like one to me. Who knows, maybe he had a hot date with the altar boys. But all the same it was nice of him to show up, real nice, real decent.

And there's little enough of decency left in the world. 'S those zipper manufacturers who're to blame.

Want another shot? Here, take the bottle.

Ya see, people go through life, lost, some never even find their "thing," they call it. And when they do find it, *if* they find it, turns out it's nothing more than the shit end of the swizzle stick, the losing Lotto number. Like when ya two got on that game show and didn't win zip. Or when ya invested in the silver—no, hear me out. . . .

How else can ya explain that maniac wrapped in herring who came for ya after ya'd just come back on the Logan–La Guardia shuttle, ya and your "Company" business, who jabbed the ice pick through your peephole—missing your retina by a friggin' quarter of an inch—who then kicks your door in and tries to bind ya up and gag ya and set ya on fire with ether? We all go a bit apeshit sometimes, but there are limits. Goddamn, there should be limits!

I'll never forget when ya called and told us Pauline'd passed out at work again, and that goddamn Yehudi doctor and his good news–bad news routine. Good news is it's not leukemia; bad news is that she's pregnant and we've just given her every X-ray series from G.I. to chest. Abortion's a sort of little suicide; on the other hand, who wants a circus sideshow for a grandkid? Boy, I wanted to give that doc a barium enema.

And that hospital, loved it. Great post-op care. Let her take a shower by herself day after so she can fall and get a broken nose and concussion.

And the Little Lady and I came back from a vacation in northern Brazil, which was no biggie, I mean, I didn't know the Amazon was a desert. "Desertification," the Little Lady said, she'd read about it in *GEO*. I could've killed that Yehudi travel agent.

So we get back just in time for Pauline's nose job. On the house—after we'd threatened to sue. She had always wanted to have a nose like that English bitch, the commie, the one who was "Julia." And she got it. She got her nose. . . .

Pauline could get things from people. The Little Lady once found a pair of handcuffs in Pauline's room while she was away, doing postgrad work. And Pauline said she'd asked a cop for 'em and he'd given 'em to her. And what about the riding crop, the Little Lady asked—she thought Pauline might be going kinko, like in Story of A—and Pauline told us about a jockey she knew. Neither of us really believed her until she brought the jockey, and later the cop, to dinner. They were polite enough, but they seemed unsavory to me. I was glad when she dropped 'em.

And after that hospital stuff, and after the nose job, she comes to stay with us a couple weeks to recuperate—ya were in Chile, I remember . . . or was it Argentina?—one day after Pauline came back here the Little Lady finds another riding crop.

I wish something was on the cable, only thing on right now's some goddamn dyke vampire movie.

I'll put some music on—that's just the ticket.

I could've sworn I closed that window, leave the room one second and it's like ya were never there. I swear.

I just found a matchbook from Umberto's in Chinatown—Joey Gallo bought it there. Me and the Little Lady ate at the table where they blasted him . . . I gave a good tip for that table, too. But why's your address written inside? Guess a cop left it.

Should I turn the music up? Lady Day—Pauline loved Billie Holiday. Wore out I don't know how many copies of her records. I saw Lady Day sing once, with Prez: "Strange Fruit," "Willow Weep for Me," "Stormy Monday," "God Bless the Child"—they just don't do 'em like that anymore. Pauline played Billie Holiday to death and back again while recuperating. It got on the Little Lady's nerves, the Little Lady never liked colored music. Said Pauline played it just to bug her.

Well, after Pauline goes back to the lab, a few years later: 'S hypoglycemia. No one in *our* family's ever had it. Then Pauline's pregnant again—terrific, we thought, really! Then your trial, that suspended sentence. The Little Lady was *sooo* relieved. Then Pauline's pregnancy turns out to be an ovarian cyst. Of course the bastards yank the ovary, yanked the wrong one, too. It's not the cold-blooded attitude that gets to me, it is the incompetence.

I tell ya now, the reason I didn't shed a single tear for Pauline when she finally passed on, it was the constant worrying and crying I did when she was alive. I mourned her on the installment plan. No collateral, low interest, paid in advance.

So when ya call again, or your secretary did, that Pauline'd started hemorrhaging at work, and we couldn't reach ya. They said ya were in the field. And the exploratory: they found her malignant from womb to intestines. So this time it's not just a hysterectomy, but a colostomy.

Ya were really great, the way ya broke it to the Little Lady.

She'd been so worried about her baby. Falling to pieces.

I'm glad ya never told the Little Lady about Pauline's colostomy bag bursting at the "Just Say No" fund-raiser.

And next to the First Lady, the First Bitch. (Wouldn't be the first time *she* walked through shit.)

God. I need another drink.

By the time I found out it'd metastasized, I just felt a numbness. A yearning. Yearning for it to be over. I felt hungry, too, damnedest thing, I felt hungry for sweet and sour pork.

And then it was over. It was over. Pauline, not the sweet and sour. Here's the shitkicker, though. . . .

Last week, I talked to Pauline's last doctor. A lady doc. Very nice. And competent. No bullshit. She asked me about that abortion. She claimed, off the record, the whole thing probably started with a D & C screwup. Tiny piece—a tiny piece of fetal tissue had been left inside her, in her uterus, and had escaped detection. Rare. But not unheard of, she said.

I made her promise never to tell ya about it. Oh—

I almost forgot, a coworker brought a bundle of Pauline's letters, postcards, Polaroids—said she found 'em in Pauline's

Clean Room locker. They were in a bag, along with frigging handcuffs, and a riding crop. The Little Lady wanted to open 'em in the worst way, but no, I said, save these letters for Sas.

Sas—Jesus in a Stuka, there's blood all over the floor here, on the couch even.

—*Crap*! You've been asleep all along—how can ya sleep in a pool of blood, Pauline said ya'd sleep through the friggin' Apocalypse. You're sleeping, and I'm just pissing in the wind, spilling my guts out. Just as well; let it lie.

I think I'll sleep on the futon couch; I'll just take your shoes off and sleep on the couch.

For Robert Frazier, "*Ein jeder Engel ist schrecklich.*"

NOTE: Toad pharmacology in "MISSING LETTERS" inspired by a passage in Akira Kurosawa's "Something Like an Autobiography," Knopf.

Hell, You Say

Deus nobiscum, quis contra?
If God is with us, who is against us?

It's stunning to think that in an age where science is daily unraveling the secrets of life and the cosmos, there remains a huge contingent of faithful who willingly put their hope and their fate in the concept of an Almighty being who directs the course of human destiny. Evidently, it is currently our destiny that far more people watch football on Sunday than attend church. Nevertheless, people cling to their faith and centuries-old systems of belief like pit bulls to a prime rib.

Many analysts have suggested the faithful are actually afraid there may be no God—but I think we're afraid there *is* a God, and He is *responsible* for everything, and when we stand before Her in the hereafter, It will know we stole Freddy's lunch money in the third grade. I find it much more comfortable to believe this is all an accident, or perhaps the Almighty has just stepped away from His desk for a millennium, and will straighten everything out just as soon as He returns.

Whatever your personal views, there is undoubted room in the universe for any number of heavens and hells. The view that earth is heaven/hell, or that we create our own heaven/hell, is well-examined territory in literature, but endlessly fascinating. We include here stories with most interesting perspectives on the age-old questions of life, death, and afterlife.

—J.H.

NEIL GAIMAN

Dark, mercurial Neil Gaiman is much like his best-known creation, D.C. Comics's *Sandman*. The wit and sense of mystery that pervades his *Sandman* scripts has translated into a successful, eccentric writing career. Neil coedited a favorite, hard-to-find volume called *Ghastly Beyond Belief*, which collected the most painful gaffs of film and literature over the last century. Neil went on to cowrite the British best-seller *Good Omens* with fantasist Terry Pratchert. Neil is currently at work on his own novel, *The Wall*. He is a poet, screenwriter, playwright, and purveyor of fantastic visions, as his story here attests.

Murder Mysteries

by Neil Gaiman

The Fourth Angel says:

Of this order I am made one,
From Mankind to guard this place
That through their Guilt they have forgone,
For they have forfeited His Grace;
Therefore all this must they shun
Or else my Sword they shall embrace
And myself will be their Foe
To flame them in the Face.

Chester Mystery Cycle: *The Creation, and Adam and Eve*. Circa 1461.

This is true.

Ten years ago, give or take a year, I found myself on an

enforced stopover in Los Angeles, a long way from home. It was December, and the California weather was warm and pleasant. England, however, was in the grip of fogs and snowstorms, and no planes were landing there. Each day I'd phone the airport, and each day I'd be told to wait another day.

This had gone on for almost a week.

I was barely out of my teens. Looking around today at the parts of my life left over from those days, I feel uncomfortable, as if I've received a gift, unasked, from another person: a house, a wife, children, a vocation. Nothing to do with me, I could say, innocently. If it's true that every seven years each cell in your body dies and is replaced, then I have truly inherited my life from a dead man; and the misdeeds of those times are forgiven, and are buried with his bones.

I was in Los Angeles. Yes.

On the sixth day I received a message from an old sort-of girlfriend from Seattle: she was in LA too, and she had heard I was around on the friends-of-friends network. Would I come over?

I left a message on her machine. Sure.

That evening: a small blond woman approached me, as I came out of the place where I was staying. It was already dark.

She stared at me, as if she were trying to match me to a description, and then, hesitantly, she said my name.

"That's me. Are you Tink's friend?"

"Yeah. Car's out back. C'mon: she's really looking forward to seeing you."

The woman's car was one of the huge old boatlike jobs you only ever seem to see in California. It smelled of cracked and flaking leather upholstery. We drove out from wherever we were to wherever we were going.

Los Angeles was at that time a complete mystery to me; and I cannot say I understand it much better now. I understand

London, and New York, and Paris: you can walk around them, get a sense of what's where in just a morning of wandering. Maybe catch the subway. But Los Angeles is about cars. Back then I didn't drive at all; even today I will not drive in America. Memories of L.A. for me are linked by rides in other people's cars, with no sense there of the shape of the city, of the relationships between the people and the place. The regularity of the roads, the repetition of structure and form, mean that when I try to remember it as an entity all I have is the boundless profusion of tiny lights I saw one night on my first trip to the city, from the hill of Griffith Park. It was one of the most beautiful things I had ever seen, from that distance.

"See that building?" said my blond driver, Tink's friend. It was a red-brick art deco house, charming and quite ugly.

"Yes."

"Built in the 1930s," she said, with respect and pride.

I said something polite, trying to comprehend a city inside which fifty years could be considered a long time.

"Tink's real excited. When she heard you were in town. She was so excited."

"I'm looking forward to seeing her again."

Tink's real name was Tinkerbell Richmond. No lie.

She was staying with friends in a small apartment clump, somewhere an hour's drive from downtown L.A.

What you need to know about Tink: she was ten years older than me, in her early thirties; she had glossy black hair and red, puzzled lips and very white skin, like Snow White in the fairy stories; the first time I met her I thought she was the most beautiful woman in the world.

Tink had been married for a while at some point in her life, and had a five-year-old daughter called Susan. I had never met Susan—when Tink had been in England, Susan had been staying on in Seattle, with her father.

People named Tinkerbell name their daughters Susan.

Memory is the great deceiver. Perhaps there are some individuals whose memories act like tape recordings, daily records of their lives complete in every detail, but I am not one of them. My memory is a patchwork of occurrences—of discontinuous events roughly sewn together: the parts I remember, I remember precisely, while other sections seem to have vanished completely.

I do not remember arriving at Tink's house, nor where her flatmate went.

What I remember next is sitting in Tink's lounge, with the lights low, the two of us next to each other, on the sofa.

We made small talk. It had been perhaps a year since we had seen one another. But a twenty-one-year-old boy has little to say to a thirty-two-year-old woman, and soon, having nothing in common, I pulled her to me.

She snuggled close with a kind of sigh, and presented her lips to be kissed. In the half-light her lips were black. We kissed for a little, and I stroked her breasts through her blouse, on the couch; and then she said, "We can't fuck. I'm on my period."

"Fine."

"I can give you a blow job, if you'd like."

I nodded assent, and she unzipped my jeans, and lowered her head to my lap.

After I had come, she got up and ran into the kitchen. I heard her spitting into the sink, and the sound of running water: I remember wondering why she did it, if she hated the taste that much.

Then she returned and we sat next to each other on the couch.

"Susan's upstairs, asleep," said Tink. "She's all I live for. Would you like to see her?"

"I don't mind."

We went upstairs. Tink led me into a darkened bedroom. There were child-scrawl pictures all over the walls—waxcrayoned drawings of winged fairies and little palaces—and a small, fair-haired girl was asleep in the bed.

"She's very beautiful," said Tink, and kissed me. Her lips were still slightly sticky. "She takes after her father."

We went downstairs. We had nothing else to say, nothing else to do. Tink turned on the main light. For the first time I noticed tiny crow's-feet at the corners of her eyes, incongruous on her perfect, Barbie-doll face.

"I love you," she said.

"Thank you."

"Would you like a ride back?"

"If you don't mind leaving Susan alone . . . ?"

She shrugged, and I pulled her to me for the last time.

At night, Los Angeles is all lights. And shadows.

A blank, here, in my mind. I simply don't remember what happened next. I don't remember. Perhaps we drove back in silence. She must have driven me back to the place where I was staying—how else would I have gotten there? I do not even remember kissing her good-bye. Perhaps I simply waited on the sidewalk and watched her drive away. Perhaps.

I do know, however, that once I reached the place where I was staying I just stood there, unable to go inside, to wash and then to sleep, unwilling to do anything else.

I was not hungry. I did not want alcohol. I did not want to read, or talk. I was scared of walking too far, in case I became lost, bedeviled by the repeating motifs of Los Angeles, spun around and sucked in so I could never find my way home again. Central Los Angeles sometimes seemed to me to be nothing more than a pattern—like a set of repeating blocks—a gas station, a few homes, a mini-mall (donuts, photo developers, laundromats, fast-foods), and repeat until hypnotized; and the tiny changes in the mini-malls and the houses only served to reinforce the structure.

I thought of Tink's lips. Then I fumbled in a pocket of my jacket, and pulled out a packet of cigarettes.

I lit one, inhaled, blew blue smoke into the warm night air.

There was a stunted palm tree growing outside the place I was staying, and I resolved to walk for a way, keeping the tree in sight, to smoke my cigarette, perhaps even to think; but I felt too drained to think. I felt very sexless, and very alone.

A block or so down the road there was a bench, and when I reached it I sat down. I threw the stub of the cigarette onto the pavement, hard, and watched it shower orange sparks.

Someone said, "I'll buy a cigarette off you, pal. Here."

A hand, in front of my face, holding a quarter. I looked up.

He did not look old, although I would not have been prepared to say how old he was. Late thirties, perhaps. Mid forties. He wore a long, shabby coat, colorless under the yellow street lamps, and his eyes were dark.

"Here. A quarter. That's a good price."

I shook my head, pulled out the packet of Marlboros, offered him one. "Keep your money. It's free. Have it."

He took the cigarette. I passed him a book of matches (it advertised a telephone sex line; I remember that), and he lit the cigarette. He offered me the matches back, and I shook my head. "Keep them."

"Uh-huh." He sat next to me, and smoked his cigarette. When he had smoked it halfway down, he tapped the lighted end off on the concrete, stubbed out the glow, and placed the butt of the cigarette behind his ear.

"I don't smoke much," he said. "Seems a pity to waste it, though."

A car careened down the road, veering from one side to the other. There were four young men in the car: the two in the front were both pulling at the wheel, and laughing. The windows were wound down, and I could hear their laughter, and the two in the back seat *("Gaary, you asshole! What the fuck are you onnn, mannnn?")*, and the pulsing beat of a rock song. Not a song I recognized. The car looped around a corner, out of sight.

Soon the sounds were gone, too.

"I owe you," said the man on the bench.

"Sorry?"

"I owe you something. For the cigarette. And the matches. You wouldn't take the money. I owe you."

I shrugged, embarrassed. "Really, it's just a cigarette. I figure, if I give people cigarettes, then if ever I'm out, maybe people will give me cigarettes." I laughed, to show I didn't really mean it, although I did. "Don't worry about it."

"Mm. You want to hear a story? True story? Stories always used to be good payment. These days"—he shrugged—"not so much."

I sat back on the bench, and the night was warm, and I looked at my watch: it was almost one in the morning. In England a freezing new day would already have begun: a workday would be starting for those who could beat the snow and get into work; another handful of old people, and those without homes, would have died, in the night, from the cold.

"Sure," I said to the man. "Sure. Tell me a story."

He coughed, grinned white teeth—a flash in the darkness—and he began.

"First thing I remember was the Word. And the Word was God. Sometimes, when I get *really* down, I remember the sound of the Word in my head, shaping me, forming me, giving me life.

"The Word gave me a body, gave me eyes. And I opened my eyes, and I saw the light of the Silver City.

"I was in a room—a silver room—and there wasn't anything in it except me. In front of me was a window that went from floor to ceiling, open to the sky, and through the window I could see the spires of the City, and at the edge of the City, the Dark.

"I don't know how long I waited there. I wasn't impatient

or anything, though. I remember that. It was like I was waiting until I was called; and I knew that some time I would be called. And if I had to wait until the end of everything, and never be called, why, that was fine too. But I'd be called, I was certain of that. And then I'd know my name, and my function.

"Through the window I could see silver spires, and in many of the other spires were windows; and in the windows I could see others like me. That was how I knew what I looked like.

"You wouldn't think it of me, seeing me now, but I was beautiful. I've come down in the world a way since then.

"I was taller then, and I had wings.

"They were huge and powerful wings, with feathers the color of mother-of-pearl. They came out from just between my shoulder blades. They were so good. My wings.

"Sometimes I'd see others like me, the ones who'd left their rooms, who were already fulfilling their duties. I'd watch them soar through the sky from spire to spire, performing errands I could barely imagine.

"The sky above the City was a wonderful thing. It was always light, although lit by no sun—lit, perhaps by the City itself: but the quality of light was forever changing. Now pewter-colored light, then brass, then a gentle gold, or a soft and quiet amethyst . . ."

The man stopped talking. He looked at me, his head on one side. There was a glitter in his eyes that scared me. "You know what amethyst is? A kind of purple stone?"

I nodded.

My crotch felt uncomfortable.

It occurred to me then that the man might not be mad; I found this far more disquieting than the alternative.

The man began talking once more. "I don't know how long it was that I waited, in my room. But time didn't mean anything. Not back then. We had all the time in the world.

"The next thing that happened to me was when the angel Lucifer came to my cell. He was taller than me, and his wings were imposing, his plumage perfect. He had skin the color of sea mist, and curly silver hair, and these wonderful grey eyes . . .

"I say *he*, but you should understand that none of us had any sex, to speak of." He gestured toward his lap. "Smooth and empty. Nothing there. You know.

"Lucifer shone. I mean it: he glowed from inside. All angels do. They're lit up from within, and in my cell the angel Lucifer glowed like a lightning storm.

"He looked at me. And he named me.

" 'You are Raguel,' he said. 'The Vengeance of the Lord.'

"I bowed my head, because I knew it was true. That was my name. That was my function.

" 'There has been a . . . a wrong thing,' he said. 'The first of its kind. You are needed.'

"He turned and pushed himself into space, and I followed him, flew behind him across the Silver City, to the outskirts, where the City stops and the Darkness begins; and it was there, under a vast silver spire, that we descended to the street, and I saw the dead angel.

"The body lay, crumpled and broken, on the silver sidewalk. Its wings were crushed underneath it and a few loose feathers had already blown into the silver gutter.

"The body was almost dark. Now and again a light would flash inside it, an occasional flicker of cold fire in the chest, or in the eyes, or in the sexless groin, as the last of the glow of life left it forever.

"Blood pooled in rubies on its chest and stained its white wing feathers crimson. It was very beautiful, even in death.

"It would have broken your heart.

"Lucifer spoke to me, then. 'You must find who was responsible for this, and how; and take the Vengeance of the Name on whoever caused this thing to happen.'

"He really didn't have to say anything. I knew that already. The hunt, and the retribution: it was what I was created for, in the Beginning; it was what I *was*.

" 'I have work to attend to,' said the angel Lucifer.

"He flapped his wings, once, hard, and rose upward; the gust of wind sent the dead angel's loose feathers blowing across the street.

"I leaned down to examine the body. All luminescence had by now left it. It was a dark thing; a parody of an angel. It had a perfect, sexless face, framed by silver hair. One of the eyelids was open, revealing a placid grey eye; the other was closed. There were no nipples on the chest and only smoothness between the legs.

"I lifted the body up.

"The back of the angel was a mess. The wings were broken and twisted; the back of the head stove in; there was a floppiness to the corpse that made me think its spine had been broken as well. The back of the angel was all blood.

"I felt myself transforming. I am not sure how I can explain it to you, but suddenly I wasn't me—I was something larger. I was transfigured: I was my function.

"The only blood on its front was in the chest area. I probed it with my forefinger, and it entered the body without difficulty.

"*He fell*, I thought. *And he was dead before he fell*.

"And I looked up at the windows that ranked the street. I stared across the Silver City. *You did this*, I thought. *I will find you, whoever you are. And I will take the Lord's vengeance upon you*."

The man took the cigarette stub from behind his ear, lit it with a match. Briefly I smelled the ashtray smell of a dead cigarette, acrid and harsh; then he pulled down to the unburnt tobacco, exhaled blue smoke into the night air.

"The angel who had first discovered the body was called Phanuel.

"I spoke to him in the Hall of Being. That was the spire beside which the dead angel lay. In the hall hung the . . . the blueprints, maybe, for what was going to be . . . all this." He gestured with the hand that held the stubby cigarette, pointing to the night sky and the parked cars and the world. "You know. The universe.

"Phanuel was the senior designer; working under him were a multitude of angels laboring on the details of the Creation. I watched him from the floor of the hall. He hung in the air below the Plan, and angels flew down to him, waiting politely in turn as they asked him questions, checked things with him, invited comment on their work. Eventually he left them, and descended to the floor.

" 'You are Raguel,' he said. His voice was high, and fussy. 'What need have you of me?'

" 'You found the body?'

" 'Poor Carasel? Indeed I did. I was leaving the hall—there are a number of concepts we are currently constructing, and I wished to ponder one of them—*Regret* by name. I was planning to get a little distance from the City—to fly above it, I mean, not to go into the Dark outside, I wouldn't do that, although there has been some loose talk amongst . . . but, yes. I was going to rise, and contemplate.

" 'I left the hall, and . . .' he broke off. He was small, for an angel. His light was muted, but his eyes were vivid and bright. I mean really bright. 'Poor Carasel. How could he do that to himself? How?'

" 'You think his destruction was self-inflicted?'

"He seemed puzzled—surprised that there could be any other explanation. 'But of course. Carasel was working under me, developing a number of concepts that will be intrinsic to the Universe, when its Name shall be spoken. His group did a remarkable job on some of the real basics—*Dimension* was one, and *Sleep* another. There were others.

" 'Wonderful work. Some of his suggestions regarding the

use of individual viewpoints to define dimensions were truly ingenious.

" 'Anyway. He had begun work on a new project. It's one of the really major ones—the ones that I would usually handle, or possibly even Zephkiel,' he glanced upward. 'But Carasel had done such sterling work. And his last project was *so* remarkable. Something apparently quite trivial that he and Saraquael elevated into . . .' He shrugged. 'But that is unimportant. It was *this* project that forced him into nonbeing. But none of us could ever have foreseen . . .'

" 'What was his current project?'

"Phanuel stared at me. 'I'm not sure I ought to tell you. All the new concepts are considered sensitive, until we get them into the final form in which they will be Spoken.'

"Phanuel was unable to meet my gaze.

" 'I am Raguel, who is the Vengeance of the Lord,' I told him. 'I serve the Name directly. It is my mission to discover the nature of this deed, and to take the Name's vengeance on those responsible. My questions are to be answered.'

"The little angel trembled, and he talked fast.

" 'Carasel and his partner were researching *Death*. Cessation of life. An end to physical, animated existence. They were putting it all together. But Carasel always went too far into his work—we had a terrible time with him when he was designing *Agitation*. That was when he was working on Emotions . . .'

" 'You think Carasel died to—to research the phenomena?'

" 'Or because it intrigued him. Or because he followed his research just too far. Yes.' Phanuel flexed his fingers, stared at me with those brightly shining eyes. 'I trust that you will repeat none of this to any unauthorized persons, Raguel.'

" 'What did you do when you found the body?'

" 'I came out of the hall, as I said, and there was Carasel

on the sidewalk, staring up. I asked him what he was doing and he did not reply. Then I noticed the inner fluid, and that Carasel seemed unable rather than unwilling to talk to me.

" 'I was scared. I did not know what to do.

" 'The angel Lucifer came up behind me. He asked me if there was some kind of problem. I told him. I showed him the body. And then . . . then his Aspect came upon him, and he communed with The Name. He burned so bright.

" 'Then he said he had to fetch the one whose function embraced events like this, and he left—to seek you, I imagine.

" 'As Carasel's death was now being dealt with, and his fate was no real concern of mine, I returned to work, having gained a new—and, I suspect, quite valuable—perspective on the mechanics of *Regret*.

" 'I am considering taking *Death* away from the Carasel and Saraquael partnership. I may reassign it to Zephkiel, my senior partner, if he is willing to take it on. He excels on contemplative projects.'

"By now there was a line of angels waiting to talk to Phanuel. I felt I had almost all I was going to get from him.

" 'Who did Carasel work with? Who would have been the last to see him alive?'

" 'You could talk to Saraquael, I suppose—he was his partner, after all. Now, if you'll excuse me . . .'

"He returned to his swarm of aides: advising, correcting, suggesting, forbidding."

The man paused.

The street was quiet, now; I remember the low whisper of his voice, the buzz of a cricket somewhere. A small animal—a cat perhaps, or something more exotic, a raccoon, or even a jackal—darted from shadow to shadow among the parked cars on the opposite side of the street.

"Saraquael was in the highest of the mezzanine galleries that ringed the Hall of Being. As I said, the Universe was in the middle of the hall, and it glinted and sparkled and shone. Went up quite a way, too . . ."

"The Universe you mention, it was, what, a diagram?" I asked, interrupting for the first time.

"Not really. Kind of. Sorta. It was a blueprint: but it was full-sized, and it hung in the hall, and all these angels went around and fiddled with it all the time. Doing stuff with *Gravity*, and *Music* and *Klar* and whatever. It wasn't really the universe, not yet. It would be, when it was finished, and it was time for it to be properly Named."

"But . . ." I grasped for words to express my confusion. The man interrupted me.

"Don't worry about it. Think of it as a model, if that makes it easier for you. Or a map. Or a—what's the word?—prototype. Yeah. A Model T Ford universe." He grinned. "You got to understand, a lot of the stuff I'm telling you, I'm translating already; putting it in a form you can understand. Otherwise I couldn't tell the story at all. You want to hear it?"

"Yes." I didn't care if it was true or not; it was a story I needed to hear all the way through to the end.

"Good. So shut up and listen.

"So I met Saraquael, in the topmost gallery. There was no one else about—just him, and some papers, and some small, glowing models.

" 'I've come about Carasel,' I told him.

"He looked at me. 'Carasel isn't here at this time,' he said. 'I expect him to return shortly.'

"I shook my head.

" 'Carasel won't be coming back. He's stopped existing as a spiritual entity,' I said.

"His light paled, and his eyes opened very wide. 'He's dead?'

" 'That's what I said. Do you have any ideas about how it happened?'

" 'I . . . this is so sudden. I mean, he'd been talking about . . . but I had no idea that he would . . .'

" 'Take it slowly.'

"Saraquael nodded.

"He stood up and walked to the window. There was no view of the Silver City from his window—just a reflected glow from the City and the sky behind us, hanging in the air, and beyond that, the Dark. The wind from the Dark gently caressed Saraquael's hair as he spoke. I stared at his back.

" 'Carasel is . . . no, was. That's right, isn't it? *Was*. He was always so involved. And so creative. But it was never enough for him. He always wanted to understand everything—to experience what he was working on. He was never content to just create it—to understand it intellectually. He wanted *all* of it.

" 'That wasn't a problem before, when we were working on properties of matter. But when we began to design some of the Named emotions . . . he got too involved with his work.

" 'And our latest project was *Death*. It's one of the hard ones—one of the big ones, too, I suspect. Possibly it may even become the attribute that's going to define the Creation for the Created: if not for *Death*, they'd be content to simply exist, but with *Death*, well, their lives will have meaning—a boundary beyond which the living cannot cross . . .'

" 'So you think he killed himself?'

" 'I know he did,' said Saraquael. I walked to the window, and looked out. Far below, a *long* way, I could see a tiny white dot. That was Carasel's body. I'd have to arrange for someone to take care of it. I wondered what we would do with it, but there would be someone who would know, whose function was the removal of unwanted things. It was not my function. I knew that.

" 'How?'

"He shrugged. 'I know. Recently he'd begun asking questions—questions about Death. How we could know whether or not it was right to make this thing, to set the rules, if we were not going to experience it ourselves. He kept talking about it.'

" 'Didn't you wonder about this?'

"He turned, for the first time, to look at me. 'No. That *is* our function—to discuss, to improvise, to aid the Creation and the Created. We sort it out now, so that when it all Begins, it'll run like clockwork. Right now we're working on Death. So obviously that's what we look at. The physical aspect; the emotional aspect; the philosophical aspect . . .

" 'And the *patterns*. Carasel had the notion that what we do here in the Hall of Being creates patterns. That there are structures and shapes appropriate to beings and events that, once begun, must continue until they reach their end. For us, perhaps, as well as for them. Conceivably he felt this was one of his patterns.

" 'Did you know Carasel well?'

" 'As well as any of us know each other. We saw each other here; we worked side by side. At certain times I would retire to my cell, across the City. Sometimes he would do the same.'

" 'Tell me about Phanuel.'

"His mouth crooked into a smile. 'He's officious. Doesn't do much—farms everything out, and takes all the credit.' He lowered his voice, although there was no other soul in the gallery. 'To hear him talk, you'd think that *Love* was all his own work. But to his credit he does make sure the work gets done. Zephkiel's the real thinker of the two senior designers, but he doesn't come here. He stays back in his cell in the City, and contemplates; resolves problems from a distance. If you need to speak to Zephkiel, you go to Phanuel, and Phanuel relays your questions to Zephkiel . . .'

"I cut him short. 'How about Lucifer? Tell me about him.'

" 'Lucifer? The Captain of the Host? He doesn't work here . . . . He has visited the hall a couple of times, though—inspecting the Creation. They say he reports directly to the Name. I have never spoken to him.'

" 'Did he know Carasel?'

" 'I doubt it. As I said, he has only been here twice. I have seen him on other occasions, though. Through here.' He flicked a wingtip, indicating the world outside the window. 'In flight.'

" 'Where to?'

"Saraquael seemed to be about to say something, then he changed his mind. 'I don't know.'

"I looked out of the window, at the Darkness outside the Silver City.

" 'I may want to talk with you some more, later,' I told Saraquael.

" 'Very good.' I turned to go. 'Sir? Do you know if they will be assigning me another partner? For *Death*?'

" 'No,' I told him. 'I'm afraid I don't.'

"In the center of the Silver City was a park—a place of recreation and rest. I found the angel Lucifer there, beside a river. He was just standing, watching the water flow.

" 'Lucifer?'

"He inclined his head. 'Raguel. Are you making progress?'

" 'I don't know. Maybe. I need to ask you a few questions. Do you mind?'

" 'Not at all.'

" 'How did you come upon the body?'

" 'I didn't. Not exactly. I saw Phanuel, standing in the street. He looked distressed. I inquired whether there was something wrong, and he showed me the dead angel. And I fetched you.'

" 'I see.'

"He leaned down, let one hand enter the cold water of the river. The water splashed and rilled around it. 'Is that all?'

" 'Not quite. What were you doing in that part of the City?'

" 'I don't see what business that is of yours.'

" 'It is my business, Lucifer. What were you doing there?'

" 'I was . . . walking. I do that sometimes. Just walk, and think. And try to understand.' He shrugged.

" 'You walk on the edge of the City?'

"A beat, then, 'Yes.'

" 'That's all I want to know. For now.'

" 'Who else have you talked to?'

" 'Carasel's boss, and his partner. They both feel that he killed himself—ended his own life.'

" 'Who else are you going to talk to?'

"I looked up. The spires of the City of the Angels toward above us. 'Maybe everyone.'

" 'All of them?'

" 'If I need to. It's my function. I cannot rest until I understand what happened, and until the Vengeance of the Name has been taken on whoever was responsible. But I'll tell you something I do know.'

" 'What would that be?' Drops of water fell like diamonds from the angel Lucifer's perfect fingers.

" 'Carasel did not kill himself.'

" 'How do you know that?'

" 'I am Vengeance. If Carasel had died by his own hand,' I explained to the Captain of the Heavenly Host, 'there would have been no call for me. Would there?'

"He did not reply.

"I flew upward, into the light of the eternal morning.

"You got another cigarette on you?"

I fumbled out the red and white packet, handed him a cigarette.

"Obliged.

"Zephkiel's cell was larger than mine.

"It wasn't a place for waiting. It was a place to live, and work, and *be*. It was lined with books, and scrolls, and papers, and there were images and representations on the walls: pictures. I'd never seen a picture before.

"In the center of the room was a large chair, and Zephkiel sat there, his eyes closed, his head back.

"As I approached him he opened his eyes.

"They burned no brighter than the eyes of any of the other angels I had seen, but somehow they seemed to have seen more. It was something about the way he looked. I'm not sure I can explain it. And he had no wings.

" 'Welcome, Raguel,' he said. He sounded tired.

" 'You are Zephkiel?' I don't know why I asked him that. I mean, I knew who people were. It's part of my function, I guess. Recognition. I know who *you* are.

" 'Indeed. You arc staring, Raguel. I have no wings, it is true, but then, my function does not call for me to leave this cell. I remain here, and I ponder. Phanuel reports back to me, brings me the new things, for my opinion. He brings me the problems, and I think about them, and occasionally I make myself useful by making some small suggestions. That is my function. As yours is vengeance.'

" 'Yes.'

" 'You are here about the death of the angel Carasel?'

" 'Yes.'

" 'I did not kill him.'

"When he said it, I knew it was true.

" 'Do you know who did?'

" 'That is *your* function, is it not? To discover who killed the poor thing, and to take the Vengeance of the Name upon him.'

" 'Yes.'

"He nodded.

" 'What do you want to know?'

"I paused, reflecting on what I had heard that day. 'Do you know what Lucifer was doing in that part of the City, before the body was found?'

"The old angel stared at me. 'I can hazard a guess.'

" 'Yes?'

" 'He was walking in the Dark.'

"I nodded. I had a shape in my mind, now. Something I could almost grasp. I asked the last question: 'What can you tell me about *Love*?'

"And he told me. And I thought I had it all.

"I returned to the place where Carasel's body had been; the remains had been removed. The blood had been cleaned away. The stray feathers collected and disposed of. There was nothing on the silver sidewalk to indicate it had ever been there. But I knew where it had been.

"I ascended on my wings, flew upward until I neared the top of the spire of the Hall of Being. There was a window there, and I entered.

"Saraquael was working there, putting a wingless mannequin into a small box. On one side of the box was a representation of a small brown creature, with eight legs. On the other was a representation of a white blossom.

" 'Saraquael?'

" 'Hm? Oh, it's you. Hello. Look at this: if you were to die, and to be, let us say, put into the earth in a box, which would you want laid on top of you—a spider, here, or a lily, here?"

" 'The lily, I suppose.'

" 'Yes, that's what I think, too. But *why*? I wish . . ." He raised a hand to his chin, stared down at the two models, put first one on top of the box, then the other, experimentally. 'There's so much to do, Raguel. So much to get right. And we only get one chance at it, you know. There'll just be one universe—we can't keep trying until we get it right. I wish I understood why all this was so important to Him . . .'

" 'Do you know where Zephkiel's cell is?' I asked him.

" 'Yes. I mean, I've never been there. But I know where it is.'

" 'Good. Go there. He'll be expecting you. I will meet you there.'

"He shook his head. 'I have work to do. I can't just . . .'

"I felt my function come upon me. I looked down at him, and I said, 'You will be there. Go now.'

"He said nothing. He backed away from me, toward the window, staring at me; then he turned, and flapped his wings, and I was alone.

"I walked to the central well of the hall, and let myself fall, tumbling down through the model of the universe: it glittered around me, unfamiliar colors and shapes seething and writhing without meaning.

"As I approached the bottom, I beat my wings, slowing my descent, and stepped lightly onto the silver floor. Phanuel stood between two angels, who were both trying to claim his attention.

" 'I don't care how aesthetically pleasing it would be,' he was explaining to one of them. 'We simply cannot put it in the center. Background radiation would prevent any possible life-forms from even getting a foothold; and anyway, it's too unstable.'

"He turned to the other. 'Okay, let's see it. Hmm. So *that*'s *Green*, is it? It's not exactly how I'd imagined it, but . . . Mm. Leave it with me. I'll get back to you.' He took a paper from the angel, folded it over decisively.

"He turned to me. His manner was brusque, and dismissive. 'Yes?'

" 'I need to talk to you.'

" 'Mm? Well, make it quick. I have much to do. If this is about Carasel's death, I have told you all I know.'

" 'It is about Carasel's death. But I will not speak to you now. Not here. Go to Zephkiel's cell: he is expecting you. I will meet you there.'

"He seemed about to say something, but he only nodded, walked toward the door.

"I turned to go, when something occurred to me. I stopped the angel who had the *Green*. 'Tell me something.'

" 'If I can, sir.'

" 'That thing.' I pointed to the Universe. 'What's it going to be *for*?'

" 'For? Why, it is the Universe.'

" 'I know what it's called. But what purpose will it serve?'

"He frowned. 'It is part of the plan. The Name wishes it; He requires *such and such*, to *these* dimensions, and having *such and such* properties and ingredients. It is our function to bring it into existence, according to His wishes. I am sure *He* knows its function, but He has not revealed it to me.' His tone was one of sarcasm and rebuke.

"I nodded, and left that place.

"High above the City a phalanx of angels wheeled and circled and dove. Each held a flaming sword that trailed a streak of burning brightness behind it, dazzling the eye. They moved in array through the salmon-pink sky. They were very beautiful. It was—you know on summer evenings, when you get whole flocks of birds performing their dances in the sky? Weaving and circling and clustering and breaking apart again, so just as you think you understand the pattern, you realize you don't, and you never will? It was like that, only better.

"Above me was the sky. Below me, the shining City. My home. And outside the City, the Dark.

"Lucifer hovered a little below the Host, watching their maneuvers.

" 'Lucifer?'

" 'Yes, Raguel? Have you discovered your malefactor?'

" 'I think so. Will you accompany me to Zephkiel's cell?

There are others waiting for us there, and I will explain everything.'

"He paused. Then, 'Certainly.'

"He raised his perfect face to the angels, now performing a slow revolution in the sky, each moving through the air keeping perfect pace with the next, none of them ever touching. 'Azazel!'

"An angel broke from the circle; the others adjusted almost imperceptibly to his disappearance, filling the space, so you could no longer see where he had been.

" 'I have to leave. You are in command, Azazel. Keep them drilling. They still have much to perfect.'

" 'Yes, sir.'

"Azazel hovered where Lucifer had been, staring up at the flock of angels, and Lucifer and I descended toward the city.

" 'He's my second in command,' said Lucifer. 'Bright. Enthusiastic. Azazel would follow you anywhere.'

" 'What are you training them for?'

" 'War.'

" 'With whom?'

" 'How do you mean?'

" 'Who are they going to fight? Who else *is* there?'

"He looked at me; his eyes were clear, and honest. 'I do not know. But He has Named us to be His army. So we will be perfect. For Him. The Name is infallible and all-just, and all-wise, Raguel. It cannot be otherwise, no matter what—' He broke off, and looked away.

" 'You were going to say?'

" 'It is of no importance.'

" 'Ah.'

"We did not talk for the rest of the descent to Zephkiel's cell."

I looked at my watch. It was gone. A chill breeze had begun to blow down the L.A. street, and I shivered. The man noticed, and he paused in his story. "You okay?" he asked.

"I'm fine. Please carry on. I'm fascinated."

He nodded.

"They were waiting for us in Zephkiel's cell: Phanuel, Saraquael, and Zephkiel. Zephkiel was sitting in his chair. Lucifer took up a position beside the window.

"I walked to the center of the room, and I began.

" 'I thank you all for coming here. You know who I am; you know my function. I am the Vengeance of the Name: the arm of the Lord. I am Raguel.

" 'The angel Carasel is dead. It was given to me to find out why he died, who killed him. This I have done. Carasel was a designer in the Hall of Being. He was very good, or so I am told . . .

" 'Lucifer. Tell me what you were doing, before you came upon Phanuel and the body.'

" 'I have told you already. I was walking.'

" 'Where were you walking?'

" 'I do not see what business that is of yours.'

" *'Tell me.'*

"He paused. He was taller than any of us; tall, and proud. 'Very well. I was walking in the Dark. I have been walking in the Darkness for some time now. It helps me to gain a perspective on the City—being outside it. I see how fair it is, how perfect. There is nothing more enchanting than our home. Nothing more complete. Nowhere else that anyone would want to be'

" 'And what do you do in the Dark, Lucifer?'

"He stared at me. 'I walk. And . . . There are voices, in the Dark. I listen to the voices. They promise me things, ask me questions, whisper and plead. And I ignore them. I steel myself and I gaze at the City. It is the only way I have of testing myself—putting myself to any kind of trial. I am the Captain of the Host; I am the first among the angels, and I must prove myself.'

"I nodded. 'Why did you not tell me this before?'

"He looked down. 'Because I am the only angel who walks in the Dark. Because I do not want others to walk in the Dark: I am strong enough to challenge the voices, to test myself. Others are not so strong. Others might stumble, or fall.'

" 'Thank you, Lucifer. That is all, for now.' I turned to the next angel. 'Phanuel. How long have you been taking credit for Carasel's work?'

"His mouth opened, but no sound came out.

" '*Well?*'

" 'I . . . I would not take credit for another's work.'

" 'But you did take credit for *Love*?'

"He blinked. 'Yes. I did.'

" 'Would you care to explain to us all what *Love* is?' I asked.

"He glanced around uncomfortably. 'It's a feeling of deep affection and attraction for another being, often combined with passion or desire—a need to be with another.' He spoke dryly, didactically, as if he were reciting a mathematical formula. 'The feeling that we have for the Name, for our Creator—that is *Love* . . . amongst other things. *Love* will be an impulse that will inspire and ruin in equal measure. . . . We are'—he paused, then began once more—'we are very proud of it.'

"He was mouthing the words. He no longer seemed to hold any hope that we would believe them.

" 'Who did the majority of the work on *Love*? No, don't answer. Let me ask the others first. Zephkiel? When Phanuel passed the details on *Love* to you for approval, who did he tell you was responsible for it?'

"The wingless angel smiled gently. 'He told me it was his project.'

" 'Thank you, sir. Now, Saraquael: whose was *Love*?'

" 'Mine. Mine and Carasel's. Perhaps more his than mine, but we worked on it together.'

" 'You knew that Phanuel was claiming the credit for it?'

" '. . . Yes.'

" 'And you permitted this?'

" 'He—he promised us that he would give us a good project of our own to follow. He promised that if we said nothing we would be given more big projects—and he was true to his word. He gave us *Death*.'

"I turned back to Phanuel. 'Well?'

" 'It is true that I claimed that *Love* was mine.'

" 'But it was Carasel's. And Saraquael's.'

" 'Yes.'

" 'Their last project—before *Death*?'

" 'Yes.'

" 'That is all.'

"I walked over to the window, looked out at the silver spires, looked at the dark. And I began to speak.

" 'Carasel was a remarkable designer. If he had one failing, it was that he threw himself too deeply into his work.' I turned back to them. The angel Saraquael was shivering, and lights were flickering beneath his skin. 'Saraquael? Whom did Carasel love? Who was his lover?'

He stared at the floor. Then he stared up, proudly, aggressively. And he smiled.

" 'I was.'

" 'Do you want to tell me about it?'

" 'No.' A shrug. 'But I suppose I must. Very well, then.

" 'We worked together. And when we began to work on *Love* . . . we became lovers. It was his idea. We would go back to his cell, whenever we could snatch the time. There we touched each other, held each other, whispered endearments and protestations of eternal devotion. His welfare mattered more to me than my own. I existed for him. When I was alone I would repeat his name to myself, and think of nothing but him.

" 'When I was with him . . .' He paused. He looked down. '. . . nothing else mattered.'

"I walked to where Saraquael stood; lifted his chin with my hand, stared into his grey eyes. 'Then why did you kill him?'

" 'Because he would no longer love me. When we started to work on *Death* he—he lost interest. He was no longer mine. He belonged to *Death*. And if I could not have him, then his new lover was welcome to him. I could not bear his presence—I could not endure to have him near me and to know that he felt nothing for me. That was what hurt the most. I thought . . . I hoped . . . that if he was gone then I would no longer care for him—that the pain would stop. So I killed him; I stabbed him, and I threw his body from our window in the Hall of Being.

" 'But the pain has *not* stopped.' It was almost a wail.

"Saraquael reached up, removed my hand from his chin. 'Now what?'

"I felt my aspect begin to come upon me; felt my function possess me. I was no longer an individual—I was the Vengeance of the Lord.

"I moved close to Saraquael, and embraced him. I pressed my lips to his, forced my tongue into his mouth. We kissed. He closed his eyes.

"I felt it well up within me then: a burning, a brightness. From the corner of my eyes, I could see Lucifer and Phanuel averting their faces from my light; I could feel Zephkiel's stare. And my light became brighter and brighter, until it erupted—from my eyes, from my chest, from my fingers, from my lips: a white, searing fire.

"The white flames consumed Saraquael slowly, and he clung to me as he burned.

"Soon there was nothing left of him. Nothing at all.

"I felt the flame leave me. I returned to myself once more.

"Phanuel was sobbing. Lucifer was pale. Zephkiel sat in his chair, quietly watching me.

"I turned to Phanuel and Lucifer. 'You have seen the

Vengeance of the Lord,' I told them. 'Let it act as a warning to you both.'

"Phanuel nodded. 'It has. Oh, it has. I—I will be on my way, sir. I will return to my appointed post. If that is all right with you?'

" 'Go.'

"He stumbled to the window, and plunged into the light, his wings beating furiously.

"Lucifer walked over to the place on the silver floor where Saraquael had once stood. He knelt, stared desperately at the floor as if he were trying to find some remnant of the angel I had destroyed: ash, or bone, or charred feather; but there was nothing to find. Then he looked up at me.

" 'That was not right,' he said. 'That was not just.' He was crying; wet tears ran down his face. Perhaps Saraquael was the first to love, but Lucifer was the first to shed tears. I will never forget that.

"I stared at him, impassively. 'It was justice. He killed another. He was killed in his turn. You called me to my function, and I performed it.'

" 'But . . . he *loved*. He should have been forgiven. He should have been helped. He should not have been destroyed like that. That was *wrong*.'

" 'It was His will.'

"Lucifer stood. 'Then perhaps His will is unjust. Perhaps the voices in the Darkness speak truly after all. How *can* this be right?'

" 'It is right. It is His will. I merely performed my function.'

"He wiped away the tears with the back of his hand. 'No,' he said, flatly. He shook his head, slowly, from side to side. Then he said, 'I must think on this. I will go now.'

"He walked to the window, stepped into the sky, and he was gone.

"Zephkiel and I were alone in his cell. I went over to his

chair. He nodded at me. 'You have performed your function well, Raguel. Shouldn't you return to your cell, to wait until you are next needed?' ''

The man on the bench turned toward me: his eyes sought mine. Until now it had seemed—for most of his narrative—that he was scarcely aware of me; he had stared ahead of himself, whispered his tale in little better than a monotone. Now it felt as if he had discovered me, and that he spoke to me alone, rather than to the air, or the City of Los Angeles. And he said:

''I knew that he was right. But I *couldn't* have left then—not even if I had wanted to. My aspect had not entirely left me; my function was not completely fulfilled. And then it fell into place; I saw the whole picture. And like Lucifer, I knelt. I touched my forehead to the silver floor. 'No, Lord,' I said. 'Not yet.'

''Zephkiel rose from his chair. 'Get up. It is not fitting for one angel to act in this way to another. It is not right. Get up!'

''I shook my head. 'Father, You are no angel,' I whispered.

''Zephkiel said nothing. For a moment my heart misgave within me. I was afraid. 'Father, I was charged to discover who was responsible for Carasel's death. And I do know.'

'' 'You have taken your vengeance, Raguel.'

'' '*Your* vengeance, Lord.'

''And then He sighed, and sat down once more. 'Ah, little Raguel. The problem with creating things is that they perform so much better than one had ever planned. Shall I ask how you recognized Me?'

'' 'I . . . I am not certain, Lord. You have no wings. You wait at the center of the City, supervising the Creation directly. When I destroyed Saraquael, You did not look away. You know too many things. You . . .' I paused, and thought. 'No, I do not know how I know. As You say, You have created me well. But I only understood who You were and the meaning of the drama we had enacted here for You, when I saw Lucifer leave.'

" 'What did you understand, child?'

" 'Who killed Carasel. Or at least, who was pulling the strings. For example, *who* arranged for Carasel and Saraquael to work together on *Love*, knowing Carasel's tendency to involve himself too deeply in his work?'

"He was speaking to me gently, almost teasingly, as an adult would pretend to make conversation with a tiny child. 'Why should anyone have "pulled the strings," Raguel?'

" 'Because nothing occurs without reason; and all the reasons are Yours. You set Saraquael up: yes, he killed Carasel. But he killed Carasel so that *I* could destroy *him*.'

" 'And were you wrong to destroy him?'

"I looked into His old, old eyes. 'It was my function. But I do not think it was just. I think perhaps it was needed that I destroy Saraquael, in order to demonstrate to Lucifer the Injustice of the Lord.'

"He smiled, then. 'And whatever reason would I have for doing that?'

" 'I . . . I do not know. I do not understand—no more than I understand why You created the Dark, or the voices in the Darkness. But You did. You caused all this to occur.'

"He nodded. 'Yes. I did. Lucifer must brood on the unfairness of Saraquael's destruction. And that—amongst other things—will precipitate him into certain actions. Poor sweet Lucifer. His way will be the hardest of all My children; for there is a part he must play in the drama that is to come, and it is a grand role.'

"I remained kneeling in front of the Creator of All Things.

" 'What will you do now, Raguel?' he asked me.

" 'I must return to my cell. My function is now fulfilled. I have taken vengeance, and I have revealed the perpetrator. That is enough. But—Lord?'

" 'Yes, child.'

" 'I feel dirty. I feel tarnished. I feel befouled. Perhaps it is true that all that happens is in accordance with Your will, and thus it is good. But sometimes You leave blood on Your instruments.'

"He nodded, as if He agreed with me. 'If you wish, Raguel, you may forget all this. All that has happened this day.' And then He said, 'However, you will not be able to speak of this to any other angels, whether you choose to remember it or not.'

" 'I will remember it.'

" 'That is your choice. But sometimes you will find it is easier by far not to remember. Forgetfulness can sometimes bring freedom, of a sort. Now, if you do not mind'—He reached down, took a file from a stack on the floor, opened it—'there is work I should be getting on with.'

"I stood up and walked to the window. I hoped He would call me back, explain every detail of His Plan to me, somehow make it all better. But He said nothing, and I left His Presence without ever looking back."

The man was silent, then. And he remained silent—I couldn't even hear him breathing—for so long that I began to get nervous, thinking that perhaps he had fallen asleep, or died.

Then he stood up.

"There you go, pal. That's your story. Do you think it was worth a couple of cigarettes and a book of matches?" He asked the question as if it was important to him, without irony.

"Yes," I told him. "Yes. It was. But what happened next? How did you . . . I mean, if . . ." I trailed off.

It was dark on the street, now, at the edge of daybreak. One by one the streetlights had begun to flicker out, and he was silhouetted against the glow of the dawn sky. He thrust his hands into his pockets. ''What happened? I left home, and I lost my way, and these days home's a long way back. Sometimes you do things you regret, but there's nothing you can do about them. Times change. Doors close behind you. You move on. You know?

''Eventually I wound up here. They used to say no one's ever originally from L.A. True as hell in my case.''

And then, before I could understand what he was doing, he leaned down and kissed me, gently, on the cheek. His stubble was rough and prickly, but his breath was surprisingly sweet. He whispered into my ear: ''I never fell. I don't care what they say. I'm still doing my job—as I see it.''

My cheek burned where his lips had touched it.

He straightened up. ''But I still want to go home.''

The man walked away down the darkened street, and I sat on the bench and watched him go. I felt like he had taken something from me, although I could no longer remember what. I felt like he had given—absolution, perhaps, or innocence, although of what, or from what, I could no longer say.

An image from somewhere: a scribbled drawing, of two angels in flight above a perfect city; and over the image a child's perfect handprint, which stained the white paper bloodred. It came into my head unbidden, and I no longer knew what it meant.

I stood up.

It was too dark to see the face of my watch, but I knew I would get no sleep that day. I walked back to the place I was staying, to the house by the stunted palm tree, to wash myself, and to wait. I thought about angels, and about Tink; and I wondered whether love and death truly went hand in hand.

The next day the planes to England were flying again.

I felt strange—lack of sleep had forced me into that miserable state in which everything seems flat and of equal importance; when nothing matters, and in which reality seems scraped thin and threadbare. The taxi journey to the airport was a nightmare. I was hot, and tired, and testy. I wore a T-shirt in the L.A. heat; my coat was packed at the bottom of my luggage, where it had been for the entire stay.

The airplane was crowded, but I didn't care.

The stewardess walked down the aisle with a rack of newspapers, the *Herald Tribune, America Today*, and the *LA Times*. I took a copy of the *Times*, but the words left my head as my eyes scanned over them. Nothing that I read remained with me. No, I lie: somewhere in the back of the paper was a report of a triple murder: two women, and a small child. No names were given, and I do not know why the report should have registered as it did.

Soon I fell asleep. I dreamed about fucking Tink, while blood ran sluggishly from her closed eyes and lips. The blood was cold and viscous and clammy, and I awoke chilled by the plane's air conditioning, with an unpleasant taste in my mouth. My tongue and lips were dry. I looked out of the scratched oval window, stared down at the clouds, and it occurred to me then (not for the first time) that the clouds were in actuality another land, where everyone knew just what they were looking for and how to get back where they started from.

Staring down at the clouds is one of the things I have always liked best about flying. That, and the proximity one feels to one's death.

I wrapped myself in the thin aircraft blanket, and slept some more, but if further dreams came, then they made no impression upon me.

A blizzard blew up shortly after the plane landed in England, knocking out the airport's power supply. I was alone in an airport elevator at the time, and it went dark and jammed between floors. A dim emergency light flickered on. I pressed the crimson alarm button until the batteries ran down and it ceased to sound; then I shivered in my L.A. T-shirt, in the corner of my little silver room. I watched my breath steam in the air, and I hugged myself for warmth.

There wasn't anything in there except me; but even so, I felt safe, and secure. Soon someone would come and force open the doors. Eventually somebody would let me out; and I knew that I would soon be home.

Heaven, Heaven Is a Place . . .

by R. V. B*ranham*

Gloria woke up wondering where she was; the last thing she remembered was eating a banana split with three cherries. There was no ache, no pain—this was wrong, she'd just been working out for the New York City Marathon.

She immediately noticed the bed she was in: brass, with head and base boards shaped like harps. There was a sort of cloying sappy string-driven idiocy being piped in from somewhere, this amplectic anathematica of sound. Gloria didn't like sappy cloying string-driven piped-in idiocy, or amplectic anathematicas, and was about to vocalize her displeasure when the music changed, to a snarling, pulsing grind, something with a ton of asbestos chips on its shoulder. Music that reminded her of every vicious shit who'd ever screwed her under, gotten her disgraced, every friend who had betrayed her to save their ass, gotten her fired, anyone who for whatever reason had mindfucked her, gotten her tossed out on her ass *not*of*the*hivenot*of*the*hive*, and left for dead in the salt flats of her skull. Yes, it could only be Throbbing Gristle, her all-time favorite Post Industrial band. After Talking Heads. And Wire. And the Violent Femmes.

"Well," a voice said—Gloria turned, and saw only white chiffon draped everywhere, everywhere like a, like a, like a movie she saw once on the Late Early about Life After Death. About Heaven. "You certainly have a feisty taste in music," this hidden voice continued. She couldn't place gender—but *knew* it was a nurse.

How did I get here?

That voice gave an aeolian sigh. "Everyone acts like this, their first twenty-four hours."

"Who," Gloria calmly inquired, "who the shit on a toothbrush are you?"

She turned and saw a fat tub of a woman, a bearded woman, dressed in a nurse's tent, with arms like thighs, hands like catcher's mitts, and a beard. And a freaking beehive. A motherlessfucking tower of babel atop her head—his head?—*its*? A biblical baseball player dressed in a tent. "You, you're my *nurse*, right?"

"Right!"

This was not what Gloria thought of as her vision of Heaven. Hell, He should forgive the word, she didn't even believe in life beyond the mortal coil . . . sometimes she'd even had her doubts about life after birth.

I'm your nurse, her nurse said, without opening its mouth.

". . . How—?" She was about to ask her nurse how it did that. And then something happened that made her realize she *was* in Heaven. *The Curse* Had Returned.

"Ahmhmhem." Her nurse cleared her throat. "If esping makes you uncomfortable, then let's chitchat."

Chitchat, she thought, God—not a chatterbox, not a V-8 Four-On-The-Floor Mouth. "I don't know what to say,"

Gloria interrupted, being, in spite of herself, embarrassed. "I'm bleeding . . .'s my monthly."

"Tampons are in the drawer by your bed." The nurse smiled, batting its batwing eyelashes. "We all bleed up here, the Curse of Eve. . . ."

She let that comment slide.

"But I'm an *ath*lete, I was *in training*! I haven't had a period since—since," Gloria counted off the months. "Well, a goddamn year at least."

Her nurse pointed at an immense artsy decoid microphone hanging downward from, well, from Heaven Central. "It might be a good idea if you cleaned your act up, profanity-wise. *He* wouldn't appreciate it."

"Next you'll be wanting me to get rid of my silver Mohawk!"

Her nurse started to say something, but thought better of it. Gloria reached over for a tampon. "Could you turn away, while I . . . ?"

"While you, while you what?"

"While I *insert* it."

"Oh." Her nurse blushed a mottled puce. "Of course." And turned away. Gloria tore the wrapper off the tampon, and was alarmed by a sigh, a *familiar* sigh. As she inserted it, this sigh turned into a moan. Joey, it was Joey, her first-fuckinglay, or layingfuck (and tristate skateboardpunk king); always in out in out, and counting sheep in five minutes flat; best enjoying the deed when his partners were menstruating (and whom Gloria had only fucked because she was wet for Joey's punkessa kid sister); and who had OD'ed on white-out a few years ago, D.O.A.

"I forgot to tell you."

"What? What was it you forgot?"

"I forgot to tell you about L.A.D., Life After Death."

Gloria frowned, picked her nose. *"What about L.A.D.?"*

"Not all who come to Glory with God come as *human* beings."

"You mean to tell me that my first and last boyfriend, my first but not last fuck, came back as a tampon?"

"For Joey that very well might be Heaven. . . ."

"Right." Gloria had to concede her nurse's point. "But this could very well be his Hell."

"For some here it is. Your philosopher Sartre was all too right when he said that Hell Is Other People. Here you have Rest and Solitude."

"Sartre was full of it, and this is not *my* idea of Heaven."

"That's the problem."

Gloria wondered what the nurse *meant* by that. "I don't remember a thing. How did I die?"

"*We don't know!*"

"Isn't it your business to know?" She was about to blow a gasket, get out of bed, raise hell, kick some ass, do some knocking of her own around Heaven's door.

"Your data file was erased during a power outage; and someone forgot to punch 'Control:/Keep Document.' " The nurse wept; the batwings drooped down the nurse's cheeks. "These things happen."

"It's not *your* fault." Gloria was embarrassed, nonplussed.

"But *I* was the data clerk. . . ."

"Oh." Gloria began to think un-Heavenly thoughts.

"This always happens to me. 'S how I got this beard—"

"That's *hormonal*—"

"—I was Sent Down, I was a Guardian Angel Apprentice then, to prevent these Greek parents from leaving their baby in the wilds to die."

"Oedipus the king!"

"You *couldn't* have known him." Gloria's nurse looked at her, then went onward: "I figured I'd use reverse psych. So I told 'em the baby'd grow up to kill his dad, marry his mom . . . I figured they'd have the common moral sense *not* to do a thing so idiotically prophesy fulfilling as trying to kill him, abandoning him."

"Right." Gloria sighed. "Like Hillel said: 'Do not do unto others that which you would not have them do unto you—' "

"That's what I figured," the nurse replied and cut Gloria off. "I met Hillel once, a very deep man, a mensch. But where was I?"

"Interrupting."

"The two fools leave baby Eddie atop a hill."

Gloria was angry: "Sounds like God's doing to me."

"Of course it was, everything was, is, and ever shall—"

"I feel sleepy—" Gloria stretched her tattooed arms and yawned.

"—Be, World Without End, For Thine—"

"Remember what Hillel said?"

"You just quoted it."

"Let me quote the whole thing: 'Do not do unto others that which you would not have them do unto you. That is the entire Torah; the rest is commentary.' "

Gloria's nurse missed Hillel's last words, "Now go and study," having gotten the hint, having excused herself. Himself? Itself?

Don't be so gendercentric, Gloria told herself. Besides, she was one to talk, with her tattooed arms and silver Mohawk.

One day, a day being as good as a month or year or eon in any of Heaven's adjoining suites, Gloria decided to escape. She got out of bed, and found an electric pink tract suit draped over a chair, and her wallet. She ripped the Velcro out and her Gold Card and State ID appeared. Gloria examined her change flap and found a subway token. Next to that was a round-trip Pan Am ticket from J.F.K. to LAX, and her watch. She looked at the watch and at the Pan Am ticket. This was the day. How could she be so brain-dead as to forget her parents' wedding anniversary? This was a weird dream she had had about being in Heaven's Lost And Found. There was also a key card, Vista Hotel. She was at the World Trade Center. She had two hours to catch the A train to J.F.K. No problem. Gloria showered, relished in the smell of Irish Spring, and dressed, putting on her pink running suit. She called the Front Desk about Checkout Time and was told Nottoworry, that the Gentleman had taken care of it. *What Gentleman?* Gloria had not had a man in years, and had never had a *Gentle*man. She took her satchel with the broken lock, and, clutching the plane ticket and her wallet, headed out the door. She had to spread her elbows to make room in the elevator down to the lobby, crowded as it was with drunken geeks. One pink-faced slob wore a badge: ''Birmingham Alabama Metrologist's Association. What's your P.S.I.?'' He tried to grope her, but Gloria introduced her knee to his groin. The door opened and she bolted out into the lobby, turning left and past a baby grand piano no one ever played, and out the revolving doors to the atrium, and left to a mall where she could have sworn she read a headline about the U.S. invading Mexico, and Iran invading the U.S.S.R.—but she was late, so it was right and left, into the subway, where she inserted her token into the turnstile slot and was allowed to pass. The A train was packed with surly people of every color and gender and economic means. Usually, they were a bit more civil about it. No matter. She just had to ride through to Brooklyn and to Queens and on to J.F.K. She thought of the old rusted globe, the old Expo grounds, where she'd shoot the shit and drink the Ripple, and later join hegiras to Forest Hills, in search of Bat Masterson or Delmore Schwartz, Sid Vicious or Boss Tweed. Those were the days. Gloria had to drag herself across a walkway and snarling traffic to an elevator, where she punched a cracked button that took her to the third floor. She barely made her flight. Just barely, and had to sit in Smoking. The flight was marred by two hideous In-

Flight Movies: *Friday the 13th, Part 13* and *Beverly Hills Cop, Part 5*. No wonder she'd given up on movies. A snoring priest had the window next to her, which he kept closed, and thus she was denied views of fruited plains or sundry clouds. She suspected she had lost her tenuous hold on reality when the lasagna didn't make her want to turn her intestines inside out for airing. As they neared the Rockies, turbulence rocked the plane and "Fasten Seat Belt" lights came back on. Finally, they landed in L.A., and after fighting John Huston and Divine at the Baggage Claim, she got a cab to El Segundo—a mere two miles away. The neat big house across the street was gone; a row of condos stood in its place. Rosita, the housekeeper, greeted her, "Gloria," and when Gloria asked where her parents had gone, she was told, as if she were a complete drooling ninny, "to Heaven, to be with you."

Gloria rushed through the door seeking her parents and found an array of video display terminals. Someone tapped away at the keyboard of an IBM personal computer. "I just can't get the bugs out of these new interactive software packages," they announced as they turned to face Gloria. It was her goddamn bearded nurse. Before Gloria could begin to properly throttle her, she exited the program and switched disks. Gloria was then plunged into an eternally momentary light and back to her suite, to her immense bed, with brass head and base boards shaped like harps. And Gloria could never stand that harp crap. And the light-suffused chiffon. Okay, Jaweh, break time.

Gloria was mad again; everything was still suffused with light. And couldn't *someone* do something about the chiffon? She blinked. The chiffon was gone, replaced by large magenta stills of Jesse Owens running at Munich, Throbbing Gristle and Talking Heads in concert, Cyndi Lauper and Germaine Greer at ringside. Her Heroes and Heroines, each and every one. *"Hi, there!"* It was Stephanie, a photographer who'd had a crush on Gloria, followed her from meet to meet—ever grateful for the one awkward mercy fuck—Stephie bought a six by four by six plot of a banana farm in Honduras seven (or was it four?) years ago. Contras. Suddenly, photos of her idols were replaced by photos of *her*, breaking records, winning bronze silver gold Gold GOLD *GOLD*!

Gloria laughed. If she'd had her medals here, they'd've wanted to talk. But she wanted to talk to *people*. . . .

Would she never be able to express her love to those who deserved it, and her hatred to those who'd earned it?

See her niece when she graduated from CalArts? Hear about a particularly vile ex-boss outliving her usefulness and being made into a scapegoat for that missing $175,000 from the Textbooks Fund? See that sawed-off cunt when she was convicted, go up to the Prosecution and thank them for a job well done?

Would she be here forever, on ice, in the data-file-erased wing?

Gloria was in a Clifton's cafeteria of the mind, done in deadly decorator silver lamé and ferns and even a jacaranda, raining purple flowers, which fell into the vats of food. The tree waved to her. It was her dad, who'd always wanted to be a gardener, but had to run an advertising agency instead.

Her father talked jacaranda, she talked esp. Tree esp tree esp tree esp. It wasn't true, Gloria thought, none of it was. *It's bullshit, but this part is good bullshit*. It was good to talk with Dad again, even if he dropped petals in her soup. Split pea.

The soup begged her to stop eating it. This soup was one of her best friends—*but Sandy was still alive*—

"What happened?" A tear, Gloria's, fell onto Sandy, who enveloped the tear, forming tiny lips that kissed it.

* * *

Gloria was in the bathroom, talking to her uncle—Lannie the bullshitter. He tickled her gums, causing her to make a mess. Gloria admired the karmic symmetry of a Fuller brush man becoming a toothbrush in Heaven.

He would have made better dental floss, though.

In the shower, she kissed mom-the-shower-nozzle-and-water. Told Mom about her father the jacaranda. Mom was always good at getting those hidden canyons of grot, behind the ears, behind the knees, under the arms, under the toes, her navel. ". . . 'Night, Mom."

On one occasion Gloria saw her nurse guiding an immense cart down the hall, a section of the flying duck–wallpapered hall she had not noticed before. She hid behind a potted palm, clutched browning fronds, then peeped out. The nurse was reconnoitering the hall, and, satisfied there were no witnesses, punched into a painting with her pinky and forefinger. A bell rang and an elevator door opened. The nurse rushed the cart in and the elevator doors shut.

Gloria left the safety of her potted palm and followed. She reached the spot where the nurse had entered the elevator. There were no doors, not the faintest sign. But the painting was still there. George Washington, Patriarch of the Oligarchy. She held her two middle fingers against her palm and pointed her forefinger and pinky straight up, in what she'd always assumed to be a dark Occult symbol. Gloria poked George between the eyes and the flying ducks parted.

Gloria rushed into the elevator. The ducks rejoined formation behind her, closing the doors. And she fell. Looking up, she realized she was in a galleria, a video arcade. She was certain she'd bumped her head, because she could not rise, try as she did, and Gloria did try. She felt as though she were flat on her back, on the gummy concrete floor, wearing fisheye glasses that brought the world to her in an acutely uncomfortable way. Gloria saw a familiar face—it was Joey! "Joey, help me up, I just escaped from God's Lost and Found!" Joey, with his hand in his pocket, fondling himself, saw her, saw Gloria. "I thought you died!" Oh, oh. No. He grabbed her, and the galleria began to spin as he picked her up and put her into his other pocket, the one without the handsized hole. Was it like this all over Heaven, everyone a prop in everyone else's set?

She could feel round objects rubbing against her. Drugs. Two Valium, one on each side, made her drowsy; further down the cotton funnel she could dimly perceive some post-psychedelic designer drug. All in all she preferred the lulling company of the Valium to some chemistry major's bumptious concoction.

This contemplation was cut short as Joey's hand reached into his pocket and retrieved Gloria. Again, everything was at a seasick angle, only there was tile, glaring tile everywhere. She made out a toilet stall, and two sets of feet. All this was quite brief, because the next thing she saw was the coin slot of a condom machine. And then she fell into the metal dark, down the chute, into a metal box, where, *clink*, she fell in with a sad assortment of despairing quarters, crying dimes, and scheming nickels. This was too much to bear. "*I'm sorry,*" Gloria finally heard herself saying between weepy sobs.

She heard approaching footsteps, then a jangling of keys. "Oh, boy, they're coming to get us," a nickel shouted.

"You'll just wind up in a roll of coins," a quarter said. All the coins were silent as a key was inserted into the outer wall of their metal prison. They all shuddered as the box was gently removed. A hand appeared and reached for Gloria.

"Hey, what about us," cried a Canadian dime.

"Don't you ever do this again, Gloria." It was her nurse. "You're going to your room, grounded for a week. No cafeteria, no jukebox or piano or harpsichord. I've had to go through every coin box in this mall. And those coins are so filthy.''

A week later, a month . . . ? Gloria was playing tic tac toe with her blanket, and listening to Bessie Smith on a Philco radio that had mysteriously appeared a few days before; and her nurse arrived.

''I've—'' Her nurse pointed emphatically upward to that microphone that looked like something out of the Big Broadcast. . . . ''—Had A Talk.'' Gloria waited her nurse out. ''Well? Would you like to join the Elect? 'S great fun, we sing hymns, contemplate creation, have spelling bees, sing—''

''You loiter around in baggy tents and sing shitty songs off-key to make an old tyrant glad?''

''Exactly!'' Her nurse had missed the irony and venom that dripped from her voice, making pockmarks in the tile floor. (She smiled at the floor, which whimpered. Those floor tiles had been her grade-school principal.)

''What about everyone else here?''

''They'll stay here.''

''And so will I.''

''Think of what you're missing.''

''I'm missing life on earth, that's what I'm missing. Running barefoot along the sand, having granola with blackberry brandy and coffee liqueur and crème de cacao, going to clubs with friends and hearing good music, taking the A train to Lincoln Center to buy my veggies or eat out, telling some jerkoff to jerk off—''

Gloria's nurse cringed.

''—I didn't mean it that way; but Hell, for Limbo, or Heaven, or whatever, this toilet isn't half-bad, even if the tampons do come on to you.''

Her nurse was about to say something, but Gloria continued: ''Look, I met and made friends with a piano who's Eric Satie, a harpsichord who's Mozart—Wolfie the Proto-Punk, a Philco radio with Bessie Smith singing dyke blues, and a jukebox who's John Lennon—*why aren't they with God*?"

"Salieri's there, and Arthur Fiedler."

"Satie told me it was a good thing I was a marathon runner and ran barefoot on the beach whenever possible, otherwise I might be a pair of Pumas or a roll of toilet paper."

"That is silly gossip." Her nurse looked away. "As I said before, your arrival was a mistake, that's why you're in this wing . . . which *isn't Limbo*—you'd find Limbo to be too Minimalist for even your taste."

Her nurse smiled. "Are you certain you won't join us? We won't make this offer again."

"Fine," Gloria said, "leave me in the casualty ward and fuck off. Please."

After her nurse had fucked off, thank you, Gloria returned to the cafeteria to talk to her father the tree and her friend and former lover the eternal soup while Mozart and Satie performed a duet. Lennon the jukebox kicked in with her favorite Talking Heads song, and David Byrne sangspoke about how, in Heaven, nothing happens, not really, not ever . . . or if it does, like a song on a jukebox, or like a kiss, it is repeated endlessly and precisely. Exactly the same. The same as before.

'S not earth, not even New York City, but it sufficed . . . overfriendly tampons and furniture with sympathetic ears . . . what more could a girl of the marathon ask for, beyond the daily terrible beatification delayed, the hourly satori postponed, the time-released epiphany unabsorbed, except, perhaps, for some fun?

HARLAN ELLISON

Most readers are familiar with Harlan Ellison—but if you are not, go immediately to a bookstore and buy all of his available short story collections and read them. *Deathbird Stories* is particularly good, as is *Shatterday* and *The Essential Ellison*; there are close to sixty from which to choose. The important thing is to get to know the work of the best short story writer there is. His talent is giant, spanning three decades now, and has not diminished an iota over the years.

Where I Shall Dwell in the Next World

by Harlan Ellison

PREPARATORY NOTE ON PROCESS: How it happens, where it comes from, why it speaks in that particular tongue, always the same damned unanswerable question. But they never give it a rest, the endless interrogation. Their cadre is never depleted. We sit under the broiling lights turned into our eyes, and they ask and ask, always the same damned question, and we plead ignorance; and when one of their number tires, she or he is replaced by another. And the question is asked again and again, without change, without compassion. We would tell if we knew, honestly we would. We would give up every secret we possess, if only they would turn off the lights for fifteen minutes, let us curl onto the cold stone floor and catch forty winks. We would tell all, divulge every tiny code number and Mercator track, drop the dime on even the dearest and closest friend or lover, spill the beans, tell the tale, give it all up if only they'd knock off for fifteen minutes, let it go dark, let us sleep.

But they won't, they're merciless; and they never wise up, because their cadre is never depleted. There's always another one warming up in the bullpen as the one on the mound begins to tire and keeps missing the strike zone. And here comes the new one, still moist from the academy, eyes bright as a Borneo Green Broadbill's, smiling ingratiatingly, plopping into the well-worn interrogator's chair, and here comes that same stupid, damned unanswerable question. Again.

Where do you get your ideas?

In a letter dated 10 July 1991, Jeremy G. Byrne of the Editorial Committee of *Eidolon*, an extremely elegant and smart literary journal emanating from Perth (which is on the coast of Western Australia), wrote to me, in part: ". . . the genesis of *Eidolon* was a long process. You might well have guessed that it was your own ANGRY CANDY piece, 'Eidolons'—with its Australian connection—that gave us the idea; and when we discovered the alternate definitions for the word, it seemed stunningly appropriate, or at least amusingly pretentious."

Where do you get your ideas?

In the liner notes I wrote for the recorded reading I did of my story "Jeffty is Five" I said:

> *My friends Walter and Judy Koenig invited me to a party. I don't like parties. I do like Walter and Judy. I also like their kids. I went to the party.*
>
> *Mostly I sat near the fireplace, friendly but not ebullient. Mostly I talked to Walter and Judy's son, Josh, who is remarkable beyond the telling. And then I overheard a snatch of conversation. An actor named Jack Danon said—I* thought *he said—something like this—"Jeff is five, he's always five." No, not really. He didn't say anything like that at all. What he probably said was, "Jeff is fine, he's always*

fine." Or perhaps it was something completely different.

But I had been awed and delighted by Josh Koenig, and I instantly thought of just such a child who was arrested in time at the age of five. Jeffty, in no small measure, is Josh: the sweetness of Josh, the intelligence of Josh, the questioning nature of Josh.

Thus, from admiration of one wise and innocent child, and from a misheard remark, the process that not even Aristotle could codify was triggered.

Where do you get your ideas?

I purposely mishcar things. The excellent novelist and critic Geoffrey Wolff has written, "Every fictioneer re-invents the world because the facts, things or people of the received world are unacceptable." So I purposely mishear things that are said. It mortars up the gaps in boring conversation. It assists in doing honor to the late architect Robert Smithson's dictum: *Establish enigmas. Not explanations.* "Jeffty is five, he's always five."

Speak to me of a Chinese hand laundry, and I visualize a large wicker basket filled with Chinese hands that need laundering. Gladly, the Cross-Eyed Bear. Tearalong, the Dotted Lion.

Where do you get your ideas?

My story "Eidolons" came from the assemblage of a congeries of misheard remarks, altered to form brief allegories or tone-poems. I did one each week as the introduction to my stint as the host of a radio show. Now, like Ouroboros, we come full circle: kindly note process, and let me sleep:

Mishearing purposely; translative adaptation of misheard remark to fictional state; assemblage of misheard adaptations to story; story as impetus for *Eidolon* magazine; request from magazine for contribution; assemblage of misheard adaptations submitted to magazine born of effects of mishearing.

The process. Where do you get your ideas?

First, the stories. Then, revelation of what was said; and what was heard. The process. At last, to sleep, the answer.

Necro Waiters

The yellow tabby had only one good eye, but that one was good enough to do the job. Cat sat on the low ledge filled with potted cacti that ran the interior length of the enormous front window of the Long Pig Bar & Grille. Cat sat no more than two steps away from me as I absently smoothed the white tablecloth, waiting for my dinner to be served. Cat sat watching a three-legged dog crossing Cyclops Avenue, staring with all the rigid attention of a coffin observing the open grave.

Body still rigid, the cat swiveled its gaze to me, the one good eye fixing me mercilessly. ''I knew that one,'' she said. ''In life, he was an Associate Professor of Comparative Religions. Smug beyond belief. Talked to God and received regular replies, often by fax, occasionally by overnight express mail.''

I said nothing. I dislike cats, have never trusted them.

''Serves him proper,'' she said, ''losing a leg. See how he can rationalize his 'personal relationship' with the Deity now, ha!'' This was a vindictive creature. I fancied she had been a switchboard operator at a New York brokerage house.

''Don't care to reply?'' she said, a feline blowziness in her tone. ''You're absolutely dead, too, you know.''

I said, ''Demise does not preclude maintaining one's ethical standards. Go away. Suck a fish head. Bother someone else.'' I looked away.

The dining room was filled, after-theater crowd and night life hangers-on crowd. Chatting, spearing hors d'oeuvres, rubbing the wounds that had killed them. I felt quite alone in the midst of pressed bodies and yammering noise level.

The cat was now attempting to insult me. I paid no notice. If a cat could stand atop a dog, would it do so gently, hoping its living perch would not bolt . . . or would it dig in like an earth-mover, drawing blood and hanging on like a dude ranch novice? Such was the quality of rumination as I waited for my dinner to be served.

I saw my waiter threading his way through the crowd, in and out, around the tables, the aluminum serving tray held high, balanced on the spread fingers of one hand. He was one of the newly-dead and yet unpenitent. A zombie, a walking dead thing, a necro waiter. He had been, obviously, a Rastafarian; his dreadlocks oiled to a gloss with the life-blood of sperm whales and dolphins, lightly scented with rose petals; a tattoo of Haile Selassie on his chest that winked as the waiter approached.

He set the heavy tray on the edge of my table, and began unshipping plates. A glass of murky water. A salad plate on which the ceremonial Greek olive had been placed midway between an arc of pignoli nuts below and a pair of sago balls above, the design forming a sort of happy face. The main course, the steaming soul of my first wife, filled the large square dinner plate, garnished with remorse, a sprig of justified annoyance, and a double portion of mashed errors, gravy pooled in the center. "Will there be any'tin else, mon?" he asked, as he swept my cloth napkin off the table, shook it into a sail, and canopied it over my lap.

I looked at the meal.

"No, nothing else," I said. "As if I were entitled."

He looked at me with nothing like compassion. Then he smiled a face without teeth and said, "I could mebbe sneak ya some lahb'ster dat dey t'rew out when de Moabites wuz slaughtered." I knew about that. I snorted and went back to my plate.

There she lay, bitter and flavorless, as she had been every night since I had died. And I was required to down every last morsel. In life we had fought; in life I had never given an inch; in life we had gnawed on each other for fourteen years. Then she had put her left hand through the glass display case in the reception area of my office waiting room, and taken a shard and opened the other wrist, all the way to the inside of the elbow. Right there in front of the receptionist, who had been too frightened to help her. And she had bled to death in the office, so the senior partners and my co-workers could see the enormity of my failure to save her from her past.

"Not to your likin'?" said the necro waiter, still standing behind and to the side of me.

"Not much," I said, lifting my fork, poking at the gray and brown substance that had been her soul. "Would it do me any good to ask for salt and pepper?"

He moved closer. He reached down and took the plate off the table, replaced it on the tray. "I got pity f'you, poor japonica. You nevuh gone get your fill on some diet lahk dat. Here," he said, removing the last small plate remaining on the tray, a plate I had not seen before. "Here. Try dis."

He put it before me. It was a new culinary treat, and its presence at my table alerted me that the next phase of what I was to know forever had begun.

I had been married more than once.

Never order hamburger at the Long Pig Bar & Grille.

PROCESS: Do you remember a roll of candy wafers, hard little circular troches, called Necco Wafers? When I was a little boy, they were a favorite sweet for the movies because they lasted so long. They came in different flavors, and all the flavors tasted chalky except for the chocolate ones. And so, because you shared the pastilles with the kids sitting on either side of you, your chums and mates and pals, you carefully orchestrated how fast you ate your Necco Wafers, so you would always be offering a licorice one, or a lemon one, or a cheery cherry. But you were always alert so the chocolate ones were retained.

One day, lifetimes ago, I felt my heart miss its rhythm when I entered a small co-op grocery store on the other side of the tracks in Painesville, Ohio, and saw for the first time the roll of all-chocolate Necco Wafers. Surely, there was a God. To this day—and they are now hard to find—I cannot resist a roll of chocolate Necco Wafers.

I was standing in a movie line. I had brought two rolls of candy with me, and as I waited for the line to move, I ate a pastille or two. Behind me, a man my age, speaking softly to his female date, not wanting to seem to have been snooping, said, with hushed awe, "He's got Necco Wafers!" and the woman, considerably younger, repeated what she *thought* she had heard, and she said, "Necro wafers?" and he corrected her and explained; but *I* had already misheard what I wanted to hear. Necro waiters. Yes. For what are they waiting? How did they die? Oh yes! Necro waiters. Process.

MARK

At forty-one minutes after midnight on the night of 28 April 1910, with Halley's Comet boiling through the ink black skies directly overhead, in a graveyard in Elmira, New York, two young boys worked feverishly digging up a freshly-laid grave. The tombstone had not yet been set; the ground had not settled sufficiently.

It was cold for April, but the boys were sweating.

It had been cold a week earlier in Redding, Connecticut, when he had died at sunset.

It had been cold as thousands had filed past the casket, as he lay there in a freshly-pressed white linen suit, in Brick Presbyterian Church, in New York City.

And it had been cold all the while they were bringing him to Elmira for burial.

Cold, past midnight, a 15¢ slice of moon not nearly as bright as Halley's Comet, and the boys dug, they dug, really dug.

"Tom," whispered the taller of the two diggers, the one wearing the crushed and chewed-out straw hat. There was no answer. "Tom? I say, Tom, you all right down there?"

A voice from below. "Except for the dirt you drop on me."

The tall boy made a *whoops, sorry* sound. "Tom, danged if'n I ain't afeared to be out here. I wisht we wasn't here. It's awful solemn like, *ain't* it?"

Tom, four feet down in the rectangular pit, jacked a foot onto his shovel, wedging it deep in the dark soil so it stood up of its own accord. He wiped sweat from his nose and forehead, but his face still shone in the dim light of the lantern at pit's edge. He looked up at his companion. "Knock off that cornball dialect, will you, 'Hucky,' and keep moving that pile of dirt away from the edge before it buries me."

Huck looked chastened. "Sorry, Tom—"

"And for pete's sake, stop calling me *Tom*!"

"Sorry, Migmunt, I just thought . . . in case there was anybody around, you know, just happened to be listening, I should stay in character . . ."

"Listen, Podlack, just keep shoveling. My back is killing me and I want to get *out* of here—"

A voice, muffled heavily by at least a foot of dirt, interrupted him. "And I want to get the hell out of *here*, you pair of imbeciles!"

The boys looked at each other with panic, and without a sound began shoveling furiously.

Fifteen minutes later, the coffin had been uncovered. There was a steady banging from inside. And the voice: "Get this infernal thing *off* me! Come on, move your weird butts!"

Podlack, also known as Huckleberry, dropped into the pit and, using a claw hammer, began prising loose the nails that held the coffin lid in place. "Just a minute, sir; we'll have you out of there in a jiffy."

"Jiffy, my groaning sphincter, you incompetent! You should have been here yesterday! Move yourself!"

Finally, with both boys straining, the lid was wrenched free; they leaned it up against the end of the pit.

The white-maned old man with the drooping mustaches sat up, cricked his neck till it popped, then got to his feet by bracing his hands against the sides of the coffin. "By god, I think my bladder will burst," he said, beginning to unbutton his fly. He suddenly realized the boys were staring at him. "Do you *mind*?"

They turned their backs. After a minute Migmunt, also known as Tom, said, very politely, "Uh, we'd best hurry, sir. The shuttle won't wait, you know."

Behind them, the old man snorted. "It took long enough to get here in 1835, and it'll be-damned well long enough poking along till it gets me home; it'll wait, or I'll have that insipid comet-jockey up on charges so fast it'll make his escutcheon tarnish!"

They peeked around, and saw he was trying to crawl out of the grave, despite what he had said. They hastily clambered out the other side of the pit and extended their hands down to lift the old man. He slapped at the hands. "Get away from me," he snarled. "What the hell's the matter with you; what do you think I am, some crepuscular, withered, senescent sack of sheep-dip, to be yanked around at your pleasure?"

As he complained, he crawled up the side of the grave, dirt slipping away under him, dropping him back two feet for every one he gained. Finally, he reached ground level and brushed himself off. He looked around carefully. "You're certain we're alone here?"

"Yessir, yessir," they both said, almost in chorus.

"Let's hope so," he replied, pulling off his clothes.

Standing buck naked in the dim amber glow of the lantern, he said it again. "Let's hope so." Then he reached down between his big toe and second toe on the left foot, grasped the sealing strip between thumb and forefinger, and unzipped his body from bottom to top. Then, shrugging off the clever plastic disguise with all four of his arms, he scratched his blunt yellow beak and drew a deep breath, a prisoner freed from a confining jail cell. He turned to look up at Halley's Comet, and smiled as best a beak could smile.

"Give my regards to Broadway," he said, and began loping off toward the pickup point, Tom and Huck pumping along as hard as they could behind him, unable, in their clever plastic disguises, to keep up with him.

"Sir . . . sir . . ." Migmunt named Tom called, wheezing heavily as he tried to shorten the distance between himself and the former owner of the estate called Stormfield. "Sir . . . could you . . . would you . . . if you please, sir . . . slow down a bit so I can ask you . . ." He abruptly felt considerable pain in his face as he ran full tilt into the beaked, feathered, webbed-and-spur-footed personage who had perspired inside the shell of Samuel Langhorne Clemens for the entire seventy-five-year tour of duty. No-longer-Mark had stopped suddenly.

"*Now* what the bleeding bejeezus do you want?"

"Sir, it's just . . . I've been on this tour a lot longer than I'd expected. I was told when I was assigned . . . that is to say, sir, I was *advised* . . . when my orders were cut . . ."

"That you'd be off this miserable duty in what, ten, twelve, maybe fifteen years?" He tapped his three-toed claw impatiently.

"Well, uh, yes. Sir. That is."

"And you want me to say something to the Archangel of the Guard when I get back, is that it?"

"If you would, sir. If you only would."

"Son," the elder entity said, reaching out with one wing and laying his five-fingered talon on Tom's shoulder, "I was told I'd be mustered out in maximum fifty years. That was twenty-five years ago. It's a job, boy, a job dirtier than most, living among these idiots; but someone's got to do it. Can't have them running amuck all over the place, can we now?"

"But . . . ."

"I'll mention your plight. Won't do any good, but I'll mention it. Now . . . do you mind if I go home?"

And, without waiting for a proper answer, he whirled on his toes, and loped off again toward the pickup point. Behind him, the two figments of his imagination pumped their knees hard trying to keep from falling too far apace.

When they reached the drop target, the slave unit from Halley's Comet was already waiting. The egg had opened, the jasmine light poured forth in a perfect pool across the ground, and three field-echelon sqwarbs were waiting, the eldest looking pointedly at his thigh clock. "Let's go, let's go, come on and let's go," he called across the clearing as the three running figures broke out of cover of the trees. "Time's on the slide, along along, let's go!"

He who had been Mark slid to a halt, threw a slovenly salute, and said, "Ready to go. Seventy-five years is long enough. Take me on home, sqwarbs!" He turned to the ersatz Huck and Tom who had come to a breathless halt behind him, there in the lee of the egg, and he saw their pathetic looks. Fluffing his pin-feathers, he said to the eldest of the echelon sqwarbs, "These two want to go home, too. Any chance, any hope?"

"Next time," said the clock-watcher.

"Next time? *Next* time!" Migmunt shouted. "That'll be almost ninety years I'll have spent here! Twelve, maybe fifteen, *that* was what I signed on for, not ninety!"

Then ensued an argument, a violence, a wrangling that would have brought the authorities, had it not taken place in the middle of a clearing inside dense woods, well past midnight, in a remote section of south-central New York state near the Pennsylvania border. Podlack actually hit the youngest of the three field-echelon sqwarbs, knocking him on his tail-feathers and crimping his comb. Migmunt and Huck tried to climb inside the egg, but were driven back by force.

Finally, when it was clear to everyone that the egg would not take their full number, Migmunt and Podlack were chivvied aside by weapons awesome to behold, Mark was hustled onboard, and the egg resealed and sped aloft, leaving the forlorn and furious Huck and Tom behind; for another seventy-five years.

As the egg soared toward the shuttle that was Halley's Comet, the one who had been Mark craned his neck and shook his feathers and said, "That wasn't perhaps the smartest thing you could have done, you know."

"What wasn't?" the echelon grenadier said.

"Leaving a pair of extremely disquieted employees in charge of an operation that big. They were angry enough to do almost anything, even let the creatures know about everything."

"Let them," the clock-watching echelon grenadier said, with a haughty curl of his beak. "How badly can they mess up a primitive society like that in just seventy-five years? What are we talking about here . . . war, famine, pestilence, plague, cheap entertainment, overpopulation, bad art?"

"Seventy-five years is a tweep in a whirl," said the youngest as he rubbed emetic on his bruise. "How hard did *you* work to bring some common sense to them? How well did *you* do; how much influence did you have?"

Mark fell silent. Very true. The creatures of that sleepless orb were highly resistant to sensible behavior. He had done all he could, but the poor dumb things were seemingly determined to stumble about blindly, like sqwarbs with their heads cut off.

He sighed and closed his eyes, hoping for some rest on the journey home. It couldn't really get much worse down there. Not in just seventy-five years. When you wish upon a sqwarb.

PROCESS: Early 1985, and all the foofaraw about Halley's coming back. And no one pairing up Mark Twain's birth in 1835 with the Comet's arrival, and his death in 1910 at its next pass, with the current swing past the Earth. And I was so fascinated with the idea, that I reread all of Twain. One night, I was reading TOM SAWYER to the son of a woman I had been seeing, he was about ten or eleven at the time, and we were both eating Hydrox cookies, and I told him this thing about how I wanted to write about Twain, and the Comet, and maybe the Comet wasn't really a comet but was possibly a spaceship, or a star, or something like that; and he had his face full of Hydrox, and he said, "When you wish upon a sqwarb . . ." which wasn't, of course, what he said; it was what I *heard* him say.

And I knew what the story should be. Except I didn't have an ending, so I didn't write it in 1985. Or '86. Or '88. Or '90. But I write it now. And it *still* doesn't have an ending. But I like the opening a lot.

Process.

The Last Will and Testicle of Trees Rabelais

My grandparents came from Poland. They came from a town, Bydgoszcz. That's in the north, right near the middle. I'm probably not pronouncing it properly. Bydgoszcz. They weren't Jewish, they were just Polish. That has almost nothing to do with me or this final statement, but I always tell everybody that my grandparents came from Poland. You never know when it might help. Once I got stopped by a traffic cop as I was speeding to the airport, and I don't know why, but I told him my grandparents came from Poland, and so did his, not from Bydgoszcz. So he let me off with just a warning.

I like to say: let any three people hose me down, and I'll wind up making friends of two of them.

Occasionally someone will ask me what that means, and I tell them, it means I'm a very friendly person.

I leave Montana to the descendants of the last surviving member of the original cast of *Gilligan's Island*. Go to Montana, if you must. You will hear more intelligent sounds by rubbing a tweed jacket.

Every beach contains the last three chapters of the story of someone's life. If you look out to sea, to see what you can see, you will see the previous pages bobbing at the top of rolling waves.

I didn't want to go without telling you what happened to those lovely symbols of the 1939 New York World's Fair. The symbols of the World of Tomorrow, the famous Trylon and Perisphere. Steel from the orb and the spire now form part of the furnace building in what was Freeport Sulphur Company's Nicaro nickel plant in Cuba. Before Castro nationalized it. Back in 1945 the plant turned out nickel oxide, an essential alloy used in jet engines. Beauty can neither be created nor destroyed, it can only be converted.

If I'd realized that creating crabgrass, spurge, chickweed, ragweed, dandelion, plantain, kudzu, purslane, knotweed, sorrel, and burdock was mostly to annoy people, I'd have given God much lower marks on the final exam.

I leave the care and feeding of all Fallacies of Substantive Distraction, including ad hominem, ad misericordiam, ad odium, and post hoc, propter hoc—which is, more precisely, a Fallacy of Causation—to the splendid Sherpa herdsmen of the Nepalese Himalayas; for it is they alone who understand that paper cannot wrap up fire; also that if one plants melons, one will get melons.

Where the hell were the cops when I needed them?

All my life I have imagined doorways as the answers, and now with gun in mouth I stand here in the middle of the great Nullarbor Plain, attesting to the truth that there are no doorways large enough for an unprotected species like myself to pass through.

I leave the face of the moon to those who look for the best ways to unsnarl knotted shoelaces and dampen bad tempers. It is always cool and quiet, the face of the moon. And from far away it appears to resemble the general appearance of young women who danced in Warner Bros. musicals in the mid-1930s.

My name was Trees Rabelais.

PROCESS: Susan and I chanced to be in the bathroom at the same time. She asked me to hand her something from the medicine cabinet. She preceded the request with *Please* . . .

I have no memory of what it was she was asking for, or how it was that I heard, "Please, grab the somethingorother" as *Trees Rabelais*. But when I repeated it, she said it sounded like the name of the tragic male lead on a soap opera. I thought so, too. And so, to be as one with Miniver Cheevy, Richard Cory, and Wednesday's child, I dwelt on the heroic, godlike, impervious nature, and suicide, of Trees Rabelais. Process.

DAN SIMMONS

As it is for many writers, Dan Simmons's ''overnight success'' was many years in the making. An introspective, well-educated easterner, Simmons drew notice in 1983 when his first professional story won the World Fantasy Award for Best Short Story. His first novel, *Song of Kali*, was also singled out for awards, as has every novel since: *Carrion Comfort, Hyperion, The Fall of Hyperion*, and his recent collection, *Prayers to Broken Stones*.

Dan's writing exhibits that rare combination of adventure, intellect, and humanity. We include here, for the many who haven't had the opportunity to read it, Dan's first and formidable short story, ''The River Styx Runs Upstream.''

The River Styx Runs Upstream
by Dan Simmons

What thou lovest well remains
the rest is dross
What thou lov'st well shall not be reft
from thee
What thou lov'st well is thy
true heritage . . .

—Ezra Pound
Canto LXXXI

I loved my mother very much. After her funeral, after the coffin was lowered, the family went home and waited for her return.

I was only eight at the time. Of the required ceremony I remember little. I recall that the collar of the previous year's shirt was far too tight and that the unaccustomed tie was like a noose around my neck. I remember that the June day was too beautiful for such a solemn gathering. I remember Uncle Will's heavy drinking that morning and the bottle of Jack Daniel's he pulled out as we drove home from the funeral. I remember my father's face.

The afternoon was too long. I had no role to play in the family's gathering that day, and the adults ignored me. I found myself wandering from room to room with a warm glass of Kool-Aid, until finally I escaped to the backyard. Even that familiar landscape of play and seclusion was ruined by the glimpse of pale, fat faces staring out from the neighbors' windows. They were waiting. Hoping for a glimpse. I felt like shouting, throwing rocks at them. Instead I sat down on the old tractor tire we used as a sandbox. Very deliberately I poured the red Kool-Aid into the sand and watched the spreading stain digging a small pit.

They're digging her *up now.*

I ran to the swing set and angrily began to pump my legs against the bare soil. The swing creaked with rust, and one leg of the frame rose out of the ground.

No, they've already done that, stupid. Now they're hooking her up to big machines. Will they pump the blood back into her?

I thought of bottles hanging. I remembered the fat, red ticks that clung to our dog in the summer. Angry, I swung high, kicking up hard even when there was no more height to be gained.

Do her fingers twitch first? Or do her eyes just slide open like an owl waking up?

I reached the high point of my arc and jumped. For a second I was weightless and I hung above the earth like Superman, like a spirit flying from its body. Then gravity claimed me and I fell heavily on my hands and knees. I had scraped my palms and put grass stain on my right knee. Mother would be angry.

She's being walked around now. Maybe they're dressing her like one of the mannequins in Mr. Feldman's store window.

My brother Simon came out to the backyard. Although he was only two years older, Simon looked like an adult to me that afternoon. An old adult. His blond hair, as recently cut as mine, hung down in limp bangs across a pale forehead. His eyes looked tired. Simon almost never yelled at me. But he did that day.

"Get in here. It's almost time."

I followed him through the back porch. Most of the relatives had left, but from the living room we could hear Uncle Will. He was shouting. We paused in the hallway to listen.

"For Chrissakes, Les, there's still time. You just can't do this."

"It's already done."

"Think of the . . . Jesus Christ . . . think of the kids."

We could hear the slur of the voices and knew that Uncle Will had been drinking more. Simon put his finger to his lips. There was a silence.

"Les, think about just the money side of it. What's . . . how much . . . it's twenty-five percent of everything you have. For how many years, Les? Think of the kids. What'll that do to—"

"It's *done*, Will."

We had never heard that tone from Father before. It was not argumentative—the way it was when he and Uncle Will used to argue politics late at night. It was not sad like the time he talked to Simon and me after he had brought Mother home from the hospital the first time. It was just final.

There was more talk. Uncle Will started shouting. Even the silences were angry. We went to the kitchen to get a Coke. When we came back down the hallway, Uncle Will almost ran over us in his rush to leave. The door slammed behind him. He never entered our home again.

* * *

They brought Mother home just after dark. Simon and I were looking out the picture window and we could feel the neighbors watching. Only Aunt Helen and a few of our closest relatives had stayed. I felt Father's surprise when he saw the car. I don't know what we'd been expecting—maybe a long black hearse like the one that had carried Mother to the cemetery that morning.

They drove up in a yellow Toyota. There were four men in the car with Mother. Instead of dark suits like the one Father was wearing, they had on pastel, short-sleeved shirts. One of the men got out of the car and offered his hand to Mother.

I wanted to rush to the door and down the sidewalk to her, but Simon grabbed my wrist and we stood back in the hallway while Father and the other grown-ups opened the door.

They came up the sidewalk in the glow of the gaslight on the lawn. Mother was between the two men, but they were not really helping her walk, just guiding her a little. She wore the light blue dress she had bought at Scott's just before she got sick. I had expected her to look all pale and waxy—like when I peeked through the crack in the bedroom door before the men from the funeral home came to take her body away—but her face was flushed and healthy, almost sunburned.

When they stepped onto the front stoop, I could see that she was wearing a lot of makeup. Mother never wore makeup. The two men also had pink cheeks. All three of them had the same smile.

When they came into the house, I think we all took a step back—except for Father. He put his hands on Mother's arms, looked at her a long time, and kissed her on the cheek. I don't think she kissed him back. Her smile did not change. Tears were running down Father's face. I felt embarrassed.

The Resurrectionists were saying something. Father and Aunt Helen nodded. Mother just stood there, still smiling slightly, and looked politely at the yellow-shirted man as he spoke and joked and patted Father on the back. Then it was our turn to hug Mother. Aunt Helen moved Simon forward, and I was still hanging on to Simon's hand. He kissed her on the cheek and quickly moved back to Father's side. I threw my arms around her neck and kissed her on the lips. I had *missed* her.

Her skin wasn't cold. It was just *different*.

She was looking right at me. Baxter, our German shepherd, began to whine and scratch at the back door.

Father took the Resurrectionists into the study. We heard snatches of conversation down the hall.

"... if you think of it as a stroke ..."

"How long will she ..."

"You understand the tithing is necessary because of the expenses of monthly care and ..."

The women relatives stood in a circle around Mother. There was an awkward moment until they realized that Mother did not speak. Aunt Helen reached her hand out and touched her sister's cheek. Mother smiled and smiled.

Then Father was back and his voice was loud and hearty. He explained how similar it was to a light stroke—did we remember Uncle Richard? Meanwhile, Father kissed people repeatedly and thanked everyone.

The Resurrectionists left with smiles and signed papers. The remaining relatives began to leave soon after that. Father saw them down the walk, smiling and shaking their hands.

"Think of it as though she's been ill but has recovered," said Father. "Think of her as home from the hospital."

Aunt Helen was the last to leave. She sat next to Mother for a long time, speaking softly and searching Mother's face for a response. After a while Aunt Helen began to cry.

"Think of it as if she's recovered from an illness," said Father as he walked her to her car. "Think of her as home from the hospital."

Aunt Helen nodded, still crying, and left. I think she knew what Simon and I knew. Mother was not home from the hospital. She was home from the grave.

The night was long. Several times I thought I heard the soft slap of Mother's slippers on the hallway floor and my breathing stopped, waiting for the door to open. But it didn't. The moonlight lay across my legs and exposed a patch of wallpaper next to the dresser. The flower pattern looked like the face of a great, sad beast. Just before dawn, Simon leaned across from his bed and whispered, "Go to sleep, stupid." And so I did.

For the first week, Father slept with Mother in the same room where they had always slept. In the morning his face would sag and he would snap at us while we ate our cereal. Then he moved to his study and slept on the old divan in there.

The summer was very hot. No one would play with us, so Simon and I played together. Father had only morning classes at the University. Mother moved around the house and watered the plants a lot. Once Simon and I saw her watering a plant that had died and been removed while she was at the hospital in April. The water ran across the top of the cabinet and dripped on the floor. Mother did not notice.

When Mother did go outside, the forest preserve behind our house seemed to draw her in. Perhaps it was the darkness. Simon and I used to enjoy playing at the edge of it after twilight, catching fireflies in a jar or building blanket tents, but after Mother began walking there Simon spent the evenings inside or on the front lawn. I stayed back there because sometimes Mother wandered and I would take her by the arm and lead her back to the house.

Mother wore whatever Father told her to wear. Sometimes

he was rushed to get to class and would say, "Wear the red dress," and Mother would spend a sweltering July day in heavy wool. She didn't sweat. Sometimes he would not tell her to come downstairs in the morning, and she would remain in the bedroom until he returned. On those days I tried to get Simon at least to go upstairs and look in on her with me; but he just stared at me and shook his head. Father was drinking more, like Uncle Will used to, and he would yell at us for nothing at all. I always cried when Father shouted; but Simon never cried anymore.

Mother never blinked. At first I didn't notice; but then I began to feel uncomfortable when I saw that she never blinked. But it didn't make me love her any less.

Neither Simon nor I could fall asleep at night. Mother used to tuck us in and tell us long stories about a magician named Yandy who took our dog, Baxter, on great adventures when we weren't playing with him. Father didn't make up stories, but he used to read to us from a big book he called Pound's *Cantos*. I didn't understand most of what he read, but the words felt good and I loved the sounds of words he said were Greek. Now nobody checked in on us after our baths. I tried telling stories to Simon for a few nights, but they were no good and Simon asked me to stop.

On the Fourth of July, Tommy Wiedermeyer, who had been in my class the year before, drowned in the swimming pool they had just put in.

That night we all sat out back and watched the fireworks above the fairgrounds half a mile away. You couldn't see the ground displays because of the forest preserve, but the skyrockets were bright and clear. First you would see the explosion of color and then, four or five seconds later it seemed, the sound would catch up. I turned to say something to Aunt Helen and saw Mother looking out from the second-story window. Her face was very white against the dark room, and the colors seemed to flow down over her like fluids.

It was not long after the Fourth that I found the dead squirrel. Simon and I had been playing Cavalry and Indians in the forest preserve. We took turns finding each other . . . shooting and dying repeatedly in the weeds until it was time to start over. Only this time I was having trouble finding him. Instead, I found the clearing.

It was a hidden place, surrounded by bushes as thick as our hedge. I was still on my hands and knees from crawling under the branches when I saw the squirrel. It was large and reddish and had been dead for some time. The head had been wrenched around almost backward on the body. Blood had dried near one ear. Its left paw was clenched, but the other lay open on a twig as if it were resting there. Something had taken one eye, but the other stared blackly at the canopy of branches. Its mouth was open slightly, showing surprisingly large teeth gone yellow at the roots. As I watched, an ant came out of the mouth, crossed the dark muzzle, and walked out onto the staring eye.

This is what dead is, I thought.

The bushes vibrated to some unfelt breeze. I was scared to be there and I left, crawling straight ahead and bashing through thick branches that grabbed at my shirt.

In the autumn I went back to Longfellow School, but soon transferred to a private school. The Resurrectionist families were discriminated against in those days. The kids made fun of us or called us names and no one played with us. No one played with us at the new school either, but they didn't call us names.

Our bedroom had no wall switch but an old-fashioned hanging light bulb with a cord. To turn on the light I had to cross half the dark room and feel around until I found the cord. Once when Simon was staying up late to do his homework, I went upstairs by myself. I was swinging my arm around in the darkness to find the string when my hand fell on Mother's face. Her teeth felt cool and slick. I pulled my hand back and stood there a minute in the dark before I found the cord and turned on the light.

"Hello, Mother," I said. I sat on the edge of the bed and looked up at her. She was staring at Simon's empty bed. I reached out and took her hand. "I miss you," I said. I said some other things, but the words got all mixed up and sounded stupid, so I just sat there, holding her hand, waiting for some returning pressure. My arm got tired, but I remained sitting there and holding her fingers in mine until Simon came up. He stopped in the doorway and stared at us. I looked down and dropped her hand. After a few minutes she went away.

Father put Baxter to sleep just before Thanksgiving. He was not an old dog, but he acted like one. He was always growling and barking, even at us, and he would never come inside anymore. After he ran away for the third time, the pound called us. Father just said, "Put him to sleep," and hung up the phone. They sent us a bill.

Father's classes had fewer and fewer students and finally he took a sabbatical to write his book on Ezra Pound. He was home all that year, but he didn't write much. Sometimes he would spend the morning down at the library, but he would be home by one o'clock and would watch TV. He would start drinking before dinner and stay in front of the television until really late. Simon and I would stay up with him sometimes; but we didn't like most of the shows.

Simon's dream started about then. He told me about it on the way to school one morning. He said the dream was always the same. When he fell asleep, he would dream that he was still awake, reading a comic book. Then he would start to set the comic on the nightstand, and it would fall on the floor. When he reached down to pick it up, Mother's arm would come out from under the bed and she would grasp his wrist with her white hand. He said her grip was very strong, and somehow he knew that she wanted him under the bed with her. He would hang on to the blankets as hard as he could, but he knew that in a few seconds the bedclothes would slip and he would fall.

He said that last night's dream had finally been a little different. This time Mother had stuck her head out from under the bed. Simon said that it was like when a garage mechanic slides out from under a car. He said she was grinning at him, not smiling but grinning real wide. Simon said that her teeth had been filed down to points.

"Do you ever have dreams like that?" he asked. I knew he was sorry he'd told me.

"No," I said. I loved Mother.

That April the Farley twins from the next block accidentally locked themselves in an abandoned freezer and suffocated. Mrs. Hargill, our cleaning lady, found them, out behind their garage. Thomas Farley had been the only kid who still invited Simon over to his yard. Now Simon only had me.

It was just before Labor Day and the start of school that Simon made plans for us to run away. I didn't want to run away, but I loved Simon. He was my brother.

"Where are we gonna go?"

"We got to get out of here," he said. Which wasn't much of an answer.

But Simon had set aside a bunch of stuff and even picked up a city map. He'd sketched out our path through the forest preserve, across Sherman River at the Laurel Street viaduct, all the way to Uncle Will's house without ever crossing any major streets.

"We can camp out," said Simon. He showed me a length of clothesline he had cut. "Uncle Will will let us be farmhands. When he goes out to his ranch next spring, we can go with him."

We left at twilight. I didn't like leaving right before it got dark, but Simon said that Father wouldn't notice we were gone until late the next morning when he woke up. I carried a small backpack filled with food Simon had sneaked out of the refrigerator. He had some stuff rolled up in a blanket and tied over his back with the piece of clothesline. It was pretty light out until we got deeper into the forest preserve. The stream made a gurgling sound like the one that came from Mother's room the night she died. The roots and branches were so thick that Simon had to keep his flashlight on all the time, and that made it seem even darker. We stopped before too long, and Simon strung his rope between two trees. I threw the blanket over it and we both scrabbled around on our hands and knees to find stones.

We ate our bologna sandwiches in the dark while the creek made swallowing noises in the night. We talked a few minutes, but our voices seemed too tiny, and after a while we both fell asleep, on the cold ground with our jackets pulled over us and our heads on the nylon pack and all the forest sounds going on around us.

I woke up in the middle of the night. It was very still. Both of us had huddled down under the jackets, and Simon was snoring. The leaves had stopped stirring, the insects were gone, and even the stream had stopped making noise. The openings of the tent made two brighter triangles in the field of darkness.

I sat up with my heart pounding.

There was nothing to see when I moved my head near the opening. But I knew exactly what was out there. I put my head under my jacket and moved away from the side of the tent.

I waited for something to touch me through the blanket. At first I thought of Mother coming after us, of Mother walking through the forest after us with sharp twigs brushing at her eyes. But it wasn't Mother.

The night was cold and heavy around our little tent. It was as black as the eye of that dead squirrel, and it wanted in. For the first time in my life I understood that the darkness did not end with the morning light. My teeth were chattering. I curled up against Simon and stole a little of his heat. His breath came soft and slow against my cheek. After a while I shook him awake and told him we were going home when the sun rose, that I wasn't going with him. He started to argue, but then he heard something in my voice, something he didn't understand, and he only shook his head tiredly and went back to sleep.

In the morning the blanket was wet with dew and our skins felt clammy. We folded things up, left the rocks lying in their rough pattern, and walked home. We did not speak.

Father was sleeping when we got home. Simon threw our stuff in the bedroom and then he went out into the sunlight. I went to the basement.

It was very dark down there, but I sat on the wooden stairs without turning on a light. There was no sound from the shadowed corners, but I knew that Mother was there.

"We ran away, but we came back," I said at last. "It was my idea to come back."

Through the narrow window slats I saw green grass. A sprinkler started up with a loud sigh. Somewhere in the neighborhood, kids were shouting. I paid attention only to the shadows.

"Simon wanted to keep going," I said, "but I made us come back. It was *my* idea to come home."

I sat a few more minutes but couldn't think of anything else to say. Finally I got up, brushed off my pants, and went upstairs to take a nap.

A week after Labor Day, Father insisted we go to the shore for the weekend. We left on Friday afternoon and drove straight through to Ocean City. Mother sat alone in the rear seat. Father and Aunt Helen rode up front. Simon and I were crowded into the back of the station wagon, but he refused to count cows with me or talk to me or even play with the toy planes I'd brought along.

We stayed at an ancient hotel right on the boardwalk. The other Resurrectionists in Father's Tuesday group recommended the place, but it smelled of age and rot and rats in the walls. The corridors were a faded green, the doors a darker green, and only every third light worked. The halls were a dim maze, and you had to make two turns just to find the elevator. Everyone but Simon stayed inside all day Saturday, sitting in front of the laboring air conditioner and watching television. There were many more of the resurrected around now, and you could hear them shuffling through the dark halls. After sunset they went out to the beach, and we joined them.

I tried to make Mother comfortable. I set the beach towel down for her and turned her to face the sea. By this time the moon had risen and a cool breeze was blowing in. I put Mother's sweater across her shoulders. Behind us the midway splashed lights out over the boardwalk and the roller coaster rumbled and growled.

I would not have left if Father's voice hadn't irritated me so. He talked too loudly, laughed at nothing, and took deep drinks from a bottle in a brown bag. Aunt Helen said very little but watched Father sadly and tried to smile when he laughed. Mother was sitting peacefully, so I excused myself and walked up to the midway to hunt for Simon. I was lonely without him. The place was empty of families and children, but the rides were still running. Every few minutes there would be a roar and screams from the few riders as the roller coaster took its steepest plunge. I ate a hot dog and looked around, but Simon was nowhere to be found.

While walking back along the beach, I saw Father lean over and give Aunt Helen a quick kiss on the cheek. Mother had wandered away, and I quickly offered to go find her just to hide the tears of rage in my eyes. I walked up the beach past the place where the two teenagers had drowned the previous weekend. There were a few of the resurrected around. They were sitting near the water with their families; but no sight of Mother. I was thinking of heading back when I thought I noticed some movement under the boardwalk.

It was incredibly dark under there. Narrow strips of light, broken into weird sorts of patterns by the wooden posts and cross-braces, dropped down from cracks in the walkway overhead. Footsteps and rumbles from the midway sounded like fists pounding against a coffin lid. I stopped then. I had a sudden image of dozens of them being there in the darkness. Dozens, Mother among them, with thin patterns of light crossing them so that you could make out a hand or shirt or staring eye. But they were not there. Mother was not there. Something else was.

I don't know what made me look up. Footsteps from above. A slight turning, turning; something turning in the shadows. I could see where he had climbed the cross-braces, wedged a sneaker here, lifted himself there to the wide timber. It would not have been hard. We'd climbed like that a thousand times. I stared right into his face, but it was the clothesline I recognized first.

Father quit teaching after Simon's death. He never went back after the sabbatical, and his notes for the Pound book sat stacked in the basement with last year's newspapers. The

Resurrectionists helped him find a job as a custodian in a nearby shopping mall, and he usually didn't get home before two in the morning.

After Christmas I went away to a boarding school that was two states away. The Resurrectionists had opened the Institute by this time, and more and more families were turning to them. I was later able to go to the University on a full scholarship. Despite the covenant, I rarely came home during those years. Father was drunk during my few visits. Once I drank with him and we sat in the kitchen and cried together. His hair was almost gone except for a few white strands on the sides, and his eyes were sunken in a lined face. The alcohol had left innumerable broken blood vessels in his cheeks, and he looked as though he was wearing more makeup than Mother.

Mrs. Hargill called three days before graduation. Father had filled the bath with warm water and then drawn the razor blade up the vein rather than across it. He had read his Plutarch. It had been two days before the housekeeper found him, and when I arrived home the next evening the bathtub was still caked with congealed rings. After the funeral I went through all of his old papers and found a journal he had been keeping for several years. I burned it along with the stacks of notes for his unfinished book.

Our policy with the Institute was honored despite the circumstances, and that helped me through the next few years. My career is more than a job to me—I believe in what I do and I'm good at it. It was my idea to lease some of the empty school buildings for our new neighborhood centers.

Last week I was caught in a traffic jam, and when I inched the car up to the accident site and saw the small figure covered by a blanket and the broken glass everywhere, I also noticed that a crowd of *them* had gathered on the curb. There are so many of them these days.

I used to have shares in a condominium in one of the last lighted sections of the city, but when our old house came up for sale I jumped at the chance to buy it. I've kept many of the old furnishings and replaced others so that it's almost the way it used to be. Keeping up an old house like that is expensive, but I don't spend my money foolishly. After work a lot of guys from the Institute go out to bars, but I don't. After I've put away my equipment and scrubbed down the steel tables, I go straight home. My family is there. They're waiting for me.

JAMES VAN HISE

James Van Hise, publisher and coeditor of *Midnight Graffiti* magazine, has turned a lifelong interest in horror and fantasy into a career. James has written several specialty volumes on television and film, edited several magazines, and now, along with his chores on *Midnight Graffiti*, has a blossoming career as a short story writer. James tackles some tough themes in the following piece, a very different sort of coming-of-age story.

Dark Embrace

by James Van Hise

The boy writhed and twisted on the ground, his head thrashing helplessly back and forth in the darkness and the dead leaves. He tried desperately to scream, but all that escaped through the hand clamped over his mouth was a strangled cry. The trees bending over him seemed to draw together to conceal what was happening here in the sheltering woodlands not two miles from his home. A hand pressed against his chest to hold him in place, and two bony knees crushed his legs flat against the ground to keep him from kicking out at his assailant. The heavy palm remained in place over his mouth while the fingers splayed out over his face like a huge spider guarding its helpless prey. His breathing came hard and fast, from fear as well as from exertion, his small twelve-year-old chest rising and falling rapidly beneath the hand that pinned it, not tightly, but firmly.

In the darkness, a face stared down at him, outlined slightly by threads of moonlight. Most of the man's face lay in shadow, so all the boy could really see well were the eyes staring back into his. Those eyes reflected Timothy's fear, but they returned expectation. The man was also breathing hard, like Timothy, but not from exertion—or fear. What could he have to fear from a twelve-year-old boy he had so easily plucked off the street, and how much exertion would it have taken to subdue him?

A hush fell over this glade and the trees that nestled it so well—so perfectly. The wind slowed to silence and the only noises were the breathing of a predator and his victim.

The man looked around, worried that even way back here in this grove someone might see. Oh, if only someone might see! thought Timothy, and he grabbed the thick, powerful hands that trapped him, and in one valiant effort tried to twist free. The hands didn't budge, and didn't have to, for all they needed to do was press harder and Timothy stopped struggling and cried out in pain and frustration.

The boy shook and trembled—fear running out of him in hot tears and cold sweat. Why, oh, why did this happen to him, and what *was* going to happen to him? He was afraid to guess—afraid to think. So many times he had been warned to be careful and not to use the shortcut through the woods and past Pine Creek at night, but he had gone this way so *many* times and nothing had ever happened before! There were the stories every child heard about people disappearing around here over the years, as well as the strange mutilation of animals on nearby farms, but they were only played up to children and played down by everyone else. Timothy had heard all these things and made of them the obvious, only nothing could be as obvious as what was happening to him now. He knew that this wasn't any monster or creature that lurked in the woods. It was a man. It was only a man. But it was a man who would, who would . . . He couldn't think about it, he just couldn't. Oh, make him go away; oh, please someone make him go away! But he didn't go away.

Timothy felt the crushing weight of the hand leave his chest while the grip of the one over his face increased in intensity so that his head was securely held in place. He felt fingers grab his shirt and bunch it up into a fist. There was a terrible crushing pain on the back of his neck and then he heard cloth tear and the shirt and the pain were gone. A slight breeze played over his chest and he shivered from the sensation of the cold sweat evaporating in the cool air—at least that's why he told himself he shivered. The free hand of his kidnapper touched the boy's bare chest, exploring the smoothness gently and carefully. He could hear the man's heavy breathing very plainly, now.

Maybe—maybe this is all he wants, and then he'll go away soon, thought Timothy, and he retreated deeper into himself, refusing to consider the alternatives, telling himself it would be over and he could go home and pretend this never happened except in the awful pits of his nightmares.

The hand moved back and forth over his chest, back and forth, back and forth, up and down, and then just down.

No! He writhed and twisted again—he had to get away! This couldn't be happening! Suddenly there was a terrible constricting around his throat and black splinters started falling in all around him and he heard a voice very close to his ear whispering in tones that were very quiet, yet very deadly, "You try anything like that again—you make another move or another sound, and I'll kill you!" The voice said nothing more. It didn't have to. Insanity all too often speaks clearly.

Tears rolled down his cheeks in an unending stream, and he felt sick to his stomach in a way so terrible he never could have imagined it—any more than he could have imagined what was happening to him now.

When the hand covering his mouth slipped away he didn't make a sound even though he wondered if death could really be any worse than this. He felt his pants being opened and two hands slipping into his undershorts to pull both them and his trousers off simultaneously. He never thought the feeling of his pants sliding down his legs and being removed could be so horrible. As helpless as he'd felt before, he hadn't felt as totally defenseless and alone as he did in that moment.

Now both hands were running over him—touching, probing, caressing ever so softly yet ever so terribly. He turned his face away and squeezed his eyes shut, trying to block it all out. The hands moved down his chest, over his stomach, and then stopped, cupping him and fondling him. Timothy's fingers clawed the ground, digging up furrows beneath his hands.

When would it stop, when would it stop, oh, where would it stop? and then he knew. In the darkness he heard something more dreadful than anything that had happened so far. He heard the man taking off his own clothes. Timothy fainted.

The moon was a high glowing scythe hanging in the sky. Bare trees swayed in the wind like black skeletons. Leaves blew across the ground and settled around the boy whose pale form shone in the deep nighttime shadows at the base of the old, rugged oaks.

Timothy heard only night sounds. When he awoke, and he was about to open his eyes, he felt the cold lick of steel against his throat.

"You were good, kid," rasped the voice, harsh and slightly muffled in the rising wind, "but not good enough that I can leave you for another time."

The boy started, his eyes jerking open to see the face leaning very close over him. He grabbed for the man's hand near his throat, but before he could push it away it moved away by itself, sliding quickly from left to right. There was an awful, blinding pain in his windpipe and suddenly he couldn't breathe, but rather felt like he was drowning somehow. Fingers of blackness reached into his brain like slivers of glass and he felt like he was falling, endlessly falling. Dimly he sensed the man walking away, vanishing off the edge of his perception to be swallowed up in the unrelieved gloom of the forlorn grove of trees.

The man was gone, he thought, *finally gone, and now he could sleep, and later . . . later . . . later . . .*

A shadow fell across him. Even though he was going to sleep, he felt it touch him. Somehow he knew this wasn't The Man again. This was something new.

The figure that looked down at him seemed to frown from a towering height. And yet, it was somehow bent and withered. It was a man even though his eyes burned with an unearthly spark deep in his skull and peered out from sockets rimmed with shadows. The clothes the stranger wore were old and tattered, rent here and there from age and covered with the dirt and filth of a thousand hiding places. When the man knelt, the image the action conjured was that of a gnarled tree bending heavily with age. The moon glinted for a moment off his chest as though this were a knight come to rescue a child. The hand that extended to touch the boy's brow had long, knobby fingers with huge knuckles, and the skin was the color of bones. He pushed the youngster's tawny hair away from the boy's sightless eyes.

The being that stared down at the defiled body had been soulless for an age beyond his shattered memory, but only now was it seeing there were things in the world of man much darker than itself or the others who wandered the night in loneliness.

The stranger slipped his long, thin arms beneath the boy's limp shoulders and cradled the head against his elbow. Life was draining from the body in a tide that ran black in the deep shadows, and the span to its completion could have been measured with a stopwatch. The being that was no longer a man bent its head to a task that for the first time in its deathless existence was being done out of some form of fathomless pity, and not from an awful need. It opened its mouth to reveal the two long incisors that closed on Timothy's neck. Deep in his dying oblivion the boy felt renewal, and something even akin to pleasure, and the pain he'd felt himself drowning in became a distant memory. A mirage of existence coursed through him. Now indeed would he sleep.

Timothy opened his eyes to sensations both strange and unnerving. All feelings of discomfort were gone, the raw pain in his buttocks, his fear. He looked up and saw the figure looming over him like a frozen sentinel. For one startled instant of constricting fear, constricted him again as he thought this was the monster who had kidnapped him, but he quickly realized that this was someone else. He had seen the face of his attacker all too clearly in the instant before—

The wind picked up with each passing moment, howling now as it swept past them, but still the figure stood motionless, only his long, unkempt hair waving wildly in the rushing air.

Timothy noticed with some embarrassment that he was still naked, although the cold September wind didn't bother him as much as he thought it should under the circumstances. He scrambled over by a tree and found his pants and undershorts and quickly slipped them on. His shirt lay in tatters, but he pulled on what was left of it anyway. It comforted him somehow. He looked over at the ragged stranger he'd seen when he woke up. The figure was still standing there as if it were waiting for him.

"Did you," Timothy began hesitantly, "did you see what happened?"

The man emitted a long, tired sigh. The glowing embers of his eyes were dimmed as his eyelids closed slightly before he replied. "Yes, I saw," and that was all he said.

The man's voice frightened Timothy a bit because it was

so rough, although the harshness seemed somehow to come less from age and more from disuse.

"Can . . . can you come with me?" Timothy asked hopefully. "I've got to go home and tell my mom and dad what happened, and I don't want to go alone. Please?"

"I cannot," the man said with obvious difficulty, "nor can you."

"What do you mean?" Timothy shouted back at him. This was all too much. First he was . . . attacked, and now this stranger refused to help him and said that he couldn't go home either! "Why can't I go home? Who are you?" and he backed away, beginning to cry, the tears burning his cheeks while he shook with choking sobs. "Are you gonna hurt me, too?"

The man seemed to slump slightly at this, as if an offered hand of friendship had been scorned and slapped away. "No, I won't hurt you. No one can hurt you anymore." The stranger's voice ached with the effort of saying so many words at once, and he had to stop for a moment. He wondered why he had helped the boy, or if he had really helped him at all, or if he had just been deluding his age-weary mind with the reason. Was it really pity that had possessed him in that moment when he found the boy's battered body, or was it his own unquenchable passion?

"Boy, hold out your hand. Let me touch it."

Timothy looked at the tall, lean man towering over him and his first instinct was to run—to get out of here—to get away from this curious individual who might even be as bad as the *other* one. He looked into the man's eyes and suddenly he felt overwhelmed, as if those two eyes shone as brightly as the morning sun. They glistened oddly and then he didn't feel afraid anymore. Why shouldn't he let this man touch his hand?

The stranger walked forward slowly, holding out his hand palm upward to take Timothy's small hand in his. The boy stared deep into twin pools of scarlet incandescence and all of his fears slipped away.

"What's your name?" a voice outside his vision asked. All he could see were eyes. All he felt was a burning need to understand.

"I'm Timothy Barnes," he replied easily.

"What did that man do to you when you woke up before I came. Do you remember?"

The boy paused, not entirely crediting his memory on this part. "I think he hurt me on my neck with a knife or something."

"Touch your throat, Timothy."

He did, but there was no wound of any kind. How could that be? "There's nothing there!" The boy was both amazed and confused.

"That's because you've been made whole again. When I said I saw what happened, I meant that I saw you killed. You were dead. He cut your throat to keep you from telling anyone about him."

"No!" He wouldn't believe it, but the voice was so persistent.

"I found you just as he ran off. I didn't understand at first. It's been a long time since I've had to think—to understand."

"How could I have been dead and now I'm not?" The conversation had ceased being confusing. Now it was simply terrifying.

Now the voice hesitated, as if it had reached the point it had planned to, but was still uncertain how to proceed. "I am one of the undead, and now so are you."

The boy's mind reeled and panicked, but the powerful influence of those uncanny eyes kept him from running off. How could this be? How could he possibly be dead when he felt so alive? Then thoughts came to him—a long train of thoughts—no longer the croaking, stumbling voice that seemed so unused to forming words. The thoughts stretched back years and across miles, to the other side of the continent and the other end of the century. Images of a nomadic existence, of wandering by night and hiding by day in caves or empty homes. The word *vampire* was there and he recoiled from it instinctively. A shudder ran through him and deep inside he felt a wave of anguish and bitter irony. At home on his dresser in the room he'd never see again was a plastic model of Dracula, a bat perched obediently on the figure's outstretched arm. His home, his mother, his father, his family that he'd never see again. How could he see them again? *"Uh, Mom, I'm a vampire and I have to sleep in the basement in the fruit cellar by day and at night I'll be going out to raid the blood bank."* What kind of an existence was that? Better they thought he was dead. No body found, just another unexplained disappearance that cripples and destroys the survivors with the pain and the torture of not knowing but eternally guessing, always fearing it's more horrible than they could imagine. In this case, it would be.

Then came more thoughts of the man. His name was Jeremiah—just Jeremiah, as his last name had been smothered in distant memory (When was the last time anyone had called him by name?) and these thoughts intruded on Timothy's reverie with shapes from the past as well as the present.

Jeremiah lived in the basement of a collapsed barn back in the hills. He wandered by night, preying on animals. There was some quirk in his personality that had always made him shun attacking human beings. It was something in his past. Perhaps something he had once had, or someone he had once known whom he had since forgotten during his dim, meaningless existence, but whom he feared he might unknowingly harm. Jeremiah seemed to recall having a family once, but it was oh, so long ago, and it hurt him to try to remember. Seeing Timothy stretched out in the clearing, used and discarded, had touched something in the old man (Was he a man anymore?) so that he was moved to give the boy another chance at living, of a sort, and also a chance to find the person who had brought him to this.

"Dead, there would be no one to avenge you. Undead, you can avenge yourself."

Tim was still under the guiding influence of Jeremiah's piercing eyes. "I never thought of that. But what can I do, I'm just a kid? Will you help me?"

"I will help. I will keep you with me by day and at night we will hunt the one who hurt you. But you are more than a child, now. You walk with the Children of the Night, and your strength is their strength, and your age is of the ageless. No one can stand before you or harm you again."

"What about all that stuff that's supposed to be able to hurt vam . . . er, us?"

"That is so, but few believe we exist anymore, so few guard against us. We roam the dark and hide in the hills in the back country. Summer, winter—it is all the same to us. Perhaps we will find others to aid."

"But how? How will we find *him*?"

"By watching. By waiting. When you aren't found, he will believe himself safe, and he'll return. Someday. Perhaps soon. Perhaps not so soon. It is all the same to us, now."

Jeremiah gently released his hypnotic touch. Now the boy finally understood. All that remained was that he accept it.

Timothy turned and walked slowly through the night-shrouded woodland. He turned once and looked toward a light far in the distance—a familiar light. He saw the distant movement of silhouettes and imagined his parents waiting for him, pacing restlessly, then frantically, then hysterically, wringing their hands, shouting at one another for letting him venture out alone, calling the police and being told that someone isn't missing unless they've been gone for twenty-four hours and how do they know he isn't a runaway? He wanted to go to them more than anything in the world, but he knew it would be worse that way. They wouldn't believe him and even if he proved it they'd try to have him "cured," in which case he really would die, and that would be for the final time.

What could he do? How could he exist like this, forever a boy of twelve, ageless and undying?

Jeremiah was alone with his thoughts. He watched the boy sitting and agonizing in the darkness. After an eternity of senseless wanderings, he had found someone. He had given the gift of darkness to another. A child. But there was nothing else to be done. The boy would have died. But was that *really* the reason he had helped the boy, if help it could truly be called?

They sat together in the shadow of the oak where two strange acts had occurred that night—one of violence, and one of pity.

Tim felt the wind rushing over him, knowing that under normal circumstances he would be shivering in the stiff autumn breeze, especially here and now, at night, and after what had happened. The fear had drained from him. The panic had fled. But hatred remained. That *man*—what he did. If not for that murderer, he could run home to his parents. But that was impossible now. Would it have been better to die than to live with this torment, this knowledge of what his existence had become and what his disappearance would mean to his parents? If only there was some way he could go to them, but that would be the crowning horror. To tell them that he was dead, but undead, and then proving it by standing unreflected in front of a mirror—or by shape-changing. Could he do that? Right now he didn't want to know.

Two hands closed over Tim's clenched fists and he looked up with a start. It was just Jeremiah. He was staring at the boy. He stared for a long time with unblinking penetration. The face wasn't really old-looking, Tim thought, just weather-beaten. It had stood up to a great deal, and it had come back.

''Where do you stay again?''

Jeremiah raised his right arm and pointed out into the blackness with a long, tapering finger. ''In the hills, beyond the woods, there is a barn. The roof is caved in, but the old cellar is still intact . . . and dark.''

Tim shivered. How could he accept this, live with this, throw everything away? He couldn't. He knew that, now. But what else could he do? There had to be something—some way. Here he sat with a man who had been a stranger just a few hours before, and now he was being told he would have to spend eternity with him and abandon everything he had ever known and loved.

''How . . . how old were you when you became . . . the way you—we—are?''

Jeremiah's hand touched his face and Tim found himself feeling amazed by the simple human gesture. ''It was a long time ago. I don't remember much, now.'' He paused, his voice sounding strained from the few words. ''I haven't talked this much, or said this many words in one night, in more years than I can recall—in more years than I want to recall.''

''I won't ever change, will I? I'll never look any older.''

''Not likely—unless you can't replenish your . . . energies. I looked much older a while ago, before I found you. Usually I stay away from people. I'd probably be stronger, quicker, if I didn't, but I just can't bring myself to . . .'' Jeremiah paused and Tim was startled when he saw a tear roll down the man's face. ''I never knew a man could hold on to life so much—be so afraid to let it go. Still, I don't love it so much that I ever would have touched you if you hadn't already been dyin'.''

Tim wanted to ask him what kind of animals he lived off of, but he was afraid. He didn't want to know that bad. Not yet.

''What happens when I grow older?''

''It'll never happen. The dead don't grow.'' Jeremiah

laughed, and it was a bitter sound. "Oh, you'll learn and grow in your mind, but your body will forever be as it is now, with the same youth that drew your murderer to you."

Tim recoiled. Having what he suspected so casually confirmed was difficult enough, but he was overwhelmed by images of what had so recently transpired. They flooded back like a cold wave. He walked off into the surrounding trees, stopping just a few yards away.

The clouds overhead parted like a tear in the fabric of the sky and the moon shone through again. Tim stared up at it, studying every glowing feature of its visible, pockmarked surface. The irony of its wicked crescent shape on just this particular night did not escape him. He had always liked the moon, but not enough to live with it forever as the only major astral body he would ever be able to gaze upon again. The sun and its summer warmth would only be a memory—something to be conjured in his dreams along with daylight and friends and school and parents.

He ran deeper into the woods, tears stinging his cheeks, memories fast in pursuit. Finally he slipped and fell at the base of a tree scarred by lightning. It hadn't asked for what had happened to it, either—it had just happened. He touched the blackened timber, felt its dead surface. Dead. Dead like him, but he still lived. That was magic, wasn't it? No, this had to be something else, something explainable, like a disease or a virus. What if that was what it was—a virus that revitalized dying tissues, but at a price?

It was all so strange—so unbelievable. Why couldn't he just go home and forget about it all? Why?

A short time later, Jeremiah came upon the boy who was curled up and weeping at the base of the old maple. The man reached out and rubbed his hands over the ruined wood. It had once been a beautiful tree, but in death it was rotted and ugly. Death did that sometimes.

He leaned over and touched the boy on his long brown hair.

"We have to go. I'm sorry."

"Go where?" Tim asked.

"To where we have to . . . stay, for the day." Jeremiah had almost said *live*, instead of stay, but he felt that wouldn't have sounded right somehow. He bent down and picked Timothy up in his arms and then walked off into the hills. The moon, such as it was, lit his path, and before long they reached their destination and were asleep.

Days were spent in a strange, troubled slumber curled up in a dank corner of the old, crumbled structure. The heat from the sunlight baked the air so that it was almost stifling, but otherwise they slept unbothered and undisturbed by daylight conditions.

Those days during the first few weeks were difficult for Tim. His dreams were haunted by images of a past now forever forsaken. Those sleeping visions were very different from what his normal dreams used to be, and it was several days before he realized that in his sleep his mind traveled. The first hint of the truth came when he saw his parents standing over a grave whose headstone bore his name. He awoke screaming.

Night had descended. The time to prowl had returned. Jeremiah explained the mind travel, which he called "soul-flights," because a soul is all they really had anymore. The man explained in halting terms that sometimes they saw things happening now, nearby, and sometimes they saw things that wouldn't happen for a long time, and he really had no idea how to tell the two apart. It was just one of those things.

It was late autumn when that terrible night passed Tim into Jeremiah's immortal company, setting them on their vengeful quest. They knew they didn't have many weeks to achieve their goal before winter set in and Tim's attacker would not likely return to the snowbound woods for any reason.

The nights of seemingly aimless wandering were tedious to the boy. He was constantly wrestling with his private anguish and searching with a helpless desperation for the one who had brought him to this.

The days continued to stretch languidly while they curled in quite somnambulance in the increasingly cooler darkness of the crumbled homestead. Winter finally came, and just as they thought, their quarry proved elusive and invisible. The months crawled past, one seeming little different from the previous.

One night something happened that altered the course of his nocturnal ramblings. It was something even more personally unsettling than the first time he drank blood from the body of a small animal they'd captured.

As they wandered down from the sparsely settled hill country and drew closer to town, they altered their route, as they always did, to try to cover different territory. Tim always found it difficult to traverse the grove where he'd been assaulted, but he realized at the same time that it was more than necessary. Nonetheless an awful coldness settled in the pit of his stomach whenever he saw it.

This time they were taking the long way around. It had gotten to the point where he seldom paid any attention to where they were at any given time because he had covered this ground so often. He was more concerned with spotting their elusive prey. This became the one time he regretted that.

They walked along a road, conversing in low tones, oblivious to any cuts or scrapes they might have sustained in scaling the wall that had blocked their path, when Tim realized something odd about the open field they were crossing. He stopped suddenly, some ethereal sense shaking him to the core of his being so that he stood there staggering for a moment, not even certain what was wrong, but knowing that *something* was very wrong indeed.

"What's the matter?" asked Jeremiah, confused and clearly concerned.

"I . . . don't know. I feel like something terrible is happening to me, but I don't know what it is." He looked around and suddenly his eyes, with a night vision more highly developed than that of any natural nocturnal dweller, riveted on something a dozen yards away. Half of him wanted to run, to flee, to hide, to die, but the other half was stronger and it dragged him to a spot that would haunt his memory to whatever bitter end his existence finally came to. He stumbled forward, tripping over both flat and upright stones until he came to the place.

There on a rough-edged chunk of marble four feet high and two feet wide was *his* name.

Timothy Barnes, Nov. 7, 1967–Sept. 17, 1980.
A son beloved more than life itself.

A stone on an empty grave bearing an inscription that mocked him and tore at every fiber of his being. It had been a year since that awful night. A year spent searching through snowless days as well as an icy winter. A year in which his parents had made the final decision on the unknown fate of their son.

He fell to his knees and gripped the cold, polished marble, running his fingers over the carved letters that spelled out his name and his fate. He pressed his face against the hard, cool surface and began pounding the stone with his fists while tears ran off his face and onto the stone. Here it stood, a monument to his future, commemorating his step from one veil of existence into another.

But where was he, really? He wasn't actually dead, and he

wasn't alive, either, but rather caught in something in-between that was neither and yet a mockery of both. What *was* this existence that he embraced and accepted so that he was forced to abandon everything he had ever known?

"I'm dead," he sobbed, his voice breaking. "They finally decided that I'm dead. I wish I could decide that. Even after all this time, I still don't know what I am."

"You're part of the night, and of eternity," said Jeremiah, gravely. The tone he expressed was neither one of triumph nor defeat—it merely stated what Jeremiah knew to be the facts, and he stated them in his sepulchral voice that, without trying, brought with it a timbre that was both charnal and foreboding.

Tim slid to the ground that covered the empty grave, digging his fingers into the soil, pounding on it with his fists. "I should be down there, under the dirt, or I should be up there, at the house, with my mom and dad. But instead I'm here, and here is no place!"

All the resentment, all the anger, and all the hate for what he was washed over him, pouring through him until finally he screamed. He couldn't stand to view the stone pronouncement anymore—those finely chiseled letters that would last hundreds, perhaps thousands of years, finally turning into dust while he still wandered the surface of a world that he could never truly be a part of.

He ran. Jeremiah called after him, but he didn't stop—he didn't want to stop—not anymore. The stone monuments in the cemetery grew larger and larger as he neared the front gate. He had to get out. He had to get away. He had to do something. He couldn't stand being like this any longer. He had to find a way out.

He ran into the deeper darkness of the world beyond the cemetery, feeling it swallow him in its silent cloak while he ran through the empty streets and fields of a world that would cast him out if it knew that he existed. But he had already cast himself out until finally even his own parents had accepted that he was gone. But he wasn't gone. Not really. He was here. Living. Breathing. Dead yet alive in a body ageless and immortal.

He felt trapped—trapped by the darkness—a prisoner of the same cloak that sheltered him. He wanted to be free, to be a part of what he once was and what he could be again if only he tried. It had to be better than this. Anything had to be better than this empty existence beyond life and death, wandering on the periphery of his former lifetime. He wanted to touch the ones he loved again—to look into the eyes of his parents and see the joy they had known at being with him. He didn't care anymore what it cost or the horrors he'd have to endure. He just couldn't go on the way he had been any longer.

It was past midnight when he turned down his old street. (Old? Was a year really old? It was a twelfth of his lifetime.) The house stood before him, dark yet inviting, seeming to reach out with a delayed homecoming, crying out: Yes, come back, we've waited so terribly, horribly long!

Tim ran up the front steps and pounded on the door.

"Let me in! It's me! It's Tim! I'm back! I'm not dead! *I'm not dead!*" The tears stained his cheeks in defiance of what he knew to be the truth. "I'm alive, I've come back, I need you; oh, God, I need you! I can't stand this anymore, please believe me!" He kept pounding on the door and trying the handle. It was locked. He looked around wildly and saw one of the flagstones in the garden. He snatched it up and smashed in the window on the front door and then reached through, oblivious of the razor sharpness of the jagged pieces of glass. Why worry about cuts? He didn't bleed, or if he did it was just tears that he bled.

Finally he got the door open and pounded inside.

"I'm here!" he shrieked. The silence seemed to gape at him in surprise, but no lights answered his cry by coming on. No footsteps sounded in the bedrooms upstairs.

Like darkness itself he crawled up the stairs, fear and denial waging an awful conflict within him. Reaching the top of the stairs he stopped and listened. Nothing. He ran down the hallway and burst into his parents' room. It yawned back at him, empty of not only his parents, but of every bit of furnishing. If he could have fainted, he would have.

"Too long. I waited too long. They're gone!" He slipped to his knees, helpless and weak. "It's all gone, now. Everything. I really have lost it all. *What use is this anymore?*"

He drew himself up to his full twelve-year-old height and began to run, not stopping even when he catapulted himself through the second-story window, glass and wood exploding outward.

He hit the ground amid a rain of debris and lay there on what had once been his front lawn. He was completely uninjured.

Lying on the ground in the shambles of his abortive suicide attempt, he looked up at the eternal stars and thought: I'm Superman. I can't be hurt—not like this, anyway. Only this Superman drinks blood and can never again gaze on the full light of day, or anything else that ever meant anything to him.

Tim buried his face in the damp grass and covered his head with his arms. Is this the way it would always be? Always frustrated? Always making the decision too late to mean anything or be of any use? Then what the hell was the use? He'd just stay there and wait for morning to come. Nothing mattered anymore anyway.

A hand touched his shoulder. He looked up quickly. Jeremiah's sunken, glowing eyes stared back at him with, what, understanding? Compassion? The old man opened his mouth to speak, and that's when the light hit them full in the face.

''Who's out there? Who is that? What was all that noise? John, you got the gun? There's somebody out here on the lawn. Looks like they broke into the old Barnes house.''

Even before Jeremiah could grab Tim, the boy was on his feet. It was old lady Wilson. She *knew* him. She'd *recognize* him. God, what a furor *that* would cause!

The two companions ran, faster than any human ever could. They heard the rifle discharge and the bullet whiz by overhead. The second shot was closer, drilling through Tim's left shoulder so that the force of it drove him headlong into the pavement. He was on his feet again immediately. No pain, just the force of impact and then immediate recovery. They crashed through a row of hedges and were engulfed by the darkness that was their only friend.

Later, in the shadows of the ruined barn, was the question.

''Why?'' asked Jeremiah.

''Why did I go back? Because I'm tired. This is meaningless. I don't have anything anymore—not even life.''

''No, I understand why you went back. I mean, why did you run? Those people would have recognized you. They would have returned you to your family.''

''I . . . it won't work. Not anymore. I thought it would when I went back, but standing in that empty house—it was like the house was dead without them. Dead like me. Existing, but empty. I'm just not who I used to be. I can't ever go back. They could never believe or understand. They'd kill me by trying to prove I was wrong, and then I'd really have nothing. But what is this? What do I have now? What use is it?''

''You have to find what use it is. Life—any sort of life—has meaning that has to be found. A purpose for existing, and a purpose beyond *just* existing. It has been a long time since I thought about that—or like that. For a very long time I've been just existing without a purpose—until now.''

Tim was startled by this statement, to say the least. Although Jeremiah had begun to talk more and more in the past twelve months, he had never said anything like this before.

"Jeremiah, what do you mean?"

"For . . . a long time—I don't know how long—when one becomes timeless one stops reckoning with time. But for all of my existence like this, I just survived—went on from night to night, purposeless, aimless other than in predatory survival, and not knowing or caring that this was so—until that night when I found you. I had never thought about *helping* someone before, until I saw you dying and realized what I could do. Maybe bringing you into this wretched way of life *was* a mistake, but I don't think so. As terrible as this is, it has caused you to grow up a little sooner, even while you've had to leave everything behind. But it also did something for me that I never realized before."

"What?" Tim asked, and he really did care to know because Jeremiah had paused as if he was fearful or ashamed to continue.

He looked directly into the boy's eyes and said, "You being here has ended *my* loneliness," and his voice cracked slightly when he said it, and Tim knew that this time it wasn't because of age or disuse. He really felt what he was saying.

"Then you've felt the way I feel?" Tim realized then that he had never considered the fact that Jeremiah really could feel on the levels and depths that he had experienced human isolation.

"For many years I have lived alone. Being apart from all mankind is bad, just as you say, but to be alone! How can I begin to describe it? It's not just existing as a shell with a dark purpose, but it's being condemned to solitude. The legends tell so many conflicting things about us, but in the most important respects they never approach the truth. All of that is difficult enough, but to be denied even the simple comfort of company, of another intelligence to relate to and share the burden that we bear . . .

''When I came upon you that night and saw you lying there, your life draining with your dying pulse, I knew what I had to do. It may have been done out of pity for you, but it was also done out of pity for myself. I have been fighting with the awful realization of that for the past year.''

Silence hung between them. Neither knew what to say next. All these months, Tim had been feeling sorry for himself—never realizing that Jeremiah understood all too well what he was going through.

''I guess there's still a lot that I don't understand, Jeremiah. I should have known that you must have felt something for me.''

The old man reached out and touched Tim's face, softly and hesitantly. It was the first time he had expressed anything like that in many years. It was the first time he had genuinely felt anything like that, any affection, in many years.

''Once I had a family, and a son much likc you, but that was such a long time ago. I don't remember much about them—just faces. I've buried that memory along with everything else I left behind. Maybe on the day I finally remember just what I lost, I'll be ready to put everything behind me and just look forward.''

''So now we have each other,'' Tim observed.

''That we do. That we do. We have, in fact, nothing but each other, and perhaps that is something after all.''

The wind and the cold bite deep when winter falls, but to those beyond humanity, such sensations as freezing are merely memories. Autumn had passed, covered with a silent shroud of snow that seemed to lend a new and brighter aspect to familiar places. This was the reason that Tim ventured into the city one night for the first time since his life had ended and begun again.

It was a busy December evening with light snowflakes drifting casually down amid the bright lights and garish decorations of the competing merchants. The streets were packed with people scurrying here and there, looking for this store or that, for this gift or that, but never at each other. What better place to lose oneself than in a crowd at Christmas when everyone else is preoccupied with everything except who they're walking past? The darkness helped, of course, and the winter coat and muffler he wore completed his public disguise.

Tim walked casually down the street, jostled and jostling, staring at the glitter and neon as if at familiar old friends. His boots shuffling through the snow and slush brought back crystal images of other times and places in winters past. He stared in at the illuminated windows that he passed, genuinely enjoying the displays and color. This was his second Christmas since the change, but as far as he could see, nothing else had changed at all. He had passed from normal existence, and whatever ripple that made on various lives had apparently been calmly absorbed.

Faces passed him like fractions of memory, moving through the crowds with angular slowness, captured for a moment in a staccato pattern only to pass and merge with the stream of humanity once more. One would pass in self-possessed rigidness, and Tim would flash on it, wishing to reach out and capture them to bring them into his world so that the loneliness and isolation would not have as keen an edge. There was Jeremiah, of course, but as alike as they were, they were still so very far apart in many ways.

Jeremiah was ancient such as few have ever been, whereas Tim was still young, truly young as opposed to just physically young, which he would always be.

Faster the faces flashed past, and faster, until they blended into a blur of motion, emotion, and memory—dancing before his eyes in movements that comprised only appearance and passage.

He ran down the street, storefront images lighting up the faces with the bright lights of gay greeting, while all around him passed people hurtling on their way through life, oblivious to the many other lives around them.

Life. Life. That which was given and so harshly denied all in the same moment. Through it all he slipped and stumbled, trying to find his way in a maze of strangers and lights and icons and sensations that were theirs but not his. He had returned to recapture something of what he had lost, but here, in the midst of it all, it was eluding him more surely than ever before. They were they and he was he, and they passed each other as completely as if each were invisible and intangible to the other. Their goals, their dreams, their hopes, were all so different that should he have stopped one of them he was sure they would have looked right through him as if he were a mist.

A mist, a shadow, a specter, an illusion—a cold shell harboring life and death but not enough of either to carry on and accomplish more than just existence.

Lights flashed. *Merry Xmas. Happy New Year. Seasons Greetings. Happy Holidays. Noel. Peace On Earth. Good Will To Men.*

Men—people—those who existed and truly lived to experience. To touch a mother's face—to feel a lover's hand.

He stumbled on the ice, choking back a cry, trapping it before it could escape, and almost falling against someone in the process. Tim looked up, straight into the face of the man who had destroyed him that cold autumn night over a year before.

At first the man had no reaction at all, seeing only a child who had fallen against him on the slippery sidewalk. He saw the boy's face, and he smiled. He saw loneliness there, and weakness—which could be exploited.

"You ought to be careful. You could've hurt yourself. Here, why don't we go inside out of the cold. If you want, I'll buy you something to drink."

A cold feeling, intense and frigid, was spreading through

the boy's limbs. When the man lightly touched his shoulder he almost cried out. He had to think. He couldn't let that one escape. He wished now that Jeremiah had come with him.

"Sure," Tim replied, his voice husky despite himself. He allowed the man to lead him through a revolving door into the interior of a department store's coffee shop. It was probably much warmer in there, but his shivering wasn't from the cold. He had to get a grip on himself. This man may have been a predator, but Tim was now much more than merely prey.

They slid into a booth at the back of the shop and the man ordered for them.

"Doing your Christmas shopping?" the man asked with feigned interest.

"Yeah, you could say I was shopping around," Tim replied. Strength—he needed strength.

"You down here with your parents?"

"No, they're out of town. I'm here by myself." Tim's cold fear was churning into hot rage.

"Say, I've got an idea. Why don't you stay at my place tonight, and then I could take you home in the morning?" This time he was playing it cool. Last time he had just snatched him off the path in the woods and to hell with the preliminaries. The comparison was not one that Tim enjoyed making. "Sure," Tim replied easily, and he tried to keep a casual manner when he added, "but I'd like to stop someplace on the way, first."

The car hummed along, its narrow headlight beams picking out the empty road in front of them. Tim knew where to stop so that the man's suspicion wouldn't be aroused. "Right here."

"Okay, but what's up?"

"I left something here which I've got to pick up. Then we'll go to your place, okay?" The man smiled and touched Timothy's leg. The boy almost screamed.

The car stopped and they both slid out and walked into the woods, the man following Tim close behind. Tim smiled to himself. The guy wasn't taking any chances on his little prize slipping away. They pushed their way through brittle, frozen bushes until they arrived at a snowy clearing. Tim stopped.

"What is it, kid? Is this the spot?"

"I'm afraid so." Tim turned and looked at the man. "Don't I look at all familiar to you?"

"No, I can't say that you do. Should you?"

"Well, you murdered me here in this clearing just a little over a year ago."

The man didn't react to the words at first—they were too insane. He looked closer at the boy. "What the hell are you?"

"Maybe if I wasn't wearing any clothes you'd recognize me."

Horror and recognition swept over the man's face and he reached out and grabbed Tim roughly by the throat. "I don't know who you really are, kid, or how you know what you know, but it's just too bad for you. You must be nuts!"

"No," replied Tim evenly, "just dead." He grabbed the man's right hand with his left, pressing and twisting at the same time. Bones cracked and splintered, and a painful adult scream split the solitude. Tim held on and he wouldn't let go.

"This is crazy!" the man whimpered. "You're just a kid!"

"I was, but now I'm something else, and I have you to thank for it!"

"No! Lemme go!"

"That's what I said once upon a time. You didn't listen then, so why should I listen now?"

"Oh, God!"

''Could someone like you possibly have one?'' said Tim coldly.

The man thrashed in a grip of steel, attempting to back away, but uselessly. He struck out at Tim's face, his fist connecting with a hard, solid thwack. Tim just grinned in evil amusement.

''I'm beyond that kind of pain, now.'' He tightened his grip on the man's shattered hand, ''but you aren't!''

The man howled and fell to his knees. ''Please,'' he begged, weeping, ''I'll do anything.''

''I know. That's why you're here.'' Tim released the broken hand and then stepped forward, planting a hard right hook on the man's chin. He watched with harsh satisfaction as the killer's body flipped over and landed with a solid thud on the frozen ground.

''You brought me pain, and so much more,'' said Tim, ''and yet, when you saw me on the street you didn't even recognize me. How many others like me have there been? So many that their faces blur and fade so quickly? It's for me and for them that I do what I'm going to do to you now.''

''Tim, no! You can't!'' It was Jeremiah, emerging from the shadows.

''Stay out of this! I've waited and suffered for this moment. I *have* to take it!''

''And what would that make you? Superior because you took his life yourself? You keep telling me how much you revere life, but now you're willing to ignore that principle just to exact simple revenge.''

''*Simple* revenge! After what he did to me? Who has more right to revenge than I do?''

''No one, but that doesn't mean that you have the right to take it, either. Life *is* sacred, whether it's the twilight existence we lead, or the life he exists with. Haven't you at least learned that much in our time together?''

"I won't let him get away!" Tim cried.

"You don't have to. Make him turn himself in. We'll follow him to be sure that he does. If he doesn't, there are other things we can do to him that are worse than death."

Tim hesitated. Maybe Jeremiah was right. Did he really want to carry the blood of another human being on his conscience, even a crazed killer like this one? He stood staring at Jeremiah. There was so much this man had given to him. He couldn't throw away that respect, now, because he knew it was so much more than just respect.

There was a sharp crack and Tim whirled to see the man lunging at him with a long, sharp staff that had been snapped off a nearby tree. Its cold brittleness had caused it to break off sharp, and it was this sharp end that was heading right for his face, held as it was in the man's good left hand and supported by his ruined right. He grinned in insane triumph.

All this registered on Tim's senses in an instant, and as the branch hurtled toward his face his left arm came up and brushed it easily aside. The man slipped and stumbled with the shaft and appeared about to fall, but then he suddenly turned and with surprising strength and agility drove the broken branch into Jeremiah's chest.

Silence. It all happened in silence. The sound of hard, frozen wood penetrating was like a harsh whisper in the frigid night air.

"Jeremiah!" Tim screamed, and he leaped for the man, catching him as he fell, and lowering him gently to the ground. Jeremiah held the branch and looked at it with dumb surprise.

Tim moaned in the night air, and turning he saw in the distance the form of a man running through the woods, darting in and out of forest shadows. In moments Tim was after him, and the thickset trees were merely blurred images passing him by as he tore through the thin layer of snow toward the distant figure. Obstacles were leaped and bypassed with lightning swiftness. Branches broke and ice splintered as he crashed through frozen overgrowth.

The figure was closer, and closer still, and once the man turned a frightened glance over his shoulder and shrieked at what he saw bearing down on him with such terrible, inhuman swiftness.

Tim saw the cover ahead thin and break as the man dashed out into the road. Blinding lights and a blaring horn that shook the air with the ferocity of its screaming exclamation met them there. The man turned in stunned surprise at the huge Peterbilt truck bearing down on him with tons of lumbering metal and screaming air brakes. The shock lasted for one split second, and then the man recovered and turned to flee. He was one split second too late. The chromed grille, caked with ice and sludge, caught the fleeing man with all the pile-driving force of loaded tonnage traveling at forty miles an hour. It impacted with solid, unforgiving velocity and propelled the body forward where it cartwheeled, spun, and twisted at a broken angle before finally falling into a bouncing skid on the lonely, icy road.

The blood on the man's face was already starting to freeze by the time the body came to rest head upward and eyes open in a glassy stare. His limbs were drawn back over him in a grotesque parody of self-protection. There was no movement—only stillness.

Tim stood in the middle of the road, staring. The truck pulled over fifty yards down and the portly driver seemed to explode from his cab and run wildly up the road to the scene of the accident. A cloud of expended breath trailed after the truck driver as he charged up to Tim. The trucker stared down at the body helplessly, running his right hand through the two-day growth of stubble on his chin, his heavy plaid coat making him look like a hunter who'd been out after deer. But this was one prize that wouldn't be tied across any fender.

"Hey, kid. You saw, didn't ya? It was an accident. Jeezus, the guy just flew outta nowhere! It wasn't my fault!"

"No," Tim replied evenly, "it wasn't your fault. You did good." The driver stared at Tim in amazement as the boy turned and walked back into the woods and their impenetrable cloak of winter darkness.

He walked slowly through the press of trees, listening to the crunch of snow under his feet and imagining it to be the disintegration of bones. The white carpet of snow stretched before him in the dark like a winter welcome mat.

Finally he reached that fateful clearing—and found Jeremiah sitting on the snow and examining the spear that Tim had seen impale him.

"Jeremiah? Jeremiah!" and he hurled himself on the old man, embracing him with all his strength.

"Take it easy, son. You don't want to break me!"

"But how? You're still alive! I saw him stab you with a wooden stake!" Tim's hands shook with relief and the release of suppressed emotions.

Jeremiah looked at Tim and then reached down and pulled open his old shirt. There was something there that Tim hadn't noticed before because it was almost the same tarnished color as the man's leathery flesh. The boy reached out and ran his hands across Jeremiah's chest. "This is chain mail!"

"Is that what that's called? I had forgotten all about it. I've worn it for a long time. I knew there was some good reason I've been kicking around so long, and I knew it couldn't be luck." Jeremiah ran his hands over it as if he were examining some amazing discovery. "Someone gave this to me once—I wish I could remember who. I've started thinking, and remembering, an awful lot since you came along, Tim, but I've got a long ways to go."

"We both do," said Tim, his voice quivering. He was finally dealing with things as they were. He had felt alone, and yet Jeremiah had always been there to cushion the darkest moments and discuss his deepest torments. He had almost lost that. He had taken him for granted—believed he would always be there while he anguished over what more his life could afford him. If he had lost Jeremiah he would have learned then what real loneliness was—the silence and the solitude unbroken by a friendly voice. Tim had been searching for a purpose in his new existence, and had discovered almost too late that he and Jeremiah were two people with a shared purpose—to make each other's life bearable and meaningful. It was Jeremiah who had saved him from the abyss and in return given him eternity. All along he had been teaching him to deal with what he was. Their sadness had been shared, linked one to the other.

Now the time had finally come to make something more of things than just a steady pointlessness, especially now when Tim had at last dealt with that one moment of his past that had stood as stark sentinel between himself and the future. Until the moment that killer had died, Tim had been restive, searching, angry—not wishing to attempt to build a future when his past was still so unresolved. But now all that was at last behind him—that and so much more.

The night they began their path away from the town where he had been born and reborn. The overcast sky made a soft, starless vault overhead. Even the city lights were just a distant glow, like a fading memory.

Their steps took them through the empty hills on the beginning of what would be a long search. There were others like themselves, and Tim wanted to find them. Jeremiah knew tales of a colony in the Rocky Mountains—refugees from the time of Cotton Mather and the Salem Witch Trials. There were many kindred spirits in the world of darkness whose fates were inextricably intertwined, but that wasn't the only reason, or even an important one. Some people search their whole lives for a kindred spirit—someone they can talk to like no other, and be near when darkness closes in and the ache of the solitary soul grows strong. Some people do indeed take a lifetime to find that kindred spirit, but Tim had a lifetime to spend with one, and he had to find a place to spend it.

He looked up at the tall, gaunt man at his side who knew himself only as Jeremiah. Tim knew him too, and for that he was at last grateful.

As they continued into the comforting darkness, Tim took Jeremiah's huge, rough hand in his.